Assumption of Guilt

Assumption of Guilt

Harold Mehling

Carroll & Graf Publishers, Inc.
New York

First Carroll & Graf edition 1993

Carroll & Graf Publishers, Inc.
260 Fifth Avenue
New York, N.Y. 10001

Library of Congress Cataloging-in-Publication Data

Manufactured in the United States of America

Chapter *1*

LILLY ROBERTSON WAS FEELING GOOD AS SHE DROVE CAROLINE HOME FROM nursery school. Two years ago, when her husband suddenly became a former marketing vice president, he made a lot of noise about living within a budget. But now, no bills she ran up provoked even a comment. Roy must be doing quite a number on those people down on Wall Street.

She turned the Mercedes two-seater into Birch Lane and brought it to a stop. Caroline had freed the seat-belt buckle and was hiding it with her hand. "Carrie," she said quietly—the books taught that there was no need to raise the voice—"please don't unbuckle your belt until we're home. We've talked about that before, haven't we?" The child clicked the belt together without responding.

In fact, Caroline hadn't said a word all the way home from Snug Arms. Talk about unusual. The five-year-old was always stuffed with energy and exhausting curiosity; words tumbled from her like gumballs from a slot. Lilly thought she'd go back to the books and look up the fussy, feisty fives.

She started up along Birch Lane and looked down the hillside at the Hudson River, which was running lazily past the marina. Caroline often sat at her second-floor window and chanted rhymes at the water. Daughter. Fought her, caught her, taught her. Inventively, she once tried to get away with sawed her.

Caroline stared at the dashboard until her mother pulled into the driveway beside the Robertsons' sprawling home. People in Hudson Ferry called it the grandest house in town. The child climbed out and stood silently in black tights and a flowered tunic with stiff shoulder pads, somewhat overadorned for a day at nursery school. Lilly wondered what was bothering her.

As the usual after-school ritual, Lilly toasted two slices of whole-grain bread from the health-food shop and placed two flowered saucers from Italy before the child. One held peanut butter, the other strawberry jam.

"Put the jam on me," Caroline said.

"On the bread, Carrie. Use the butter knife."

"Put jam on me."

"What are you talking about? Don't be silly."

The child picked up the jam saucer and ran across the kitchen, twirls of black curls flying. Pulling a stepstool to the sink, she leaped up and smashed the dish into the stainless-steel basin. Porcelain splinters bounced against walnut cabinets as Caroline shouted, "Laurie puts strawberry on my peepee." She was laughing. "Laurie licks it off. With her tongue. Sung-rung-hung. I want you to do it, Mommy!"

Lilly Robertson took a step. "Carrie!" She grabbed the back of a chair. The child blurred and the Roman numerals on the wall clock danced. She had never felt a pure adrenaline rush of fear in her life, not even two years ago when Roy kept turning away from her and she finally asked what the hell was wrong with him. She thought the end had come, he must be involved with some woman. But he had only been ditched from his big-time job, eased out by a new man in a corporate shakeup. Before he got into stocks and bonds.

She knew she was speaking to Caroline but heard no words. Filling a cup from a bottle of spring water, she drank it in a gulp. Words came. "Carrie, sit down, please. What are you talking about?"

The child was laughing wildly. "Laurie calls it Sweet Time. Neat-feet-seat. And we play Bottoms Up. She kisses our bottoms."

Lilly thought of the teacher and was sure she would faint. Laurie Coles was one of the staff of three at Snug Arms. She was a pleasant young woman who had been there for the better part of a year, Caroline's second year at Snug Arms. The children all liked her.

She composed herself and tried to smile. "Did you play Sweet Time today, Carrie?"

The child was looking into the sink. "I put strawberry on Laurie's peepee. She told me to." She jumped down from the stool, pulled off her tunic, and ran from the room screaming.

Terrified, Lilly waited a moment, then hurried into the living room. Caroline had removed all her clothes and was arched on her hands and outstretched legs. "Bottoms up!" she shouted.

The child was lifted, carried upstairs, and put into pajamas without a word. The best thing that could happen to Caroline at the moment, and to Lilly, was for the little girl to take a nap. She did, after saying, "Laurie choked a rabbit, Mommy."

Lilly Robertson went out onto an upper terrace and gazed down the hillside from Birch Lane. April's afternoon sun was slanting across the splendid river, speckling its tranquil surface with glints of gold leaf. Up here in Hudson Ferry, give or take a hundred miles from New York Harbor, the water barely registered the attack and retreat of the tides. And the swirl of the big city was distant. Hudson Ferry was serene. About half the locals were native to the area; they were the permanent party that repaired shoes and toilets and ran the service establishments and mom-and-pop stores. Most of the rest were like Roy and Lilly Robertson. They arrived as refugees from metropolitan tumult, or when companies opened facilities here. A few were weekenders or had summer homes; on Nantucket they would be called off-islanders. They loved the tranquility of it all.

Lilly went inside, called Ellen Strand, mother of Bonnie, four and a half years old, and told her what Caroline had said about Laurie Coles. Sweet Time. Bottoms Up. She forgot about the rabbit.

Bonnie Strand, a few months younger than Caroline Robertson, pushed her peach halves away and looked up into a very tight face. "Ellie, you look scared," she said. She called her mother Ellie. It was allowed, and there was no father to correct her. Bonnie had a faint recollection of seeing tight skin on Ellie's face before, all stretched out, as if somebody was squeezing her neck, or grabbing her hair hard. In a TV movie. It happened on the morning Ellie sat her down and explained that Daddy Mickey would not be living with them on Oak Lane any more. When Bonnie grew up, Ellie said, she would understand that things like this happen sometimes. But Daddy might pick her up on weekends and take her to interesting places. He never did.

On the first Saturday morning after Daddy Mickey left, Bonnie ran to her room and sobbed so hard that her hair was soaking and her favorite blanket was damp hours later. But the shock did not persist because, in fact, Mickey Strand had rarely been around the house on weekdays when he did live there. He worked in another city, Ellen said. And when he arrived on weekends—Bonnie wished she didn't remember so many things—Mickey and Ellie would shout at each other all the time. And he never played with her. Once, on an evening just before he went away forever, she peeked down from the stairway and saw him push a long needle into one of his arms, on the inside, near the elbow. Ellie was yelling something like, "It'll be better for Bonnie if you get out of here! You're crazy!" Bonnie was not sure that's what her mother said, or what it meant.

Then, with no father to help her mother, Bonnie ran out every morning to get the paper, with the comics in the second section. She could make out a few of the words and imagine others from the way Calvin and his tiger friend Hobbes acted. She saw the boy's mouth twist up as he scowled at the pesty little girl with the ribbon in her hair. Stealing glances as she followed Hagar's antics, she would watch her mother grind a cigarette into an ashtray, the oval one with the swan's head, and light up another.

Now Ellen Strand turned to the stove, filled her coffee cup, and lit up. Trying to smile, she said, "Tell me about school, Bonnie. Did you have fun today?"

"No." Her bright face squeezed up and red curls bounced around as she shook her head. "You shouldn't smoke, Ellie."

"I know. Why didn't you have a good time?"

"Laurie says smoking hurts you."

"I know. I'm trying to stop. Tell me why you didn't have a good time today?"

"It wasn't today."

"Eat your peach. It's delicious." She sliced it into quarters with a small, sharp knife. "What wasn't today?"

"I want a pop stick."

Ellen Strand sighed and removed an orange Popsicle from the freezer. Instead of eating it, Bonnie took the knife and hacked away at the frozen sugar water, holding the stick until it was bare. Her mother drew deeply on her cigarette and waited. Then the child seized a slice of peach and pushed the stick into it.

"It hurt," she said.

Her mother dropped her cigarette, retrieved it, and threw it into the sink. A hand came up to her chest as she felt her heart pounding. "What hurt, sweetheart?"

Bonnie stabbed the peach with the stick. "Laurie put it in my peepee!" She pushed the plate off the table and ran from the kitchen, shouting, "Carrie says tickle-stickle, tickle-stickle! It hurt!"

She was clumping up the stairs as Nanny, bustling and cheerful morning, noon, and night, came through the kitchen door. Ellen, having taken her usual afternoon hour off, had to get back to Far-Flung Fashions, her boutique on River Road. Business was brisk between four and six o'clock.

"Bonnie's upset," she told Nanny. "Ask her about her nursery school. Pay attention to what she says and tell me when I get back."

Nanny laughed. "That's all we ever talk about."

"Listen to what she says. And tell her I'm bringing her some new books."

Nanny laughed again. "You need a bigger house. There's no room for more books."

Bonnie's mother walked out without replying, lighting a cigarette, and Nanny wondered what was bugging her.

Ten minutes later Ellen Strand parked on River Road, in the midst of what was called downtown Hudson Ferry. She sat in the car breathing rapidly, fighting off panic. During the drive she had talked to herself about a missing shipment of ankle-length skirts from Morocco and some embroidered blouses from Sri Lanka, and whether she should switch from the gold card to the platinum, which had a classier look. She had been trying to keep two words, Snug Arms, from reaching the front of her mind.

This was Friday, the last day before Easter vacation, so Bonnie would not be at the nursery school for a week.

Suddenly she saw pictures of the child's rosy body, still so wonderfully innocent of the cruelties that life might and sure as hell would impose, pain and sorrow that no one could prevent. More images floated before her. Bonnie, sitting at a table in the Snug Arms cafeteria, next to a young woman. Bonnie, telling one of her marvelous stories, eyes closed to block out unexciting thoughts. The young woman slipped a hand beneath the table; it came to rest between Bonnie's legs.

She yanked at the car door, then stopped and stared ahead, trying to become invisible. The rear-view mirror showed a man coming along, swinging a malacca walking stick that rarely touched the sidewalk, going by the coffee shop on his way to the courthouse two blocks away. The Honorable Johnson Gillies Mathes, justice of the New York State Supreme Court, Princess County division. Jacko's calendar must be slow, or he was just goofing off. Oyez and oyez and hear ye and hear ye. She wondered who the honorable one had fucked after lunch today.

Mathes passed her with the stretching stride of a golfer, but she waited until he reached Dutch Street, at the Third Federal Savings Building, then ran into the Copper Kettle and calmed herself with the help of more coffee and another cigarette. She wasn't sure about a lot of things in life, but of one she was certain: Nothing terrible could have happened to her Bonnie. No hand had slipped under a table and touched her. And that story about a Popsicle stick was nonsense. Crazy kiddie talk. She hurried into Far-Flung Fashions and started tracking down the missing items from Morocco and Sri Lanka, wherever those places were.

* * *

Harry Hull and Hudson Ferry liked each other. His brand of lawyering might have explained why he had been drawn to the town five years ago—there was a lot of real-estate action up the river. He billed himself as a general practitioner, but most of his time was devoted to home-sale closings and contract writing. And he privately admitted to another reason—he had practiced for a couple of years down in New York City without enjoying a day of it. Negotiating settlements with opposing lawyers was a form of street fighting, in-your-face talk, threats, the law of the jungle. If you won't settle, I'll see you in court in two years, counselor, if you haven't starved to death. The courtroom was worse. Hot shots bombarded the bench with one motion after another and *brash* wasn't the word for their style. Simple cases were diverted, subverted, and perverted. The more convinced those lawyers became of their genius, the pushier they became. Hull tolerated it as long as he could but in the end found himself unable to believe, as they did: "I will win. You will lose. I am the greatest!"

He said the hell with the city and left. Or had he fled? It was an uncomfortable question that nagged him, especially during the loneliest times. It was a sense of defeat. Sometimes another beer would chase it for a while.

No lawyer had to handle criminal cases, and in Hudson Ferry Hull avoided them when he could; defending felonies was an arcane art. He carried out modest chores nimbly, collected solid fees, and down at the Ferry Ale House, the Saturday night retreat, he joined the laughter over barrister jokes.

"Harry, what's five thousand lawyers at the bottom of the ocean?"

"I give up."

"A good beginning."

As did others, Hull considered Hudson Ferry the headquarters of peace and quiet, a refuge from the turbulence of big-city life. But he also remembered that six months ago today a pair of drug-tilted teenagers, members of prominent, that is, important, families, held up a 7-Eleven in the middle of the night and slugged the owner unconscious. One of the boys was raping the man's wife in a back room when a policeman happened in. The teens were tried as adults, and an expensive, imported defense could not save them from stiff prison sentences.

Hull shared the town's desperate desire to erase its shame, but the ugly recollection hovered behind all conversations, censored from speech by pain.

On this gorgeous afternoon, Hull, who had never married, sat in his office, drank awful coffee, and thought about women. He considered them to be very complex cases. Sometimes he wished he had been born back when chicks weren't as smart as they seemed to be nowadays. Those he ran into were so confident and knowing, or sounded as if they were, that he was intimidated. So he said little while recognizing that when he was in the midst of couples, he chatted more with husbands, about sports and what was going on around town. It bothered him, but that's how it was. There had been escapades, of course, with hot stuff Sal of Speedy Sally's and some real-estate agents, but those were flings in the night and why don't we do it again sometime? Sometimes they did.

Hull had had it up to here with bacheloring. He wanted someone to talk to about ups and downs, triumphs and heartaches, and the other stuff. Once in a while his mind wandered to pretty Polly Lennon, who ran the bookshop across from his office. She was filled with enthusiasm and humor and often greeted him with lines from heavy literature. He walked into the Book Nook one day and Polly pulled down a volume of Shakespeare and recited a line: "The first thing we do, let's kill all the lawyers." That was from *Henry VI*, she told him, and he almost said, "Who?" Polly stirred his juices, but he was afraid of her.

Today was Harry Hull's birthday, which, he realized, was the reason for all this interior browsing. He abandoned it, but not before the thought registered that at the age of forty he was wishing more than anything else that he felt surer of himself. He also wished, occasionally, that he would stick to his now-and-then vows to cut down his beer-guzzling. I can't stop the hair from ending up in my comb, or the tiny lines from creeping in under my eyes, he told himself, but I could at least cut back on the dozen brews a day, most of them sucked up in the evening at home, alone. I don't want to turn into a beer-belly, do I? I could go down to a half dozen a day. So why don't I?

A week later Hull was shaving, the old-fashioned way, with a razor, when he flipped on a nine-inch TV that was always set at channel 22 for the morning news. At the first words, his razor dropped into the sink. Corky McGonigle, news hound, said, "Scandal hits Hudson Ferry. Last night a teacher at the Snug Arms nursery school was arrested and charged with sexually molesting little children. Laurie Coles was indicted yesterday afternoon on twenty-three counts of assault for invading the bodies of four- and five-year-olds. She will be arraigned this morning before Justice Johnson Gillies Mathes."

Hull scraped the whiskers from his face and went out in his bathrobe to get the *Hudson Ferry Tribune* and read the disgusting story. He was shaking his head until an amusing thought struck.

The astronauts would have to fly in an attorney from another planet to handle this case. No lawyer within five hundred miles would touch it.

Up and down River Road, through the business district and out into the residential areas of the town, population forty-five hundred, everyone was discovering that grotesque crimes had taken place in their midst. The story was being promulgated by print, air, and telephone. Parents clicked off the news and slipped newspapers into drawers. They lingered over their little ones but did not ask questions, dreading what they might hear.

Chapter 2

LAURIE COLES WAS TO BE ARRAIGNED IN AN HOUR, AND PETER HARMON, district attorney of Princess County, of which Hudson Ferry was the seat, pulled out a report filed by the investigating detective. The mother whose complaint had initiated the case said her daughter, just home from the Snug Arms nursery school, had asked for jam to be placed on her vagina, as her teacher had done. Another mother reported that her child said Laurie Coles inserted an ice-pop stick into her vagina. "Laurie put it in my peepee," she said. "It hurt." The mother rushed the child to a physician, who said it indeed appeared that her vagina had been invaded; the doctor was on the prosecutor's witness list.

The D.A. dropped the document back into the file and consulted an edited version that omitted a pledge from the first mother: "I'm going to get this bitch thrown in the river," a statement followed by more explicit and rather colorful threats. The remarks were clearly inspired by anguish and in any event were irrelevant. And they could be troublesome.

Harmon walked to his window and looked down onto River Road, which ran parallel to the Hudson River and whose century-old red brick surface had just been restored. The river, lying just a quarter of a mile west, had once made the town a fishing center and a bustling port. Progress had claimed the fishing grounds, but Hudson Ferry had survived.

His attention focused on two vans parked before the red-brick criminal courts building, trimmed with white marble. Cables snaked out of the vehicles and television technicians were shaking hands with the courthouse super, who understood he would find beer money in his palm. Moments later, extension cords and connection boxes emerged from the building and linkups were made.

Reporters were flicking cigarettes and swapping the latest jokes. "What's the difference between Dan Quayle and Jane Fonda? She's been to Vietnam."

He sighed. Here we go again.

In a line of work filled with surprises, he thought, at least there would be none from the bench. Justice Johnson Gillies Mathes would not look favorably on foxy legal ploys. He would clear the path to the guillotine and cut down anyone who sought to block the way. Enter, Laurie Coles.

The first person to walk into the courtroom seated himself in the back row, on the aisle near the wide double doors. He was one of those men who move through life unremembered. Neither chunky nor spare and not tall without quite being short, he was what average meant. And he had a face, topped by hair whose brown had surrendered to gray. His freshly pressed suit belonged to a bygone decade.

Fred Coles had dropped off the bus in Hudson Ferry after a night-long ride from Portsmouth, New Hampshire. He hoped he would lose only one day's pay at the shipyard, where he threaded pipes, and where some years ago he had left half the small finger of his right hand.

Laurie Coles's father stared at his freshly buffed black shoes as townspeople began filing into the imposing courtroom whose dramas were rarely enacted before sellout crowds. Terrified, he wished he could remain and disappear at the same time.

Laurie's call had come at seven o'clock in the evening, just as he was finishing off a pork sausage. He was looking into a passbook for no reason; he knew that every cent he had was represented by the two thousand one hundred and ten dollars in a savings account. The total was once ten times higher, but then Mother suffered a stroke, collapsed, and broke a hip. Laurie, who was finishing up at the University of Maine, came home on weekends and looked after her. After a long illness, Mother was dead and the savings were depleted. Fred Coles said damn the money, I want my wife. Now contracts had dried up at the shipyard, there were layoffs, and he wasn't saying damn the money any more.

Laurie had spoken rapidly and said there was only two minutes for the call. But she didn't sound like his daughter. More like a voice behind a desk at the shipyard, a hire-and-fire person, hurried and brisk. She said she was in the police station in Hudson Ferry. She had been arrested and would be taken before a judge tomorrow morning. "Can you get here, Dad?"

He remembered dropping the bankbook and looking across the living room at his wife's photo, the one he pressed to his cheek each night on the way to bed. He tried to speak reassuringly into the phone but no words emerged. He could not understand what Laurie was saying. Finally, in a voice he did not know, he asked what she had done. She said, "I didn't do anything. Can you get here, Dad?"

He called Trailways, then went around the neighborhood and borrowed seventy-five dollars. He ran to the station and his eyes did not close during the trip. Looking out at the landscapes, he saw nothing while thinking about Laurie. He had not sent her money for a year. Not that she had asked for any. She didn't earn much at the nursery school, but enough, and she liked the job. Had she stolen something? Impossible. But okay. If she took something, he would square it up. He had brought the bankbook along, and the paid-up deed to the house, to show he had assets. But Laurie couldn't have done anything wrong.

A man in front of him ruffled a newspaper and Coles saw words of a headline:

SNUG ARMS TEACHER ARRESTED
FOR SEXUALLY MOLESTING TOTS

He shivered in the perfect temperature of the courtroom.

The room filled quickly, and as each of the one hundred and sixty seats was occupied, many by unfailing attendees known as the courthouse regulars, the doors were clamped open to permit a jostling overflow in the corridor to see and hear. Two women in the second row were speaking in animated bursts. The short, wiry one on the aisle was whispering with energetic head shakes while brushing long black hair from her eyes. Suddenly she stood and canvased the room, the largest public space in town except for the movie theater, which had been carved into six cubicles. Her lips were closed tightly and her face advertised her anger. A man murmured to his wife, who whispered back, "Lilly Robertson. She has a daughter at Snug Arms."

Coles looked up from his shoes and caught Lilly Robertson's attention. Her glance swept by him, then returned and held. She stared until his eyes returned to the floor. He closed his eyes and squeezed his thigh muscles with fingers made strong by a life of labor. The taut backs of the hands, all the way to the edge of the remaining digit of the little finger, were void of color. He squeezed harder as he pressed his heels against the floorboards.

The chatter hushed as a door to the right of the bench opened and a youngish man walked in. D.A. Peter Harmon came forward with a long but not quite coordinated stride; there was a gangliness to him that caught the eye. He had the commanding look that is expected in a prosecutor as he swung around the long counsel table before the elevated bench. He sat down and his nails drummed the cover of a thick file.

The court reporter entered with her QuickWrite machine and sat in a cubicle before the podium. Several spectators smiled; she often seated them at the Hendrik Grill in the evenings. She was followed by the clerk, then a bailiff who emerged from the judge's chambers to the left of the rostrum, near an American flag whose red stripes were faded; the rest of the décor was shipshape. The bailiff remained standing and chanted, "All rise! Hear ye! Hear ye!" They still did it that way. "All those having business before this Supreme Court of the State of New York in and for the County of Princess draw near and give your attention. Presiding, the Honorable Johnson Gillies Mathes."

Jacko Mathes was magnetic as he entered briskly from his chambers. He was a flaming redhead with a pursed mouth and a strong chin. His tailored black robes held to his body as he moved with quick, long steps and mounted the bench smartly; the malacca walking stick never appeared in court. Waving spectators back into their seats, he spoke in an authoritative manner. "Present the defendant."

The bailiff touched a buzzer and the door of the holding room at the windowless side of the court opened. A young police officer stepped in, followed by Laurie Coles in handcuffs. Her father's legs stiffened, then jerked.

"No!" the judge shouted. "Uncuff her!" Those at the press table heard him add, "Is somebody crazy around here?"

The policeman halted and Coles collided with him. He grabbed her arms and pushed her back through the door. Seconds later she reentered, rubbing her wrists. But she seemed calm as she was led into the open area between the judge and the jammed press table. A reporter, carried away by inspiration, wrote, "Petite as she is, she was further diminished as she faced the massive, elevated bench." It was the first time in the town's history that the media had invaded the courtroom in battalion strength.

As Justice Mathes looked down at Coles, his sharp tone sent a message that he wanted no sloppiness. "Read the indictment."

The clerk fumbled for an elastic ribbon around her neck, set her glasses in place, and cleared her throat.

The people of the State of New York versus Laurie Coles. A grand jury, properly impaneled and sitting in Princess County, has found cause to believe and here makes public the following accusations:

On at least five occasions at the Snug Arms Preschool in Hudson Ferry, the defendant removed the clothing of and engaged in sexual activities with children of the ages of four and five years under her care. On two more occasions, the defendant appeared nude in the presence of children. Each of these acts constitutes sexual abuse in the first degree, a class D felony.

The defendant is further accused of performing bodily functions in the presence of children on six occasions and of inducing them to play with her waste matter or suggesting that they consume it. Each of these acts constitutes aggravated sexual abuse in the second degree, a class C felony.

Sharp intakes of breath sounded in the courtroom, as well as the scratching of ballpoints among the reporters. The clerk stopped reading and looked down at Coles. She stared up at Justice Mathes, who rapped his gavel.

On three occasions the defendant placed a food substance in the area of her vagina and attempted to force a child to remove it with her tongue, and on four occasions she inserted foreign objects into the vaginal orifices of children. Each of these acts constitutes aggravated sexual abuse in the first degree, a class B felony.

On three occasions the defendant issued threats to the effect that if her acts were revealed to parents, she would kill the parents and, if imprisoned, would return to harm the children themselves. Each of these acts constitutes coercion in the first degree, a class D felony.

The clerk cleared her throat again and regarded Coles, whose eyes had never left the judge's face.

The above findings are attested to by Peter Harmon, District Attorney, Princess County.

One court buff nudged another. "Here's the count. Thirteen aggravated sexual assaults, seven sexual assaults, and three coercions—the terroristic statements. That's eighty to three hundred and thirty-five years in the pen. How old is she? Early or middle twenties? The doll is dead."

"If she's proven guilty," said his colleague.

"Yeah. Well, she might get parole in twenty or thirty, but I doubt it."

"Mr. Prosecutor," the judge announced, "we are here for the process of arraignment. Is the state ready to proceed?"

Harmon rose, moving with less dispatch than he might have, perhaps displaying an unconscious distaste for Mathes, who was not his model of an impeccably fair-minded jurist. He thought of Jacko as carried away by the broad powers of the bench, and sometimes he hoped the judge would realize his dream; insiders knew he was hoping for a seat on the court of appeals, the state's highest court. That would not advance justice, Harmon conceded, but it would be a plus for Hudson Ferry.

"The state is ready, Your Honor." His coolness toward Mathes also accounted for his choice of gray tweed jacket and blue slacks instead of the proper suit the judge favored.

Mathes was aware of the prosecutor's unfriendliness, but he was also sensitive to vibrations in the local power grid. Harmon was one of the few district attorneys in the state who were still appointed, and if the pols wanted him, don't make waves. However, the D.A.'s term would expire in four months, and there was still time to drop a discreet word into the right ears.

He pointed to a chair at the far end of the counsel table and told Coles, "Sit there." She scanned the courtroom before doing so. Her father lifted his chin as a hello. As spectators turned to find him, and glared, he lifted a hand defiantly.

"Where is your lawyer?" Mathes asked. Sitting rigidly, she shook her head and said, "I don't have one. I have no money."

Mathes crooked a finger and the clerk handed him a list. He studied it, pointed to a name, and the clerk went into chambers. "Recess," he announced, heading for a coffee. The young bailiff stationed himself behind Laurie Coles.

Seats were too precious for spectators to risk losing, and amidst the buzz that started as the judge left, Harmon stared up at an acoustically tiled ceiling whose vastness was a tribute to cordial relations between town officials and local building contractors. Scores of tiny plastic cubes hid neon lamps and a single spotlight was set into the ceiling at an angle that cast a bright glow on a particular site, the bench; the judge was always slightly illuminated; Harmon wondered if Mathes had ordered the fixture installed.

The district attorney scanned a memo from a psychologist who had interviewed not only the little girl who had told her mother about the strawberry jam, but several other Snug Arms children. "We spent many hours together," the report said, "during which the child confirmed the incident. She supported it with details and provided further accounts of sexual molestation by the teacher." The psychologist noted that the child's information was useful in conducting interviews with her classmates and helped overcome the resistance that children of this age employ when they are asked about acts that they already understand are no-no's. "The material elicited was by far the most shocking I have encountered during numerous investigations of this kind," Dr. Amanda Roth commented. "I would also point out that these children have been seriously injured from an emotional standpoint. As a result, all efforts should be made to protect them from further damage as the investigation proceeds."

Harmon wondered. Who would want a job like Amanda Roth's? Grave-robbing would be more fun. On the other hand, thank goodness these professionals were around to help clean up such messes. The gruesome article in the *Tribune* this morning had ignited the town—the rage was everywhere—and he who did not deliver the goods in court would be forever cast out.

He walked over to the jury box, which was vacant except for a tall, thin man wearing brown slacks and a beige jacket with a small blue-and-gold emblem in the lapel. It was Vincent Garafolo, the detective who had investigated the first report of scandal at Snug Arms and come back convinced that the school was a house of horrors.

They chatted, but Harmon suddenly moved off as a man elbowed his way into the courtroom through the throng at the double doors. He hurried down the aisle and pushed through the swinging gate. He was studied by two courtroom haunters who represented opposing camps among the legal buffs. One was an avenger who ached for a return of capital punishment, hoping he might some day win a front-row seat at an execution. The other was a bleeder to whom defendants' stories often seemed to be plausible and who spoke of the overabundance of human imperfection.

The avenger informed his colleague, "Harry's going to be her lawyer? Harry? He has to throw her on the mercy of the court. This one's over before it starts." The bleeder demurred. "I could get that sweet-faced girl off myself. Look at her and tell me she would do sex stuff with children. Res ipsa loquitur." They were given to such talk.

Justice Mathes reappeared and announced that the court had appointed Harry Hull, attorney-at-law, to represent defendant Coles. Without sitting, he asked if there was any reason Hull could not accept the assignment. The attorney hesitated, then shook his head slowly before rising. "No, sir." Any other reply was out of the question. Mathes told Hull to consult with his client and went off to his chambers once more. It was said that Jacko would beat all

Colombians and Brazilians hands down in a coffee-drinking competition.

Hull introduced himself to Laurie Coles, then asked the court clerk for a copy of the indictment. The veteran clerk had seen horrendous crimes portrayed in the courtroom, but this was the worst by far. She shook her head and handed him the document, then led lawyer and defendant into the jury room and closed the door behind them.

Hull sat at the table around which fates were decided and read the indictment word for word. As he finished the first paragraph, his head came up and he looked at his client with astonishment. She was staring ahead. He finished the document, then read it again and sat silently, sullen questions ricocheting through his head. "Why did Jacko do this to me? When did I give him a hard time?"

Aware that he was stalling to avoid a distasteful conversation, he surveyed his client. Her ash-blond hair was trimmed compactly and there was a fullness to cheeks that flanked a nose slightly on the small side. Finally he said, "I want to ask you a couple of things, Miss Coles. Have you been asked any questions about these charges? And have you said anything to the police?"

"The detective only said he had a warrant for my arrest." She had a cool voice, soft but clear.

"Did they read you your rights?"

That did not have to be explained these days. "A policeman read something that sounded like that."

"Did they ask you any questions at the police station?"

"No."

"Okay, here's the rule. You don't answer any questions unless your lawyer is present. Now, I have to tell you, these allegations they've made sound very specific. I mean, as if they think they've got a lot of evidence."

She shook her head and looked away.

Hull nodded at a response that did nothing to ease his task. He looked down at the indictment and said, "I know the prosecutor. Pete Harmon. He's a careful guy. He wouldn't go to trial without hard stuff. Follow me?"

She said, "I didn't do it."

He nodded again. "Here's something to think about. When the D.A. gives me his witness list, we're going to see names of children from Snug Arms, and names of their mothers and fathers. Now, they're going to say you did things, when they testify." He hesitated. "They're going to swear to it, under oath. You know what I'm saying?"

She did not reply.

Hull's reasonableness persisted. "I'm taking your word for what you tell me. But we're up against a big problem. People talk, and they say a lot of things when they're angry. They panic and get each other going. Harmon knows that. He's too smart to bring charges he thinks a jury wouldn't believe. So he'll press the strongest ones. Now, look around you. This is the room the jurors will sit in after they hear all the testimony. I'm sorry, but that's how it is."

She had swiveled away, but she suddenly turned back and said, "I didn't do it!"

He sighed. How about a surprise, for once. "I didn't say you did. I said it's reality time. I have to tell you the facts. If they go to a verdict, you could get the limit. In the big place." He realized he was banging the table with his pen and took a time out. Could this rap be beaten? Coles seemed likable enough with those big, appealing eyes and a healthy look. Why would she fuck with infants? He could imagine the wind-up of his summation to the jury: "If there ever was a case of confusion, surely that's what we have here, ladies and gentlemen. We know children have the greatest imaginations in the world. Give them an idea and they'll run wild with it. Let's remember that as we consider this ca: . As you judge this young woman, consider that no one, no one at all, may be guilty in this matter. We have an innocent defendant, and children who don't mean to harm anyone. Bless them. But we can't take Miss Coles's liberty away on the strength of wild stories."

Still, there was a bigger problem. The pressure would be enormous. This town did not want to hear fancy talk and it didn't want the children of Hudson Ferry put down as a pack of liars. The folks wanted to hear *guilty*. The town was at war, and Hull could become a casualty.

"Look, Miss Coles. I want this to come out the best it can for you. But there may be a limit to what we can do. I can talk to the prosecutor. He'd probably drop the toughest charges and the judge would go along. You'd be out in two years, three or four at the outside. Maybe you should think about that."

Hull saw pleading eyes and felt uncomfortable. "In the end," he said, "it's your plea. You'll decide and I'll stand up and say it. But I have to go through these things with you. And all that's left except not guilty is a plea of temporary insanity. It happens to people, and sometimes the jury buys it. You'd say you can't remember anything." He paused. "I mean, if that's true. It might give you a chance."

She turned to him and said, "I didn't do it."

"Let's go back in," he said.

*   *   *

Watching them enter, the D.A. assumed he would be approached with the familiar hondle. "Pete, what do you want? Blood? She'll take a plea. You win. So reduce the charges and she'll cop a guilty to a lesser. And it's over." Harmon stared up at the plastic cubes. No way, Harry. I've got the detective's interviews with the kids, about the jam and the stick and the other stuff, and the psychologist's interviews back that up. And have I got a witness? Lilly Robertson, dynamo mother. Tiger Lil. And more ammo on the way.

Hull did not approach the prosecutor. With his client, he marched directly to the end of the table and sat down as all eyes tracked Laurie Coles's movements.

Justice Mathes entered the courtroom and found the audience in agitated conversation. He put his gavel to work but did not threaten to clear the court. "Counselor," he said, "how does the defendant plead?"

"Good morning, sir."

"Get on with it."

Hull rose and said firmly, "Your Honor, the defendant pleads *not guilty.*"

Fred Coles stared at his shoes and the audience studied him. Murmurs sounded again and so did the gavel. The judge looked out at the spectators and his puckered lips conveyed his reaction to the plea. No one ever does anything. He turned to Harmon. "Does the state have motions to present?"

The D.A. rose. "Yes, sir. But I would like to say first that the investigation of this case is continuing. Because of the nature of the charges and the delicate ages of the children, we felt it was important to have grand jury action as quickly as possible." The court buffs noted that he was choosing his words with unusual care. "So I am serving notice now that there will probably be further indictments in time. More counts will be added to the true bill."

His use of that term would reignite an old argument among the buffs. Why is an indictment called a true bill? How does anyone know what the truth is before a trial is held? Isn't the term unfair to defendants? Many a drink went down as the rights and wrongs of that one were debated.

Justice Mathes did not want to hear about an expanded indictment. He was aware of the notorious case out on the West Coast, where half the staff of a nursery school was accused of playing lewd games with children. But five years and many millions of dollars later not a single person had been convicted. Was the D.A. going to convert Hudson Ferry into Sodom? He held up a hand and his eyes narrowed. "Are you saying that more defendants will be added to this case, Mr. Harmon?"

A low buzz broke out at the press table. Had only a sketch of a shocking picture been revealed? Would Snug Arms rival the serial killer epics? This assignment was a dream. There might even be time to put a poker game together.

Harmon wished Jacko would pay closer attention and wondered if that was a copy of the morning crossword puzzle lying before him. The judge was an ache. "No, sir. I apologize if I was unclear. I'm saying that we will be presenting additional evidence to the grand jury and we expect new charges against the defendant to emerge. I am merely alerting defense counsel to the situation. He will be notified promptly as new counts are added to the indictment."

A warning note sounded in the judge's voice. "We don't want this case to go on forever, Mr. Harmon. The court strongly suggests that the indictment process not be dragged out."

Harmon nodded. It was clear that the pols had told the judge: Limit the damage and cut the losses. The town will get a bad name. Real estate prices and all that. He had received a subtle suggestion himself from Bob Kirk, the top man on the board of supervisors. "Be nice to have this over with as fast as possible, Pete."

"Trial will begin ninety days from today," the judge said. "Mr. Hull?"

The lawyer rose and Harmon couldn't decide whether he was hearing a touch of stubbornness or if Hull was putting on a bit of a show. Maybe Harry thought the cameras had been admitted. "Your Honor, I think I will need more time than that to familiarize myself with the facts of the case and organize an effective defense. Just a little more time. If you please."

Jacko was displeased. "You are familiar with the recent directive from the court of appeals that cases involving allegations of child sexual abuse should be tried promptly. Three months is a reasonable period. And I direct the prosecution to be expeditious in turning over its witness list and exhibits to the defense. Is there anything else on your mind, Counselor?"

The district attorney's assent had not even been asked. An enormous amount of preparation lay ahead and Harmon would also have liked more than three months. Knowing he would not get it, he remained silent. It was his way of coping with the system.

Hull was still on his feet, shifting his weight from side to side. "Yes, sir. Now, on another matter. We request bail pending trial, Your Honor."

Harmon started to rise but the judge cut him off. "Bail is set at seven hundred and fifty thousand dollars."

Hull laughed aloud. "That's a denial of bail, sir. Miss Coles would have to put up seventy-five thousand in cash, and collateral for the rest."

Mathes tried to stare him down. "Bail has been set."

"Bail has been denied," Hull said.

Coles's eyes had not left the counsel table, but now she shifted in her chair toward the courtroom windows and the western exposure. The April sun was high and shimmering on the river.

Hull felt the unaccustomed onrush of a filibuster. "Your Honor, the prosecutor has given me his witness list and I see the name of at least one psychologist. I would like to know if this person has spoken to the children named in the indictment."

Harmon saw what was coming, but he rarely said more than was necessary, feeding out information as it was demanded by opposing counsel or the judge. "The children have been seen by a detective"—he pointed to Vincent Garafolo, who came to attention in the jury box—"and by an investigator and a psychologist."

Coles was staring at the judge, whose eyes occasionally flicked to her and then quickly away.

Hull was wondering again why he had been chosen for this assignment. "I move that we be permitted to talk to the children. We can't prepare a defense if our experts can't see them. The jury will simply assume, without hard evidence, that they've been injured if all they hear is one-sided testimony. And the only one they'll be able to punish is the defendant, because she's the only one available. They'll believe that because she's been charged, she must be guilty."

The judge motioned to Harmon, who spoke quietly. "I appreciate the problem, Your Honor, and the state wants fairness for the defendant. But we are dealing with special circumstances. These children are immature, and they have been traumatized by their experiences. Emotionally injured. Our experts advise us that they should not be subjected to endless interrogation, and especially not by representatives of the person who is accused of harming them. So they are also entitled to fairness, and we ask the court to safeguard the well-being of these minors."

He waited, as did Justice Mathes, and finally Hull got to his feet. "Your Honor, our experts could be supervised while they're interviewing the children. There is no way they could be harmed. Our experts do not even have to be identified as having been engaged by the defendant."

Harmon eked out more salve. "We will submit transcripts of the interviews to the defense the instant each one becomes available. And I now deliver to counsel the transcripts of the interviews that have already been conducted."

Mathes gestured to the court clerk, but she was already on her way to chambers. She returned with a thick file of Court of Appeals rulings and he flicked through pages. This time there was no sound in the room as he read. Then he looked up and said, "The possibility of emotional injury to the children exists, and a high probability of embarrassment. That decidedly outweighs the defendant's right to access. Prior decisions support this conclusion and the motion is therefore denied."

Hull climbed to his feet with a quizzical expression. "Exception," he said. "We have a right to see the children, to find out if they really are afraid of the defendant. Sir."

"Exception noted but not the speech," the judge replied. Snapping a law book shut, he said, "I rule further that the children will not testify in open court. They would be subject to harmful emotional stress. We will use closed-circuit television. The children will testify from my chambers, where they will be questioned by the prosecution and defense attorneys. The jury and I will observe the testimony from the courtroom, and so will the defendant. The children will see the accused via a monitor and she will be able to see them and communicate with her attorney during their testimony."

Hull felt his decorum depart and tried but failed to rein himself in. "No! The defendant has a right to confront her accusers directly, Your Honor. The Sixth Amendment. It's clear." He turned to the court reporter and spoke for the record. "The defense moves that all witnesses in this case be required to take the stand in open court."

"Objection," said the district attorney, needlessly.

"Sustained," Jacko said curtly. "The defendant is hereby remanded to the custody of the bailiff." He banged the gavel smartly and stood up.

So did the audience and Laurie Coles. But she startled the judge by shouting, "My father is here. I want to talk to him!"

Mathes looked out over the room and Fred Coles rose. "Five minutes," he said. The robes exited to chambers.

Coles came down the aisle, elbows moving this way and that, as if daring anyone to block his passage. A policeman led the two to the witness holding room and locked them in.

Most of the audience departed, leaving only Lilly Robertson and two young men who had been attracted to the proceedings by the photograph of the defendant in the *Tribune*. They remembered spotting her a couple of months ago, having a beer in a bar near the movie house. The more imaginative of the pair thought she might be a member of a motorcycle gang. They asked if she was in the mood to do some kinky things to a couple of big guys who'd pay top dollar. She sloshed her beer in their faces and walked out. They liked seeing her in a place she couldn't walk out of.

Lilly Robertson, small and taut-waisted, was still seated, as if she thought the proceedings would go on, or needed to be reminded that the wheels grind exceeding slow. Her eyes remained on the chair Laurie Coles had occupied, and finally she was alone as Fred Coles emerged from the holding room. As he passed with tears streaming down his cheeks, she shouted, "You dirty son-of-a-bitch! You animal! You and that piece-of-shit daughter of yours!"

He continued out of the courtroom. The reporters and cameramen were ready, but he swung wildly at those in his way and landed a fist on a photographer's shoulder. The cameras caught him running toward the depot.

As he waited for his bus, he told himself that his daughter was innocent. Why were those children and their parents saying those filthy things about her? It couldn't be true. Could it?

Chapter 3

SANDWICHES FROM SPEEDY SALLY'S ARRIVED AT THE LOCKUP IN THE BASE-
ment of the criminal courts building at six o'clock. Only two of the
five cells were occupied, one by a drunk past whose lips no food
could make its way, the other by Laurie Coles. But meals had
been ordered for both the prisoners, as a perk for the attendants,
a man and a woman, both hungry. One of them wrote the drunk's
name on the check; he was in such awful shape that they would
have breakfast on him, too.

As Coles ate quickly from her Styrofoam plate—knives and
forks not allowed—the matron watched her and said, "Eat good,
honey. The food's lousy up in the big place. You're going on a
long diet." She gripped a leather-dressed billy club at her belt and
added, "Rest up. You won't get much sleep up there. You'll wish
you were deader than a rock when they start the treatment. Every
night they'll give you a new cellmate to shove something in you.
They know all the tricks and the guards are deaf."

Coles stared at the bars until high laughter trailed away.

The furnishings in her six-by-seven room consisted of a fold-up
bunk, a sink with a drip, and a wheezing toilet. Her only belonging was a card that carried Harry Hull's name, address, and office
and home numbers.

She stretched out and closed her eyes until the voice of the male
attendant roused her. "Don't give her any lip," he said softly.
"Keep quiet. She'll get tired of it."

She thought of her mother, Mary, a Down Easterner. From the
way Mom read, no one would know she hadn't quite made it
through high school. Sometimes she went through three books a
week, one after another, as if she feared there would never be
enough time to catch up on things missed. History was her pas-

sion. She could tell you the name of every signer of the Declaration, and what the War of 1812 was really about, and the Civil War stuff and how Labor Day started and who shot McKinley, and about Roosevelt and the other ones.

Mary Coles was a constantly encouraging mother who said that Laurie was the only one who could set limits on her own future. "Work hard," she said. "Read every book you can get your hands on. Explore everything and do whatever you want to. Sometimes people may laugh at you, but do it anyway." She wrote many letters, and Dad, who was not a word man, always added a brief P.S., including one she would never forget. "Whatever you end up doing, you'll be darned good at it, little girl. Excuse me. I mean young lady." Another note addressed her as "Dear Wonderful Person." Mom said Dad wouldn't know what eloquent meant, but that's what he was.

She did well in college, but then Mom's stroke came, and another one followed. She could not speak or care for herself and finally she died. Laurie returned home and stayed with Dad as long as she could, and they had remained close.

A while ago, when he was sitting with her in the holding room upstairs, beside the courtroom, she knew Dad wanted to ask what this was all about, how she could have been accused of doing such terrible things. But he just cried, almost silently. The only time she had seen tears in his eyes was when Mom died. Then, as the police officer came back into the room with a pair of handcuffs and snapped them on her wrists, he looked ancient.

Lying on the bunk, she became aware that until this moment she had sealed off her memory from the time last night when she opened her door to a series of loud knocks. Detective Garafolo and a man in uniform walked in and told her she was under arrest.

Then she realized that it was ten days ago when the first sign appeared that trouble was on the way. Caroline Robertson, who never missed a session at Snug Arms, was absent for three days. She might have had a spring cold, but Laurie noticed one morning that the director's door was closed, which was very unusual. And at noon that day a tall man, a stranger with a take-charge stride, came down the hallway toward her; he stared as she approached and suddenly ducked into the director's office. More children began missing school, a lot of them, and the next afternoon, on the way home she crossed a downtown intersection and saw Mrs. Robertson in her Mercedes, waiting for the traffic light to change. Lilly Robertson saw her, for sure, but turned away quickly.

She hurried home and waited nervously for Allison, with whom she shared her apartment and some of her deepest feelings. She wanted to talk about how scared she was, but this was Allison's day to work late.

Screened by a curtain, she stared into the kitchen of an apartment across the street. A man and a woman often appeared during the hour before dinner to peek into the oven or pour a drink. As she watched, the man slipped into the room and grabbed the woman from behind. She turned and they kissed each other again and again, as if they would never stop. His hands were all over her, and for a reason Laurie did not understand, her tenseness increased and she snapped the curtain closed.

Evening came, and Allison was still at work when the detective, Garafolo, pounded on the door.

At eight o'clock she rose from the bunk and called for the matron. She wanted to call her lawyer, she said. Hull's home number was busy and she was told that she had used up her telephone privileges for the day.

A half hour later word finally worked its way through the circuits that Defendant Coles's trial date had been set for three months off. She was removed from her cell and placed in the back of a squad car, handcuffed behind a wire screen, for transfer to the larger county jail, five miles out of town. Not the big place, upstate, that the attendants had described so pointedly, just a facility with more cells.

They crossed the town line in the darkness and the driver, a very large man, caught her eye in the mirror. He called back, "Chick, how about I pull over behind some trees? I'll come back there and you can do tricks on me. If I'm not too old for you, I mean. I'm going on seven."

Chapter 4

IN HIS OFFICE ON THE AFTERNOON OF ARRAIGNMENT DAY, THE DISTRICT attorney of Princess County contemplated a weakness in his case that Harry Hull would probably spot sooner or later: While the indictment overflowed with filthy counts, few juries would take the unsupported word of tiny children to send an adult off to the pen for most of the rest of her life. Their accounts would have to be corroborated by other compelling evidence. And while new cases at Snug Arms would no doubt turn up as the investigation progressed, they would be variations on the theme and would not solve the shortcoming.

And what if some children balked at testifying, out of fear, embarrassment, or plain cantankerousness? Or what if in the end the parents would not cooperate?

There was no escaping the fact that the available proof in the Coles case consisted of words that would be spoken by, as that headline called them, tots. Under oath, of course. He could hear Hull addressing a child with a smile: "Let's play a quiz game, young lady. Here's the first question. What does telling the truth mean?" And Justice Mathes would have to allow that line of attack. Hull would have no trouble demonstrating that some children hadn't a clue to the difference between telling the truth and telling stories.

The biggest problem was the lack of hard evidence. A doctor would testify that a child's vagina had been bruised and showed signs of having been penetrated. But the defense would establish, correctly, that the size and structure of vaginal apertures varied widely among small children. Moreover—and scientific literature would be cited—bruise marks did not necessarily mean penetration. The jurors would be cast adrift in the jargon of the medical trade.

Nor did Harmon have an eyewitness to Coles's misdeeds, even though that was no longer a rigid requirement in cases of this kind. A molester was not expected to commit crimes against children on a busy street corner at noon. In the language of a precedent-setting decision, "Crimes involving sex are not perpetrated in public view. They frequently happen in seclusion and in the shadows." So this case would have to depend almost wholly on circumstantial evidence, and on testimony about what children had told parents and investigators. In other words, hearsay, a lot of which was admissible when the sexual molestation of small children was involved.

The D.A. was walking through what he called the desert area of the law—arid stretches full of hidden gullies, treacherous expanses that had to be negotiated with great care.

Harmon's guest interrupted his contemplation. Dr. Amanda Roth had already talked to two Snug Arms children. And she had been involved in many similar cases and testified often as an expert witness. Roth was the one who had sounded a national alarm over the hidden incidence of child abuse in nursery schools. Mothering used to be a full-time task, she pointed out. Now, with so many two-job families, little ones were more and more cared for by strangers and the opportunities for sexual abuse had multiplied.

She was stout and had a strong, businesslike manner. When Harmon asked if she had enjoyed the springtime drive through the Hudson Valley, she did not reply. She was not here to exchange pleasantries, which was fine. With juries ever in mind, he liked the way she sat down wordlessly, snapped open her briefcase, and set herself up to take notes.

He had decided not to open the conversation with an elaborate explanation of why he wanted her assistance. He would feel much more secure if she got the point herself. It was a test. So he merely displayed the information that Detective Vincent Garafolo had brought in. There was his chat with Caroline, Lilly Robertson's daughter, who described the jam-on-the-vagina incident. And Bonnie Strand told him that Coles had inserted a stick into her vaginal orifice.

And there was an impressively articulate statement from Billy Andrews, about defecation and what he called the making of poop cakes. Harmon felt something crawling up his back.

Dr. Roth compared Garafolo's transcripts with her own interviews, and her eyes moved down the documents quickly; Harmon noted that she was not a stopper and gasper. She finished and spoke in a series of rapid runs, shaking her head. "The allegations support each other in the main. Nevertheless, this just won't do. The age factor. There's a credibility problem. You need collateral testimony. From more parents. Believable supporting evidence."

Of course. She had passed the test. He pushed a contract form across the desk. "The state wishes to extend its retainer on your services, Dr. Roth. We would like you to consult with more Snug Arms children and with parents. Will you accept the assignment?"

She ignored the form. "On one condition. I am basically a therapist. Some parents may want professional help for their children. Treatment of their emotional injuries. I must be free to treat as well as investigate. When a district attorney doesn't permit that, I decline to participate."

Harmon thought about it. He didn't care if she rang up some fees, but he wanted no conflict between the roles of investigator and healer. The defense could score heavy points on that one. ("Dr. Roth comes in here and says the children needed treatment. That means they were injured. It's circular reasoning and there's no way the accused can defend herself, especially when our own experts have not been allowed to see the kids.") Could Harmon trust Roth not to mix up her functions?

He abandoned that tack. He needed her and would have to take a chance. "You may also act as a therapist, Dr. Roth, so long as you don't volunteer your services," Harmon said. "You must be asked."

He had left her no wiggling room. She signed, and after calling Lilly Robertson to make a date, she left with a nod and no words. The D.A. took off the rest of T.G.I.F.

Harmon climbed to a study in the tower of a gray-shingled Victorian house on a hillside. Against a wall, or as against it as a curved wall can accommodate a rectangle, stood his small desk on which lay a single sheet of reminders; the rest of his papers were filed. Across the room was Serena Wiley's large table covered with piles of paper. He considered her method haphazard; however, she had no trouble finding anything.

She did not hear him enter the study, which gave him an opportunity to observe her unseen. She was sitting in a deck chair out on the widow's walk, a brick-red circular deck that surrounded the tower. A sun visor shadowed her eyes, which were gray-green and had a translucence that was characteristic of near-sightedness. Her exquisite nose and strong chin were in full sunshine, and her hair lofted in a lazy breeze. She was a brunette who had clearly been born a redhead; the fair, freckled skin showed it. And there she was, wearing his sneakers again, a habit that delighted him. Two notepads lay before her and the thick draft of an appeal brief sat in her lap.

They were an odd match. She stood just below his six feet and her torso was strong and fluid. He verged on skinny; she said he was slim. His hands were large and bony and his arms ever so slightly long for his body. His hair was crew-cut and dark, except for strands of gray that she exorcised now and then. And there was a smile-enhancing gap between his upper front teeth; she liked to explore it with the tip of her tongue.

And stranger yet, they were loving adversaries, and he took note of a particular blessing. He did not have to face her in courtrooms since he prosecuted cases and she appealed convictions with the submission of heavyweight briefs. He put people in jail, she tried to get people out. When his head reached the pillow at night—she didn't use a pillow—he was exhausted less from the day's work than from an evening of mixed quarrel and banter over this case and that. But she was exhilarating. Serena's brain had a high-quality motor. And there was all the rest of her, which was captivating. You are one lucky guy, he reminded himself frequently. Take care not to forget that.

He went out onto the walkway and offered some advice. "Keep your brief brief, Serena. It's spring, and judges' fancies turn to golf. They read the last ten pages of appeals."

She continued to write and he understood he was being dismissed.

Later, over a gin on one cube, no vermouth, no nothing, he broke the news that was bound to stir an eruption. "Jacko has assigned the Laurie Coles case to Harry Hull."

Serena never referred to Mathes as Jacko. She called him the Hangman of Hudson Ferry and said he believed that those who appeared before the bar were guilty until proven innocent. He agreed and added a complaint that reflected his own view of courtroom propriety. Mathes had difficulty hiding his scowls at defense lawyers as he found favor with prosecution motions. A district attorney did not want a jury to begin sympathizing with a defense lawyer who was being put down day after day. However, they both conceded, the honorable one was adept; he was not often reversed by the appellate courts.

She shook her head sadly. "Mathes is a shameless hypocrite. Harry Hull is an all-right guy, but he's a civil litigator, a commercial lawyer, and he gets contract work from the town and county. How many criminal cases has he handled? A dozen? I think he's won five and lost seven, which ain't bad in criminal law, but he's not what the Coles case calls for. She needs someone who's been around the block with you guys."

"Of course. But I will say Hull put up a good fight this morning."

She glanced at her watch. "Six o'clock, Pete. Turn on the news. Let's hear the inadmissible evidence that a town full of potential jurors is getting."

He tuned in channel 22 and there was Corky McGonigle with the lead story.

The words: "Heaven became hell today in Hudson Ferry. This serene hideaway has become the scene of a sickening scandal. Unthinkable, almost unspeakable, crimes have been committed against tiny, defenseless children, according to an indictment made public today. The children are not even old enough for grade school. They are enrolled in the Snug Arms Preschool, where the crimes are said to have taken place. We advise parental guidance as we report the allegations."

"Do you love it?" Wiley said. "He called the charges almost unspeakable so he could go on and on about them."

"The indictment alleges that children's orifices were invaded by foreign objects, that small animals were sacrificed to terrorize them into silence, and that there were attempts to force them to eat and drink human wastes. We'll see."

Harmon switched to a network channel: "After Laurie Coles's lawyer stood up in court and proclaimed her innocent of a multitude of charges of child molestation, District Attorney Peter Harmon told us he felt he had a very strong case." There was the suggestion of a tolerant smile on the lips of the newscaster. "Evidently Justice Johnson Gillies Mathes was not impressed by Miss Coles's plea of not guilty. He did not seem confident that she would show up for trial if released on bail, so he made sure she wouldn't be able to meet it."

The pictures: A long-lens shot, a sneaky angle from the corridor while Mathes was in chambers having one of his recess coffees, showed Coles as a rigid rod at the defense table. And there was unsteady footage from a hand-held camera. Fred Coles was reaching out to grab a lens, rage over his face, the berserk father of a child abuser who had been impaled on the bar of justice. Cut. Lilly Robertson came slowly down the steps of the criminal courts building. She halted before the cameras and used the words, the ugly words, through tears as she told of the abuse to which her daughter had been subjected at the Snug Arms school.

Harmon raised a long foot and kicked it toward the TV. "Stop it, Tiger Lil. You could pollute the legal ecosphere." He did not want her to lay the basis for a claim that the trial should be moved to a less inflamed jurisdiction.

Serena zapped the TV. "Here's how it works these days, Pete.

The defendant is tried and convicted over television, then goes into court for a show trial. Joe Stalin could have learned something from the way we do it. And when a skeptic asks if that's fair, the answer is, 'Do you want the government to run the press?' "
She let up. "At least you had the good sense to keep your handsome face out of the camera."

He smiled. "Thank you. But take my word for it, love. Dershowitz for the defense couldn't win this one. The verdict is, excuse the expression, locked up."

She jiggled a sliver of an ice cube against her empty glass. "How cocky we are tonight! You sound pretty sure of yourself."

He thought he had heard the opening shot of a new set of hostilities whose outcome was predictable: In the end they would agree to disagree, again. Meanwhile he fired back by reviewing the evidence, piece by piece, and concluded with a brief summation. "However you want to cut it, Laurie Coles, sex freak, is going down. But don't get the idea that I've got a cinch here. A lot of this case will depend on little children's testimony. And children say this and that. They're con artists and you're never sure when to believe them. And neither are juries. A defense attorney can make kids look like babbling idiots. So I'm not home free. But never fear. She'll go up."

She thought about that. "I don't doubt it, Pete. She won't walk out of court, not with the heat that's stirring up in this town. But there are a lot of hidden traps in a case like this and cooler heads on appellate benches look for them. It's so easy to walk on a defendant's rights in a dirty case. I'm not saying you'd do that, but the Hangman would. He'd rather take a reversal than go against the local sentiment." She paused. "And if you help him kick Laurie Coles around to get a guilty verdict, this caretaker of underdogs just might help with her appeal. That would be a first for us, wouldn't it, sweetheart? Don't say I didn't warn you."

He wished he could be sure she was joking.

She changed the subject. "It's your turn to cook, isn't it? What's to eat?"

"I ordered your favorite. General Ho's spicy chicken. It ought to be here in ten minutes. Let's have another drink and fight some more."

Serena Wiley was the reason Peter had elected not to pursue the law down in the big city, also known as action central. For jungle warfare, drop into any courtroom in the five boroughs, where lawyers were expediters. Live bodies were piled and stacked. Drugs and thugs. Hundreds of new cases every day and almost all the accused were guiltier than sin and hell was full to the ninth circle. There was no room at the jailhouse and the creeps and judges and lawyers all knew it. A defense attorney said, "You have nowhere to put my client. Make a deal." An assistant D.A. replied, "You want to bargain? Give me a guilty and I'll let him off with a lesser. But you make the first offer. Give me a hard time and I'll get him a spot close to the fire. Negotiate and go. I'm busy."

The rest of the routine was predictable. The A.D.A. would add, "Do you think there might be a spot for me in your law firm? Just kidding, guy. Don't repeat that. But let's do lunch."

Harmon would have liked Hudson Ferry for no other reason than that Serena loved it, and he loved her. She was a Yalie who had been an editor of the law journal and he was a Harvard grad who had clerked for the chief justice of the Massachusetts Supreme Court. He often tried out his toughest cases before her, those with weaknesses that a keen defense might use to beat the rap, and waited for her to spot the flaws. Then he repaired them as well as he could before facing a jury. He suspected, however, that she did not point to every lapse she found.

She was like no one Pete had known. Both thirty-five, they had come together a year ago in a rush of passion and debate and were still exploring each other feistily. He remembered her predecessors—terrific girls, intelligent and with looks that would draw a crowd. But he maintained a certain distance; when the topic of marriage surfaced, tension followed and bonds loosened and parted. The child of a drearily unhappy union, he feared that wedlock dispelled mystery, ended intrigue.

Serena had her own reason for never having married and had come to recognize it as a product of her errors. She had known many congenial guys who shared a tendency; they rarely challenged her and soon lost their attractiveness. Pete Harmon had shredded that pattern.

They had decided to share the house with the tennis court, on which he ran her legs off, because they wanted to be together. And they were aware of gossip over the fact that they had not appeared before a justice of the peace. Serena had fashioned a reply in the event she was ever asked: "I'm too busy. You see, Pete brings his cases home and I spend a lot of time sneaking looks at them and figuring out how to help the defendants get off." She wouldn't actually say it, but she savored the thought.

Given all that, Harmon had recently been surprising himself by muttering, privately, "Pete and Serena Harmon." He thought he might present the subject in the guise of humor.

"Serena, how about a tennis tournament? If I beat you in straight sets, I get the grand prize."

"What's the prize?" she would ask.

He would look into the gray-green eyes he wanted to penetrate more deeply, to explore hidden landscapes behind them. "You marry me." He would see how fast she wanted to run.

He enjoyed their squabbles. For her, the deader the duck, the more attractive the case. "Pete," she would say, "the grimier the accused, the more he's entitled to the best defense because he's a goner before he walks into court. Tell me about the kicks you get out of putting people in jail."

He would reply, "Tell me about the joy of keeping hoods *out.* Here's what you really want to ask. 'Do prosecutors use human lives as currency to buy career advancement?' The answer is no. We help keep civilization together."

Their feuds had prompted friends to ask questions for which answers were elusive. "Why do some lawyers like to prosecute while others prefer to defend? Are D.A.'s we-will-have-order types? Are defense lawyers cranky mavericks?" The trouble was, lawyers had been asking those same questions for ages.

On Saturday morning he had his bait ready for another tussle. "Love, last night you started to tell me about the loser you're trying to get out of jail this time. But you fell asleep."

She responded as if she had been interrupted in midsentence. "It's the kind of case prosecutors dream of. A horrible rape by a thug with a record a yard long. And then he beat hell out of her. She I.D.'d him and a semen test showed it could be his. Three residents of her building identified him as the man who boarded the elevator at her floor ten minutes after the rape. And they saw blood on his hand, where she bit him. The blood matched his type and it added up to a solid case. He got fifteen to thirty." She smiled. "So he was guilty as hell, wasn't he, Mr. Prosecutor?"

The district attorney was aware that he was being set up. "What are you holding back, Counselor?"

The arrow flew. "The assistant D.A. overlooked something, the son-of-a-bitch of a defendant clammed up, and his lawyer talked to him for a total of nine minutes. His alleged lawyer."

Harmon decided to enter the trap. "Why do you refer to your client so harshly, love?"

"Because he's a pimp who beat up his girls so badly that one needed cosmetic surgery. And he was picked up the afternoon of the rape on the beating charge. He was in a holding pen waiting for arraignment from an hour before until two hours after the rape. And he'll even beat the assault charge in the end because the girls are too scared to testify against him. That's why I call him a son-of-a-bitch."

He couldn't resist. "Okay, so he didn't do that particular rape.

Why not let him decompose in jail? Wouldn't everybody be better off—especially his girls?"

"No good, Pete. If they want to seal him away for society's good, they have to get him for the right crime. Otherwise, nothing makes sense. I'm going to get him out."

Then came one of her jabs. "Did you know that a law was once introduced in Nevada under which all D.A.s would have to do time in jail, so they'd have a better idea of what they were asking juries to do to defendants?"

"Gosh, I didn't know that. Did it pass?"

She laughed. "Almost. It got three votes out of fifteen."

Harmon had much to do on the Snug Arms molestation case this morning, so he kissed her and hurried off, stopping only to perform a ritual. Sitting on Serena's work table was a brass replica of the scales of justice, the blindfolded lady perched at the top. A heavy metal bar stamped PROSECUTION pressed one tray down; a bar half its weight, propelled on high, was stamped DEFENSE. He reversed the weights and left.

A half hour later he was at work on the file of the case known as *The State of New York versus Laurie Coles.*

Chapter 5

Harry Hull had spent Friday night in fitful sleep with a leg kicking and a tremor running up his back. Giving up at dawn, he sat out on the back terrace, where he found himself still wondering why Jacko Mathes had fingered him for the Laurie Coles case. *A broad who messes with lollipoppers? Strawberry jam on her strawberry? I could have been a baseball coach.*

He tried to concentrate on a strategy, which still eluded him. The problem was, Coles needed a defense *team*—several experienced lawyers plus paralegals and researchers. Instead she had a wanderer in the legal forest.

He gave it up and faced up to the real reason for his sleeplessness. Whenever pressure closed in, he embarked on fitful trips into his past the moment his head touched the pillow. They were reruns of dreams that had begun in his boyhood. It was on his twelfth birthday that Eddie Hull, a man whose heavy drinking fueled violent outbursts toward the child, was running him down at dinner, as usual, when he suddenly blurted an incredible revelation. "You're not our boy, Harry. We ain't your Mom and Dad."

Despite Edna Hull's futile protests, the alcohol-driven tempest went on and the child was told that when he was six months old, he and his parents were coming home from a drenching weekend in the Adirondacks when their bus skidded and crashed into an overpass. The parents were among many fatalities, but the boy survived.

He still recalled a sour laugh at the end of Eddie Hull's story: "We took you out of an orphanage because we thought you looked bright. *Wrong.* You're not smart enough to be ours."

The dream cycle began that night and went on and on, and in the mornings the boy remembered a terrible screech and a stunning crash. But he could never figure out whether those were actual recollections trying to emerge or fanciful products of a yearning to solve the mystery of his origins. Much time was spent imagining what his mother and father might have looked and sounded like.

At home the subject was never mentioned again, except that Eddie Hull said the names of his true parents had been lost; Edna Hull never contradicted her husband. He persevered—that's how he thought of it afterward—and joined the army the day he finished high school. Off he went to Vietnam, where he was terrified by the strangeness of the land and numbed by the ferocity of the killing. Then came the American withdrawal, as defeat was called, and like many others he tried to obliterate the experience from the day he was discharged. He had an extra reason. In the dream scenes in Nam, the screeching of tires was loudest and the crash of the bus most piercing.

Hull ended up in New York by chance and never saw his adoptive parents again. But one day he met a lawyer and found the courage to ask for help in locating his mother. The attorney dug out his past, which provided still another shock. As was Eddie Hull's alcoholic way, he had told some of the truth and inexplicably fabricated at the same time. Harry was actually the son of a woman named Ann Morgan who was sixteen years old at his birth and had put him up for adoption. No trace of her, nor a clue to his father's identity, could be found.

Harry Hull kept the name and looked no further for branches of the true family tree.

The attorney cottoned to the confused young man and offered a lot of advice. Taking some of it, Hull used his G.I. Bill money to enroll in college, then went on to a law school at which little time was spent analyzing the decisions of justices Holmes and Brandeis. It was an institution whose graduates knew how to file motions, subpoena documents, and obtain trial delays—the ingredients of meat-and-potatoes lawyering.

It was then that he had practiced law in New York and abandoned or was driven out of it. Up in Hudson Ferry, enjoying the rewards of real-estate tinkering, he built a reputation as a straight-shooter who got the job done and understood the importance, in a small town, of getting along with the influentials.

Finally he dressed and drove over to Crestview Park for a softball game. Hull played a good third base for the River Raiders, rarely committing errors and consistently delivering a batting average of .330. He was a singles hitter, using lunging swipes to punch the ball between infielders. But the Raiders' manager never quit. "Harry, pull the bat back and swing through. You'll knock the ball across the river." Not one to quarrel with success, he went on punching out singles and driving in runs. The manager concluded that Harry was not a high-risk taker.

The Raiders took the field against the Red Hook Rumblers to an ovation from forty fans. The Raiders' pitcher struck out the first Rumbler but walked the next three hitters. With the bases loaded, the manager said, "Move up, Harry. They'll try to squeeze in a run with a bunt. Cut him off at the plate."

Hull moved in. Ball one. He edged back. Strike one. Another step back. Ball two. At ball three he had retreated almost to the base, ready to dash in if he had to. He heard a woman's voice in the crowd yelling for him to move in but had no time to look. The pitcher was already in his windup. The batter swung and the ball rocketed to Hull's right. He launched himself, gloved it, and collapsed onto third, doubling the base runner off. The inning was over, the crowd cheered, and the Raiders went on to humble the Rumblers as Hull maneuvered four singles through the infield.

Over beer, the manager said, "You were lucky on that line drive, Harry. You couldn't have defended against a bunt. Sometimes you have to gamble. You can't play it safe all the time."

Chapter 6

ROY ROBERTSON MOVED A LITTLE TOO SPEEDILY ALONG MARINA ROAD IN his Infiniti, which he called his rickshaw from Osaka so people would ask what it cost. Grant Burney, the man from IBM, was pulling into his driveway and received a greeting from a horn with a wide repertoire; this time it was the opening notes of the theme from *The Godfather*. But Robertson was distracted and omitted the usual wave. His wife Lilly had called an hour earlier at his downtown office and gone on and on about how Carrie was driving her crazy, crying, slamming doors, and running from room to room. The frantic behavior had begun the day the child first mentioned the strawberry jam and Laurie Coles, and it was getting worse. Roy had held the phone away several times, when Lilly seemed to finish and then started all over again.

On Birch Lane he eased into his driveway, grabbed his briefcase, and did not go into the house. Instead, he rushed out to his retreat, a cottage overhung with leafing elms that sat a half-acre behind their grand home. Lilly heard the car and banged on his door minutes later. There was no answer and she pounded again and shouted. "Get out of there, Roy! Dr. Roth is coming and we're going to talk about Carrie. You won't duck out of this one!" Hearing only the clicking of a computer keyboard, she rattled the knob and pounded again, then hurried back to the main house and buzzed him on the intercom. There was no answer. She stood in the kitchen and remembered the month of silence and inaccessibility before she learned that he was no longer a dashing marketing vice president. Now, as a stock-market player who described himself on his tax returns as Investor, he was minting money.

But Roy had become strange. On mornings when she was in a mood to recall intimacies of the night in colorful detail, he would remember something he had meant to tell her about index futures, and a new stock-picking program he was developing that would bring Wall Street to its knees. The fidgeting started the evening Lilly told him what Carrie had said about Laurie Coles at Snug Arms. He crossed and uncrossed his legs, then fussed with the well-adjusted air conditioner and entered his cocoon. Roy Robertson had a list. Blindness. Heart attack. Stroke. Cancer. Cancer. If such words found their way into the mind they were to be cast out. And now there was Laurie Coles.

From the composition of the eight people who formed a circle at one end of the commodious living room, it was clear that Robertson was not alone in his reticence to become involved; the only Snug Arms father present was Grant Burney. He and his wife sat beside Dr. Amanda Roth, who occupied a high-backed chair near the bay windows. On her other side were detective Vincent Garafolo and a young blond man who Dr. Roth introduced as chief of the child protection unit at the general hospital. In the center, with Lilly, were Ellen Strand, Bonnie's mother, and Letty Andrews, whose son Billy said the teacher had defecated in the presence of the children. Mrs. Andrews was an attractive woman despite a deep frown that intruded lines into her face and an intensity that was marked by unrelenting knuckle-cracking.

The doorbell rang and a maid led in a tall, bony woman who sat down without greeting anyone and placed a briefcase across her lap. It was Mildred Cross, owner and director of Snug Arms, or what had been Snug Arms. Mrs. Robertson did not want this irresponsible person in her home, but Dr. Roth had insisted.

The most common expression was apprehension, but Grant and Marla Burney seemed more puzzled than tense.

Dr. Roth had seen these small initial turnouts before. "It's normal," she said. "Parents, this will be difficult. Understand that. You will need all your love for your children and all your courage. Many people were too terrified to come tonight. Parents don't want to believe that their children's bodies have been invaded. They hide the truth to chase it away. So, if you please, Mrs. Robertson, would you tell us how this all began?"

Lilly Robertson glanced through the living room portal at a curving red balustrade and spoke in a hushed voice. "When I brought Caroline home from school that day, she told me she didn't want any jam with her toast. She said I should put the jam on her vagina—on her peepee, she said. She told me that Laurie Coles did that and licked it off. I tried to stay calm when she said Miss Coles put jam on her own vagina and asked Carrie to—" she paused "—lick it off. It was a game the teacher called Sweet Time.

I didn't know what to say. I asked her if there were other games
like that and she said they played something called Bottoms Up.
The teacher took off their clothes and kissed their behinds. She
wouldn't say anything else. She was angry because I wouldn't—
you know. But she said Miss Coles did the same thing with other
children." She dried her eyes. "So I went to the police, and detective Garafolo talked to Carrie and she told him the same thing."

"Thank you. Now, Mrs. Strand, would you tell us what happened to your daughter?"

Ellen Strand spoke softly. "Yes. Bonnie came home and asked
me for an ice-pop. She took the stick and stabbed it into a slice of
peach. She said Laurie Coles put a pop stick into her vagina and
that it hurt. I took her to the doctor. He found marks in her
vagina that could have been made that way. So I went to the
police, too."

The group studied the furnishings as Ellen Strand regained
control. "Bonnie hasn't been the same since she told me this." She
stared at the director of Snug Arms. "Now she sits with her cray-
ons and all of a sudden she starts crying. So I look at what she's
drawing and I see violent pictures."

She stopped. "Please go on," Dr. Roth said.

Mrs. Strand displayed a drawing that showed a series of green,
jagged lines. Each streak ended in a fiery red ball.

"We see this often among sexually traumatized children," Dr.
Roth said. "It's their way of depicting blood, which is a metaphor
for violence."

Grant Burney had a thought. "Maybe it represents jam."

Dr. Roth was familiar with denial. She looked past him and
spoke to Marla Burney. "Have you noticed any behavioral
changes in your child recently?"

She shook her head and Burney said, "Tom's as wild as ever."

Dr. Roth returned to Mrs. Burney. "Nothing?"

She shrugged, uncomfortably, it seemed.

"Has he talked about animals?"

"Yes. He's learning the names of the dinosaurs."

"Small animals. Dead animals, perhaps?"

The Burneys looked bewildered.

"Tantrums?"

"Once in a while," Marla said. "The usual."

"Nightmares?"

"Now and then. About dinosaurs."

"Inappropriate screaming?"

"That's hard to say. Tom might not agree about the inappropriate part."

As Dr. Roth turned to the others, Grant Burney remembered

the morning it all started. He had made thumping and growling sounds as he came down the carpeted stairway, and as sure as taxes Tom came flying into the hallway, arms stretched out, and landed on his chin, which the thick carpeting saved. The four-year-old whooped as his father picked him up and slung him across a shoulder. The altitude was two inches over six feet, so Tom enrolled in the air force and gunned down every enemy who had the bad fortune to fall within his sights. "Captain Tom-Tom!" he announced. "Ace fighter pilot!"

At the breakfast table Burney reminded the boy of the penalty for missing a tackle. Tom gulped a spoonful of bran flakes and opened his book. "The pilot saw the other plane. Zzzzz! He dived and zzzzz! The other plane fell in the ocean. Captain Tom-Tom went home."

Marla laughed as she glanced at the open book and saw only pictures on the page. Burney walked out to fetch the morning newspaper and thought about that Tom-Tom business. The boy's name was Thomas, and Tom was okay, but Tom-Tom had trailed him home from nursery school and he wasn't comfortable with it. Who was Tom-Tom? Some kind of a jungle boy? He wondered if any white nursery school Thomases were known as Tom-Tom.

He removed the *Hudson Ferry Tribune* from its orange tube, saw the headline about little Tom's nursery school, and shivered. April had become December.

Dr. Roth was telling the group, "Sexually molested children suffer from stress disorders that block them from revealing what is on their minds. Sometimes they feel they might have done some-thing wrong themselves. Or they're so disturbed that they just can't talk. They scream or wet their beds. And there's fear. Many children are threatened by their attackers. If they tell, something terrible will happen to them or their parents. These cases don't differ much in detail."

She turned to the woman who could not stop cracking her knuckles. "I'm sorry. What is your name, please."

"Letty Andrews."

"And your son Billy told Detective Garafolo about a room at Snug Arms in which some of these acts took place?"

"Yes."

"All right. Do you mind if Mr. Garafolo tells the group what Billy said?"

She shook her head and Garafolo read from his notebook.

Laurie took me to the secret room during playtime. The monster room. Downstairs.

Mildred Cross's head snapped up. "There is no downstairs," the director of Snug Arms said. "I told you that, Detective!"

Garafolo continued.

Billy: There's a table down there. Like our picnic table. She did poo-poo on the table. She told me to make poop cakes. She said they tasted great. I didn't eat them. I ran upstairs. Laurie ran after me and caught me. She said if I told anybody about the poop cakes, the monster would get me. I started crying and I said I wouldn't tell.

Garafolo: Can you remember any other games like that one?

Billy: She did peepee and said it was good to drink. Some of the other kids drank it but I didn't.

Garafolo: Did that happen in the secret room, too?

Billy: In the monster room.

Garafolo: Why do you call it the monster room?

Billy: There's a dragon down there. It lives in a cave under the ground and it comes in the room when Laurie calls it.

Garafolo: Did the dragon ever come in the room when you were there, Billy?

Billy: The other kids saw it.

Garafolo: How old are you, Billy?

Billy: I was five years old on my birthday party. How old are you, Mr. Giraffe? I want to go home. I want Mommy.

Mildred Cross jumped to her feet. "Now, let's get something straight. There's no basement at Snug Arms and no secret room, Mr. Garafolo, and you know it. You told me you were going to get a warrant and search the building and I told you you didn't need one. Search it." Her hands were trembling and her voice rose. "You went through the whole place, knocking on walls and picking up carpets and examining the floorboards. And you didn't find a secret room. So why are you spreading this nonsense?"

Garafolo turned to Dr. Roth, who responded in a gentle tone. "No one is accusing you of anything, Mrs. Cross. Dealing with abused children is a complex matter, and we have to listen to all the victims."

"Do you put someone in jail every time a child fantasizes?" Mildred Cross shouted. "And wreck a good school? Snug Arms is dead. I got a call this afternoon and a man said he was going to torch the property. I called the parents of the only three children left of the thirty-five enrolled and asked them to pick up their children. Then the bank called in the mortgage. I have to pay it off within ten days or they'll foreclose. Snug Arms is gone. What else do you want? A child uses a red crayon and your twisted minds see blood. If she used a black crayon, would you say she was drawing death?"

Grant Burney raised a hand. "She's got a point." His wife reached for his arm, then stopped.

Liam Gunn, the sex-abuse investigator from the hospital, ended his silence. "Mrs. Cross, we know children imagine things. We hear it all the time. But we have to talk to them. And to their parents, too. Then, when the interviews are finished, we can sift through the material and separate fact from fantasy. You see, there are rarely any eyewitnesses to crimes of this kind. So we have to check out everything, and we may discover that nothing happened. I doubt it, but it's possible."

Mrs. Cross sat down, hands still shaking.

"Here's the problem," Gunn said. "We have even more evidence. Some children have told us that Miss Coles sacrificed animals at the school, in front of them. So we must conduct a thorough investigation. We have no choice, I'm sure you'll agree. And to investigate properly, we need a list of all the Snug Arms parents."

"And if I won't give it to you, you'll subpoena it, right?"

Lilly Robertson understood now why Dr. Roth had insisted that the director be present.

"We need not only the names of current parents," Gunn said, "but of those whose children were in the school last year, when Miss Coles joined the staff."

"Or else a subpoena." She stared at Robertson, then thrust a hand into her briefcase. "I brought the lists with me. I wasn't born yesterday." She crossed over to Gunn, handed him several sheets, and walked out of the room. The door slammed.

The session broke up five minutes later. As Vince Garafolo and the parents left, Mrs. Robertson turned away from Grant and Marla Burney, who she felt had been less than cooperative. Then she sat down with Dr. Roth and Liam Gunn and watched them prepare a covering letter for a questionnaire that would be sent to Snug Arms parents, past and present.

She listened, and as a draft was completed she argued that the message ought to be tougher. No doubt should be left that parents would be harming their children severely if they did not cooperate. The language was hardened and the meeting ended. Dr. Roth and Gunn left with the impression that while Lilly Robertson would be a great organizer, she would need attention. Good intentions could get out of hand.

The Burneys stopped for a bite on the way home. Then Grant walked the babysitter home and stopped on his way back to take in one of his favored sights across the river, a palisade of staunch, green-clad pines. He thought of them as a battle formation that symbolized his personal march toward professional success. He had just learned that he would soon leapfrog some gifted colleagues. On the first of the month, Gray Matter Burney, as he was known down at the IBM research center, would take command of a design group that was transforming tiny bits of arcane materials into products with miraculous capacities, microchips that would bring about another revolution in the world of computers.

In the morning, at breakfast, the Burneys told Tom he could never do anything that he should be afraid to tell them, or that he should be ashamed to talk about. They reminded him that he had never been spanked. They didn't think hitting was a good idea. When he tossed a tantrum, he was exiled to his room until he felt better. Then Mom or Dad sat down with him and figured out what was bothering him.

Tom said they were the best mom and dad in the world and on the sun and the moon.

After a while they told him they were interested in Laurie Coles and asked him to tell them about her. Tom told them what went on at Snug Arms—minute by minute, it seemed. The children drew pictures and learned letters of the alphabet and some numbers, and they played games in the backyard.

Grant Burney wondered if they had done anything different when the weather began turning warmer. Had they ever taken their clothes off, either in school or outside?

Tom was amazed. "Dad! Not in school!"

Marla asked if he had ever heard of a game called "Sweet Time."

He shook his head and asked for a cinnamon doughnut.

Marla said that once in a while even the best grownups do dumb things. "Did Laurie ever do anything dumb? Or do a bad thing to you?"

He frowned. "Laurie's great. Captain Tom-Tom likes Laurie!"

With the boy in bed, Grant asked Marla, "What the hell is going on?"

"I don't know," she said. "Maybe nothing. Maybe something awful."

* * *

The days passed quietly. Spring continued to push through the earth; crocuses could be seen, and signs of gold appeared in the forsythia.

On a Sunday an afternoon shower pitted the surface of the river. Dusk beat eight o'clock by five minutes, and at eight thirty, with the moon in a blackout, darkness enveloped Hudson Ferry. But caution reigned and not until midnight did a pickup truck brake down silently before the Snug Arms school on Linden Terrace. The driver waited. Another car pulled up behind him, then a van and two more cars.

The drivers climbed out. One was Lilly Robertson, who knew the lay of the land. Snug Arms sat near the town line on a plot that realtors wished they had spotted during the economic doldrums. Mildred Cross had snapped it up while they were dealing in acres closer to the center of town. She had Snug Arms built at the bottom of a slope, and because spring and fall rains could cause inundations, the structure was built on a single level. Behind it was a drainage gully that was fenced off because it became a gushing stream twice a year.

The men, carrying sledges and pickaxes, advanced on the frame building in the darkness as Mrs. Robertson remained at the curb and watched the road. The front door was whacked open. They went to the rear, pounding the floor as they moved along and stopping at each suggestion of hollowness to chalk the spot with an X. At the rear they started forward and pickaxes went to work. The flooring was ripped and splinters flew. No word was said as the planks were torn loose. But each excavation ended with tools clanking harshly on cement.

They moved back through the rooms, checking the depth of each wall, searching for a space large enough to accommodate a hidden room. None could be found and they retreated, sweating. But a man at the rear of the group saw a circular scoring in a wall and smashed a one-way mirror that sat below it. Behind the mirror was a video camera, which he demolished with his sledge. They climbed into their vehicles and drove off.

Lilly Robertson stood on Linden Terrace and cursed her husband. Roy would have figured out a way to solve the mystery. He was a very smart coward.

Chapter 7

THE ABSENCE OF TELEVISION VANS FROM THE CENTER OF TOWN CALMED
Hudson Ferry as it waited for the trial of Laurie Coles. The *Tribune* wanted to do a profile of the district attorney, but Pete Harmon would not cooperate. A promise that the case would not be
mentioned stimulated a smile but no words.

Harmon was on edge. Each time he called Liam Gunn he received reassurance. Parent questionnaires come in slowly at the
start of this sort of investigation. Dozens will soon pour in; they
always do. Harmon wondered what made Gunn so sure.

He had to give the grand jury evidence of more crimes committed by Coles, and though the process of adding new counts to the
indictment was uncomplicated, charges could not be added end-
lessly. "Give us a break," Harry Hull would say. "You're putting
the defendant in endless jeopardy. Let's look at the old parch-
ment we celebrate. The Constitution." That's what Harmon himself would say. And while Jacko would not be pleased with such
oratory, he would have to bow to the framers. And he would grant
no postponements. This town wanted justice on schedule, not
stalling by legal beagles.

There was another time element. A trial on such serious charges
would normally consume at least a month. But there were reasons
aside from pressure to shorten this one up. Children were unpre-
dictable on the stand, as their testimony in divorce cases so often
demonstrated. So Harmon would keep his witness list as brief as
possible and accelerate the proceedings.

He read Gunn's covering letter once more:

Dear Parent: A heartbreaking situation has come to light in
our community. Children have been sexually molested at the

Snug Arms Preschool, either recently or at some time over the past several months. We are alerting you to this tragedy and asking for your help because your child may be among the victims.

As you have no doubt heard, Laurie Coles, a teacher at Snug Arms, has been indicted on charges of sexual assault and making threats. The district attorney has considerable evidence that crimes have been committed against three pupils, but we believe that many more have been molested. We need your cooperation urgently. Please fill out this questionnaire and return it as quickly as possible. Give special attention to the questions about unusual behavior by your child, such as tantrums, sulking, emotional withdrawal, persistent nightmares, and fighting with playmates and siblings. Thank you.

It was to the point, omitting the psycho-babble referred to as scientific language. And it should meet the goal of just about doubling the twenty-three counts against Coles.

Harmon decided he would use only two experts, Dr. Roth and Liam Gunn, both of whom had talked to the Robertson, Strand, and Andrews children. There was no need to clutter the case with redundant testimony. Besides, repetition dulls the edge.

Scanning a report of what was known of Laurie Coles, a line caught his eye. She shared an apartment with a woman named Allison Wright. Should Wright be interviewed? Had Coles brought tales home? Poop cake stories? His imagination widened. Just a minute. Might something else be going on? Could Laurie and Allison be sharing anything in addition to an apartment? Such as each other?

He let those questions wander to the rear of his mind and shuffled through the mail, piling the nut stuff on a table. The kook postmarks ranged from New York to California and Hawaii to Berlin. He usually let the stack mount until, as now in the late afternoon, he would sift through it and copy one or two that might provoke acidity in Serena.

Unfortunately the letters were as boring as junk mail and should have been sent to Justice Mathes since they dealt with suggestions for the punishment of the Coles bitch, as she was invariably referred to. Harmon got the drift from the opening lines and usually skimmed the balance. Tie her down every day for an hour, put cheese between her legs, and send in the rats. In addition, rat time should be changed frequently so she'd never know when to expect the nibbling.

He had told Wiley he seriously considered sharing this mail

with Justice Mathes. Why shouldn't Jacko suffer, too? She said that would be downright risky. The Hangman of Hudson Ferry was too suggestible.

In the latest heaping pile was an envelope with a local postmark. That was unusual. He read a typewritten note.

Mr. DisTericT ATTorney:

This is hardesT leTTer I ever wriTe. I know This Coles biTch is inocenT. In Snug Arms. I know who is gilTy. Me.

He pushed the rest of the trash into a cardboard box and sat down again. The letter was unsigned, of course, but it could not be ignored.

I work for gardner who Took care of Snug Arms. To Take away dead Trees and mow. ThaT kind of Thing I did iT Home, before I come To This CounTry. Illegal sTaTus.

I Take childs wiTh me To back of properTy when They are in yard playing and puT my organ in Their mouTh. I have sexual dysfuncTion and need childs.

I don'T Tell you whaT is my name. You know why. BuT This Coles biTch, she did noT do iT.

That much too clever. Where did this illiterate immigrant get "illegal status," and "my organ" and "sexual dysfunction?" On the way home Harmon concluded, uncomfortably, that nuts were sprouting in the treetops of Hudson Ferry. Here in sleepytown, where "Good morning" and "Excuse me" were still part of the language. Next time he walked down River Road he would try to figure out which gracious lady or gentleman would get the tickles out of sitting down and composing such sickness. The hail-fellow manager of Third Federal Savings? How about bouncy Sal of Speedy Sally's? Sex cases stimulated mysterious undercurrents in people. He grinned. Serena, if you don't mind, do not tell me that a sweet young thing like Laurie Coles could not have done those things.

Serena minded. It was her turn to cook, so she attacked in the kitchen, where an all-vegetable dinner was on the menu; she had gained an annoying pound during the week.

"Pete, this case lights up a terrible problem. I'm sure kids are being sexually abused. It's one of the aberrations of human conduct. And there are few worse things parents could be told than that their child has been molested. The idea makes my skin crawl and I've wondered what I would do if I was up against that fear. But that doesn't mean an accused person is guilty."

"Who said it did?"

"Your investigators." With Liam Gunn's questionnaire in hand, she went on. "I don't know if Coles is guilty or innocent, but I know unfairness when it insults me. This questionnaire is a packet of fertile seeds. It plants allegations in parents' minds, which they'll soon transplant into their children's heads. And testimony will grow like crabgrass. Will there be a prize for the four-year-old who can tell the wildest story, Pete?"

She would not get away with that. "You're off base. We're not dealing with adults here. How else can we get the kids to speak up? They're scared."

"How do you know?"

He was just short of sharp. "Qualified investigators say they are. That's how the system works. If you can think of a better way of doing things, run for president." He couldn't resist. "Or district attorney."

"Touchy-touchy! Why aren't you looking at another possibility? Maybe more children haven't spoken up because there's nothing to talk about. You're out hunting and fishing."

"Jesus! We have juries to decide whether witnesses are believable, and whether the prosecution has made a case."

"Yes, after the facts have been cooked and strained by a judge with a low-priority interest in the truth. Keep bringing this stuff home, Pete. My interest is rising."

Amanda Roth and Liam Gunn had given Lilly Robertson the names of parents to whom the questionnaires were sent. They suggested she wait three days, then begin calling. The scenario never varied, they said. Everyone in town who could see or hear knew of the scandal at Snug Arms, but humans were masters at evading what they did not want to believe. Thus, the questionnaire would touch off fresh shock waves. Then fear would set in. Some mothers, anticipating scoffing responses from uncomfortable fathers, would even hide the letters. A catalyst was required.

Lilly Robertson made the calls and closed off avenues of retreat. "If we don't act," she said, "our children could be vulnerable to emotional crippling later in their lives. Meeting this situation head-on might save them from serious illness."

Each evening, with Roy hidden away in his cottage, she showed groups of parents what her Caroline and Bonnie Strand and Billy Andrews had told the investigators. And, she said, every child should have an immediate physical and psychological examination.

She watched the slow erosion of denial, especially among mothers. One woman said another nursery-school child had slept over and she found the youngsters nude in a bedroom; the boy was on top of her daughter. Others remembered behavior of a sexual nature, and talk they had ignored, about poop cakes. Now they said they would question their children more closely. Lilly Robertson delivered new batches of questionnaires, sat in homes while they were completed, and delivered them to Liam Gunn.

Still, with little time before the opening of the trial, Gunn had given the district attorney only twenty-one completed forms. From these, Harmon harvested evidence for only four more counts at most. Gunn said there were problems. "We showed three kids a photo we doctored up. It was supposed to be a class picture, with the Snug Arms teachers. But we substituted movie stars for the other two teachers. Laurie Coles was in the picture, but when we asked who did those things to them, two of the kids pointed to Jodie Foster. We checked with the parents and they said the kids watch a lot of TV movies. But that's the quirkiness you get at these ages."

Harmon sighed and threw out one of the four new charges he had counted on.

"The big snag," Gunn said, "is that a lot of children are clammed up. They know Coles is in jail, but she told them she has magic powers. She'll get out and hurt them if they tell. That's the classic molester's weapon. But we're taking care of that problem today."

There was another snag. The other two Snug Arms teachers were not available for questioning. Knowing they were tainted forever, they had left town immediately after the indictment was handed down. One teacher, Teresa Vane, sent the D.A. a statement saying she had never observed any wrongdoing on Coles's part. But the letter was not notarized. Harmon suspected that if the teachers ever returned, it would not be until the scandal had exhausted itself.

Nor was he happy over the attitude of Mildred Cross. The director of Snug Arms, still furious over the demise of her school, gave strangled and uncommunicative answers to his questions. He could subpoena her, but he was not anxious to put a hostile witness on the stand; he placed Cross in the wait-and-see category.

That afternoon Liam Gunn and half a dozen mothers drove twenty-one children to a roadside ice-cream parlor in the neighboring village of Riverview. As they enjoyed their treats, the parents brought up the terrible trouble at Snug Arms and told the children that in September they would be going to a new nursery school. Mothers had warned Gunn that their children would be reluctant to talk about what happened at their school, and the group became silent as he explained that sometimes kids were afraid that a person who had done bad things would get at them and hurt them. Tom Burney and Billy Andrews began to shout and throw ice cream at each other.

On the way back to Hudson Ferry the caravan pulled off the highway at a bus shelter across from the county jail. Gunn—some of the children were calling him Uncle Liam now—pointed to the towering walls and said, "Wow, is that high! I couldn't climb over that wall in a thousand years. Could you kids climb over it?"

They looked up and told him they couldn't climb over that wall in a *million* years.

"Laurie's in there," Gunn told them. "And she couldn't get out in a *billion* years."

He explained what a jail was, and how sad it was that sometimes people hurt other people and had to be kept behind bars and high walls. He pointed to the guard towers. "They're watching the bad people all the time," he said. "No way they can get out. Maybe in the movies, but those are made-up stories."

Dr. Roth set up a schedule. First Gunn would talk to the children who had seen the jail and remind them of how secure it was. Then he would ask questions about Laurie. When he finished, she would take over.

Three days later Harmon had enough information from children and their parents to add a dozen new charges to the indictment against Laurie Coles; he looked forward to thirty-eight counts.

In the evening, with Tom Burney in bed, Marla interrupted Grant's endless work with a disconcerting story. "This afternoon Tom called me into the bathroom. He was naked and he asked me to touch his penis."

Burney set his pencil down.

"It was a stiff little thing." Tears were forming. "You know how he gets when he waits too long. So I asked him why he wanted me to do that and he said Laurie touched him in the bathroom, at school. I didn't know what to say, Grant. I felt as if the air had been sucked out of me."

Burney shook his head silently.

"I asked him when it happened and he said he couldn't remember. Then he started laughing and I asked him if it was just a story. He said no, it was true. And he said she did the same thing to other kids. I don't know what to believe, Grant."

He paced the living room. "You talked to him, Marla. What do you think?"

She dried her eyes. "I don't want to fill out one of those morbid questionnaires, and it's possible that the kids are telling each other stories. But I've decided I should go to the district attorney and tell him about it. I don't think we have the right to hold it out."

He sat down with her. "I asked you to decide because I have a story for you, too. Evidently a rumor's been going around that we've been slow to cooperate with the law on this matter. Anyway, Don Hobson came up to me at work this afternoon."

Don Hobson lived up the road in Greenwood. He was black, too, and junior to Grant.

"Don said, 'What you're doing is bad for us. Bad for our image.' I didn't like that, so I said, 'Who's *us*?' And he said, 'Oh, I'm sorry, Grant. I thought you were trying to pass for black.' He walked away and I went after him and said I do what I do because it's the right thing." He smiled. "I told him not everything is black or white."

They had been over that topic many times and determined that they would not be stereotyped. As Grant put it, "I am not guilty of being embarrassed by making it."

Marla sighed. "And you didn't want to pressure me."

"Right. We're not on trial, and we shouldn't act as if we are. You've made up your mind and I agree with you. The right thing is not to hold out information."

In the morning Marla made her coffee stop at Ellen Strand's, and Tom and Bonnie raced into the backyard to hunt for dinosaurs, also known as raccoons. Marla, too distracted to press her stop-smoking campaign with Ellen, said she wanted the truth. "The night we were at Lilly Robertson's with the investigators. I know Lilly was upset, but did others feel that Grant and I were holding out?"

Ellen poured coffee and lit up. "I think it was only Lilly. You know how she is. I thought you and Grant were doing what you always do. Sort of exploring. You were trying to get people to stop and think." She smiled. "But maybe you sounded a little too cautious."

Marla recounted Tom's story about Laurie Coles and Ellen looked scared. She agreed to watch over the children while Marla went downtown.

"Mr. Harmon," Marla said, "the truth is, my husband and I have been a little skeptical about some of this Snug Arms business. We've had trouble taking all the stories seriously and we still think some parents may be going off the deep end."

The D.A. was careful. "You don't have to believe either way. Why don't you just tell me what brings you here?"

She told him, and added that she didn't know whether to take little Tom literally; he was quite a storyteller.

Moments later Harmon had the thirty-ninth count for his presentation to the grand jury.

Justice Mathes had to be circumspect. He never paraded his dates around town. A divorced man who wanted a seat on the court of appeals did not want his wanderings chatted about. So they frequented a fine restaurant down the road in Poughkeepsie.

If there was one topic that fascinated women, he had discovered, it was life in the black robes. He told lively stories and always fudged identities because you never knew. But this evening he was in a more philosophical frame.

"Lawyers are actors," he told Sylvia. "Prosecutors and defense attorneys, both of them. Some of them are pretty good, but see one act, you've seen them all. I fight off the yawns all the time." He poured wine. "So I do crossword puzzles and they think I'm taking notes."

She was surprised. "Jack! You make it sound as if it's all a big fake!"

He was taken up with her. She was a knockout. "It's a big show. Lawyers are never honest about anything. Drop in some day and watch them drip with sincerity when they tell jurors that all they want is an open mind. One of these days I may interrupt and tell the jury that all they want is to win and they don't give a damn how. That's the period end of it."

Over six months' time, Jacko had become increasingly interested in Sylvia's possibilities. Not only was he wearing out on the carousing life, but she had once married money and stayed with it long enough to reap a rich harvest at divorce time. And she owned nothing short of a castle at river's edge and hopped off to the Caribbean or Florence when the urge visited. She also talked of having a child and kept asking if he was sure he could produce one. No problem, he told her.

She picked up on his theme. "What does the way a lawyer acts have to do with whether a defendant is innocent or guilty?"

She was enjoying the wine and he signaled for another bottle. "Look, I can tell you whether a criminal is guilty before a trial starts. Before the hambones take the stage."

"Wait a minute. Why did you say a criminal? What about the innocent ones?"

He remained patient. "People don't understand the safeguards that are built into the system. One in a hundred didn't do it. And prosecutors don't want to spoil their records by bringing bad cases into court. Look at the Snug Arms case. Do you think the town wants a black eye? It would be terrible if the whole thing turned out to be a mixup. I assure you that's not the case. Hey, let's order. You want me full of energy, don't you?"

They returned to her mansion and Jacko marveled again as they entered the living room, thirty feet by twenty-five with a lofty beamed ceiling and white walls hung with modern paintings. The furniture was uniformly a stylish gray, and high open arches led into large adjacent spaces. He was most impressed.

Sylvia decided to forego birth control on this night. Jack was becoming more and more serious, so why not find out just *how* serious he was? She was back in a marrying mood, and it sounded as if he would soon become a big man in the legal world.

In the morning he went home swinging his malacca, elated. He had been finding most women like most lawyers; their acts tended to resemble each other. But Sylvia had introduced new evidence that called for reconsideration of that impression. And she had large money.

Still, he remembered, in one way it made no difference whose bed he shared. The moment he closed his eyes, he thought of a particular someone else. But she was in the past and that's where she would stay.

Chapter 8

ASSIGNMENT TO THE SOLITARY CONFINEMENT BLOCK OF THE COUNTY JAIL was a mixed blessing for Laurie Coles. She did not have a cellmate. But on the way back from each meal she had to pass through the men's area and endure screaming taunts. "Baby fucker!" "They should tear your tail out! I've got something here that'll rip it!" When she reached the women's section, doors slamming deafeningly behind her, the messages changed. "Suck me! Drown in my blood!" "Come on out of solitary. I want you, honey!"

She wondered how long she could take it.

Her father caught the bus two hundred miles away in New Hampshire on Friday nights and reached Hudson Ferry early on Saturdays. He stayed in the terminal until noon, moving from seat to seat and drinking corrosive amounts of coffee. Then he wandered around town, stopping for a sandwich. At one o'clock he boarded a local bus and rode to the end of the route. Walking the rest of the way by two, when the thirty-minute visiting period began, he arrived at the county jail.

Laurie was brought out and placed behind a wire barrier. They talked about everything but what was on his mind. He told her about his job and she told him, too many times to be convincing, that jail was not as bad as she had feared. When their time was up, she touched a finger to her lips and pressed it against the screen. He met hers with his.

Fred Coles checked into a motel near the jailhouse where only cash was accepted, which was fine; he did not believe in credit cards. Then he stretched out on a bed, stared at a blank television screen, and thought about his wife, wondering what she would have been saying to Laurie.

On Sundays he paid his bill at eleven o'clock, ate some corned beef hash, walked back to the jailhouse, and saw Laurie. Then he caught the bus back into town and made the six o'clock to Portsmouth. On the return leg of one of those trips he decided to talk to a bank about a mortgage on the house. If he got ten thousand dollars, he could handle the payments, if his job held out. On Monday mornings, he fried an egg and went to work.

Harry Hull visited the jail regularly and asked questions, some of them over and over. "How many kids attended Snug Arms? How many classes were there? How many rooms were used? Tell me about the other teachers. Where's the director's office?" He had gone through the school before its destruction, but said, "Draw a picture of the layout. Have you ever heard of a hidden room? I know that's silly, but did you hear talk about it?" And, "Who took the children to the bathroom? Was the door left open when they were in there? Again and again: "Was the door always left open? Was that a rule? I have to ask these questions."

On a morning three days before the trial was scheduled to open, Hull put down his breakfast spoon and told himself, "Get this straight. Whether Laurie did the crime is something to ask God about. What I've got to figure out is whether I should go all out defending her."

At the prison he was taken to a large visiting area instead of to the small room in which they had been meeting. Laurie was led in handcuffed and sat on the other side of the wire screen. The visiting hour had not begun and they were alone, except for a male guard who patrolled behind Hull and a matron who walked back and forth behind the prisoner.

He opened the session by telling Laurie what she might expect when—sorry, if—the jury brought in a guilty verdict. The actual sentence was beside the point. She would do no less than twenty-five years, twenty at the very least, before parole would even be considered. "I have to tell you about that," he said. "You have to know."

But he did not suggest that she might change her plea to guilty when the gavel came down and opened the proceeding.

"Laurie," he said, "here it is. I'm going to bust ass defending you. Now, let's get to work."

She started to reply, but he saw the matron moving slowly toward them and held up a hand. "This is an attorney-client conference," he said loudly. "We want privacy."

He heard steps behind him and his shoulder felt a hand with the grip of a vise. "Get off me!" he shouted, trying to rise. "Take your hand off right now!"

The grip tightened and he heard, "Watch your mouth, Lawyer."

The matron stepped back and he saw her speak into a walkie-talkie. A door at the far end of the room opened and two male guards came running into the area.

"Get the superintendent in here!" Hull shouted. He felt his legs quiver and saw fright in Coles's eyes. His voice took on a drill sergeant's tone. "The senior one of you get the superintendent on that phone. I want him in here now or you'll be standing before a judge in an hour."

A guard with a stripe on his shoulder signaled and the shoulder was released. The senior man took the phone from the matron and spoke into it. Hull turned and saw that the man who had been roughing him could have been a tackle for the Chicago Bears.

The far door opened and an oval of a man in a black suit came in. Hull said, "Sir, I am this prisoner's attorney and I demand privacy. This matron was snooping on our conversation and I won't stand for it."

The superintendent smiled. "I'm sure there's been a mistake. Your name, sir?"

"Harry Hull. And if you mess around you'll be explaining the mistake to Justice Mathes. I demand a private room. And if the prisoner is mistreated when we're through talking, there'll be hell to pay. You people are not above the law."

The superintendent waved the guards out, whispered to the matron, and said, "There's been a misunderstanding." He left and Hull and Coles were taken to a private room, where he told her, "Forget about that. But keep your voice down."

He opened a line of questioning that sounded more casual than it was. He had been wrestling with a problem that defense attorneys wished would go away. Should the defendant take the witness stand. "I want to know more about you, Laurie. About your life, things you do."

She settled down and talked about her mother. "Mom always said, 'Be curious. Try things out.'" She went on and described her father; she could not remember his ever having raised his voice, she said.

Hull noticed that she was telling him about her parents instead of herself. He waited for a break and eased into a topic he had encountered in his midnight reading of articles about child abusers in psychology journals. "What about guys and dates, Laurie? Tell me about boyfriends."

She looked down at the table and shook her head but said

nothing, then glanced up and said, "Why are you asking me that?"

The response was too guarded. "I'm trying to anticipate everything the prosecution might pull. I'll tell you straight out. I'm worried about you taking the stand. If you testify, you open the door into your private life. It's called character stuff. They can find out if you've been married or had children. Or even, sometimes, if you've been sleeping around."

She turned away and he said, "Talk to me, Laurie. We don't want to be ambushed."

She looked him in the eye. "Boys just wanted one thing. They didn't even care who I was. As long as I had a place they could stick it into. That's all they were interested in. You asked me, I told you."

Hull was shaken by what sounded like an extreme reaction to a problem many young women face. He wanted to ask her if she had never met a nice guy. Instead, he took a detour. "What was your salary at Snug Arms?"

She looked surprised. "Three hundred dollars a week."

He calculated. "That's about two and a quarter in take-home pay. What's your rent?"

"Four hundred dollars."

"That's almost half your take-home. How do you pay it?"

He thought he saw a hesitation. "I share an apartment, so it's just two hundred."

"Who do you share it with?"

Her voice rose. "A friend. Allison Wright. Is that what you're trying to find out?"

"I don't know what I'm looking for. Now don't get mad. How many bedrooms are there?"

She jumped to her feet and he said, "Sit down, Laurie!"

She remained standing.

He stood, too. "Listen to me. I told you I'm going to bust ass defending you. But I have to make all kind of decisions and you're going to have to trust me or get rid of me. Tell me about Allison Wright, and don't hold out."

Their eyes met again and her voice was firm. "We were lovers. Are you satisfied now?"

He shook his head. "Laurie, I'm not trying to butt into your personal life. I don't care what anybody does. I'm asking these lousy questions because I have to know more than the district attorney does. Or at least as much. So I've got another one. Do people know about you and Allison?"

She shook her head angrily and he went back to the routines at

Snug Arms. But he was no longer really listening and wound up the session quickly.

In her cell, stubborn because her anger remained strong, she was glad she had not told Hull of a decision she and Allison had agreed on shortly before her arrest. They had decided to live apart for a while because neither was ready to say she had reached a firm decision about lifestyle. For Laurie, at least, repelled by constantly groping guys, the liaison had been an experiment.

But that had nothing to do with the fact that Allison had not visited her since the arrest. Given her attorney's questions, she understood why.

Lying in her bunk, she suddenly thought it was just as well that her mother was dead. No matter what Mom said, she couldn't have stood this.

On the way back to town, Hull tried to weigh the benefits of putting Coles on the stand and showing the jury that she was likable plain folks against the risk of opening up her private affairs to cross-examination. Would the prosecutor try to get into her sex life and play to prejudices? Of course he would. Did people still look on lesbians as freaks? A lot fewer than in the old days, but Hudson Ferry was not quite the capital of broad-mindedness, was it? On the third hand, would the jurors hold it against Coles if she declined to testify? Would they feel she might have a lot of dirty stuff to hide? He couldn't find answers he trusted and put the dilemma on hold.

Pete Harmon studied Allison Wright closely as she entered his office. Dark hair was closely cut and she had restless dark eyes that checked out the room quickly. As she sat down, he reminded himself to avoid the typecasting that cast lesbians as wrestlers. He was helped by the fact that Wright had all the grace and good looks of a starlet.

"You don't have to answer my questions," he told her, "and you don't even have to speak to me without an attorney. But if you decline to answer my questions, I can subpoena you to appear before the grand jury. That's how it works."

She nodded and said, "Ask whatever you want to."

"How long have you and Miss Coles shared an apartment?"

"About six months."

"Did she talk much about Snug Arms?"

The reply was quick. "All the time."

"Did she say anything about the children?"

"She never stopped."

Harmon drove on. "You know the charges against Miss Coles,

so I'll ask you if she ever mentioned any of the acts she is accused of committing."

There had been a smile on her face; it vanished. "Of course not! It's all nonsense!"

He nodded. "Juries decide those things." But the message was received and he altered course. "Do you still consider yourself a friend of Miss Coles?"

She spoke sharply. "Of course. Look, let's stop pretending, Mr. Harmon. Go ahead and ask me if she was my girlfriend."

He saw that she had not come to his office without careful preparation. "Were you and Miss Coles having sex?"

"If you subpoena me, this is what I'll tell the grand jury. I love guys. They turn me on. And the same goes for Laurie. I've never seen a girl pant after studs the way she does." The smile returned. "May I leave now, Mr. Harmon?"

The D.A. tried to be pleasant. "Thank you for coming in."

Alone, he considered. If Coles testifies, I'll be entitled to get into personal things. Character stuff. If the door to lesbianism can be opened a fraction of an inch, I can call Wright and pound away at her. Then I'll find a psychiatrist who'll testify that many lesbians fit the model of child molesters. Helpful opinions are available, always.

He would tell Serena that Allison Wright had the cool of dry ice and should have been an actress. But then he decided not to discuss the matter with Serena at all. Since he really didn't give a damn who was straight and gay, this part of his job was bringing on an attack of ethical embarrassment.

On the Saturday before the trial date, Allison agreed to have a sandwich with Fred Coles if they could meet away from the sporting goods shop at which she worked. In a coffee shop he told her, "It won't be long before this crazy thing is over." He thought she looked at him oddly. "Look," he said, "about the rent. I'll send you money for Laurie's share."

She shook her head. "Don't worry about that. The landlord made me get out last week."

He was angry. "Because of Laurie? Where are her things?"

"I have them and you can pick them up any time. I'm sorry, Mr. Coles, but I can't do anything to help her now."

He did not understand. "What do you mean?"

"If I visited her in jail just once, people would start talking." She hesitated. "Do you see what I'm getting at?"

He was perplexed. "Mr. Coles, the best thing I can do for Laurie is stay away from her now. I love Laurie, but—" She stopped and stared at her sandwich. Then she jumped up and ran out.

When the point finally penetrated, Fred Coles sat in the coffee shop, horrified. After a while he went out and walked to the edge of town and back and was still walking as the day ended, wondering what could have happened to his dear little girl.

Chapter 9

Summertime real-estate closings were unusually slow in the Hudson Valley and that was one reason Harry Hull was giving the Coles case more and more of his time and attention as the trial date closed in. There was another reason. He had discovered that he did not give a damn what anyone thought. He was going into court to win.

He took a lot of heat as spring gave way to summer and did not suffer it easily, at least during the first few weeks. He was putting away an onion omelet at Speedy Sally's when a real-estate agent who sent him a lot of business tapped his shoulder. "You going to try to get the bitch off, Harry?"

He swallowed egg and onion unchewed and said, "Jacko sat me down at the table. Should I tell him to go fuck himself?" Maybe that would restore some flavor to the omelet.

The real-estater freed Swiss cheese from his incisors. "You don't have to go bananas in court."

He swiveled his stool. "Why don't you say it straight?"

"She should go up. That's where she belongs."

He lost his cool. "She hasn't got a chance. She'll go. Everybody in town knows that. So what's the hard time for? Off my back!"

"See that she does."

A week later it was a Spanish omelet and Sal clucked at him. "How can you go ahead with this thing, Harry? Everybody's going to hate you."

The fork hit the plate. "Everybody off my case! Is your memory failing, Sal? Don't you remember when you needed a lawyer, when that guy got hurt in here? You had a shaky situation, with that pipe sticking up out of the floor. What did you want your

lawyer to do? Walk into court waving a white flag? Off my back!"
He threw money on the counter and walked out.

Time passed. Hull was taking his cleaning in and found himself
explaining that he was a court-appointed lawyer. He went down
the street and bought a shirt and had to point out that he'd be
lucky if he got five hundred dollars out of this case. The judge will
set a fee the size of a gnat's eye.

Lilly Robertson accosted him along River Road that morning
and asked if he would be happy when he got Laurie Coles off and
little Caroline grew up to become a pervert instead of a woman.
The rest of the day he greeted friends and acquaintances with a
brisk opening line. "Say one word about the case, one word, and I
walk away."

On the Saturday afternoon before Trial Monday, Hull did not
tune in the ball game. He was exhausted from long nights in law
books, where he reviewed procedures in criminal cases and
sought the expertise he did not have. Enough. He stretched out
on the back terrace and regarded his acres. Abundant elms and
sycamores surrounded the house, and Mr. Sod, the lawn doctor,
had created a billiard table of a landscape. He found himself con-
templating his future. What will they do to me when the Coles
trial is over? Send the word to clients and make me an untouch-
able? The longer he thought about such matters, the more often
he returned to the kitchen for another beer and, steadily, the
angrier he became. Is that what they do when you decide to do
your job? Beat you into the ground?

He sloshed a can across the lawn and said it out loud. Is that
what they're doing to Laurie Coles? They're mad and they could
care less whether she's guilty or not. I don't know if she's guilty,
either, do I? It's none of my business.

He stretched out in the living room and sleep came with a final
thought: Jacko Mathes had chosen him to represent Laurie Coles
because the pols thought of him as Old Reliable. He was being
counted on to go through the motions for his client. That's all.
Forget the heroics, huckleberry.

And there was another thing. Would he ever find a wife?

At eight o'clock he awoke, showered, and drove off to the Saturday night haunt, the Ferry Ale House on Water Street, with the
bright red awning and the name spelled out in chipped ivory
letters on the windows. It was a jumping joint, but this evening, as
he entered, the sound level declined abruptly.

He walked up to the long, varnished bar, ordered a beer and
two hot dogs, and put them away while studying a huge, illuminated painting that hung over the the glassware of the backbar. It

was a rendition of the Ale House, with Big Bert loading a stein
from the old-time tap handle. The brass rail gleamed under the
light and the artist had caught the adornments on the sheet-metal
ceiling. Everyone loved the painting but no one ever mentioned
the artist's name. Bert used to tell how the city fellow who had a
summer home in Hudson Ferry would sit at a table and sketch for
hours. Then one day a truck arrived and the painting was
brought in. But the artist was never seen again and no bill was
ever submitted, although Bert would not have argued over the
price. It was learned that the man had sold his home and was back
in the city. Then an obituary reported that he had died of AIDS.
Arguments started and some patrons wanted the painting removed. Bert wouldn't take it down and Hull backed him up with a
plea that ended: "Christ, he's dead. Rest in peace. Isn't that what
we should be saying?"

Now he turned to face the buddies and the wives; he was one of
the few bachelor members of a gathering known as the Saturday
Night Live gang. But the rest of the cast was wearing gags for this
performance.

"Bert," he told the bartender over his shoulder, "pick up the
checks from the following twelve people." He roamed the tables
and called out names. Then he addressed the dozen. "Run up any
tab you want, friends. Your evening is on me. Provided you don't
punch me out. Whoever decks me pays his own tab. Okay, citizens
of Hudson Ferry." He walked across the room and yanked the
jukebox plug from its outlet. "You're the jury and I'm Harry Hull,
Laurie Coles's attorney. The bitch's lawyer. And I'm here to find
out how we feel about justice in this town. So I'm going to ask you
some questions."

Not a chair scraped. Hoist-a-beer Harry was a favorite, even if
he had been acting zonky about that awful case of his. He approached the nearest table, picked up the early edition of the
Sunday paper, and read out a headline: "CHILD-ABUSE TRIAL OPENS
TOMORROW." Two of the table's foursome were women, one of
whom was his designated juror. He told her, "You don't have to
sit through this trial, Joan. You've been reading the papers and
watching TV and you already know the facts. Right?"

She looked at her husband, then agreed. "I know what happened, if that's what you mean, Harry."

"That's what I mean. Is there anybody on this jury who doesn't
already know the facts?" He waited. "Good. Then I won't need
too much of your time. So drink up. Bert, another round. All
right, you've heard the evidence. How do you vote, Joan? Is Laurie Coles guilty or not guilty?"

She did not hesitate this time. "You know she's guilty. Bert, change mine to scotch. Don't come around begging for sympathy, Harry."

"Thank you. Make it a double, Bert. As for you, Dick. How do you vote?"

Joan's husband, a Hudson Ferry policeman, was miffed. "The same way you would if you were on the jury instead of trying to get in the way of justice. Guilty."

It went fast, slowed only by irrelevant remarks that were quite relevant to the future of Laurie Coles. Guilty, beyond any lawyer's help. Guilty. If she's not guilty, I did it. Guilty. When you find a rat in your basement, shoot it. Guilty. Why waste the taxpayers' money? Guilty. Put her down. Guilty. You lawyers are all the same. Guilty. Thanks for the beer, Harry. Guilty. Bert, give me another one before he gets to the end. And one for the wife. Okay, Harry? Guilty. And go to hell for sticking up for her. Guilty, but I'll switch my vote if you'll pop for a gin, Harry. Make it Bombay, Bert. Laughter.

Hull returned to the bar, finished his Bud, and turned back to his audience. "Ladies and gentlemen of the jury, I didn't come here for a good time tonight. I'm planning my strategy. We're going to choose a jury in this case on Monday and you've helped me figure out how to do it. But I've got one more question for you, and it's a tough one." He walked over to the wife of the Hudson Ferry policeman, the woman who had told him not to come around begging for sympathy. "Joan, are you a friend of mine?"

She was embarrassed. "Of course I am, Harry. It's just that, you know."

"I know. And you know I wouldn't put you on the spot. But I've got a good one for you. Have you ever seen those movies in which someone is charged with murdering thirty people and cutting them up and mailing their bones to the relatives?"

She laughed. "I never miss those flicks."

"Don't you love the scenes that close in on the accused because you want to see how he's taking the testimony? You want to see the look on his face when a witness says, 'I was watching when he cut off the nose and wrapped it up and I followed him to the post office and saw him mail it. And he was laughing all the time.' Aren't those scenes great?"

She agreed. "I try to figure out what the killer will do. Laugh or cry or jump up and scream at the jury."

"Sure. And how would you act if *you* were sitting there? What kind of a look should Laurie Coles have when they testify that she did those things to the children? Should she smile? Or scream? Or look shocked that anybody could say such things?"

He had their full attention. The Ferry Ale House was silent as the patrons thought. Then Joan spoke. "I don't know, Harry. I just can't put myself there."

"All right," Hull said. "It's a nightmare, isn't it? Anybody want to help?"

No. "Okay," he said. "It's my problem. But I'm going to disappoint you about something. I'm not going to tell you whether I think she's innocent or guilty. I wasn't put on this case to decide that. And if you were on trial and I was your lawyer, that's how you'd want me to feel. Thank you all and good-night. Bert, I'll stop by tomorrow and settle up the bill."

As he walked out under the red awning, the Ferry Ale House was still. Moments later, normalcy returned and theories were exchanged on the best way to pick winning numbers in the lottery.

On Sunday morning Hull told himself that his client could not get a fair trial. Most people tried to be open-minded, but the pressure was enormous and few would want to see a person who just might have committed such terrible crimes walk away. At noon he was walking the downtown area and feeling closer to serenity than he had since the court clerk called and said come on down. On a whim, he walked into the Book Nook and told Polly Lennon, "I want to ask you a question. Is Laurie Coles guilty?"

She smiled. "You're in a bad way, Harry."

He was riled. "Is she guilty? You're the only one in town I haven't asked yet."

She became serious. "How would I know? But I'll tell you this. A couple of people were in the shop yesterday and one of them said this case was making a whacko out of you. And a few minutes ago someone said you flipped your lid at the Ale House last night. News travels fast in this town, Harry."

He leaned against the counter and felt the glumness return. "Yeah. I have to cool it, Polly. The case is taking me over. But I'm mad. You can tell anybody who asks that I'm an attorney-at-law, and Mathes is not going to turn me into his houseboy!"

"Why take it out on me, Harry?"

"I'm sorry. You happened to be standing there. Listen, at first I was bothered because Jacko put me on the case. But I'm over that. Now I'm boiling because I see how Coles is being set up. They're not going to give her a chance."

Polly walked over to a bookshelf and said over her shoulder, "Do you know who was called the attorney for the damned?"

"Harry Hull?"

He heard the laugh he liked so much; sometimes he thought it was Polly's sound that drew him into her shop. "Wrong, but you're in good company. It was Clarence Darrow."

He remembered as she handed him a book. "Darrow did a great job cheating railroad employees out of money when they were injured on the job," she said. "But one day he got fed up with being a legal crook and from then on he represented only people whose cases no one would touch. And it made his life. It's a biography, Harry. Read the first chapter, and if you like it you owe me twenty-five dollars." She laughed. "If you read the whole thing, I'll give you back five dollars."

He liked the first chapter and decided to go on.

Chapter 10

THE COURTROOM WAS BEING INVADED BY THE MOB, WHICH IS HOW HARRY Hull had come to regard many of his neighbors, and since it was too late for a refresher course in criminal law, he remained outside the swinging gate and mingled with the front-row buffs. Immune to the shuffles and struts of legal showboats, sometimes they were sharp observers, and as students of imperfection, their major interest was in the mental machinations of the juries on which so many fates depended. At the conclusion of a trial they pounced on the panel with comments in the guise of questions. "Yeah, but the defendant really did it, didn't he? There were too many holes in the prosecution's case, right? But wasn't the defense guy too cocky? Or did the D.A. turn you off more?" And always, "Who held out the longest? What hung you up?"

Hull seemed looser than at the arraignment ninety days earlier. A sprightliness was noticed as he maneuvered about the buffs, trying to distinguish the avengers from the bleeders. "Coles is bye-bye," said a regular. "She'll get the limit." A woman cut in. "Probably. But first she has to be found guilty beyond a reasonable doubt." Hull turned away. Sympathy would not aid his cause; the nattering of the hard-noses might.

Detective Vince Garafolo and District Attorney Harmon entered the courtroom, Harmon with briefcase, and sat down at the jury side of the counsel table. The prosecutor sits closer to the jury and gets in the last word. As the buffs said, "Go ahead. Ask why. Waste your breath."

"Here's the thing," an avenger told Hull. "Go for the heart. Forget the head. Find a juror who looks like a forgiver. Pluck the strings. Sure, juries listen to evidence, but they're human like us. Soft in the brain."

Hull asked, "What's that got to do with the Coles case?"

"You're not listening, Harry. The bitch is a butch. You know that. And the jury'll know it. Who else would fuck with babies?" He turned to a bleeder. "Excuse me. And I hope she goes up forever, Harry. But you want to find a closet tough on the panel. No balls showing, but never married and no children. If she doesn't give a little sigh with the answer about no kids, keep her. She could be your holdout. Jesus, you can't expect better than a hung jury. If the kids were screwed around, somebody has to pay. Tune in, Harry."

A strident voice broke in. "With all respect, my learned friend is full of shit. Pardon me, honey. You can't tell a butch from a bunny girl just by looking. Anyway, let's get one thing straight. I hope your client gets two hundred years, Harry. On the other hand, my friend is right about one thing. What you need is a holdout. A back-to-the-wall juror. The kind you could put against a wall and throw a thousand rocks. No surrender."

The bleeder said, "I would concentrate on the fact that she has to be found guilty beyond a reasonable doubt."

A reply silenced her. "You think they'll let her off? You want to bet a piece of your Social Security check?"

The advisers seated themselves to preserve their places and Hull stood before them. There was a new look to the courtroom today. Most trials were like ballparks. Hometowners on one side, enemy on the other. Here it was all home team. Lilly Robertson and Letty Andrews sat side by side in the front row and behind them were Marla Burney and Ellen Strand. In the last row on the right he recognized Laurie Coles's father, who had been calling him in the evenings, when the rates were lower, asking how the case was going. Also at the rear was Pete Harmon's girlfriend or wife or whatever. The tall one. Serena Wiley. She was a lawyer, too, wasn't she? And the reporters were at their table. Outside, back on duty for the big event, were the cameras. He saw Corky, Cornelius McGonigle, from channel 22, grinning and waving. Corky was a newshound who was known for putting a hard eye on official versions of events.

"Keep talking," Hull told his consultant.

"Get an academic on the jury, Harry. The kind who counts angels on pins. From his face you can't tell what he's thinking. He doesn't care if he loses the popularity contest. Prove it, he says. Prove it, prove it. People bore him when they give opinions. So here's what you do when you spot a guy like that." He turned to the female buff. "Excuse me. She could be a woman, I guess. These days. The lib thing. Look for the long face and the glasses and the suit, Harry. Sideways eyes. Don't ask him about his education or what he does for a living. Maybe Harmon will forget. He might be thinking about last night, if he got, you know, his woman he's shacked up with. So play your hand right and you'll get El Professoro on the jury. He might be your nitpicker. I hope it doesn't go that way, I'll tell you the truth. She ought to hang in public. But."

Hull dismissed most of it but filed away some. There were those who said psychological gurus could help select the best jury. Who said the fairest? The best for your client. Others said that was all self-promoting hogwash on the part of the shrink types with cash registers in their offices. Fate evens the odds, and in the long run protracted niggling doesn't help. Making his way through the gate, he was convinced that the law journals would still be debating the point on New Year's Day 3001.

"Oyez!" the bailiff shouted. All rose and Johnson Gillies Mathes strode in, red hair vivid against his trim black robes. A side door opened and Laurie Coles entered. Decorum having been learned since the arraignment, she was not handcuffed this time. And she looked like a corporate woman walking into a boardroom. Blue suit, white blouse, blue bow-tie hanging down the front, ash-blond hair freshly trimmed, curiosity on her face.

Hull squeezed her wrist. He yanked open his accordion file and the ordeal of Hudson Ferry was gaveled to its opening. The court would now find twelve good and true men and women blessed with blank minds.

Harmon was scanning the voluminous indictment, pleased that the grand jury had come through; the original twenty-three counts had grown to thirty-nine. But he was interrupted by Hull, who rose and spoke loudly. "Your Honor, we move that the defendant be released on reasonable bail during trial. She has been a model prisoner over the past three months, as the prison records will show. And no evidence has been offered that she would fail to present herself in court each day."

"Bail has been set," the judge said. "I thought you knew that. Let's move to jury selection."

Hull spoke in a rush and directed his words at the court reporter. "I advise the bench that I will ask the appellate division to order reasonable bail."

Mathes's eyes dilated. Had Hurry Hull forgotten his place? "Thank you, Counselor. Be *seated*."

Harmon was staring at Hull, who did not sit. "Your Honor, you appointed me counsel to Miss Coles and I am going to represent her to the last inch." Still speaking to the reporter, more slowly now, he was surprised by his words. "I don't see why I'm being forced to appeal for realistic bail. I'm asking you to reconsider your decision. She should not have to sit in jail and wait for the outcome of my appeal."

The bleeder winked at her avenger friends and Mathes said abruptly, "Recess. Counsel, join me in chambers." He strode out, followed by Hull and a startled district attorney.

Mathes poured himself a coffee as Harmon sat down. Hull remained on his feet. The judge's face was almost as red as his hair. "Are you loony, Harry? Do you want me to kick your ass around the courtroom and out of town?"

Hull's opening line was reminiscent of a gentleman at the club requesting a taste of the finest brandy. "Your Honor, if my manner was offensive, I apologize." Then his chemistry turned acid. "But you are treating me like a dead man or a flunky in this courtroom. I'm not dead yet and I'm not your caddy, sir."

Harmon was embarrassed as he saw the coffee mug shake in Mathes's hand and heard contempt. "You *will* be dead, Harry. Why do you think I appointed you to represent this defendant? Do you think you're a *lawyer?* Play ball or you're finished around here. Do I have to spell it out?"

The D.A. rose. "I waive my right to sit in. I don't think I can contribute to this conference."

"Go!" Mathes said. As the door closed he told Hull, "Get this straight. Some cases don't need trials. Coles is only here because that's the drill. The legal system. But I'm not running a county fair. Forget about bail. Get it out of your head. You know she'd be in Canada overnight. And even if she doesn't run, we don't want her walking our streets. She'd be shot! So if you keep up this nonsense, I'll put you on food stamps. You'll never get another piece of legal work in this town. Do you understand, you asshole?"

Hull thought it over. He started to take a deep breath, then stopped. He did not want to exhibit panic. But he realized he felt elated. This was the first time he could remember causing a ripple in these parts. What could Mathes do? Put him in a cell for ten days after the trial? He might become known as the lawyer who wouldn't be pushed around. Henry Fonda. Or Spencer Tracy or that lefty William Kunstler. Well, not that guy.

He looked around the room, searching for a recording device and finding none. "Jacko, why don't you put up a sign on my lawn. 'Don't even think about defending your client.'" He considered his next remark carefully. "Drop dead, Jacko." Then another word slid out. *"Asshole!"*

No one missed the fury on Hull's face as he came back into the courtroom. Coles whispered, but he shook his head and scrawled across a pad. She looked and nodded.

Five minutes passed before Justice Mathes mounted the bench, during which spectators awaited the throaty rumble of a famished lion who would swallow this cheeky barrister in a single gulp.

They heard the purr of a pussycat. "If you please, Bailiff, is our first panel ready?"

The bailiff had no chance to respond. A clamor broke out at the rear of the room, just inside the open doors, and spectators leaped to their feet. Those before the bench could not see. Nor could Mathes, who jumped up and pounded his gavel. Neither the pounding nor his shouts could be heard over the bedlam. He pointed to two policemen, who shouldered their way through the crowd in the aisle as a third officer tried to get spectators back into their seats.

Mathes's voice was finally heard over the din. "Bring those people before the bench!"

The officers reached a pair of figures struggling on the floor between the last two rows of seats. Fred Coles was sprawled across the body of a younger, chunkier man, with one arm stretched along the other's body. A hand that had gripped shipyard pipes for so long was locking the younger man's hand into a jacket pocket.

"A gun!" Coles shouted. His daughter jumped up at the counsel table. The man's elbow came up and smashed Coles in the nose. Blood spurted and a policeman seized Coles's arm. But he would not let go and officers had to pry him loose. They pushed him away and fell on the younger man, who was laughing wildly.

The officers came lurching down the aisle, holding the men with their arms pinioned behind. Laurie Coles tried to rise, but Hull held her back and said, "Don't move. Not a hair!"

As they came through the gate, a woman in the first row stood up, pushed her way into the aisle and through the throng and ran from the courtroom. It was Ellen Strand, mother of Bonnie.

Harmon was shaking his head and staring up at Mathes.

Standing before the bench, arms still restrained, were Fred Coles with bloody nose and the younger man, who wore a neat gray suit and appeared to be relaxed despite the grip on his arms. The officer holding Coles released him and laid a .38-caliber revolver on the bench.

"Get it out of here," Mathes said. The bailiff placed a handkerchief over his hand and picked up the gun. He snapped the cylinder open and flicked bullets onto the bench. Mathes gestured and the bailiff, hand still covered, moved the items to his own desk and slid them into an envelope.

Coles was wiping blood from his face as the judge asked, "Are you the defendant's father?"

"Yes, sir." He ran his fingers through his gray hair.

Mathes turned toward the other man but not quite at him, it seemed, more at a point vaguely over his shoulder. "What's going on?" He paused. "State your name."

The man just laughed.

Mathes hesitated. He wore a disconcerted look as he said, "Identify yourself for the record."

"Michael Strand, Mathes. Mickey Strand." He stood erect and spoke clearly, with a quick laugh, as if everyone would catch on to a hidden joke before long. He tossed his head and black curls were flung about.

"How did you know he had a gun?" Mathes asked Coles.

"When he sat down next to me, I heard metal bang against the seat. So I was watching him. Then he put his hand in his pocket and pulled out the gun. I pushed it back in and held his arm."

Voices rose again and the judge stood and looked across the room threateningly; the babble subsided. Coles, still wiping his nose, turned and nodded to his daughter as Mathes asked Strand, "Why did you bring a pistol into this courtroom?"

"I have a permit," Strand said. He seemed quite at ease.

"Search him, Officer."

Strand received a thorough frisking and a number of articles were laid on the bench. Two sets of keys, a wallet, currency and change, and a small white packet. He was released and, arms freed, he reached for his wallet and laid a card on the bench. The judge inspected it and said, "This is a New York City license for a handgun. It's not valid here. Anyway, you can't bring a gun into a courtroom, permit or no."

Strand was smiling. "Bite my ass."

The officer behind him moved forward, but Mathes shook his head and pointed to the white packet on the bench. He beckoned to detective Garafolo, who hurried forward. "Have the contents of this envelope analyzed and direct the laboratory to send the report to the district attorney." Then he told the officers, "Commit this man for psychiatric examination. Restrain him, and if he opens his mouth, gag him."

The smile had not deserted Strand. "Jacko, you son-of-a-bitch!" he said softly.

"Get him out of here!" the judge shouted. "Now!"

Strand was led away. He appeared less upset than dazed as he nodded to one person, then another, and moved along the aisle between the policemen.

"Go back to your seat," Mathes told Fred Coles.

"My daughter was sitting here with a gunman after her," Coles said. "Are you going to protect her, Judge? Is she safe here?" His

voice gave way. Mathes did not reply and Coles turned and
walked down the aisle.

Hull rose but Mathes cut him off. "I am not declaring a mistrial.
Forget it and sit down."

Hull did not sit. "I was not going to ask for a mistrial, Your
Honor. The jury panel wasn't in the room when this happened."
Mathes raised his gavel to abort the lecture, but Hull became
louder. "I rise to ask how Laurie Coles can get a fair trial in this
town with the atmosphere the way it is. Everybody knows that Mr.
Strand is the father of one of the children the state says was
abused."

There went Mathes's cool. "This is my last warning. I will find
you in criminal contempt if you do not remain within bounds."

"Yes, sir. But my client is in danger in this courtroom. We have
just seen an example of the passions that have been aroused by
this case. I move that the proceedings be moved from Hudson
Ferry to a venue in which Miss Coles will be safe." He sat down
and the district attorney rose.

"*You* sit down!" the judge roared. "Motion denied. Bailiff, clear
the court. And be sure that all who enter are searched. When the
room is secure, we will proceed." He strode out.

A half hour later the spectators had been readmitted one at a
time, an extra delay occurring because the matron had to be
called from the basement lockup to frisk the women. Pete Harmon looked around and would have sworn that not one person
had been frightened into leaving.

Serena, however, had changed her seat and was now sitting
beside Fred Coles.

Mathes reappeared and spoke gruffly. "Bailiff, is our first panel
ready?"

"It is, Your Honor." Fifteen men and women came in and sat
down in high-backed chairs that would bring sobriety to the most
frivolous. Harmon and Hull observed the panel with the intensity
of neurologists studying the president's brain scan after an assassi-
nation attempt.

Mathes scanned the room as he explained the outlines of the
case. The jurors would be asked to consider grave charges against
the defendant, accusations that some might find embarrassing.
The sexual abuse of little children was involved. "If any member
of the panel wishes to be excused for this reason, raise your hand
now."

No hand went up.

Hull had pleaded with his client to try to look relaxed. Pleasant.
But during the judge's remarks her lips were clamped.

Mathes launched a search for those who should be dismissed immediately for cause. "Were any members of the panel in the courtroom during the pretrial proceeding, the arraignment of the defendant?" Heads wagged. Passing over this probable untruth, he continued. "Of course none of you has a child at the Snug Arms Preschool? Or had one there in the past?" No. "Have any of you heard of this case before coming into court today?" Heads wagged. "If you should realize in the next few minutes that you have indeed heard something about this case, ask yourself if you have formed an opinion. If the answer is yes, come to me and tell me about it." Nods. "Does anyone know a mother or father who has or has had a child at Snug Arms?" No reaction. It was one of the most hermetically sealed groups imaginable.

"So far, so good," Mathes said. "Now listen carefully. The defendant is not here to prove she is not guilty. She does not have to do that. She is innocent of the charges and will remain innocent unless the state can prove that she is guilty. The prosecution has the entire burden of showing that and cannot leave any reasonable doubt about it in your minds. You must never forget that and I will remind you of it again at the end of the trial."

Mathes asked if the defense counsel wished to put questions to the panel and Hull requested time to confer with his client. "Certainly, sir," Mathes said. "Take all the time you need."

Drop dead again, Hull thought. I see how you're going to play it. The fair-and-square look. Can there be any doubt what the verdict will be, Jacko? Not after the Saturday Night Live performance. *That* was Hudson Ferry speaking. You know you'll get a conviction. You just don't want to be reversed.

He whispered to Coles. "Each side has twenty peremptory challenges. We don't have to give a reason to knock them off. I point and that one is gone." He stopped. "Laurie, look up at the jury and smile while I'm talking to you. Nothing big, just a cheerful look." On a pass-or-fail standard, she failed, but he gave her a C-plus. He had told her in jail, "Don't be a cold fish, as if you're waiting for the last rites." Now he said, "When you're up against a town in this kind of hysteria, a lot of jury selection is luck. There's no cinch formula for getting the right people. We'll do the best we can. So I'm going to try to chase some of them for cause and save the peremptories."

He reminded her again. "No grim looks." He had to loosen her up, strip away the mask, and the best way to do that was by forcing her to participate in her own defense.

Consulting his list, he approached the panel members and passed up Chair Number One, a thirty-five-year-old word processor who returned his smile. He remembered her name and knew she had worked on an occasional contract of his. If she didn't bring it up, he wouldn't. Passing familiarity couldn't hurt.

He recognized Number Two. She was forty years old and a loan officer at Third Federal Savings, the bank beneath his office. They crossed each other's paths about once a week and exchanged nods. She was married, had no children, and had sat on juries before. And she had hunched-up shoulders, he noted. Either she was built that way or had never learned to let down.

Chair Number Three was a man who should not have started chewing tobacco sixty years ago. He had been rocking with a slight motion, but stopped as Hull asked him what his occupation had been before he retired.

"Railroad engineer."

"Have you been called for jury duty often, sir?"

He nodded and the judge said, "Please answer."

"Yes."

"Have you served?"

"No." The rocking resumed.

"Why were you excused the last time, sir?"

"A ratty guy stuck up a drugstore. His lawyer asked if I could give him a fair trial." He laughed. "I said sure, but he looked like a thief to me. They told me to go home."

Hull was pacing nervously. He stopped and turned to the judge, but Harmon was on his feet again. "Your Honor, may I ask the panelist a question?" Mathes gave him a wave. "Sir, do you know of any reason why you could not give this particular defendant a fair hearing?"

Chair Number Three stared at Laurie Coles and rubbed white stubble on his cheeks. "I guess I could."

Harmon said, "I see no cause for dismissing this panelist."

The judge did. "Chair Number Three is excused." The elderly man went off with a grin the shade of tobacco.

Many lawyers found the name for this part of the jury selection process amusing. It was called voir dire, truth-speaking.

They wrangled over Number Four, a well-dressed man who replied wordily to questions and volunteered opinions that were unrelated to the interrogatories. Mathes would not dismiss him for cause and Hull used his first peremptory challenge.

Chair Number Ten, youngish and with hair the shade of the judge's, was incensed when Hull banished her with another peremptory; he was not taken up with her snappish responses. "I'm qualified to sit on this jury!" she told the judge. "I'm fair!"

Hull did not like that outburst and asked Mathes to clear out the entire panel and start over. He declined and lectured all present on the fairness of the peremptory-challenge system. To be dismissed was not a reflection on one's character, he said. As the panelist's mouth opened again, he said, "You have been excused, madam. Step *down.*" She glared at Hull and left.

He stopped pacing as he reached his major point. "Ladies and gentlemen, this is the most important question I have for you. Please think about it carefully, keeping in mind that our objective is fairness. Much of the testimony you will hear in this case will be sordid. Dirty. There will be explicit references to unnatural sexual acts. So you must be able to put aside embarrassment when you hear that testimony and continue to give the defendant the benefit of reasonable doubt. If you feel you can't do that, we must hear from you now."

No one was heard from.

He focused on Number Two, the bank loan officer. "Madam, you will hear charges—allegations—that little children's bodies have been violated. That this defendant invaded the intimate organs of defenseless little kids." He wanted to be the one to utter the words, now, to soften the pounding of the D.A.'s guns. "Will you be able to put the subject matter aside and ask whether those acts were actually committed, or only alleged by the prosecution?"

Number Two looked him in the eye and said, "I always try to be objective."

"Thank you." He wandered over faces slowly. "We're all human," he said. "It's not a reflection on anyone's character if you don't think you can overcome emotional feelings when you hear the testimony we expect to be presented. So if anyone cannot feel the same way Number Two does, please tell the court now."

No one was heard from.

Hull bowed, returned to Coles, and whispered, "We've got a lot of peremptories left, but I want to use only one more. They're waiting for me to get rid of them one by one. You heard what the judge said. People who are knocked off juries take it personally. So when I go after just one, the others will relax. We think they're honest and fair. They'll start out with a good attitude. Do you see anyone with a really grim face? I don't particularly care which one it is."

Coles smiled at the jury, weakly, then wrote, "Grandmother, next to last seat on right, first row. Looks hostile."

He consulted his list and said, "Your Honor, we ask that Number Six be excused." She was.

The bailiff gave his box a spin and extracted the name of the man seated in Chair Number Nine. "Raise your hand, please."

Justice Mathes asked if Nine had any problem with the questions asked of the other panelists. He did not.

Hull was struck. Chair Number Nine was the image of the juror the court buff had described, with the long face and narrow eyes. The holdout type. He looked as if he could say "Prove it!" a thousand times while under missile attack. Checking his list again, Hull noted that Number Nine was chairman of the mathematics department at Wadleigh University, down the river road. A plastic pouch was protruding from his breast pocket; it contained two pens and three pencils.

He said, "We find the panel satisfactory, Your Honor."

D.A. Harmon surprised few by announcing that he was also satisfied with those sitting in the jury box. Of course, Hull thought. What does he have to worry about?

Harmon was aware that a subtle shift in the audience's focus had taken place over the past half hour. He was not the star of the drama; Harry Hull had seized center stage and the D.A. would have to recapture the momentum.

The jurors, including two alternates who would be dismissed when deliberations began if an act of God or man did not disable any of the first twelve, were sworn in, married for the duration and for better or worse. Six women and six men. Sales clerk, loan officer, construction chief. Ad man, postal clerk, jeweler. Word processor, health-food retailer, retired secretary. Grocer, plumber, and university math chairman. Hull wondered how many secrets lay behind those faces, how many human vices were hidden in these humans. He tried to guess who would be elected foreperson and become the hardener of sentiments that would quickly form. Was there anyone left who thought jurors began deliberating only when the testimony ended?

Pete Harmon was less concerned with such matters. He made a note of what he was wearing today—brown jacket and tie, beige slacks. That's exactly what he would wear on the day he stood before the jury and delivered his summation, the last day of the trial. He told Serena: "Superstitious? Me?"

Justice Mathes wove the rest of the web without which the legal system could not function. He told the jurors he was sure they would not read or listen to news about the case and would not discuss it with anyone, especially with any attorney they might know. Nor could they even talk about the case among themselves until they began their deliberations. No chats over coffee and no phone calls in the evenings. Then he called a fifteen-minute recess.

The lockup matron, the one who had promised Coles a thrilling reception up in the big place, led her to the bathroom. Hull went out into the buzzing corridor and saw Serena Wiley, Pete Harmon's whatever, watching as a TV camera closed in for a tight shot of Corky McGonigle, the man from channel 22. McGonigle was moving toward the courtroom door with long strides and it was clear from a button microphone on his necktie that his voice was going out live over the air.

Pulling one of the doors open by its brass handle, he said, "This is the hall of justice in Hudson Ferry, where Laurie Coles is about to be tried for the sexual abuse of children. The room was invaded this morning by a man carrying a loaded gun." The camera rolled up to the portal and trailed McGonigle as he strolled down the aisle. "Michael Strand, father of one of the Snug Arms children who is said to have been molested, was seized by the defendant's father, Fred Coles, after he pulled a thirty-eight from his pocket. Fred Coles held on to Strand until he was disarmed. Then Strand cursed Justice Mathes, who had him taken away for observation. So Laurie Coles remains safe in this hall of justice—for the moment, anyway."

McGonigle held up a hand. "There's more." He strode back out into the corridor and another camera picked up the elderly woman who had been the original Chair Number Six in the jury box. "Why do you think the defense took you off the jury?" the newsman asked.

She shook her head. "I don't know. I wish I was serving. Miss Coles looks like such a nice girl."

McGonigle, who did not think Harry Hull was the worst guy in the world, said, "We can't read minds, can we? But the defense might have blown its chances this morning." Pause. "More at six this evening. Corky McGonigle at the criminal courts building in Hudson Ferry, 'Channel Twenty-two News at Noon.'"

Serena Wiley intercepted Hull and introduced herself. He was surprised as she extended a hand and said, "I think you're putting up a good fight against the Hangman. He is pure son-of-a-bitch. But I'd like to make a suggestion."

Remembering that she was a criminal-appeals attorney, he was nevertheless puzzled. Harmon's girlfriend?

"Mathes will give the parents the run of the witness stand," she said. "He'll admit almost anything they say. And he'll probably get away with it. You know the higher courts give a lot of leeway when children are involved." She handed him a copy of the United States Supreme Court's decision in *Maryland versus Craig,* in which the justices trimmed the rights of defendants accused of sexual crimes against preschool children. "There's a section of *Craig* that might hold some paydirt. About children testifying over TV. The law's still being being written, even if Mathes doesn't know it. It's a long shot, but I'd read the decision carefully. And you might consider looking into the parents in this case, running a check on their private lives. Strange things have a way of turning up."

He looked away. "What's going on? I mean."

"You mean Pete Harmon and me. Pete's Pete. I'm Serena. So you might want to think about those things."

He reentered the courtroom recalling that he had seen Wiley chatting with Polly Lennon, who ran the Book Nook. Polly with the soaring laugh. Well, any friend of Polly's couldn't be all bad.

Wiley had a point, about a private investigator. Who knew what a snoop might turn up that could challenge the credibility of a prosecution witness? Was there a family anywhere that did not keep a hush-hush in a locked box in the attic?

He tucked away *Maryland versus Craig* and stopped before Fred Coles, who was sitting on the aisle. "Hell of a job you did there," he said loudly. Then he dropped his voice and told the man who had nowhere to go, "Stick around at the lunch break, will you? I need a minute with you."

Chapter *11*

CHAIR NUMBER ONE: *My last case was boring, but that won't be a problem this time. Okay, here we go with the first opening statement. I wonder how the district attorney is going to play it. I'd be restrained, even look a little embarrassed. But can he resist getting into the dirty details?*

"This is a sad day for Hudson Ferry, ladies and gentlemen. The defendant sitting before you is said to have committed aggravated sexual assault against minors who are four and five years old. Laurie Coles is accused of violating felony laws that were enacted to protect youngsters like these."

The defendant is trying to look like Saint Joan at the stake, and I don't blame her. It's not easy sitting there, is it? There ought to be a training school for defendants, where they can learn how to act.

"Members of the jury, we all know it's easy to bring charges. But we may not all know that it's not as easy to prove them beyond a reasonable doubt, as the judge said.

"It is the state's responsibility to convince you of the truth of these charges. And we will do that. We will show you that Laurie Coles harmed these children in ways from which they may never recover."

I'm going to keep an open mind if it kills me. But it won't be easy. Could she actually be not guilty?

"Now as to the specifics of the charges. Laurie Coles exposed herself before the children, ladies and gentlemen. We will prove that. And she placed a substance on her private parts and asked children to remove it with their tongues. I'm sorry. This is a sordid affair."

He means disgusting. *This case is going to take a strong stomach.*

"Further, Laurie Coles defecated before these children and asked them to play with her waste material. The state will prove that she committed that perverted act.

  "She inserted a wooden object into the vagina of at least one child. We will prove that. And she appeared nude before the children and handled a child's penis. We will prove those acts beyond a reasonable doubt."

God! Kinky is one thing. But with little kids? Is this whole thing possible?

"Laurie Coles made terroristic threats to the children. And that is a crime. She said she had magical powers. If they told anyone of her acts, she warned them, she would come back, no matter where they put her, and kill their parents. And then she would haunt the children for the rest of their lives. You will hear from the parents and we will prove these charges beyond *any* doubt."

Somebody said the defendant's father is at the back of the courtroom. I've read about fathers sexually abusing children and turning them into freaks. Could that have happened to her?

"Ladies and gentlemen, we will show you that the injuries Laurie Coles inflicted on these children may affect them the rest of their lives. I will not overstate the case and say that no child will ever recover. There will be no need to exaggerate anything in this trial. But we will prove severe and lasting emotional damage."

He means expert witnesses. Not too many, I hope. They can cure insomnia. But a D.A. has to cover all bases. And what can Harry Hull do? He should have broken a leg to get out of this thing.

"We are not looking for winners or losers here, members of the jury. No one can win in this ghastly case. We are simply looking for justice."

The D.A.'s sitting down. That's it? All right, give us a break, judge. It's almost noon. Why do they have to run trials in the middle of summer? Let's get this over with. All right, she's entitled to a fair and speedy trial. We're going to have to listen hard to both sides. But right now it doesn't look good for Saint Joan.

Chapter 12

WHEN THE COURTROOM CLEARED, HULL WAVED THE MAN IN THE REAR UP to the counsel table and shook his hand. "Mr. Coles, you did a good job on the gunman. I hear he does drugs and gets loony. But listen. I want to confess something. I was dragged into this case. I didn't want any part of it. To be honest, I've been taking it for granted that your daughter is guilty."

"She didn't do it," Coles said. Under his dreary suit lay a crinkly new white shirt and a dark tie.

"That's not for me to say. And I shouldn't be talking to you about this because a lawyer's not supposed to speculate on a client's guilt or innocence. I'm doing it because you've probably wondered, and I want you to know that I'm going all-out to defend Laurie."

Coles said nothing and Hull went on. "Look, the prosecutor's going to dump testimony all over this courtroom. And there's a limit to how tough I can be with the children when they testify. The tougher I am, the more the jurors will turn off. I don't care if I'm the bad guy, but I don't want them taking it out on Laurie. If they do, even off-the-wall testimony from a kid will sound like it came from on high."

"Is that what you wanted to tell me?"

Hull scanned the room and saw that the door to the judge's chambers was ajar. He walked over and pushed it shut. "No, there's something else. If I have to go easy on the kids, that leaves the prosecution's expert witnesses and the parents. I want our own expert to talk to Laurie. Our own psychiatrist. I want to put him on the stand. He has to be paid, but I can get money from the court for that."

He looked around and dropped his voice. "That leaves the parents. I want to hire an investigator to look into them. Try to find something. I'll say it right out. This is a dirty case and two can play that way. I'm looking for material that would attack the parents' credibility, so every word they say won't be sacred. It's a long shot, but it makes sense and I need some money to do it."

Coles was uneasy. "Can you do that? Are you sure Laurie won't get into more trouble?"

"There's no law against looking. When people charge you with a crime, you can find out if they're believable."

Coles said with obvious embarrassment, "Would five hundred dollars be enough?"

Hull sighed and shook hands again. He watched as Coles went through the swinging gate and up the aisle. If this whole matter was a comedy, five hundred dollars would be humorous. A private investigator would cost maybe twenty times that. What the hell. He did not want Coles to feel it was over before it started, even if that was the truth. With hope in his bones, Fred might be able to get his daughter to warm up a degree in front of the jury.

On the way to a pay phone, he debated. Is she guilty? It looks that way. Is she innocent? I hope so. The good news was that the latest prosecution witness list still did not carry the name of Allison Wright. So Harmon had decided that Coles was not going to testify and he wouldn't get a chance to sneak in a lesbian sex number, or Wright had clammed up on him. Hull didn't care which version was correct.

He called Albany and reached Anthony Sgueglia, who had chased down a crooked mortgage broker for him last year. The Squail got back Hull's twenty thousand missing dollars in return for not turning the thief in to the Princess County constabulary. Hull briefed Sgueglia on the case and read him the names and addresses of six Snug Arms parents. "Tony," he said, "I want something that'll louse those people up when I rub it on their faces on the witness stand. Call it smear stuff. Oh, and write down the name of a psychologist. Amanda Roth, Ph.D., from New Jersey. Start with her."

Sgueglia interrupted. "Roth? Is she the one who got caught eating her mother?"

"You do jokes on my credit card? And listen, Tony, don't make any moves that wouldn't look right. Whatever you do has to stand up in court."

"You didn't tell me to be a nice guy when I went after your money, Harry. Just kidding. Okay. Everything on the up and up."

"Check's in the mail. A thousand down."

Pleased, he hurried over to Speedy Sally's.

* * *

In the basement of the courthouse was a cafeteria that needed a warning sign: DANGEROUS TO YOUR HEALTH. Serena Wiley, restricting herself to what she hoped was canned pea soup, asked Pete Harmon if armed men broke into many of his trials.

The D.A. decided he owed her one. "I was against him shooting the defendant, love. I don't want to lose a conviction."

"Amusing. Is that nut really one of the fathers?"

Harmon nodded. "Ellen Strand's ex. He's off his rocker. But I was afraid Mathes might say he had no choice but to move the case out of the jurisdiction."

"You don't want to lose this one, do you, Pete?"

"No. Only an incompetent could mess it up. But I don't want to see Coles shot up, either."

She was perplexed. "Sometimes I don't understand anything about people. Why would a man with a gun barge into a courtroom and bang it around his seat? The shrinks say those people are dying to be caught, but I don't buy that."

"He's walking around with cocaine in his blood. That's what the stuff in his pocket will turn out to be. He's stratospheric. Those people fly down the Thruway at ninety miles an hour and get pulled over with a trunk full of drugs. They're not connected."

She changed the subject, asking if Harmon had run his eye over the U.S. Supreme Court's *Craig* decision lately.

"Confrontation," he said. "Um." They often spoke in code. "Sandra Craig. She ran a school in Maryland. Accused of molesting children. The judge ruled the children should not have to testify in open court, with Craig sitting there in front of them. Intimidation. So the defendant's right to face-to-face confrontation was outweighed by probable harm to the children." Just as mistrustful of the menu, he chewed on an LT, without the B.

Wiley said, "You might want to read the whole thing again, Pete. About the circumstances under which closed-circuit TV is allowed." She sipped and gave him the penetrating eyes. "Hey, I don't know why I'm helping you. I'm a defense attorney."

Harmon stopped chewing.

"The gods on high amended the Sixth Amendment. They said confrontation wasn't absolutely guaranteed at all times. Not all kids have to face their alleged tormentors. But Pete, every child must be assessed individually. The judge has to decide that harm might be done to *each child* before he can rule that any one of them doesn't have to face the accused in open court. The Hangman didn't do that. He just said closed-circuit will be fine, thank you."

Harmon took another bite. "Am I Harry Hull's professor?

Should I ask Mathes to stop the trial every ten minutes so I can tell the defense counsel when to object?"

Wiley had been under the growing and uncomfortable impression that the Coles trial might lead to rambunctious exchanges with her guy. "You're right, Pete. It's not your job." She searched for offhandedness. "So I gave Hull a copy of *Craig* and told him to study every word of it."

"What the hell. You're helping me, love?"

"You'd rather be reversed on appeal? Because Mathes is so prejudiced he paid no attention to precedent?"

"What kind of games are you playing? When did you talk to Hull?"

"A few minutes ago. I'll come clean, Pete. I also told him to think about hiring a private eye. Dum-da-*dum*-dum."

Harmon was not amused. "He'll find out the Snug Arms kids were running a prostitution ring. They were bringing call girls in from Zanzibar."

"Finish your sandwich, sweetheart. And think about what those parents are going to get up there and tell the jury. Are you in a gambling mood? I'll give you ten dollars every time Mathes upholds one of Hull's objections. You give me five every time he denies one."

The D.A. felt his sense of humor ebbing as his words tumbled out. "I know what they're going to say. What their kids have told them. What the hell are you doing, Serena? Why don't you run the goddamn Coles defense for Hull?"

She raised both eyebrows, carried her tray to the barrel, and went home. She had to finish up the appeal for the son-of-a-bitch who would have raped that girl down in the big city if he could have but couldn't have because he was locked up when it happened, except that no one gave a damn.

Harmon was drinking coffee and thinking about private eyes when Vincent Garafolo walked in, having delivered Mickey Strand's little white packet to the General Hospital laboratory. The D.A. told him to stay on the case and began reviewing—rehearsing, some might say—Garafolo's testimony. He wanted to be certain the prosecution's lead-off witness would not testify from a hazy memory.

Juror Number One, practitioner of the word processor, got her two cheeseburgers out of the bailiff but only one order of shoestring fries. Delicious, she announced to dead silence in the jury room. What was this, a gathering of mutes?

Suddenly Chair Number One understood. Her companions were speculating on who was going to take charge. The judge had instructed them to elect a foreperson during lunch. He said *person* with a touch of the lip. Mathes was a member of the old-boy club.

It was obvious that none of the men wanted the job. She glanced at Chair Number Nine, the long-jawed math man from Wadleigh U., with the squeezed eyes of a mouse. He was over at the window, staring down at the TV vans. Mr. Blank Face. He hadn't said a word.

Chair Number One noted that Chair Ten, the postal clerk, had broken his silence but once, having belched and excused himself.

She broke the silence. "Does anybody want to be the foreperson of this jury?" She grinned. "Don't all of you raise your hands at the same time."

Not a finger wiggled, except for that of Chair Nine, who was tapping. He turned from the window. "Why don't you be the foreperson? You're sitting in the first seat anyway."

Well, so Chair Nine did have the power of speech.

"Any objection?" she asked.

Silence.

"Okay. Let's take the first ballot."

They all looked scandalized.

Number One laughed and checked her watch. "We'd better get back to court. Coles's lawyer wants to tell us how much his client loves children. Especially little children."

Ellen Strand rushed home from the courtroom and tried to avoid chain-smoking in front of Bonnie, with little success. It was enough that Mickey had suddenly surfaced back in Hudson Ferry, but now a radio bulletin said that her ex-husband was armed. She had not seen him since the day their divorce decree was handed down and wondered if he was still cooking the powders. Well, she told herself, he had better remember their private, out-of-court agreement no matter how zonked he got. It was uncomplicated. Mickey, you shut up about Bonnie and I'll keep quiet about the drugs, and why the man in Albany fired you. Unless you want to go to jail.

She moved closer to the radio and turned the volume down so Bonnie could not hear the speculation that Michael Strand appeared intent on shooting Laurie Coles, the Snug Arms teacher who was accused of sexually molesting his daughter.

Ellen didn't believe that version. She called Marla Burney, who knew why she and Mickey had broken up. Marla didn't believe that Mickey Strand was after Laurie Coles, either.

Chapter 13

CHAIR NUMBER NINE: *I'VE SAT ON JURIES AND HEARD PROSECUTORS PROM-*
ise the moon and deliver fog. Their opening statements are like checks that
bounce—insufficient evidence in the bank. That's why I tell my faculty
colleagues in the soft fields, like sociology, that mathematics can't get away
with promises, promises. It has to prove every claim the instant it's made.
Well, the prosecutor made a lot of promises this morning. But the defense
counsel had better get with it. He's shuffling papers and the judge is eying
him. I hope he does a good job for the young lady. She looks decent and the
charges are wild. Okay, here he goes.

"Ladies and gentlemen, you have heard the prosecutor say
he will prove the charges against the defendant beyond a
reasonable doubt. He has a tough job ahead of him, and I'll
tell you why. The defense is not going to sit here quietly and
let the state use emotion instead of evidence. I serve notice.
We won't let that happen. I don't care what anybody in this
courtroom thinks about the defendant at this moment. She
has a fair trial coming to her and she's going to get one or
else."

When he said anybody, *he looked at the judge. Settle in for a contest.*
He says they've got to prove it, prove it. Like a theorem. Lay out the
numbers for all to see. I think we've heard a declaration of war. And
what's that fierce look on the judge? Neutrality, sir!

"I want to explain why there are probably no more than a
dozen people in this town who don't already believe that
Laurie Coles is guilty of the crimes charged. I hope, members of the jury, that you are that dozen."

*He's asking us if we have the guts to do the right thing. What's hap-
pened to this Hull fellow? Somebody said that if he represented a robbery
victim, the victim would end up in jail.*

"Many people feel that Laurie Coles must be guilty because
she's been indicted. But an indictment is not evidence. All it
means is that a grand jury has heard enough to decide that a
trial should be held. That's all. No more. But we've all been
brainwashed. I'm going to prove that to you with a quiz question: Who made the statement that not many suspects are
innocent, that if a person was innocent, he wouldn't be a
suspect, would he? Who told that joke? Well, it wasn't David
Letterman. I'm going to give you thirty seconds to come up
with the answer."

Send the money, counselor. I read the papers.

"It was not a joke. The man who made that statement in all
seriousness was Edwin Meese, while he was attorney general
of the United States. Our country's number-one prosecutor.
Gosh, why would they arrest the man if he wasn't guilty? I'll
tell you why, ladies and gentlemen. Because good, honest
policemen can make mistakes. Okay, so they'll knock me off
the softball team for saying that."

"But more important to Laurie Coles, and to everyone
who lives in Hudson Ferry, our town, *prosecutors* can make
mistakes, too. They are told that something happened, and
that X was in the room when it happened. And they say, then
X did it. He's guilty. He wouldn't be a suspect if he wasn't
guilty, would he?"

*This is how I'll explain the problem to my colleagues on the jury: A
equals B and B equals C, so A also equals C. Right? Certainly, but only if
you've proved that A equaled B in the first place. You learn that in the sixth
grade. Say, the prosecutor didn't like Hull's attitude on that one, did he?
He's looking at the judge. And Hull is glaring at the prosecutor. Harmon
wants Mathes to belt Hull for getting personal.*

"But it's possible that something much simpler happened in
this case. Mr. Harmon is too intelligent to make serious mistakes, and I've always found him to be fair, too. I mean that.
Pete Harmon will not take advantage of you. But he can be as
wrong as you and I can. So maybe what happened is easily
explained. Someone complained about Laurie Coles. It was
said that a revolting act was committed against children. The

police investigated. What could they do? Come back empty-handed? No way. And what is the prosecutor supposed to do? Stand up in front of the folks in our town and say, 'We couldn't get a case together. Sorry.' Rule that out, too. There *has* to be a case. And here it is before us in this courtroom."

He's got a point. It's easy to get an indictment when everybody is convinced a crime has been committed and wants it solved.

"Members of the jury, I'll finish by saying, as Mr. Harmon did, that this is a sad day for Hudson Ferry. There can be no winners in this case. We do have a tragedy. But its chief victim is the young woman sitting here before you. Laurie Coles. I know the prosecution will not be able to prove its case and that when you've heard all the testimony you will find her innocent. Because she is. But will she ever be able to recover completely from the assault that has already been committed on her good name, and on her emotions? That's impossible. Can we find a way to salve her wounds and restore some of her health? Maybe. At least we can try. The most this jury can do is to make sure that her future is not completely destroyed. And there is a way to do that. It is by listening carefully to every word that is said against Laurie Coles, and by trying to separate facts from assumptions and emotions. In other words, by demanding that the prosecution prove every charge, not by repetition, but with facts that convince you *beyond a reasonable doubt*. Thank you for listening."

He really believes in her, doesn't he? Okay, Mr. Prosecutor. Your adversary has challenged you to put convincing evidence on the table. Prove it, prove it.

Chapter 14

THE OVERTURE HAD ENDED AND THE SPECTATORS WERE RUSTLING WITH impatience. The curtains parted, the judge mounted the bench, the defendant and the jurors were in place, and Vincent Garafolo was in the witness box, swearing to tell the truth and omit no part of it. He was closely shaved and his hair was freshly trimmed. The detective had selected a dark blue suit for the occasion and the blue-and-gold service pin gleamed in his lapel. The district attorney fingered papers, which gave the jurors an extra few seconds to take in the lead-off witness's precisely professional appearance.

With a few questions, Harmon established Garafolo as a member of the Hudson Ferry police force for eleven years, the last five as a detective. Answering in a crisp monotone, the plainclothes officer added that he had also studied psychology at the state police academy.

"At what point did you enter this case?" Harmon asked.

"When we received complaints of sexual abuse at the Snug Arms Preschool. I was assigned to investigate."

Harmon consulted his witness list and asked, "Did you speak to Mrs. Ellen Strand?"

"Yes."

"And what did she tell you?"

Harry Hull: "Objection! The mother can testify to that."

"The answer is admissible subject to corroboration," the judge said.

"Exception."

"Noted. Proceed, Mr. Harmon."

"What did Mrs. Strand say, Detective Garafolo?"

"That her daughter Bonnie, who is five, told her that Laurie Coles, a teacher, had placed a stick in her vagina." He turned to the jury and his tone did not alter. "I asked Mrs. Strand's permission to speak to the child and it was granted. Bonnie repeated the story almost word for word, except that she said 'peepee' instead of vagina."

As if responding to a prompter's direction, the jurors all looked at Laurie Coles, as did the spectators. She was taking notes; Hull had warned her against presenting the jury with looks of horror and denial each time a charge was made. Expressions of outrage wear out with repetition.

"Tell us," Harmon said. "Who first brought up the name of Laurie Coles? You or Bonnie Strand?"

Garafolo's voice sharpened and Harmon liked that. "Bonnie identified Miss Coles as the perpetrator on her own."

"Thank you, Detective." And please, Harmon thought, don't start with the perp word. "One more thing. Was Bonnie's mother present during your conversation with the child?"

"No. We try to avoid outside influences."

"Objection," Hull said. "The witness is adding self-serving irrelevancies as he answers."

"Sustained. Limit your replies, Detective."

Harmon asked if Garafolo had interviewed any other Snug Arms parents or children.

"Yes. For example, Letty Andrews and her son Billy."

"Why did you see Mrs. Andrews?"

"Because Ellen Strand said other children were abused. She told me her child was not the only victim of the perpetrator."

"Of the what?"

"The defendant."

"And what did Mrs. Andrews tell you?"

"Objection! Hearsay."

"Denied, exception noted."

"Billy told her that Laurie Coles removed her clothing, defecated on a table, and told him to make cakes of the waste material."

"Did he follow those instructions?"

"Yes."

"Did Miss Coles give him any further instructions?"

Hull was on his feet. "The prosecutor means, did the child's *mother* say there were further instructions."

"That's assumed," the judge said.

Harmon asked, "What did Mrs. Andrews tell you that Billy said those instructions were?"

"That he should eat what he called the poop cakes. But Mrs. Andrews said that Billy ran away, and that the defendant caught him and said a monster would attack him if he told anyone about this incident."

Coles was scribbling at top speed and passing notes to Hull.

Harmon said, "Did you then speak to Billy Andrews, and did he repeat what his mother said? And how old is he?"

"He's almost four years old and he told the same story, but he added something. He said Miss Coles urinated and told him it tasted good. And that some children drank the urine, but he didn't."

"Thank you, Detective. The state has no further questions."

Justice Mathes nodded to Hull, who rose slowly for cross-examination. He was looking over Coles's shoulder as she finished a note. Picking it up, he circled the counsel table, approaching Garafolo without haste and speaking in a voice that sounded almost friendly. "Sir, would you explain why you told the court and the jury that you had studied psychology?"

"It's part of my qualifications. I've learned a lot about how to handle children."

"You thought the jury should feel that you are specially equipped to deal with small children. What did your studies consist of?"

"Evening courses."

"Oh. How many?"

"Three."

"So you're not a psychologist."

"I didn't say I was."

"You didn't. That's true. But the jury might have misunderstood. I know you would want me to clear that up."

The detective gave no indication of how he felt about that.

Hull handed him a sheaf of papers. "Do you recognize this document, sir?"

Garafolo's eyes flicked to Harmon as he scanned each page. "It looks like a transcript of my interview with Billy Andrews."

Hull spoke to the jury. "You're not sure it is?"

Pete Harmon spoke up quickly. "Your Honor, the state stipulates that Mr. Hull is holding a document we gave him. It is a transcript of Mr. Garafolo's interview with Billy Andrews."

Hull addressed the judge. "The district attorney has not entered the document as an exhibit—"

Harmon rose. "I planned to, Your Honor, and I do so now." He handed the original transcript to the court clerk and she marked it *State No. 1*.

Hull asked if Garafolo would read out the exchanges he had marked up.

The detective was almost his composed self as he recited Billy's description of the downstairs room at Snug Arms in which he said defecations had taken place. The secret monster room, the one the dragon entered at Laurie Coles's command.

The eraser of Harmon's pencil was tapping the counsel table as Hull asked, "Did you visit the Snug Arms school during your investigation, Mr. Garafolo?"

"Yes."

"Please tell the court what the monster room looked like, and whether the dragon was friendly or hostile."

"Objection to the form of the question," Harmon said. "And to its sarcastic nature."

"Withdrawn. Mr. Garafolo, did you find a room on a lower level of the school?"

"No."

"Is there a lower level?"

"No. The monster room is one of those stories that children make up as they go along. A lot of kids do that."

Hull nodded, dropped the document onto the counsel table, and turned quickly to face the witness. "Detective Garafolo, why do you dismiss fantasies about a monster room and then accept tales that this defendant performed acts that could send her to prison?"

Judge Mathes waved Harmon off before he could rise. "The witness may answer."

"It's well known that children fantasize. They have wonderful imaginations."

"They do? Is that something you learned from your psychology courses? Or from chatting around town?"

Mathes called Hull to order angrily. "Counselor, the courtroom is no place for sarcasm. You will not frame your questions in a frivolous way. You are representing a defendant who is facing serious charges and you are expected to conduct yourself in a professional manner."

Hull exploded. "This court has no right to make that statement in the presence of the jury. Your Honor, you have suggested that I am not being serious about the defense of Laurie Coles. Those are grounds for a mistrial and I move for one."

The judge stroked his mustache. "Denied. Proceed."

"Exception. And the defense now moves that Your Honor remove himself from this case. You have exhibited prejudice on the side of the prosecution."

Mathes blinked. "Denied, exception noted." Then he smiled and said, "Counselor, never in all my years on the bench have I been accused *successfully* of being biased."

If Hull had been lifting beers with friends, he would have con-

ceded that the judge had provided no grounds for a mistrial. He
didn't care. His strategy now was to keep Mathes honest, lob shells
at every opportunity. He executed an agonizingly slow circle, first
turning to the jury and staring into each face, then gazing out at
the audience, smiling, and finally facing Coles and winking. "Shall
I repeat my question, Mr. Garafolo, or do you remember it?"

The detective said, "You learn to tell the difference between
whether a child is telling the truth or just inventing things as he
goes along."

"How do you do that?"

Garafolo smiled. "You watch closely. When a child is making up
a story, he keeps looking around and avoiding your eyes. Or he
twists his hair or jumps up and down. He's excited. But a child
who's telling the truth is calm and straightforward. You get steady
eye contact."

Hull was pacing the zone between the counsel table and the
witness stand. His hands were clasped before him, palms up, fingers entwined. One of the court buffs said it reminded him of a
movie. Actually, he had devised the technique of camouflaging his
midriff; it was easier than cutting down on the beer. He turned to
Garafolo and said, "Tell us how Billy Andrews acted when he told
his, uh, story."

"When he told me what happened to him, he was calm and to
the point."

"But we've been informed that Billy was emotionally traumatized by the treatment he received from the defendant. It doesn't
sound as if he was very wounded."

Garafolo opened his mouth, closed it, then replied angrily.
"Oh, he was injured, all right. But he's one of those children who
bounces back."

Hull was satisfied. The jury had seen and heard Garafolo reach
for a way to justify his earlier testimony. "I see. Then he's no
longer traumatized."

"I didn't say that. I'm not qualified to offer an opinion of that
kind."

"I agree. I notice in the transcript, sir, that at one point Billy
said, 'I want to go home. I want Mommy.' But the interview goes
on for another four pages. Why didn't you send him home when
he said he wanted his mother?"

"We weren't finished."

"But Billy said he wanted to go home. Was he a prisoner?"

"Objection."

"Withdrawn. What do you mean by 'finished'? When you get
what you want?"

Garafolo shrugged. "It means finished. That's all."

Hull rummaged through his papers and found a transcript of conversations held with Lilly Robertson and her daughter Caroline. "I'm puzzled, detective. You testified that Mrs. Robertson said: 'Laurie Coles placed jam on her vagina and asked Caroline to lick it off.' But later the child told you that the defendant placed the jam on *her,* Caroline, and that Coles removed it with *her* tongue. Why did you not tell us about the differences in those two accounts?"

The D.A. and Garafolo had reviewed this variance several times and the detective was prepared for the question. "Because children make mistakes when they're talking to adults."

"But how do you know which statement is a mistake?"

The detective employed his smile of confidence. "You know from experience."

"Oh," Hull told the jury.

"Anyway, Caroline straightened it all out when I spoke to her again."

Hull adopted his perplexed expression and searched through the transcripts. "I don't see the correction here."

Garafolo was staring straight ahead. "There is no transcript of the last conversation. I didn't notice that my recorder batteries were dead."

"Oh. Well, Detective, you have confirmed what a lot of people already think. Children make mistakes. Do you think they might have made mistakes when they described the actions of the defendant?"

"Objection," Pete Harmon said. "It is the province of the jury to decide what to believe."

"It sure is," Hull managed to say before Judge Mathes upheld the prosecution. He went on. "Your Honor, I have no further questions at this time, but I reserve the right to recall the witness in the event that new documents raise more questions about his testimony."

"There's no need to make a speech. You have that right." He stifled a yawn. "It's past four o'clock. We'll take a fifteen-minute recess."

In the corridor Hull was puffing on a cigarette as he received a tentative verdict from one of the buffs. "*Yes,* Harry! Go for the jugular. That's the way to play it. Be outraged. Keep showing the jury how the cards have been stacked against your client."

A contrary opinion was heard immediately. "Mistrial? Mathes should disqualify himself? Watch your ass, Harry. Jacko never forgets."

"Judge Mathes is not an elephant," Hull replied. "He's a

horse's ass." The cautioning buff wondered if counsel was asking for it.

Harmon, who remained at the counsel table, was assessing Vince Garafolo's testimony. He was satisfied. The detective was not qualified to render expert opinions on child behavior and Hull had done the right thing in trying to weaken his story. But Vince had stood up well, and witnesses with heavier credentials were coming up. In particular, a physician would describe his examination of Bonnie Strand and the D.A. had not wanted Garafolo to touch on the topic of ice-pop sticks in vaginas; Hull would have tried to lead him into making medical judgments. And he might have succeeded. Sometimes Garafolo did not know when to stop.

As for the jury, Harmon was reasonably confident that the prosecution had done well. Never one to thrash about on the stage, he had avoided looking as if he would collapse when the crimes were described. But he had also kept the jurors in a corner of his eye, and he wondered about the woman in Chair Number One. He had started to worry about her, and if there was one prospect he did not want to face, it was a deadlocked panel. The trouble was, reading a jury was like predicting the future. Probing the palm was more reliable.

Chapter *15*

As in a street gang, corporation, or baseball team, the jurors in the Laurie Coles case quickly became leaders and followers. Ten members already regarded chairs One and Nine as their mentors, and when Judge Mathes called the coffee break, One and Nine sat apart, at one end of the long jury room, where One said, "Hull's got a one-two punch, but that won't help the defendant, will it?"

The mathematics professor rumbled at the throat. "We can't discuss the case."

"Are you married?"

"What?" Nine felt a stirring. Why had she asked that? And why hadn't he replied? Did she have something in mind for a beautiful evening in July? "I wouldn't be surprised if the judge locks us up for the duration at the Champlain," he said. Whenever his wife went off to Syracuse to visit her sister, he waited for her call at nine o'clock—no later, he told her, I'll be asleep—then hurried down to the cozy lounge of the Hotel Champlain, with the old-time music.

"So what do you think?" One asked. "How do you vote?"

"We can't discuss the case." The Champlain lounge was a hangout for couples, but there was usually a stray or two at the bar. Now, if twenty-five couples were sitting in the lounge and three women were roamers, they represented twelve percent of the total. And if only one of the three was worth pursuing, that was four percent. A weak number, but it beat watching the tube.

One said, "This whole town didn't just wake up one morning and say, hey, let's go out and get this Coles bitch. She's here for a reason."

"We can't discuss the case," Nine replied. "But that was an interesting remark Hull made when he quoted the attorney gen-

eral who said if you're a suspect, you did it. It shows how careful
we have to be with prosecution witnesses."

She grinned. "I'd love a drink. Sure, but that stuff about suspects has nothing to do with this case. You'd have to say the cops
just decided to hang all this sex stuff on somebody, no matter
who. And that doesn't make sense."

"We can't talk about this specific case, but those things have
happened before. Kids say something, the pressure's on, and the
police have to make a move."

"Do you ever drop in to the Champlain?" Chair One wondered.

A coffee cup banged the table at the far end of the room and
covered Chair Nine's surprise. "Why do you ask? Is that a haunt
of yours?"

She gave him a severe look. "Am I desperate? Once in a while,
maybe." She lowered her voice. "You didn't say if you were married, but I don't want to get personal. Remember that case last
year? The teenagers who stuck up the deli and one of them raped
the owner's wife? The jury was out two days and they were seques-
tered for the night. I know somebody who served. I'm not saying
who, but he gave the bailiff a twenty-dollar bill and connecting
rooms were arranged. Can you beat that? I mean, shameless!"

Nine said, "Here comes the bailiff. We're going in."

"I can't wait to hear the kids," Number One said. "Coles is
going to wish she never walked into this town."

"Maybe," said Nine. "We have to keep our minds open."

Chapter 16

PETE HARMON MISCALCULATED. WITH THE CLOCK SHOWING ALMOST FOUR thirty and with Justice Mathes's reputation for being out of the courtroom well before five, he was anticipating a quick departure. Instead the judge said, "We have time for one more witness, Mr. Harmon. Brief testimony."

It was a command. The D.A. checked his list and said, reluctantly, "The state calls Mr. Ike Brendelski."

A buff said, "Ike the strange one? What the hell!"

A door at the front of the court opened and a short, burly man walked, or swaggered, in. He was given the oath and Harmon spoke. "Your Honor, I want to say that this witness appears under subpoena. In return for his testimony, Mr. Brendelski has been granted immunity. He cannot be prosecuted for the actions he is about to testify to."

After a quick exchange with Laurie Coles, Hull objected. "I don't have a Brendelski on my list. And is the jury supposed to believe somebody who's made a deal with the district attorney to escape prosecution?"

"Sidebar," the judge said. The attorneys approached the bench, out of the jury's hearing, and Harmon could be seen speaking. Hull. Harmon. Hull, gesturing. Then Mathes's lips moved briefly, red mustache in concert.

The attorneys stepped back and Hull spoke fiercely. "I have a motion to make. The prosecution proposes to take testimony from a witness we have never heard of. We are told that he has new information, freshly discovered. That's a tired excuse for not informing the defense in good time of witnesses to be called. I move that Mr. Brendelski be excused until we have been shown his deposition. And I move further that he be barred from testifying because he is tainted with a crime for which he is being let off."

"If you have problems with the witness's testimony," the judge said, "you may recall him at any time. In that way, the defendant's rights are preserved. The motions are denied. Proceed, Mr. Harmon."

"Exception," Hull said. "And I was not finished, Your Honor. From the bare explanation the prosecutor gave at the sidebar, I cannot see how this witness's testimony can be related to any count in the indictment. I move that Mr. Ike Brendelski be excused."

Mathes checked the time. Sylvia pouted when he was tardy. "Motion denied. We don't know if his testimony will be relevant because we haven't heard it yet. Counsel's exception is noted. Let's move on."

They moved away from the bench. Hull sat down and Harmon asked Ike Brendelski what he did for a living. He replied in a throaty voice that he was a road builder. Did he have a child at Snug Arms? Fixing a stare on Laurie Coles, he said he did. "Until this mess started."

"Now, on April twenty-six last, at approximately midnight, did you appear at the school, along with others, and were you equipped with construction gear?"

"I sure did. And I won't tell you who else was there."

"And did you and the others enter the building by force?"

"You bet." The hoarseness was pronounced.

"Would you tell us why?"

"Yep. We were looking for a room. My boy told me about it. Where that one"—he pointed—"took the kids."

"Objection!" Hull shouted. "Irrelevant and prejudicial. I renew my motion that the witness be excused as unreliable."

"Sustained and denied. Restrict yourself to answering the questions, Mr. Brendelski."

"And there is no point to this line of questioning. As I suspected, it doesn't relate to any charge before us."

"I have already ruled on that. Be seated, Counselor. The witness may continue."

"We were looking for a hidden room," Brendelski said. He was glowering at Hull and breathing rapidly.

"Did you find it?" Harmon asked.

"No."

"Did you know that a search had already been conducted for such a room?"

"Yep."

"Then why did you do what you did?"

"What would you do if your kid was nastied?"

The judge intervened. "The jury will disregard that remark. Mr. Brendelski, this is a court of law. Just answer the questions that are asked."

"We weren't taking anybody's word."

"So you found no hidden room."

"Wrong."

"Please explain." Harmon wished he had declined to start off a witness at this hour. The hell with Mathes.

Brendelski glared again at Laurie Coles. "It's behind a fake mirror. I smashed the glass and found a video camera back there and I sledged it."

"Why did you do that?"

"Because my boy told me that perverted bitch took the kids' clothes off and put the camera on them. That's why!"

"No, no!" Hull roared. Then he reconsidered. "I withdraw the objection. Let him rave on. No guilty verdict will stand up with this kind of nonsense going to the jury. Your Honor, why waste time? Why don't we send out to Andy's Hardware for a rope?" There were few courts in which an attorney could get away with such remarks, and this did not rank among them. But Hull felt that the record would show he had been provoked.

Laurie Coles was pale. And the judge's mouth was pinched as he addressed the jury. "I will instruct the court reporter to strike parts of this witness's testimony. And you are to ignore the witness's characterizations of the defendant. Such remarks are not evidence."

"Why not?" Brendelski asked.

"Quiet!" the judge snapped. "And I'll tell you something else, Mr. Brendelski. You may have immunity for vandalizing the Snug Arms school, but I will have you committed to jail immediately for contempt if you continue to disrupt the legal process. Have you got that straight?"

Harmon rose quickly. "I have no further questions, Your Honor. But I want to add that I was not able to explain to Mr. Brendelski what could properly be said before a jury. I did not expect to have to call him as a witness this afternoon. I apologize to the court and the defense."

"No cross-examination," Hull said. "But I still want to know what deal the state made with Mr. Brendelski. What did he agree to say in order to get his immunity?"

The volume of the judge's voice startled the spectators. "*Order!* As far as I'm concerned, this witness has nothing further to say in this case."

He motioned the bailiff to the bench and whispered. The officer nodded and Mathes addressed the jury; no one in the room could have doubted the depth of his anger. "Ladies and gentlemen, because of the inflammatory nature of the charges before us and the potential for violence that has been demonstrated in the courtroom, it will be necessary to sequester the jury."

Ten faces in the jury box revealed dismay; they did not include those belonging to chairs One and Nine.

Brendelski's eyes remained on Harry Hull as he stepped down and passed the counsel table. Halfway up the aisle, he turned for a final look.

"I did not want to sequester you," Mathes told the jurors. "I'm sorry, but I have no choice. Officers will drive you to your homes before taking you to your hotel. I suggest you gather up personal items that will last several days. And I direct you to remember this: You are not to discuss the case with anyone else or among yourselves until it has been concluded. Have a pleasant evening. This court is adjourned until ten o'clock in the morning!"

He slammed the gavel three times and everyone rose except for Hull, who was the picture of a cat after a meal of canary. Mathes ignored him.

Fred Coles struggled to reach his daughter through the crowd and told her he could not stay longer. He had taken Monday off but had to be back at the shipyard in the morning. They hugged and he left for the depot with a promise to return on Saturday morning. She went to jail for dinner.

Chapter 17

"SERENA, LET'S GET MARRIED."

Wiley's pencil dropped and rolled off the desk. "That's a proposal, Pete? Where did you learn to do that?"

"In law school. I was taught to take the offensive."

"Why are you so late?"

"You mean, in talking about getting hitched?"

"No, from court. How about a drink, sweetheart?"

"How about a drink over dinner, love, while I'm proposing to you properly. Let's clean up and go out."

They showered together. To save water.

Dinner at the Champlain began awkwardly. "Damn!" Harmon said. "Change places!" They were seated in a corner of the dining room and he had just seen the maître d' bow to the bailiff of the court, who was followed in by the twelve jurors and two alternates. The D.A. groaned. "I plain forgot they'd be put up here. I'm slipping."

Wiley was amused. "Pete, the woman on the bailiff's left just winked at me. Number One on your jury."

"We're not leaving, Serena. My back is to her now and she's forty feet away. She can't see me."

Wiley was enjoying the scene. "She winks at me and doesn't know we're together? You think she's warm for me? You know, I think they're seated in their order in the jury box. They're already trained. Hey, what in the world went on this afternoon? I didn't think the Hangman would sequester them since he doesn't have to do that anymore."

Harmon downed a second gin. "Lava flowed just before we shut down. Jacko pressured me and I had to produce a quick and dirty witness. Well, Garafolo tracked down one of the guys who ransacked Snug Arms. Ike Brendelski. He confessed without even being asked. I think something's missing in his head. He said he found a camera and wrecked it because his son told him Coles videotaped the kids naked. So I offered him immunity to testify." He flagged the captain and ordered wine.

"Who is he?"

"Ike Brendelski. So—"

"Ike? What's his real name?"

Harmon laughed. "He said he changed it from Isaac because somebody asked him if he was Jewish when he was a kid. People are strange? Anyway, he was full of prejudicial remarks and Hull went bonkers. I don't blame him, but I think he was just trying to get the judge to blow his top. And Jacko obliged."

"Not so fast," Wiley said. "The indictment says nothing about nude videotaping. How can such testimony be admitted?"

"Subject to connection."

"Are prosecutors still pulling that trick?"

They ordered. Caesar salad for him, soup and lobster for her. "What do you mean, subject to connection?" She could read embarrassment.

"I think I can make a connection, love. I'm going to try."

"The prosecutor thinks he can connect it. After the jury's ears are full of it." She eased up. "Number One has cut me dead. She's working on Nine."

They were served, that much too quickly for Harmon's taste. "I move we change the subject."

"Have your way with me, Pete."

"The motion before us is that we get married. Serena, I'm through squiggling around that subject."

She filled her mouth with soup to prevent herself from saying she had never pressed the topic.

"Do you remember bringing in a package on Saturday? You knew it was from my father but you didn't say anything."

"Your father the stranger? When I met him last year, I got the impression he didn't think I was God's gift."

"You offended him. You didn't faint with admiration every time he spoke. And you actually expressed opinions."

She remembered. "So what did he send you?"

"Two hundred and fifty pages of rambling. And a note that said, 'I'm proud of my accomplishments.' He's very modest."

She reached over and tapped the strong arm that held her so gently so often. "No wonder you were so quiet Sunday afternoon. I thought it was because I beat you in that first set. So get on with it, Peter!"

She had called him Peter a year ago, when he insisted on fixing a leaky rainspout himself. "Get off that ladder. You'll get hurt, Peter!" Minutes later he fell and fractured two fingers. And it was *Peter!* six months ago when he failed to express sufficient outrage over an appeals court ruling that a murder conviction need not be reversed just because the police deprived a defendant of food and water until he confessed.

"It's Dad's version of his greatness. He didn't have a nickel when he started repairing brakes. But then he figured out how to make better brake shoes and sold them by the bushel. He made a lot of money and bought a bus route that ran between Salt Lake City and Denver. Then it was real estate and millions. Every deal and the exact amount it was worth is in the manuscript. And he explains several times how smart he's been. Dad's never been wrong, you know. Not once ever."

"It sounds like a best-seller."

He pushed the Caesar away. "And the last twenty pages are about what he's done for me. College and law-school money to the penny. It's like a bill for services rendered. Say, did I ever tell you I didn't want to be a lawyer? I'm not saying I don't like it. It's just that I wouldn't have picked it. But I had no choice. Dad decided that's what I'd be and that's all he would pay for and that's what I became."

"You never told me. I'm getting a peek into Pete."

"But I got even. The law saved me from being like Dad. When I lost my first case, I knew I blew it with cockiness. That loss was an arrogance vaccine."

"Somebody up there works in wondrous ways."

"But get this. Nowhere in all those pages was there a mention of my mother. Not one."

She said nothing.

"Here's what I remember. She never said a word. He talked for her. He told her over and over, 'Be quiet. You don't understand.' He said it once too often and one day I told him to shut up. He went after me, but I was sixteen and I was taking boxing lessons. I just stood there and all he could do was bang away at my arms. He quit when his hands fell off."

"Maybe you should have been a boxer, Pete."

"Be quiet, love. You don't understand. So I was sitting on the porch reading this stuff and a light went on. I realized why I've been so skittish about marriage. After watching Dad turn Mom into a zero, I was afraid of getting too close to people. As in marrying them. But I'm over it and I want to marry you. You're the most marvelous thing that's ever happened to me. I said it. Sue me."

She looked him in the eye and said, "Wow, I love you, Pete! Let's keep talking." She didn't say Peter, he observed.

Chair Number Two, the loan officer, was known at Third Federal Savings as nobody's nerd. She once noticed something odd about certain bank policies. Newer employees were being let go as they approached the end of their first year of service, when their best benefits would kick in. And they were being replaced by people who had worked at nearby banks, but, coincidentally, had also been let go as they neared better-benefits time. The banks had teamed up to skin their employees and she told her manager she was going to court. The thievery ended.

She had seen Number Nine, the math man, slip something to the bailiff in the lobby of the Champlain and whisper in his ear. Now Nine was ignoring the rest of them and speaking only to the foreperson, who was spinning one distasteful joke after another. The bailiff laughed so hard he almost choked on his T-bone.

At the end of the meal the bailiff announced that they would go to the public telephones, where those who wanted to call home could do so. The room phones were disconnected, but the police had his room number in case of emergencies. And no one could leave a room until breakfast time.

Chair Number Two, the loan officer, was last off the elevator at the seventh floor. She watched the bailiff lead One and Nine to adjoining rooms. Nobody's nerd did not have to be told the rooms were part of a suite. And on the very first night! So she had their number, and the bailiff's, too.

Chapter 18

THE SECOND DAY OF TRIAL WAS TO BEGIN AT TEN O'CLOCK BUT DIDN'T. Barnard Rooney, the assistant district attorney, greeted Harmon with the news that the grand jury had failed to produce an indictment against Michael Strand. Perplexed, Harmon called the court clerk and said he would be held up for fifteen minutes. Please tell His Honor it's unavoidable.

Rooney explained. Strand carried a loaded gun into court. And even if that were legal, it was not properly licensed. A substance was found on Strand's person that was thought to be an illegal drug and was being examined at the hospital laboratory. Three felony counts and seven witnesses: Judge, bailiff, prosecutor, defense attorney, police officer, court clerk, steno.

Harmon was baffled. "They wouldn't even indict on the gun counts?"

Rooney shook his head. "I'm not sure what happened, Pete. It was the last day of their term, so I felt I could chat it up when they came back with the no-bill. One said they thought Strand was under extreme stress because his daughter is in the Snug Arms case. You can't walk around with a gun, but the parents are strung out. He says there was a lenient mood."

Harmon banged his desk. "So it would have been okay if Strand shot Laurie Coles? Where did they get the idea that he was under more stress than any other parent? The shrinks haven't even said anything about him yet."

"It doesn't make sense, Pete. But you can't argue with a grand jury, right? Another juror said they didn't want to be held over for the drug charge. If they did Strand on the gun, they'd have to do the drug business. And they know it'll take days for the lab reports. They said they'd put in enough time, so I had to turn 'em loose."

"How did they figure out they might be held over? They know beans about procedural stuff. What going on? This is only the second turndown we've had in a year."

Barney Rooney, two years younger than Harmon, shrugged. "Pete, both those jurors were jumpy as hell. I wonder if we should leave the whole thing alone."

Harmon remembered Strand's surly confidence as he stood before Mathes, and his calling Jacko a son-of-a-bitch. He told the assistant D.A., "Something is odd—" He stopped and said, "All right, what's done is done. But lay the drug charge on the new panel the minute it sits. I mean, I assume the lab report will be positive. Let me see it when it comes in and keep this thing strictly between us."

He had a sudden thought. "Barney, do you play golf?"

Rooney was surprised. "Sure. Why?"

"Are you good at it?"

Rooney laughed. "Handicap of six. What's on your mind, Pete?"

"I've been thinking I might take up the game. Maybe I'll ask you to give me a lesson or two."

"Any time. Look for me at the Rhinebeck Club."

Harmon went down to the courtroom in an uneasy frame of mind. The failure to indict Strand made no sense.

Harry Hull used the delay to phone his private eye in Albany. He heard a recording. "Squail," he told the machine, "wherever you are, get down to Hudson Ferry fast!"

He reentered the courtroom through a metal detector that had been trucked over from the airport at Albany.

As Harmon arrived, Justice Mathes said, "Thank you for joining us." Chuckles escaped the spectators. "May we proceed in the matter of *The State of New York versus Laurie Coles?*"

Harmon watched the judge closely. "Sorry, sir. I had a grand jury matter to dispose of." He saw nothing in Mathes's face. Smiling apologetically to the jurors, he said, "The state calls Letitia Andrews."

Hull wondered why Harmon was not leading off with Lilly Robertson. Tiger Lil, after all, had lit the fuse that was crackling through Hudson Ferry. Suddenly he understood. It was Mrs. Andrews's son who told Vince Garafolo about the nonexistent monster room, downstairs at Snug Arms, which had no downstairs. She would have to testify, so, aside from Ike Brendelski having been forced on Harmon, he was putting her on first among the parents, to bury the memory of her under all the testimony that would follow. He whispered to Coles, "Now don't look like you're being hit by a car. Glance at the jury once in a while. Move slowly from face to face and then go back to your notes." She began to write.

Hull edged his chair back from the counsel table, positioning himself to fire objections.

Letty Andrews came in from the witness room cracking her knuckles. She was about thirty, an attractive, energetic brunette with wide, inquisitive eyes. Harmon pointed her toward the witness stand and sensed a warning in the air: Handle with care. He spoke softly and at a slow pace to relax her during the identifying preliminaries. "Mrs. Andrews," he said, "this may be a difficult ordeal for you."

Hull rose. "No need for that, Your Honor. The witness is just here to testify."

Mathes nodded in agreement and Harmon was annoyed. Being a nice guy in front of the jury was standard. He said, "Please tell us what your child said about Miss Coles."

"Double objection," Hull said, earning snickers from the audience. "First, vagueness. Second, here we go on hearsay again. If the children are going to testify, they'll tell us what they claim happened to them. We don't need help on that."

The judge was ready. "Sustained on vagueness. Overruled on hearsay. It's the tender-years rule, Counselor. Small children are often frightened and the child involved is barely five years old. Still, the prosecutor must corroborate the parents' testimony. If he does not, I will strike it. Proceed, Mr. Harmon."

"You'll strike it, Your Honor, but the jury will have heard it. I will object to hearsay evidence from every parent. It must not be admitted."

"Exception noted. All right, Mr. Harmon."

"Mrs. Andrews, did your son talk to you about an act that Miss Coles is accused of committing?"

Letty Andrews opened her bag and extracted a small notebook. As she opened it, Hull was on his feet. "What's going on? Are witnesses going to read to us from diaries instead of just answering questions?"

"Sidebar," Mathes called out, and up to the bench went the attorneys. "Explain, Mr. Harmon."

"When the investigation started, sir, the children were very reluctant to talk about acts described in the indictment. It took many conversations before the parents could get them to open up. We will present expert testimony to explain this problem. But because of it, the parents were asked to enter their children's statements into diaries, to avoid confusion."

"That won't work," Hull said. "Adult witnesses are required to give their best recollections, without prompting and memory-refreshing devices."

The judge thought about that. "Nine times out of ten I'd rule for you, but this also falls under the tender-years exceptions to the hearsay rule. I'll allow it."

Harmon backed away but Hull stood before Mathes shaking his head. "Stop that!" the judge hissed. Hull retreated, read a note from Coles, and pocketed it.

The stenographer repeated the question and Mrs. Andrews consulted her diary. "Billy said that Miss Coles removed her underclothing, squatted on a table, and defecated."

"In the children's presence?"

"Yes. How else would he know?" A knuckle cracked.

"Please just answer the question."

She turned a page. "The next day Billy said Miss Coles told the children to make mounds out of her waste matter. He said she called them poop cakes."

Hull heard Coles's breath and touched her hand.

"And that she told the children they tasted good."

"Did she say anything else about this waste material?"

The witness hesitated. "She told them to eat it."

Angry sounds erupted and Mathes gaveled several times. The witness tugged at her fingers.

"Did Billy do that?"

"No. But he said one child did." She turned another page. "And he said she urinated into a cup and asked the children to drink it. He said, 'I ran away, but she caught me. She said that if I told you, Mommy, she would kill you. And she would torture me. So I didn't tell you.' That's what Billy said.

"And it reminds me of something else." She leaned forward and her voice rose. "Several times I tried to sit in during play time at Snug Arms." She pointed to the counsel table. "And Miss Coles wouldn't let me. I guess she wanted the children to herself."

The judge's eyes shifted to Hull, then back to the witness when the attorney did not object to the speculation. Harmon, also surprised by Hull's silence, shrugged and went on. "Mrs. Andrews, do you recall Billy telling you anything else about the defendant— that is, anything that involved his body?"

"He said she kept asking him if he wanted to go to the bathroom and he said he didn't have to. She told him she would help him urinate and when they were in the bathroom she put a little pointed stick into his penis. He wanted to show me how she did it, but I wouldn't let him."

Hull reached for Coles's arm.

"I see. Is your child receiving any medical treatment at this time, Mrs. Andrews?"

"Yes. I asked a psychologist to talk to him."

"Why?"

"Well." She looked at the jury, then away. "Billy wants to sleep with my husband and me. Between us. We don't think that's right." She blushed.

"I have no further questions, Your Honor."

Hull kept his distance but was full of cheer. "Good morning." She did not reply. "Mrs. Andrews, I have just a few questions, to make sure I understand your testimony." Buffs rolled their eyes at that familiar remark. "You said that when Miss Coles asked the children to drink her urine, or that your son reported that she asked them to, Billy ran away. My question is, did he run upstairs?"

Harmon studied the counsel the table. He knew Mrs. Andrews would be looking at him. "I don't remember," she said. "Away or upstairs. But she threatened him."

Hull nodded. "I see. But didn't this act attributed to Miss Coles, that is, the urination, occur in a lower-level room that Billy referred to as the monster room?"

"I don't know. What difference does it make?"

"Well, we have to get a clear picture of events. If you'd like to consult your diary, go ahead."

She stared at him and tightened her grip on the book.

"Let's let that pass for the moment." He directed himself to the jury and spoke very deliberately. "All right, you testified that Billy said he did not ingest any of Miss Coles's waste matter, but that another child did. Do you recall who your son said that child was? Does your diary show that?"

"I don't know."

"Oh." He turned from the jury to Mathes and said, "Here we have another case of the defense having to prompt the prosecution to introduce material as an exhibit. Your Honor, I—"

Harmon was standing, thinking he was going to have to take Hull more seriously. "The state wishes to place Mrs. Andrews's diary in evidence, Your Honor."

The clerk approached and held out her hand, but the witness said, "No! This is personal property."

The judge shook his head. "I'm sorry, Mrs. Andrews, but you testified from it, so it becomes part of the record. Please give the diary to the clerk."

She handed it over.

Hull removed a sheet from his pocket and closed in on the witness box. He stood, reading, eyes moving from line to line, slowly, until no one could doubt it contained the secrets of the universe. Then he moved a foot closer. "Mrs. Andrews, you testified that on several occasions you tried to sit in with the children during play time. And that Miss Coles"—he pointed—"the one accused of these crimes, would not let you do that. And you said, 'I guess she wanted the children to herself.' Do you remember that?"

He saw anger and considered himself fortunate that she did not have Mickey Strand's .38.

"I'm going to ask you to search your memory," he said. "Can you think of any other reason, no matter how remote, that Miss Coles would have wanted to keep you from sitting in?"

"No!"

Hull smiled. "None? Let me see if I can refresh your memory. Isn't it a fact that you did sit in on two occasions before you were barred?"

"I don't know."

"Well, when you sat in the first time, do you recall that you continually interrupted Miss Coles? And disrupted the activities she was directing?"

"What the hell are you talking about? Of course not."

"Objection," the D.A. said. "Counsel is harassing the witness. And anyway, I think we should know where all this is leading, Your Honor."

Hull grinned at the judge. "I'm going to make a connection. Like the connections the prosecutor has promised to make. Mrs. Andrews, when you were present during playtime on the second occasion, did you not say repeatedly to the children, 'These are lousy games. What kind of a teacher is this?' Do you recall saying anything like that?"

The witness stood up and Justice Mathes asked her to be seated. But Hull did not wait for an answer. "No further questions, Your Honor. But I assure you I will introduce corroborating evidence."

"You may step down," Mathes said. "Court will recess until one thirty."

Hull glanced at Chair Number Two as the jurors rose to file out. She looked away, but he caught enough of her expression to worry. Would she be one of those wrung-out ones who think there's just too much crime going on these days and we've got to put a stop to it?

He turned and saw a muscular man hustling down the aisle. It was Anthony Sgueglia, his private investigator. "Where'd you get that black thing on your lip?" Hull asked. "Did you dig up Groucho? And where have you been? I need you!"

"I'm here, I'm here," Sgueglia said. His facial muscles operated to produce grins, regardless of mood. "And I've got a piece of info already. You'll love it." He handed Hull an official-looking memo and the attorney scanned it, then noticed that Laurie Coles was being led away. He threw her a wave and gave his private eye a high five. "Nice start, Squail. Now get after the moms and dads. Kick off with Letty Andrews, the doll who just left the witness stand. Her husband Nick is an architect down in the city. That's all I know. But something's bugging that little lady. She's full of jitters."

So am I, he thought.

Nor was Pete Harmon feeling upbeat. Serena didn't have it right. True, this was an open-and-shut case. Laurie Coles was certainly guilty as charged. On paper. But it would not be a snap in the courtroom, even with Jacko, who's dying to put her away. We're dealing with children, who can mess you up. They'll give one account and then a whole other one and the new version will still be the gospel. They're full of stories about flying witches and princesses in great danger. But in court every contradiction is seized and exploited until it looks as if the witness wouldn't recognize the truth if it was swallowed. And jurors can start down one road and change direction without signaling. No, this won't be a cinch.

He dropped it and wondered if the day would come when Serena would be called Mrs. Harmon. Or, married, would she remain Wiley? No big deal. Would they have children? Two would be just right. So of course Serena would want one, or three. And what brawls there would be, choosing names for the little ones, however many.

During lunch he chewed over another topic. Why did the grand jury refuse to indict Mickey Strand, on the gun charge? That was another open-and-shut case, wasn't it?

Chapter 19

CHAIR ONE GAVE NUMBER NINE NO CHOICE BUT TO JOIN THE REST OF THE jurors for lunch by sitting with them herself. She had something to say. "You know, if they knock you off a jury, you feel like something's wrong with you. Like they think you're brainless." She tested her sandwich. "But I wish they'd sent me packing. I don't like this case. Or this alleged tuna, either."

Number Nine, the man of mathematics, showed surprise. "Why not? You thought she was guilty before we heard a word. Don't tell me you're swinging over?"

Two, the loan officer at Third Federal Savings, said, "We can't talk about the case yet."

"Those witnesses are like my word processor," One said. "I tell it what to say and it never says anything different. When they testify, out comes the same story, except for a slip here and there. And what about the downstairs room that isn't there? It's getting hard to know what to believe."

Nine shook his head. "The defense is fussing too much about that. It looks like something happened somewhere."

It was Number One's turn to be taken aback. *"You're* switching? But you said they had to prove it, prove it."

"That Andrews woman was convincing," Nine said. "She had a hard time talking about that mess-on-the-table stuff, but she was believable. What reason would she have for walking into court and making up stories like that?"

Number Two intervened, crisply now. "Look, we all have to live with each other until this is over, so I'll try to be polite. Please stop talking for a minute and listen. You're totally into yourselves. How you feel about everything, from your hamburgers to your tuna sandwich. Meanwhile, someone's life is in our hands and this is a very complicated case. We have to keep our minds open and not reach conclusions about the testimony until the case ends."

"Don't get excited," One said.

Two's voice became noticeably calm as she replied. "All right, I didn't want to have to say this, you've forced me to do it. The next time I hear you discussing the evidence before the trial ends, I will notify the judge."

"Get off your horse," One said. She turned to Number Ten, the postal clerk, who was holding a paperback book. "What are you reading, friend?"

He smiled. *"Anatomy of a Murder.* About an army guy and a lawyer. The lieutenant shot a bartender who raped his wife, and I think his lawyer's going to get him off."

"Check out the video," Number One said. "It's a great rent. The lawyer believes in his client and gets him off, but at the end the army guy says, Sure I was guilty, sucker, and the lawyer stands there wiping egg off his face. You'll love it."

Ten was irate. "You give the whole thing away? Now what am I going to do all afternoon?"

One shrugged and Two said, "Do you always act this way? Or is the strain too much for you? Don't we have enough to think about without playing games? Try to concentrate on the case."

One smiled. "It's boring."

The case did not seem boring as it consumed much of the afternoon in Number One's room. She and Nine haggled over the saintliness or depravity of Laurie Coles. In the course of their crossfires, they discovered that each was digging at the foundations of once-immovable beliefs. Nine thought the prosecutor was starting to prove it; One argued that the defense had started to cast reasonable doubt on the state's case.

Chapter 20

PETE HARMON HANDED HARRY HULL SEVERAL DOCUMENTS. THE DEFENSE counsel glanced at the top sheet and turned the stack over to Laurie Coles. "While they're testifying," he said, "start reading these transcripts of the sessions between the investigators and the children. Look for who said what first. Did a child use your name or did an investigator say it? And make notes of where the kids say things happened but where they couldn't have. Architecture and layout. And give a lot of attention to Chair Number Two, in the front row, the one with the high shoulders. As if you feel she must understand how zany these charges are. Can you do that?" She nodded.

"Another thing." He turned, saw that the courtroom was sold out again, and winked at a buff. "I'm going to wake up the jurors when Jacko comes in. Just so you won't be surprised." He squeezed her shoulder. "You were great this morning. Keep it up, Laurie."

All rise and so on and in came the jurors, gravid with hamburgers. Hull rose quickly. "Your Honor, during the lunch break I was given a copy of a warrant issued last April twenty-eighth that authorized a search of the defendant's apartment. I ask the court to determine from the prosecution why we were not notified of this action in a timely way."

Justice Mathes looked surprised. "Mr. Harmon?"

The district attorney seemed nonplused. "I don't know anything about it. My office didn't ask for the warrant."

Hull flipped a page. "The report says that a search of Miss Coles's premises discovered nothing incriminating."

The judge asked, "Then what's your complaint, Counselor?"

Hull ignored Mathes and spoke to the jury. "What am I complaining about? We had testimony yesterday that a hidden video camera was found in the Snug Arms school on April 26, and that a pupil said Miss Coles taped children in the nude. That part of the testimony was stricken, of course, but the jurors heard it. Now, Miss Coles's apartment was searched two days after the school was wrecked. So it's obvious that the police were looking for tapes of nude children. But no such evidence was found. My point is that underhanded methods are being used to tear down the defendant's character, and that the atmosphere in which this trial is being conducted is thoroughly polluted. I move again for a change of venue so this trial can be heard in an environment that has some chance of being fair."

Mathes did not bother to recognize the D.A., or to veil his sarcasm. "Mr. Hull. Most attorneys would know that a change of venue cannot be granted once a trial is under way."

Hull's gaze had never left the jurors. "I'm aware of that, Your Honor. I just felt that the jury should understand what's going on around here. So if you want to strike my remarks from the record, I won't object."

The mustache on the bench quivered. "Call your witness, Mr. Harmon."

The district attorney had finished dashing off a note to the police chief: "Here's how you can help: Don't help." He said, "The state calls Lilly Robertson."

Everyone had been waiting for the star's entrance, and here she came. The primmest matron in the county could not have outdone Caroline Robertson's mother in the choice of apparel. A gray tweed suit. The neckline of a canary silk blouse met her throat and its sleeves reached her wrists. Expensive silver and turquoise jewelry. Advancing swiftly in low-heeled shoes, she offered the jurors a brief smile, seated herself in the witness chair, and looked up at the prosecutor.

A search for anyone who did not already know what Lilly Robertson would say would turn up no one. Still, there was not even the scrape of a foot in the audience. And Harmon was aware that the jury also wanted to hear it all over again. But he was apprehensive. Tiger Lil was a key witness and he had spent long hours with her, reviewing her testimony and urging her to chill out. "You have every reason to be furious," he told her, "but to get justice you must act calmly and objectively. You don't want the jury to get the idea that you're in court for revenge and will say anything to get it."

She replied, "Whose side are you on? Aren't you the district attorney?"

He would calm her emotions by wording his questions as

blandly as possible. "Mrs. Robertson, approximately three months ago you felt that a physician should examine your daughter. Please explain why you reached that conclusion."

She spoke almost in a murmur. "I brought Carrie home from Snug Arms and she said, 'Laurie put strawberry jam on my peepee.' And that person sitting there"—she pointed to Coles—"asked my daughter to lick it off. Carrie said Miss Coles called it Sweet Time. And when my daughter wouldn't lick it off, she was threatened." Her voice rose. "I almost went crazy—"

"Objection."

"Sustained," Mathes said. "Please try to control yourself, Mrs. Robertson. We realize this has been a difficult time for you."

Hull broke in. "No, Your Honor! You're appealing to the emotions of the jury! It has been just as difficult for the defendant. Maybe more difficult."

Mathes was almost shouting. "Approach the bench!" Hull started forward and Harmon followed, but the judge waved the prosecutor back. Harmon stopped, startled. It was highly unusual, to say the least, for a judge to speak to an attorney in mid-trial out of the other's presence.

"Around here." Mathes pointed to the side of the bench away from the jury box and the jurors cupped their ears to try to make out the whispers. They heard nothing but saw the judge's lips moving swiftly and his mustache wiggling as Hull's head bobbed as if in genial agreement. Mathes stopped and the attorney moved back. "Yes, *sir!*" he said loudly and returned to his seat, raising his eyebrows at the jurors.

Laurie Coles, head down, was paging through the transcripts Hull had given her.

Harmon resumed. "Mrs. Robertson, would you tell the jury the circumstances under which your daughter brought up this act of sexual abuse."

She struggled for composure. "I always prepare toast and peanut butter and jam for Carrie after school. But on that afternoon she said she wanted me to put it on her vagina. When she saw the shock on my face, she ran to the sink and smashed the jam plate in it. Then she told me what happened at the school."

Harmon fielded a problem before Hull could reach it. "I'd like to clear up what may sound like a contradiction. Caroline told detective Garafolo that Miss Coles placed the jam on her own vagina, and that she asked Caroline to lick it off. You're aware of that?"

The witness nodded. "Carrie told me that, too. When I asked her more about it, she became angry and ran to her room. Then she said she wished she hadn't told me anything. She was crying and she said she was afraid that person over there would hurt her for telling. She was scared, and when she talked to the detective, she got mixed up again."

"Thank you. Now, did your daughter say that the jam incident occurred just once, or several times?"

"She said it happened only once with her, but that Miss Coles did it with other children."

Harmon changed the subject. "Mrs. Robertson, did your daughter tell you anything else about Miss Coles? And would you speak up just a bit?"

"Carrie said she took a box from a shopping bag and pulled out a rabbit by its ears. She put her hands around its neck and choked it until it wasn't moving. And then she took a knife and stabbed it. Caroline yelled 'Blood!' at me. And she said Miss Coles cut off the rabbit's feet and put all the parts back in the box and cleaned up the mess."

Harmon was pacing. "Did Caroline tell you what Miss Coles said at the time? That is, did she explain why she choked the rabbit and dismembered it?"

"Yes. She said she wanted them to see what she would do to their parents if anyone told about the, the jam in Caroline's vagina."

"Thank you, Mrs. Robertson. I'm almost finished. Did your daughter say whether incidents with animals took place just that one time, or many times?"

"She said Laurie did the same thing to a squirrel, and to a bird. She cut out the bird's eyes. And she warned the children again not to say anything to their parents."

"What exactly did your daughter tell you Miss Coles said?"

"She said she would burn our house down. And if they put her in jail, she would come back and torture Caroline when she got out." The witness stared at the D.A. "Wouldn't you consider that a threat?"

Harmon turned to Justice Mathes. "No further questions."

Hull rose but did not leave the counsel table. "Just one or two questions," he said, looking down, as if at notes. "Mrs. Robertson, did your daughter tell you what room she was in when the jam was allegedly placed in her vagina?"

"Oh, you're going to start up that stuff about a secret room? That's just how children talk."

"I see. Well, did she ever tell you if other children were present when these alleged acts took place?"

"Of course. About a dozen."

"All right. Now, were you in contact with other Snug Arms parents in the weeks after your daughter told you this story?"

"Of course." Her voice rose. "Do you think I just sat there and did nothing?"

"No. Now, when you spoke to the other parents, did any of them say whether their children had seen the defendant put jam on your daughter's vagina? Or theirs?"

The witness was openly angry. "No. Children don't like to talk to their parents about such things."

"But we've heard that a dozen children were present when the jam incident occurred. Not one of the dozen mentioned it?"

Mrs. Robertson's self-control departed. She stood up and shouted, "You see what we're up against? This lawyer and the district attorney. But I'm not surprised by the prosecutor. A man who's shacked up with a woman who's not his wife."

Coles stopped writing and looked up. Hull's eyes were fixed on Harmon. Juror Number One seemed exasperated. Number Nine, the math chairman, rolled his eyes.

The courtroom was agitated and the gavel hammered the bench several times. "Mrs. Robertson, you will restrict yourself to answering the questions."

Still on her feet, she pointed to Hull. "We're talking about little children, you damn fool! Can they remember everything? Are you going to give them an I.Q. test? This pervert has hurt our children and we get technicalities!"

Harmon asked himself the same question Harry Hull had propounded earlier. What did I do to deserve this?

The judge looked at Hull, who turned away quickly. He wanted so badly to explain to Mrs. Robertson that, yes, indeed, the children had to pass a test. They had to convince the jury that they were believable. But he would not take the chance of undoing any of the damage he felt Lilly Robertson was inflicting on the prosecution.

Hull turned back to the witness and said, "First we hear that Miss Coles placed jam on your daughter's vagina. Then we're told that the defendant placed it on her own vagina. How can you or the jury tell which one of your daughter's two stories is the right one?"

"Objection. Speechifying."

Justice Mathes said, "Sustained. Mr. Hull, just ask questions. You are abusing the cross-examination process."

"I am? Excuse me, sir. No further questions."

The judge saw the witness's mouth open. He lifted a hand to shut her off but failed.

"I was told to act like a lady and not blow up," Mrs. Robertson said. "I'm not a lady. I'm Carrie's mother!" She turned to the jury. "If you don't convict this bitch and send her to jail, you're all chickenshit and you'll rot in hell, with my husband!"

Hull, who had been gripping Laurie Coles's arm, released it. "I hope she never stops," he whispered.

Lilly Robertson was suddenly speechless. She looked out over the audience and found Ellen Strand. But Ellen was shaking her head.

The judge tried to control his frustration. "There are no more questions, Mrs. Robertson. You may step down."

She stood, then sat again and found her voice. "What are you talking about? Don't you want to know what happened? What she did? She played a game she called Bottoms Up. The children took off their clothes and she took hers off. And the kids leaned over and put their hands on the floor and she went around and kissed their, their buttocks. She told them their mommies and daddies do that."

That was a new one on Harmon, and on Hull, who made certain the jury recognized his wonderment.

"You don't want to hear that, do you? And there was—"

Mathes's tone was now loud and firm. "The witness will *step down* immediately!"

She continued to sit and he spoke to the jury. "We have a difficult situation, ladies and gentlemen. The acts alleged here are bound to provoke extreme reactions. You are instructed to disregard the witness's emotional outbursts and consider only the facts of her testimony."

Hull asked, "How will they tell the facts from the fictions, Your Honor?"

Mathes ignored him and Lilly Robertson remained in place.

The judge motioned to the bailiff and the jury was led out, moving slowly and looking back. "Now," Mathes said, "leave the court on your own or an officer will remove you, Mrs. Robertson."

The clerk suggested gently that the witness step down. She rose, spat in the direction of Laurie Coles, and walked out.

Harmon could hear Serena chiding him. He passed Hull a sheet on which the names of three parents had been crossed out. Hull was pleased. The D.A. knew he might lose more than he could gain if many more parents took the stand and chewed the scenery.

It was only a few minutes past four, but Mathes called it a day. "Court will resume at ten o'clock in the morning." He departed with an aggravated shake of his head, the jury rose, and the jail attendant moved up to the defendant. Hull waved her away and asked Coles for her notes. "Take the rest of the transcripts with you and read them tonight. Listen, we almost broke even today. Keep your chin up, Laurie."

Hull stayed off the beer for the second night in a row. He spent most of the evening reviewing Coles's notes and checking the transcripts of conversations between the Snug Arms children and prosecution investigators. Then he drove over to Sgueglia's motel, where he had a couple of brews and wrote another check.

At the Harmon-Wiley homestead Pete found Serena halfway through what he recognized as the record of the Coles trial, Day One. He reached for a casual tone. "You're buying the daily transcripts? And nobody has even retained you?"

"I'm not buying them, sweetheart. Your secretary dittoed your office copy for me. I was sure you wouldn't mind."

"Listen, love. I don't care how involved you get in this case. Just save time for my daily marriage proposals."

Chapter 21

CORNELIUS MCGONIGLE COULD HAVE WORKED FOR ANY CHANNEL DOWN IN the big city, but he preferred the Hudson Ferry pace to the rat race. He was a ferret of a reporter who delivered the goods, received a lot of airtime, and was responsible for much of channel 22's headlock on the local ratings.

McGonigle was an enormous man, well over six feet and big-boned, and his energy was inexhaustible although he rarely slept; he was a stimulation addict. He carried his own camera, and more than once he had videotaped a story, then laid the voiceover back at the studio. High tech made it sound as if he were speaking on-scene. He usually spoke with great foresight since he had already seen the future, live on tape.

It was cockcrow time and McGonigle was already prowling the downtown area, briskly, camera on a shoulder, when he spotted a familiar face in a car, waiting for a light to change. What was Anthony Sgueglia, the private eye from the state capital, doing in our burg?

McGonigle's bark could awaken a neighborhood. "Tony Snoop!"

"Corky the dogcatcher!"

They had worked together, when McGonigle was with a channel up in Albany. An arena was being operated at which locals bet on which pit bull would shred its opponent. But no slaughter was ever in progress when the cops arrived, so Sgueglia was retained to gather evidence. McGonigle hid a camera in the barn that housed the arena, and that evening blood poured from TV screens and indictments followed.

"What're you doing in town?" McGonigle asked as he climbed in and dropped his camera onto the backseat. "You're not here to check the tides. Who're you working for?" he bellowed. "On what? No lies now, Tony!"

Sgueglia laughed. "You were talking when you left Albany, Corky, and you're still doing it. I was going to look you up."

"You must be on the Coles case. The shame of Hudson Ferry. Which side are you working for?"

Sgueglia pulled out and rolled down River Road. "I'm tired of sneaking around," he said. "I want to retire, and maybe I'll do it around here. I'm looking the area over, Corky."

"Tony, I said no lies. You're here on the Coles case, yes? All right, I'll show you around. Go up the hill."

In five minutes they were in residential Hudson Ferry, verdant, subdued. "Left on Utopia," McGonigle said. "Then your first right." They came onto Marina Road and he asked, "You want to live here in heaven, do you, Tony?"

"Maybe. Does the town have cable TV?"

"Why do you ask?"

"I saw one of those deep-dish antennas in a backyard."

"Turn right into Birch Lane. Sure there's cable. But I've got the ratings. I murder the cable news shows. Where did you see an antenna?"

"Back there. Listen, I saw a piece in the paper about this Coles. Is she guilty?"

"You won't tell me who you're working for, right, Squail? And you want to know if she's guilty. You're the most devious snoop I ever ran into. It doesn't make any difference. Guilty or innocent, she'll get it. But I'll tell you 'cause I'm impartial. She's innocent and they're full of shit. This case is a frame-up, but I'm not blaming the D.A. Pete Harmon's straight, but what can he do? It's his job."

"Harmon? Who's the defense lawyer?"

"Pull over, across from that two-by-four, and look at it." Sgueglia parked and took in a sprawling mansion surrounded by towering trees and manicured shrubbery. "The one who started the whole thing lives there. Tiger Lil Robertson. A one-woman firing squad. Her husband does stocks, but he's gone underground. She'd throw his ass out if it wasn't for the money."

Sgueglia grinned. "Where have I heard that before? So how'll she get even? Does she run with a kinky-sex crowd?"

"What makes you ask a question like that, Tony? I figured you were working for the prosecutor. And then you ask me who the defense lawyer is and now you want to know if there are any strangers in Lilly Robertson's pants. I know you can't tell me. Just nod. You're working for Pete Harmon."

"Which way is nodding?" Sgueglia inquired. "Show me some more homes."

McGonigle slumped in his seat, a Herculean feat in view of his size. "I give up. Harry Hull is for the defense. He's over his head, but he's giving it a big shot. He's trying to get the judge to blow his stack and he may pull it off yet. It's his only chance. Oh, shit! You're working for Hull, Tony."

"Which way is nodding?" Sgueglia asked.

They drove down to the marina and were surveying the sloops when Sgueglia asked, "What about Andrews? What's Mrs. Andrews like?"

McGonigle extricated himself from the car. "You're really looking for shit, aren't you? We went by her house, you know."

Sgueglia remembered the mailbox and made a note. The deep-dish antenna was behind the green house on Utopia Lane.

"She's an overwound spring. You bastard, if you turn up anything on Letty and Nick, you owe me a first. So you're working for Hull. The Andrewses have been here three or four years. Came up from the city where Nick's an architect. But he's not interesting." He grinned. "Letty's a string of firecrackers in the sack. Bang-bang. She never stops. Ask a man who knows."

"Who might that be?"

"I came by for a visit one morning and a pickup truck was in the driveway. A half hour later it was still there. And it was there for a half hour three times a week. I parked down the block and watched and once *two* guys came out. Round-robin, I guess. So I dumped her. She smelled like big trouble."

"I like to hear you talk," Sgueglia said. "Let's see more of the town, Corky."

They were back up the hill when McGonigle said, "Tell Hull you saw Ellen Strand's house, Tony. He'd probably like to check her carburetor, but he can't because he's lawyering for Coles."

"Ellen Strand? Mickey Strand's wife? What is this, Corky? Small-world time? Tell me more."

McGonigle grinned. "I got your attention. The gun in the courtroom? You remember Strand from Albany, don't you, when he raised campaign funds for the senator who runs the banking committee? He was good, but one day the man threw him out on the street. Mickey and Ellen moved here and had a baby, but he divorced her a year ago and left her with the kid, the one in the Snug Arms case. Anything else you want to know, Tony? Are you writing a history of Hudson Ferry?"

"Yeah. But it might be too dirty to publish."

They were driving near the north edge of town when a muffled boom filled the air; it seemed to come from up ahead. Sgueglia slowed and McGonigle said, "No, hit the gas! Move it, Tony! Take a left at the second crossing." He reached behind and seized his camera. "Sweet Jesus! I think it's Snug Arms!"

Sgueglia swung onto sparsely occupied Linden Terrace and heard McGonigle's videocam whir. A bloom of smoke rose and they saw a van racing toward Sgueglia's car. The newsman locked his lens onto the gray vehicle until it shot by. Then he swiveled and caught the receding rear license plate. "What did the driver look like, Tony?"

"Too fast. And I was scared."

"It was Ike Brendelski. I'm sure of it. He's lost the few marbles he ever had." McGonigle swung the camera around, struggled out of the car, and stood across the road from Snug Arms.

They watched the flames, McGonigle through the viewfinder of his camera, as streaks flew from the rear section of the roof. The sky had gone gray and was steadily darkening as wild new streaks of fire flashed through it. And a low roar reached their ears as the temperature rose and smoke poured out in rolling puffs.

"What am I doing here?" Sgueglia asked. "I'm not a volunteer type."

"Tell me who you're working for or I'll throw you in the middle of it, Tony."

"Where's the fire department? Does this town have one?"

Then they heard a different noise. It sounded like a fat-fingered chord on an organ, two keys instead of one, blaring. "Somebody's in there!" Sgueglia yelled.

McGonigle lowered the camera. "No. It's shut down."

"Somebody's inside!" Sgueglia yelled over the roaring of the flames. "Yelling!"

The newsman placed his camera, carefully, on the roadside. "Let's go, Tony."

Sgueglia didn't move.

"Let's go!"

Sgueglia's lips were moving. He said, "Okay. I'm trying to to pray."

They heard distant sirens as they dashed across the road and the lawn of the school. McGonigle hit the front door and it gave. They went into the smoke and McGonigle heard Sgueglia say, "For Christ's sake! What am I doing here?"

Fumes entered their nostrils and they fell back to the door. Then Sgueglia seized McGonigle's arm and they went through the first room, trying to remember about smoke, bending over as they advanced. The sound of sirens was closer. "Let's get out of here!" Sgueglia yelled. "They've got masks."

McGonigle pushed forward and they edged into the second

room. But a sudden force, followed by a blast of air and an explosion, this one louder than the boom on the roadway, threw them back and Sgueglia bounced off a wall and said, "Get on the floor! There's somebody ahead of us!"

They dropped to their knees and scrambled through a doorway. Before them lay a woman McGonigle recognized. Her legs were spread-eagled and held to the flooring by ropes fastened to metal stakes and she was screaming. They looked along her body and saw that her arms were also tied down.

Sgueglia took a deep breath. It was a mistake and he passed out. McGonigle, lungs saturated with smoke, shouted for the firemen. He passed out seconds later as Mildred Cross was freed and gurneyed to an ambulance.

McGonigle screamed at a man in a white coat, "Where's my camera? If you son-of-a-bitches didn't get my camera, you're dead!"

"Try to be still," the doctor said, reaching for his stethoscope. "You're fine."

"Where's Sgueglia?"

"Who? He wouldn't give his name. But he was released a few minutes ago."

"I probably got the name wrong. Where's my camera?"

"The other gentleman has it. He's resting on a bench in the corridor."

McGonigle sprang out of bed and pushed past the doctor. He rushed through the door and found Sgueglia stretched out, the camera between his legs. "What time is it, Tony?"

"Seven thirty."

"We've only been here an hour?" McGonigle snatched the camera and started running. "I can still make the morning news!" He coughed. "Give me a lift, Tony. Quick!"

"Are you crazy, Corky? The tape has to go to the police. You've got pictures of the guy who bombed the school!"

McGonigle had other ideas and Squail delivered him to channel 22 before driving over to the courthouse. The newsman was intercepted on the street level by a tape editor who said, "Take the back way. The place is full of cops and they want your tape!" He raced to the rear and dashed into the cellar, where he laid his commentary over the pictures. Shortly before eight o'clock he slipped into the studio unseen, waved to the standard blond, blue-eyed anchorwoman, and tossed the tape to a technician.

Anthony Sgueglia caught Harry Hull in the courthouse cafeteria at five minutes before the hour. Hull said, "Squail! Were you boozing all night? You look like warm shit."

Sgueglia shook his head. "Harry, you haven't got a lot of time. If you turn on the TV you'll find out the school was bombed this morning. Write down this name. Mildred Cross. She owned Snug Arms, right? A guy named Ike Brendelski tried to kill her in the place. Don't interrupt me. You'll find out on the news. And I'm working on Letty Andrews, but I haven't got anything solid yet. Tell me what I told you."

Hull repeated it and said, "You're a piece of merchandise, Tony. I'm going to buy you a beer."

"This job'll cost a hell of a lot more than a beer, Harry. What the fuck is going on? I don't want any more of it."

"Hang in, Squail. You'll be rewarded in heaven."

"Don't negotiate with me!" He walked off, shakily, and Hull ran to the nearest television screen.

Cornelius McGonigle's loyal fans were soon watching the firebombing of the Snug Arms Preschool on tape with the look of live action. Viewers saw ribbons, flashes, then balls of smoke flare across the screen and heard Corky remark, as if the newsman had been out buying roses for the girlfriend, that he and a buddy from Albany happened to be driving by. Mildred Cross, who directed Snug Arms when it was in business, had been found bound to the floor. She was being treated for smoke poisoning but was expected to recover. McGonigle's composure in the midst of the carnage was amazing. He was the greatest; he knew that.

The camera cut to the newsman live and smiling as he pointed to a studio door. Noise was heard and the cameras swiveled. The door burst open and six policemen came through. A camera dollied in and caught the scene as McGonigle delivered a tirade to the officers, something about freedom of the press. Risking a fine for overacting, he asked that the videotape now be turned over to the police. It might help in their investigation, he said. One cop who did not realize he was on the air uttered an epithet that was not normally heard on family TV. Then came the ritual close. "Corky McGonigle, channel twenty-two. Stay tuned."

Hull went up to the courtroom entertained by a fantasy. There they were, Corky and Sgueglia, in the Snug Arms school, gasping for breath in dense smoke. They groped around and saw a man staked to the floor. He had a bristling red mustache and was clad in black robes. Corky and the Squail winked at each other, walked out, and drove away.

Chapter 22

It was August and ninety-six degrees without a breeze in Hudson Ferry. Justice Mathes entered the cool courtroom and the jurors were led in, energized by conversations about the firebombing of Snug Arms. An informal vote, taken after a scan of forbidden news programs, had convicted Ike Brendelski.

The buffs were taken up with Corky McGonigle's coverage of the disaster. One said, "He'd do anything for a story. The cops should check· him out." Then it was learned that a three-state alarm was out for Brendelski, for attempted murder, aggravated assault, and arson. The police had viewed McGonigle's videotape and found the opening footage useless because the rising sun had shone into the windshield of the gray van. But an enlargement of the rear license plate sent them rushing to Brendelski's home, where his wife said he had left before sunrise; her added remarks strengthened the idea that he was loco.

Hull was contemplative. He noticed that Old Glory, the one at the front of the courtroom with the faded stripes, had been replaced by a vivid new flag, and he tried to believe that was an omen for the defense. Something about freedom.

Laurie Coles handed him the last of the transcripts of the investigators' interviews with the Snug Arms children and he winked. At nine o'clock the evening before he had received a call from her. The jailers had seized the material, saying she could not have it in her cell. Hull spoke to the prison superintendent and asked how he would like to appear in court in the morning and explain his interference with a prisoner's right to defend herself. The transcripts were returned.

This was Trial Day Three and Harmon was anticipating a compelling performance by Marla Burney. Mother of Tom and wife of

Grant, she did not have a story that sounded practiced; nor was she overwrought. In their few talks she had listened, thinking over the D.A.'s questions before replying. Reading jurors' minds was futile, but Harmon suspected they would size her up as he had. She was credibility itself.

Hull was also studying slim and pretty Mrs. Burney, whose name had come to him well after those of other witnesses. He knew about the rumors that she and her husband had been laggard in assisting the prosecution. The folks in Hudson Ferry felt good about their upscale black family, but Marla and Grant would not receive acclaim at the moment.

"Mrs. Burney," Harmon said, "I think the jury should know that you were not sure until recently that you would appear as a witness in this case. Why did you decide to come forward?"

She saw Grant in the audience; he had taken the morning off without mentioning it. "My son Tom had never said anything negative about Snug Arms or Miss Coles. So when we first heard about these charges, Grant and I were shocked, and we decided not to talk to him about it. He's not even five. Then we attended a parent meeting and went home worried. Everyone was upset, understandably, but there seemed to be pressure to make accusations against Miss Coles. So we wondered if shock was becoming hysteria."

She paused and Harmon waited while stealing a glance at the jury, where he thought he saw expectation.

"We were very concerned, as you can imagine. Finally we sat down with Tom and talked to him. We asked if the children ever took their clothes off at school, because we had heard that said. He laughed at us. We asked him about Miss Coles and he said, 'Laurie's great.' So again we thought that maybe the situation was being exaggerated. But a couple of weeks ago Tom called me into the bathroom." She looked out again at her husband. "He had taken off his pants and he asked me to touch his penis."

Hull leaned over to Coles. "Start writing. Write anything and don't look up. Do it!"

"I couldn't think of what to say, so I just laughed. Tom laughed too, but he repeated it. So I asked him if someone had touched his penis." She hesitated. "It was enlarged. Sometimes he waits too long to urinate. And he said, 'Laurie did. When I go, she always stays by the bathroom door, but once she came over and touched me.'"

In the audience, Grant Burney received sympathetic glances.

"Tom tells a lot of stories, so I asked him if this was just another one and he said yes. But when I asked him again, he said it was true. Grant and I decided we shouldn't try to judge whether it was true or made up. I still don't know whether to believe Tom, but we thought we should tell his story."

Hull searched the jurors' faces and found what he read as belief.

Harmon said, very quietly, "No further questions."

Hull rose. "Mrs. Burney, I have only one thing to ask. Could you be more specific about when this act was supposed to have occurred? You said about two weeks ago. Today is August first. Could you place the date more precisely?"

She considered, then said, "Yes, it was on a Saturday. I know because Mr. Burney goes fishing on Saturday afternoons. So it was on Saturday, July twenty-first."

"Thank you," Hull said. "I have nothing else."

Pete Harmon would have liked to close out the parents at this point. No one could improve on Marla Burney, who had expressed misgivings and then given an account with a convincing sound. But his next witness's story was graphic, and he needed the heavy stuff, too. "The state calls Ellen Strand."

Bonnie's mother entered, cigarette smoke in her trail, and took small, rapid steps to the witness box, halting to stare at the jurors before seating herself. Harmon was counting on her to help build the case; she was not one of the hotheads. He opened in a subdued tone. "Three months ago you told the police about an incident at the Snug Arms Preschool. Would you tell us about that, Mrs. Strand?"

"Bonnie—" she coughed and cleared her throat. "Bonnie came home from school one day and chopped up a Popsicle. Then she stabbed peach slices with the stick and said Miss Coles put a pop stick in her vagina."

Hull rose and said, "Your Honor, I don't want to repeat my objections to hearsay testimony any more than you want to hear them. If the court will stipulate for the record that I object every single time a parent is asked what a child said, I will not rise again on this point."

"A pleasure, Mr. Hull. The court reporter is so instructed." The reporter typed phrases she had come to know well. Defense objection. Hearsay evidence. Denied. Exception.

"I won't linger on that subject," Harmon said. He wanted his witness to relax. "Mrs. Strand, has your daughter spoken of the killing of animals?"

Ellen Strand smiled for the first time. "She said the kids made up that story. They were scared, too, so they tried to change the subject when they were being questioned. And they said anything terrible they could think of, or that they had seen in a movie."

Harmon had not included the sacrificing of animals in the indictment. Unlike the physical molestation of a child, it would not be admissible without corroborating evidence, such as the body of a bird or squirrel, of which there were none. But Ellen Strand's testimony had defanged some of Lilly Robertson's excesses. He returned to the subject of the pop stick. "Mrs. Strand, you testified that after your daughter said Miss Coles inserted a stick into her vagina, you had her examined. Please tell us what the physician said."

She hesitated. "I want to get the words right. He said there were abrasions on the inside of her vagina, and the marks were consistent with penetration. By an object."

"Look at the jury," Hull whispered to Coles. "Don't sit and sulk."

Harmon nodded. Ellen Strand had done her job and he would get corroboration from the physician. "Thank you, Mrs. Strand. I have nothing further."

Hull could feel the witness's animosity as he rose and approached her. "Mrs. Strand, did your daughter continue to play with other Snug Arms children after the school was closed?"

She looked away, toward the jury. But he also noticed that she had not looked at the judge since sitting down. "Yes. They often played at my house."

"And do you know whether they talked about Sweet Time and Bottoms Up and other incidents that have been mentioned during this trial?"

"I'm not always home, but the nanny told me they did."

"Do you feel it's logical to assume that Bonnie and her friends talked about the pop-stick incident?"

"I don't know."

"Well, if you can agree that they might have, why do you think no other child told a parent about such an incident?"

"Objection!" Harmon said. "Asking for a conclusion."

"Sustained."

Hull gave it up. "Mrs. Strand, a final question. Has Bonnie ever mentioned a secret room at Snug Arms?"

The witness's composure departed. "No. But why did the police leave it to Ike Brendelski to look for it? Why didn't they dig up the place themselves? Well, now that it's burned down, maybe they can find the room!"

She halted abruptly and Hull said, "Oh, one more question. Just to be sure, would you tell us just once more what the physician said about the signs of abrasion he found in your daughter's vagina?"

She looked at the jurors. "He said they were consistent with penetration by an object."

"Thank you. Nothing else."

As Ellen Strand hurried down the aisle, Marla Burney left her seat and they went out together.

Mathes banged the gavel. "Recess. Ten minutes."

The physician who had examined Bonnie Strand was a portly man to whom the prosecutor put just three questions.

"Did you find marks in the Strand child's vagina?"

"Yes."

"They were consistent with penetration by a foreign object?"

"Yes."

"Could that have been a small stick?"

"Yes."

"Thank you, Doctor."

This time Hull did not pass. "Doctor," he asked, "have you testified previously in a criminal case?"

He looked at his watch. "This is the first time."

"I asked that because I don't want you to feel that when I ask a question, I'm attacking your credibility." Hull smiled and the doctor seemed puzzled. The notion that his credibility could be questioned was novel. "Do you specialize in gynecology, sir?"

"No, but I know gynecology."

"Oh, I didn't mean to imply that you didn't. Is pediatrics your specialty, sir?"

"No, but I see a lot of children."

"Of course."

"Well, what is your specialty, sir?"

"I'm a general practitioner."

"Ah. You don't have a specialty."

"Incorrect. General practice is a specialty."

"Despite the word *general*. All right. Do you frequently examine the vaginas of small children?"

"Frequently? How often is that?"

There was a faint titter in the room.

"I don't exactly know. I'm trying to get an idea of how many times, in a year, say, you have occasion to examine a child whose vagina was invaded by a foreign object."

The doctor strolled into the trap. "I didn't say the Strand child's vagina was invaded by a foreign object." He smiled.

"Nor did you say it had been *penetrated*. Am I correct?"

"I say things the professional way. The signs of abrasion in the child's vagina were *consistent* with penetration."

Hull nodded. "Perhaps you could help those of us who have

not been trained in medicine, Doctor. Is there a simple way of defining what *consistent* means in this particular context?"

"It means the act could have occurred."

"Does it mean it did occur?"

"Of course not. That's why I didn't say that."

"Thank you, sir. I'm beginning to understand. Now, did you also determine whether the opening of the Strand child's vagina was correct for her age?"

The physician smiled. "There's no such thing as correct. The size of children's vaginal openings varies considerably. It's surprising how lay people—"

"Thank you, Doctor. So if a child's vaginal opening is somewhat larger than you might have expected, it would still be difficult to say that the area had been penetrated."

"One could not be certain."

"Fine. Let's assume that the signs were such that you believed penetration did in fact occur. Would you be able to identify what the penetrating object was?"

He thought about that. "Sometimes a penis is thrust roughly into a vagina before it has been lubricated."

"This child is not even five years old, doctor."

"Yes, but you asked a general question. It could be almost any object of an admissible size."

Hull faced the jury. "And would you say that a child might possibly have inserted something into her own vagina? Would the abrasion marks be the same?"

"Objection," Harmon said. "There is no evidence of such an act by the child in question."

The judge thought about that. "We have an expert witness here. Questions can be broader than usual."

"Would the marks be about the same if the child did the penetration herself, doctor? While playing in the bathtub, say?"

"Well, yes."

"Thank you, sir. I have no further questions."

Harmon was satisfied. The jury would remember the abrasions in Bonnie Strand's vagina. And the child herself would testify to what caused those marks.

Mathes spoke. "Due to other obligations, it will be necessary to adjourn court until tomorrow morning." The robes flared as he left the bench.

In the corridor, Hull's secretary handed him a fax message from the appellate division. His appeal from the stratospheric bail figure set by Mathes had been denied.

Hull said he would be in the office in a few minutes with another fax for the appeals court. He would ask the appellate judges to remove Mathes from the case and declare a mistrial. It was a hopeless request and he knew it. But his goal was to keep the case of Laurie Coles up front in the appellate judges' minds, in the section that regulates the conscience.

Chair Nine caught Two emerging from the ladies' room. "The defense guy backed off that doctor, didn't he? The doc had to admit that the child could have put the stick into herself."

Chair Two decided it was time to unhorse Nine. "It's easy to be taken in by defense attorneys. At first I thought the prosecutor had a weak case. Nobody would keep doing those things to kids without expecting to be caught. Kids talk. But then we find out that Coles shut them up by threatening them."

Nine sniffed. "You're right. It's easy to be taken in."

On the searing steps of the criminal courts building, Corky McGonigle was pointing out Ellen Strand to Anthony Sgueglia. "Mickey's ex," he said.

"Who's the couple with her?"

"You're so curious about the locals, Squail. That's Marla Burney, who testified this morning. And her husband. He's a whiz kid at IBM. You want more? Ellen doesn't get invited around much these days. The ladies worry about a dame who isn't hooked to a guy. Marla's an accountant. She does the books and taxes for shops around here and she and Ellen are thick. Now cut out the bullshit and tell me who's paying you, and what for."

Sgueglia checked the time. "It's a long story, Corky, and I'm due in Albany in a couple of hours. See you, pal."

McGonigle went down to the cafeteria, spotted Hull, and said quickly, "Tony Sgueglia's working for you. Right, Harry?"

"I've heard that name. Is he the one who rescued Mildred Cross this morning? Or did he get in your way?"

McGonigle laughed. "You don't have to con me, Harry. The Squail's already told me he's on your payroll."

"Who's the Squail? You wouldn't make up stories, like the kids, would you, Corky?"

Hull, perspiring heavily, walked over to his office in the Third Federal Savings Building. He was looking forward to tomorrow, when he would shoot it out with Pete Harmon's expert witnesses. But he had to dig into the law books. There were rules about what qualifies an expert, and about the hypothetical questions that could be put to such a witness.

"As I understand your reply, sir or madam, which was based on your wide-ranging experience in such complex matters, you say that the defendant sitting before you could indeed have chewed off the victim's head even though the defendant is toothless and had dropped his choppers down the drain, where, as the defense has shown, they were lying at the time the victim's head was severed. Your answer, based on extensive professional experience, was that such an act would nevertheless have been entirely possible. Thank you."

He had some extended hypothetical questions in mind.

Chapter 23

Pete Harmon was annoyed that Justice Mathes had shut down the trial until morning. Yes, Lilly Robertson had made a frazzled fool of herself on the stand, although he didn't give half a damn about her reference to his living in sin with Serena. I mean, does anyone care about such things anymore? But Tiger Lil had also scattered dust over the landscape. Still, he had not wanted to lose an afternoon of testimony. His experts were on hand, and there was something called momentum.

He stared at a new pile of crank mail, which he no longer bothered to read, and conjectured. At one o'clock he wandered down the corridor and looked into Barnard Rooney's empty office. The assistant district attorney was out to lunch. He returned to his own office and reflected anew. A few minutes later he called the Rhinebeck Club. "Hi, I'm in town for the afternoon and somebody said my old buddy Barney Rooney was out there hitting the ball. Has he teed off?"

"Barney, Barney," came the answer. "Yep. He's on the front nine with Justice Mathes. Any message?"

"Nah. I'll catch him next time I come through. No sweat."

Barnard Rooney, who had failed to get Mickey Strand indicted for toting a loaded gun into the courtroom, was out on the links with Johnson Gillies Mathes. Harmon asked himself, "Am I missing something?"

Antenna quivering, he checked his calendar. His term as D.A. expired in less than a month and he had not seen a reappointment notice. He hadn't lost sleep over it, but those forms usually arrived sixty days before a term expired. He considered that, then called Bob Kirk, chairman of the county board of supervisors. "Bob," he said, "I know the mail service has gone to hell, but my secretary hasn't seen the reappointment." He laughed. "I'm so worried I can't get any work done."

Kirk laughed, too. "Pete, that's some case you're working. Well, let me look into that."

He had not heard Kirk say, "Hey, Pete. You're our D.A. The check's in the mail."

The superintendent was told there was a long-distance call for prisoner Coles from her father. Should it be put through? He said, "Give it to her. Don't give that smartass lawyer a chance to make trouble."

She was led from her cell to a telephone. "Hi, Dad!" she said. "Can you make it down here Saturday?"

"Bitch," a voice replied, "you better pray they send you up. If they turn you loose, you won't get out of town. I've got a dozen guys lined up to fuck you to death."

She hung up, remembering the gravelly voice of the man who had torn Snug Arms apart looking for a hidden room.

She told the attendant, "I think that was Ike Brendelski, the man the police are looking for."

"It wasn't Daddy? Get back in your cell and don't worry about it, honey."

In fact, Fred Coles did not even know how to call Laurie at the prison. He had been reading the papers, about her waste matter and the kids, and that jam stuff and the stick in the vagina. And about threats to kill the children if they told on her. And the man who tried to shoot Laurie in the courtroom. He thought about what he would say if someone at work figured out that Laurie was his daughter.

The afternoon was interminable for most of the jurors. They were escorted to the Hotel Champlain but not permitted to leave their rooms after lunch. At three o'clock Chair Number Two walked out into the corridor and found the bailiff with his chair tipped against the wall. She was going down to the gift shop, she said. "Forget it," he told her. "I can't follow you down there and watch the rest of the jury, too."

She said, "You want to keep track of the jurors? Why not start by finding out if Number Nine is in Number One's room?" The front legs of his seat hit the carpeting. He stood up and she went by him to the elevator.

Nine's mouth had risen from the lower reaches of One's inner thigh to a field of fur. Her eyes were wide and her face drawn. "Come on!" she urged him. "Get *in*. Hurry up!" Then she giggled. "Do you want jam on it?"

Minutes later, hearing a rush of breath, he reached up and placed a hand over her mouth. She bit his finger as she tried to squelch a scream and he removed himself from her as punishment. But he was too late. She lay rigidly, except that her pelvis was jolting, as if electric shocks were being administered.

Nine was on his knees, hovering over her when her eyes opened. "My turn," he said. "Do it!"

It went on and time passed and they lay side by side, placid in their dampness.

One's attention returned to the case. "Look, Coles is guilty, but I don't get something. Why would anyone want to get it off with babies? That part doesn't make sense. Guys are walking all over town with big bulges. I see 'em a block away."

Nine had returned to his methodical self. "First, I've said from the beginning that it's all too much to believe. And those parents. One thing just leads to another with them. But the Burney woman made sense. She's not crazy. Hey, cut that out! I'm beat." He groaned. "Maybe before dinner."

Number Two returned from the gift shop with a box of chocolates and showed them no mercy.

Hull sped off a new brief to the appellate division, then drove over to the general hospital, where he was told that Mildred Cross had just emerged from intensive care and could not have visitors.

"Why not ask her?" he said.

The nurse abandoned her professional tone. "You're not going to bother her with that case of yours, Mr. Hull."

He smiled. "Ask her if she wants to talk or I'll do it myself. Don't mess with me."

The patient, in a chair at the window, greeted him with a sigh. "The police were here and I'm sick of answering questions, Mr. Hull. What can I tell you that I haven't said? How Ike Brendelski put a gun in my face and drove me to the school? Or how he gagged me and tied me to the floor?" She shuddered. "God! If those men hadn't come by."

"I'm glad you're coming out of it, Miss Cross. No, I don't want to ask about that. I'd like to know more about that video camera Ike Brendelski referred to. Did the Snug Arms parents know it was behind the one-way mirror?"

She nodded impatiently. "Of course. We put it back there because parents like to watch their children, and the kids ham it up as soon as they see a lens. We wanted to catch them relaxed, being themselves. Many of the parents knew about it. They've watched the children from behind that mirror many times. That awful Lilly Robertson. And Letty Andrews, the hysteric. And Marla Bur-

ney. She's not one of the nuts. Why do you want to know all this?"
She looked at him suspiciously. "Are you another one who doesn't
believe me?"

He sat down with her. "I believe you. And I'll be honest with
you, Miss Cross. I'm not trying to save Snug Arms. It's gone. I'm
trying to get Laurie Coles a fair shake in court. You believe she's
innocent, don't you?"

She shook her head mournfully. "None of what they're saying
could have happened. I was almost never away from the school.
And have you thought about all this undressing they're talking
about? Do you realize that no parent says a child ever came home
wearing another kid's socks or missing some underclothes?" She
coughed sharply. "Over months and months?"

"One more thing. Letty Andrews testified that Miss Coles
wouldn't let her into the classroom during playtimes, and she
made it sound as if Laurie was trying to be alone with the kids.
What can you tell me about that?"

Cross's anger was rising. "Letty Andrews was disruptive. She
put down the teachers and interrupted class routines all the time.
I felt she should stay out and I told Mrs. Andrews she had to
remain behind the one-way mirror or else remove Billy from the
school. She became very agitated and walked out and I haven't
seen her since."

"Thank you very much. I'll leave you alone now. And I hope
you're out of here soon."

"Out of here? I want to get as far away from this town as I can
get."

"Well. I may want to call you as a witness."

She closed her eyes again, then said, "Of course I'll testify.
Look, I'll do whatever I can to help." The nurse came in and Hull
left.

"I'll tell you straight out, Tony. If you told me what you wanted
when you called, I wouldn't even have seen you. I'm not going to
talk about it."

Sgueglia was at home in Albany, and a big, muscular fellow, the
chairman of the banking committee of the New York State Senate,
was his target. He asked, "When was the last time I let you down,
Joseph? When I convinced that young man he was mistaken
about—"

"Stop it, Tony! I was drunk."

"Did I shoot off my mouth when the S&L guy thought he was
being asked for a bribe? What's his name, doing five years for
looting his bank? Did I tell him he would only hurt himself if he

went public with his accusations? And did he back off? Remind me, Joseph. When did I sell you out last?"

"Stop it, Tony!" Joseph rose and looked out at the mall. "All right. What do you want and how are you going to use it?"

"It won't go public. Can I explain?"

Joseph did not leave the window.

"Mickey Strand walked into a courtroom down in Hudson Ferry with a gun and drugs in his pocket. I'm trying to make a connection between his habit and the reason you threw him out. I'm not after Strand. I could care less if they put him in jail, which I don't think they will. I want the information to get his ex-wife to open up to me privately. It's her I'll be pressuring. So tell me what happened and it'll stay between us."

Joseph turned a worried face. "Strand was running my campaign committee and I didn't find out until it was too late that he was crazy. Jumpy, always on the edge. He was high half the time, with a very expensive habit. So he was taking contributions in cash to pay for it. Big numbers, way outside the limits. And putting a lot in his pocket. When I found out, I told him to come up with every cent and then I checked with the givers. He collected eight hundred thousand and turned back a little over six hundred. I pushed him against the wall there and put my knees in his balls with my hands on his throat. Then he told me. The money was gone. He was in all kinds of trouble. Bribing narcs and more. And I think he was being blackmailed. You bribe 'em and they squeeze you for more. Anyway, it all went somewhere. So I papered it over and threw him out. He's down in the city now running his own public-relations agency. One of the TV networks is his big client. All right, Tony? Now, for God's sake, will you leave me alone?"

Sgueglia said, "Joseph, stop worrying. I'm not going public with this stuff."

"I'm dead if you do, Tony."

"I won't. And thanks, Senator."

He drove back to Hudson Ferry, to find Harry Hull, all the while hoping he would not have to go public with his private information.

Pete found that Serena had already received the transcript of the morning session of the trial. He convinced her to devote the tail end of the afternoon to tennis; she wouldn't be able to talk about the case while he moved her from side to side. He enjoyed her fierce, reckless lunges as much as he did the game, even though she returned a surprising number of shots. They returned soaked and had one of their frisky showers.

Over a gin, Serena said her day had begun with an interesting phone call, followed by delivery of a document from the court of appeals. "Let me read to you from the dissent, Pete."

That meant she had won her appeal in the case of the pimp who been in jail at the time he was supposed to have committed aggravated sexual assault. He raised his glass to her.

"The dissent says, 'Although the appellant's guilt of the crime before us may not have been established to everyone's full satisfaction, the majority opinion ignores a lengthy criminal record. This man is clearly a continuing menace to society. A means must be found to prevent such habitual offenders from remaining at liberty.' Can you beat that, Pete?"

"No. He must want to run for mayor of somewhere."

"Exactly. There's talk of it."

"Congratulations on the majority, love. You're piling up an outstanding record. I just hope you don't run into your client on a dark night."

"If I do, it will be because the police didn't do their job right. But thank you for your concern." She ruffled her copy of the Coles transcript. "Interesting time in court today. Did you wish you had a muzzle for Lilly Robertson?"

He groaned. "And Hull was cute. He might have torn her apart, but he passed on cross-exam. He figured she had already done his job for him. But tell me where I scored today. I'm dying to hear it."

"Marla Burney. She was perfect, and a tip of the hat for recognizing that her shade of doubt made her the perfect witness. Pete, it's against my principles, but let's talk about guilt and innocence. I'm curious. What do you think about Laurie Coles at this point?"

He poured another drink. "Once in a while I wonder. Then I go over the evidence again. And I know exactly what the experts are going to say. And don't forget the interviews with the children. There are problems, but no case is perfect. All in all, the evidence of guilt is overwhelming, and that's what the system is about. Okay, you're on."

"You were great in the shower," she said. "I didn't think such things were anatomically possible."

The gap showed as he grinned. "Stop it. What do you think?"

"I can't do it just on the evidence. I have to see how the case developed. Whether one worried parent hyped up another one and then they went to work on the kids. Although I think they all believe they are telling the truth. But the case is tainted. The evidence is compelling, but I don't think you've overcome reasonable doubt yet, and that's also what the system is about."

"You haven't answered the question."

"I don't know. I have a hunch she's innocent."

"If you think that's going to stop me from proposing to you again tonight, you're wrong. Let's get married, Serena."

Chapter 24

IT WAS DAY FOUR AND LAURIE COLES WAS LOOKING GOOD. SHE WORE A light gray blouse with a blue scarf and skirt and seemed relaxed as she greeted the jurors with a brief smile. Hull was pleased.

It was time for the calm and composed experts whose task it is to unscramble the confusion wrought by the passions of lay witnesses. Big, blond Liam Gunn took the stand as the leadoff witness and the district attorney asked the investigator how he had become interested in the problem of abused children.

"My son was in a nursery school in California—"

"Objection!"

Justice Mathes peered down at Harry Hull. "You're objecting to what?"

The audience recognized that Jacko's capacity for wrangling was approaching its nadir.

"To what he is about to say, Your Honor."

"We don't know what he's going to say until he says it. Go ahead with the answer, please."

"My son was a victim of sexual abuse in his school and I became interested in the field."

Hull's tone reached a high note on the derision scale. "And you're going to strike it now, sir?"

"Strike the answer as irrelevant and prejudicial. The jury will disregard it." There was murmuring among the monitors of judicial fairness; Hull had shown up the judge on that one.

Nor did he let it pass. "Your Honor, it was clear that the answer would be prejudicial. And now you've stricken it from the record. But how can you strike it from the jurors' heads? I don't see how you can conduct this trial—"

Mathes interrupted. "Enough. Proceed, Mr. Harmon."

Privately, Harmon agreed with Hull. He had merely wanted to establish Gunn's background and would not have asked the question if he had known of the personal experience. "What is your training and position, Mr. Gunn?"

"I hold a degree in sociology and have had specialized training in child abuse. I am chief of the child protection unit at the Princess County General Hospital."

"How many cases of child sexual abuse have you investigated?"

"About fifty, around the country."

"Did you appear as a witness in some of those cases?"

"Yes, in about thirty."

"And in how many were the defendants convicted?"

"Objection. Miss Coles was not a defendant in those cases."

The judge looked unkindly at Hull. "The witness is an expert, counselor, so broad questions may be put to him. That is a well-established legal maxim." He smiled. "You may wish to research the point."

Hull sat, then rose again. "No. The fact remains that Miss Coles was not a defendant in the cases the witness is being asked about. He must not be permitted to answer, Your Honor."

"Your exception is noted," Mathes said.

Hull took his seat. He heard a whisper and turned to read a buff's lips. "He'll punch you out, Harry."

"The conviction rate has been about eighty percent."

"Mr. Gunn," Harmon asked, "how many children from Snug Arms have you spoken to?"

"Six boys and five girls."

"Let's begin with a child named Billy Andrews. What did he tell you about the school?"

The high sun coming through the slatted blinds was heightening the golden glow of Gunn's hair. "He said Miss Coles defecated on a table and asked the children to make cakes of her waste matter, and then to eat them. But he also said that those acts took place in a basement room of the school. I explained to him that that was impossible."

"How did you know it was impossible?"

"I had seen the plans of the structure and knew there was no underground level."

Hull passed a note to Coles: "He's trying to detox the Andrews and Garafolo testimony. And take the sting out of Lilly Robertson's nuttiness."

Harmon attacked the child-credibility problem, a necessity before the children appeared. "How do you account for Billy's reference to a nonexistent room?"

Gunn nodded. "That sort of thing is common. Abused children

undergo severe shock. Their nervous systems have been injured
and they become disoriented."

"Objection. It has not been shown that Mr. Gunn knows any
more about the nervous system than anyone else in this room."

"Overruled. Proceed."

"Children learn at home that certain body functions are to be
conducted privately. They know, for example, the difference between sneezing and defecating in public, or at least outside the
family. So they are jarred when a grownup violates those norms.
But an adult can integrate a certain amount of shock and a child
can't. He is not sure who to trust anymore. So while he's getting
the story off his chest, he discards other rules, such as adhering to
the strict truth in serious matters. It's easier if he can make up
some elements of the story. The experience becomes less threatening."

The jurors were nodding and Coles passed a note to Hull: "I
wouldn't pursue that one." He had a churlish thought that the
defendant ought to mind her own business.

Harmon had not made a move during Gunn's explanation.
Now he saw heads bobbing among the jurors. "Mr. Gunn, what
did Billy say when you told him that Snug Arms had no basement?"

The witness smiled. "He said I was a dumbbell and that he
wouldn't call me Uncle anymore. But later he said he was mixed
up and I had it right."

Harmon nodded pleasantly. "Who was the next child you interviewed, and what did you learn?"

"Bonnie Strand. She's four years old and she said the defendant placed a stick in her vagina. Her own vagina. According to
Bonnie, Miss Coles said it was a game called 'Stick 'em Up.' "

"Did she tell you where this incident occurred?"

"She just said, at school. She's very bright."

"No one asked if she was bright," Hull said; the judge ignored
it, but the attorney received a glare from Chair One.

So it went and the jury heard once more about the sacrifice of
animals. That topic held Pete Harmon's attention. "Sir, we have
had earlier testimony about small animals. Based on your experience, how much reliability do you place in such accounts?"

Gunn studied his hands as he replied. "I've thought a lot about
it and I find those reports different from dungeon-and-dragon
tales. There's hardly a child I've talked to who doesn't understand
that dragons are just products of the imagination, and that rabbits, birds, and squirrels are real. This is not the first time I've
heard about the mutilation of small animals—"

"Objection. This is the only time we care about."

"Overruled. The witness is testifying as an expert."

"In many cases, stories about animal sacrifice have been verified," Gunn said. "As a result, I finally concluded that the reports in this case might be accurate."

Harmon wound it up, having placed the animal stories in the jury's mind without including them in the indictment. "A final question, sir. Would you be able to rank the severity of injury suffered by the Snug Arms children against injuries suffered in similar cases?"

Hull was on his feet shouting. "There are no similar cases. Every case is different, and so is every defendant, Your Honor."

Mathes shook his head. "You may reply, Mr. Gunn."

The witness pursed his lips. "The extent of the emotional injuries suffered in this case is new to me."

"No further questions, Your Honor."

Hull advanced on the witness stand. "Mr. Gunn, you believe the stories about the mutilation of animals at Snug Arms, cutting out birds' eyes, chopping up rabbits and squirrels. What makes you believe one story but not another? Why do you think those acts occurred when you know they could not have taken place where the children say they did? How do you pick truth from fables?"

Gunn pursed his lips. "You learn to watch children's faces. Their expressions change when they're making up things. Or they concentrate on something in your pocket. A pen. It's a matter of experience."

Hull strolled in small circles between the counsel table and the witness. "Do their eyes dance around when they're making things up?"

"Yes. Quite often."

"Do they twist their hair when they're making things up?"

"Yes, often."

"Do you know detective Vincent Garafolo, Mr. Gunn?"

"I've met him."

"Do you know that he also testified that when kids are making things up, their eyes dance around or they twist their hair? Did you and Mr. Garafolo discuss your testimony?"

"Of course not!"

"I guess it was just a coincidence, Mr. Gunn. Well, if you're describing methods of distinguishing fact from fancy, and those procedures are widely accepted, I'm sure you can cite references from the literature to support your statements."

Gunn glanced at Harmon, then said, "Unfortunately, the problem of child abuse has not received the attention it deserves. Journal articles tend to report observations that are often contradictory. Those who work in the field have drawn conclusions based on widely varying experiences."

Hull's voice softened. "Is that another way of saying that science hasn't figured out how to tell who is from the village of the truth-tellers and who is from the other place, Mr. Gunn?"

The witness did not reply. But he knew the drill, which required conferring a look of sympathy on those who simply don't understand scientific matters.

Hull said, "I trust the court will note that Mr. Gunn did not answer the question. And I believe we should note a facial gesture toward the jury. A sneer, to describe it."

"Objection," the D.A. said. "Uncalled-for comment."

"Sustained," Jacko said. "I direct you once more to control your comments, Counselor."

Hull saluted and went on. "Mr. Gunn, you testified that the children's nervous systems were injured and that they became disoriented. Well, they're going to testify. How much time would you say it takes wounded kids to get straightened out and become credible again?"

"That's hard to say. They're all individuals."

"But how will the jury be able to tell who is okay and who is still disoriented?"

Gunn sought an avenue of retreat. "I believe someone with more expertise would be able to give you a better answer."

"I see." Hull turned to the jury. "So your expertise can tell you when a child is disoriented, but not when he's not?"

"Objection," Harmon said. "The witness has answered to the best of his ability."

"Sustained."

"Mr. Gunn, you said you have interviewed eleven children. The defense has seen none of them and we envy you. But the judge has ruled, unfairly, I believe, that we can't."

Justice Mathes stood up. "Chambers!"

Hull went for broke. "Why chambers, Your Honor? Why don't we discuss my conduct in front of the jury? I tell you now that I'm going to go on fighting for a fair trial unless you put me in jail to shut my mouth!"

Mathes strode from the room and Harmon came over. "Harry, you're asking for the ax. If you force him to take you out of the case, it'll be a mistrial and you know we'll have to do it all over again. And you'll be disqualified to represent the defendant. I don't see where this is going to get you." He followed the judge out and so did Hull.

In chambers, Harmon spoke first. "May I be excused once more, sir? I don't think—"

"Go." Harmon went.

Mathes poured coffee, for himself, and Hull asked if he might have a cup. When the judge ignored him, he walked over to the hotplate, poured a cup, and sat down.

"Stand up!"

"You sit, I sit," Hull said. "This is not a formal proceeding since the state is not represented." He was awed that he was speaking this way. Was he passing a point of no return?

Mathes laughed for some reason. Then he spoke in what seemed to be a jovial manner. "Harry, I'm begging you to use your common sense. You can't win this case. Why are you going berserk when you know I can't let you get away with it? I've got to enforce discipline. If you don't cut it out, you're damned sure going to be in jail when this trial is over."

Hull sipped his coffee. "I wish I could reach you. This is no game. I'm almost convinced my client is innocent. That's irrelevant, I know, but she's not getting a fair shake. You're letting the prosecution get away with murder and I won't sit there like a potted geranium."

Mathes pulled at the red mustache. "I thought you had some smarts. You asked the appellate division for lower bail and you lost. And now you want them to remove me from the case. You can't win that one, either. Look, I don't really give a damn about that. I understand lawyer games. But you're full of shit about Coles being innocent, Harry. She's guilty and she'll be convicted and you know it, so what's going through your head?"

"It's a waste of time, but I'll tell you. You wanted a patsy when you put me on this case. And I was. I tried to get her to plead guilty, God forgive me. She wouldn't do it. So I'm her lawyer. But this is an inquisition. You're upholding me on nothings and giving all the important stuff to the D.A. Doesn't that bother you even a little bit?"

Mathes sighed. "You're hopeless. Let's go back. But count on it. You're going to jail when the trial's over."

Laurie Coles looked up anxiously as Hull returned, but his expression revealed nothing. The jurors and the spectators were examining the judge's face but could find no clues to what had happened. Mathes said, mildly, "Carry on, Counselor."

Hull rose. "Thank you, sir. Mr. Gunn, you've interviewed many children who attended the Snug Arms school. Correct?"

"Yes."

"On more than one occasion?"

"I talked to some several times."

"Why were several meetings necessary?"

"They get tired. Or cranky."

"I see. And were you the first investigator who talked to those children?"

"I believe Mr. Garafolo had spoken to some of them."

"And so did their parents. But were you the first professional investigator to interview them?"

Harmon thought he saw the direction Hull was taking, a suspicion confirmed by Gunn's pause before he responded.

"I believe I spoke first to four of them."

Hull was navigating his small circle. His hands were behind his back, clutching a sheaf of papers. "And who saw them next?"

"Dr. Amanda Roth. A psychologist."

"And did she see the others first?"

"Yes."

"Am I correct that those conversations were recorded?"

"They were."

Hull changed course. "And did some of the children call you Uncle Liam?"

"Yes."

"How did they happen to do that?"

"I told them they could."

"Why?"

"To relax them. They were tense."

"It helps if you're thought of as a member of the family?"

"Something like that."

The witness was relaxed and Hull tacked back. "Did you and Dr. Roth discuss each other's experiences with the children?"

"From time to time."

"Could you be more specific? Did you see the transcripts of Dr. Roth's interviews before you spoke to children for the first time, and did she see your transcripts?"

"Yes."

Hull nodded amiably. "Well, here's a puzzler. If you and Dr. Roth interviewed eleven children, why are only seven mentioned in the indictment?"

"Objection," Harmon said. "Mr. Gunn did not draw up the indictment."

"Sustained."

Hull switched. "Something is odd, Mr. Gunn. The mystery of the missing children. Did those who are missing from the indictment say that Miss Coles did anything to them?"

"No, they didn't. You see—"

"Thank you, Mr. Gunn."

The witness rebelled. "But I want to explain—"

"Of course. You want to explain that your expertise allows you to believe those who said what you wanted to hear and not—"

Harmon was on his feet. "Your Honor, counsel is testifying."

"Sustained. Cut it out, Mr. Hull."

"Excuse me, sir. Go ahead and explain, Mr. Gunn."

Gunn caught himself. "You see, some children just won't make accusations. They're embarrassed, or frightened."

"Uh-huh," Hull said. He turned to the bench. "Your Honor, we have only received transcripts of interviews in which children accuse Miss Coles. We want to see the interviews that exonerate her. The jury should know about them."

"Sidebar."

The attorneys approached the bench and Mathes told Hull, "First, saying that the other children exonerated the defendant is a conclusion. Okay? Now, if the state puts those children on the stand, you will be entitled to see their transcripts."

Hull returned to the witness stand. "The defense objects to the ruling that the jury may not see the missing transcripts, the interviews that do not support the charges."

"Overruled and exception noted. Proceed."

Hull scanned the sheets before him. "All right, Mr. Gunn. Let's talk about what the defense has been permitted to see." He waved the papers. "These are interviews you conducted, and I will quote from some of the conversations. Do you recall this exchange? You said to Bonnie Strand, 'Sure you'll tell me a story about Laurie. Your friends have already told me great stories.' And Bonnie said, 'I don't know a story about Laurie.' Do you recall that?"

"It sounds familiar."

"I guess you're saying you recall it. Can you tell us who brought up Laurie Coles's name first? You or Bonnie Strand?"

"I don't really know. Doesn't the transcript show that?"

"It sure does, but I'm not supposed to testify. Your first words to Bonnie were, 'Hi, I'm Uncle Liam. We're going to talk about your school today. There's a teacher we want to know more about. Laurie.' Do you remember that?"

"No, but if that's the transcript, it must be so."

"Thank you. When Bonnie said, 'I don't know a story about Laurie,' you replied, 'Of course you do.' Instead of accepting the child's answer, you pressured her. Am I correct?"

"Objection to the accusatory nature of the question."

"Withdrawn. Bonnie said she knew nothing. Why did you contradict her, Mr. Gunn?"

"It may sound like a contradiction, but it wasn't. Children always say no at first."

"Until you get them to say what you want to hear? Isn't that how brainwashers get the answers they want?"

"You may interpret it any way you wish."

"The jury will do the interpreting. Let's go on. You told Bonnie, 'You're beautiful, honey. I wish I wasn't so much older than you are.' And you said, 'Would you like to sit in my lap?'" He handed the page to Gunn and pointed to the words. "Can you explain what you were up to?"

"I was trying to put her at ease."

"With seductive talk? You wish you weren't too old for her? Mr. *Gunn!* Are little girls safe with you?"

The gavel fell. "Counselor!"

"Excuse me, Your Honor. I was shocked."

Harmon looked uncomfortable.

Gunn said, "I might have been careless that time. Okay?"

"Okay. And would you agree that you were careless in using the name of the accused before the child did? Detective Garafolo knew better and you have specialized training. But you also said, 'Now, as soon as you tell me what Laurie did to you, we'll go out for an ice cream.' Isn't that a one-two punch? First the pressure, then bribery?"

"I don't think so. Remember the ages of these children."

"I'm remembering. We all know these are impressionable little children, so easy to manipulate. And you're the voice of authority in these conversations, Mr. Gunn. One more question. You worked with Dr. Roth on these interviews. Have you worked with her before?"

"Yes. On a few cases."

Hull stopped his circling and looked downright cheerful as he said, "No further questions, Your Honor."

"Lunch," Justice Mathes announced. "Resume at two."

Hull went off to have a hot dog in his office, where he spent an hour marking up the transcripts of Dr. Amanda Roth's interviews with the Snug Arms children. As his secretary was collating the pages, Anthony Sgueglia walked in, clearly pleased with himself.

"We can't use it," he said, "but this guy Mickey Strand is so hooked on coke that he stole for it, Harry. I got it from the horse's mouth. The man he stole it from. But I know we can't use it."

In his mood, Hull was properly playful. "Keep telling me we can't use it, Squail."

"He was fired in Albany for pocketing almost two hundred big ones, swiping it out of campaign funds. He was gone on drugs."

"If we can't use it, why are you telling me about it?"

"So you'll tell me to go see his ex. Beat her over the head with it. She'd never live it down around here if it got out. And maybe she'll remember her daughter's story differently."

Hull thought about that. "You're forgetting, Squail. I said no rough stuff. On the other hand, I guess I can't watch you every minute."

"You're beautiful. My kind of people. Say, has the law put the arm on the mad bomber yet?"

"Brendelski? Not that I've heard."

"Maybe you should watch your ass. That guy is crazy, Harry."

Chapter 25

As Justice Mathes called the afternoon session to order, Hull saw Sgueglia among the spectators, sitting directly behind Ellen Strand, leaning forward to hear any comments she might make, checking her out. The Squail, looking for an edge.

Dr. Amanda Roth commanded attention as she came in from, or barged out of, the witness room. Her hard and clumpy stride sent a signal: I'm not here to waste time and I won't be manipulated by lawyers. Her elbows swung awkwardly as she mounted the stand and Pete Harmon thought she might take Mathes to task if the proceedings did not move expeditiously.

The D.A. adapted to her style, speaking briskly, and established that Dr. Roth had graduated from Rutgers University and spent several years as a therapist in private practice, where she discovered that many children were being sexually abused in their own homes. She handled cases in which divorced mothers accused fathers of molestation and vice-versa. "Then," she said, "I found that children had become prey to perverted teachers in preschool environments—nursery schools."

Hull, surprising Harmon, did not object to her extended responses, as he had when Liam Gunn testified. Nor did the psychologist's generalized reference to teachers as perverts provoke the defense counsel. Justice Mathes dared hope that Harry had come to his senses.

Harmon set out to balance the testimony, or as Serena would say, to weight the balance in his favor. He asked if the Snug Arms children had spoken well of Miss Coles.

"Indeed. At first. They said they liked her." Harmon waited. "But those versions changed as they broke out of their emotional bondage and told the truth."

"Would you explain that, Dr. Roth?"

She said, "Untrained persons would not recognize, of course, that the sexual abuse syndrome is a two-stage process. In the first stage, the molester lures the victims by ingratiating herself. That enables her to proceed to the second stage, in which abuse takes place. We see the process constantly."

"But why would the children start off by saying they liked the defendant if the abuse had already taken place?"

Dr. Roth's left palm received her right hand, on which the forefinger was extended. "Children undergo their own process." Hand thumped palm. "Children know right from wrong, so sometimes they feel guilty for having taken part in forbidden acts. Others are so traumatized that they repress the memory of their mistreatment. And still others have been threatened. Whatever form the reaction takes, it results in denial or repression. So they lie. But prevarication is identifiable. They suck their thumbs or yawn."

Chair One whispered, "It's that simple?"

Number Two said, "Shh. Please!"

Harmon did not want a rerun of the lurid tales of sexual abuse. Hold the jam. But he needed corroboration of Liam Gunn's testimony, so he asked what Caroline Robertson had told Dr. Roth about her experiences at Snug Arms.

"I spoke to her twice before she told me the defendant had placed jam on her own vagina and asked the child to lick it off."

Hull seemed to have lost his tongue.

"How do you feel the children have been affected, Dr. Roth?"

"Of the cases I have handled—close to two hundred—these children have suffered the most trauma of all. I have grave fears about the directions their sexual development may take as they reach puberty."

"I see. Now would you describe your conversations with other Snug Arms children?"

"Several reported that Miss Coles undressed them, and then herself, and handled their sexual organs. One boy showed me, graphically, how she touched his penis. Evidently she was teaching them to masturbate."

"She was *what?*" Hull asked.

The judge frowned and the witness went on. "Such children become uncommunicative at home. And rebellious."

Harmon asked, "Has such conduct been observed in many Snug Arms children?"

"Yes. Their behavior has been aberrant. You see, when small children are betrayed by someone they believe in, they are at sea and rebel against authority. Parents. And unfortunately, the worst may be yet to come. Some children may suppress their rebellion until they reach adolescence, when antisocial behavior is far more dangerous."

And Hull did not object. "Thank you, Dr. Roth," Harmon said. "I have nothing else."

Hull fumbled with papers before getting them in the right order. Mathes was pleased to see him klutz around, but the D.A. was apprehensive. He knew that attorneys often play the nerd to disarm the witness; Harry must have been reading books by those exhibitionist criminal lawyers who try their cases in court and then all over again in the form of literary reminiscences.

Hull finally found the page he wanted and smiled at the witness. "Tell us, Dr. Roth, do you recall a child telling you that Miss Coles showed him her penis?"

"Of course. Such slips are not unusual. Those are strange words to children."

Hull nodded. "Do you recall a child telling you that his father played with his private parts?"

"Clearly. That's the transference mechanism."

"The what?"

There stood Harry Hull, receiving pity from yet another expert. "Transference is well-understood in the field of psychology. Adults use it regularly. When people are uncomfortable about an experience, they often shift the source of their pain. Patients who cannot handle the hostility they feel toward their mates frequently transfer it to their therapists. In this case, the child was ridding himself of bad feelings toward Miss Coles by replacing her with his father." Her expression was gentle. "I hope I have made myself clear."

Hull was doing his nodding. "Yes, and thank you. Now, I'd like to remind you that Billy Andrews told you at one point, and I quote from the transcript, 'Laurie didn't do bad stuff to me. Helen did it. The babysitter.' Was that another example of what you call transference?"

"Yes, surely."

His geniality thinned. "How do you know? Maybe Helen the babysitter needs the prosecutor's attention."

He received a reply he could not have wished for. Dr. Roth said, "You're barking up the wrong tree on that one, sir. Billy Andrews is a severely wounded child. He was having tantrums, and his mother asked me to treat him."

Hull returned to the counsel table and wrote a note. Coles looked at it and at him. She saw nothing but scratches.

The judge cleared his throat.

Hull went back to the witness and his voice became a growl.

"Are you telling us, Dr. Roth, that in addition to acting as an investigator, you accepted Billy Andrews as a patient? Please tell me I misunderstood you." Sharp ears among the spectators heard him emphasize Roth's title. *Doctor.*

"You did not misunderstand. I am a therapist, and when a parent asks me to treat a child, I take on the task if I can."

"When were you asked to treat Billy?"

"After my first meeting with some of the parents."

"In other words, before you had talked to the child the first time."

"Yes. But if you're implying that I cannot separate my roles as investigator and therapist, you are incorrect. A psychologist learns to make those distinctions."

"Well, hold on a moment. Isn't there something odd and peculiar about all this?"

"Argumentative," said the D.A.

"Sustained."

"I'll rephrase the question. Is it a fact that you decided that Billy Andrews was wounded before you talked to him?"

"I soon established that fact."

"If you hadn't established that fact, as you call it, you would not have had a patient. It would be unethical, after all, to take on a patient who didn't require therapy. Isn't that so?"

Dr. Roth bristled for the first time and snapped, "You know it's so!"

"But didn't you form a closed circle from which nothing could escape? If you decided a child was not wounded, Miss Coles couldn't be accused of wounding him. But once you say he needs treatment, he must have been wounded and you have earned a patient. Correct?"

"Again argumentative," Harmon said.

"Sustained." Mathes was disappointed. "That's the second breach on that one, Counselor."

"I'm going to be more careful, sir." He returned to the counsel table and picked up several sheets, sorting them once more as he approached the witness.

"Dr. Roth." There went the *Doctor* again. Here is a passage from an interview you conducted with Caroline Robertson, who is a playmate of Billy Andrews. Your first statement to Caroline was, 'Your friends have told us yucky stories about Laurie and that's what I'm going to ask you about today.' The child replied, 'I don't know yucky stories.' You said, 'Of course you do. Your friends say you do.' Caroline said, 'I don't know yucky stories.' Well, why in the name of common sense didn't you take Caroline's word for it? *Why?*"

"Because she wasn't telling the truth."

"Did God put you here to decide— Strike that. Instead of letting it go, you said, 'That can't be, Caroline. You're afraid Laurie will do something bad to you if you tell me, aren't you?' And she said, 'I'm not afraid of Laurie.' You said, 'Don't worry about her. We've got her locked up tight, so you can tell me.' She tells you she's not worried and you tell her she doesn't have to worry. This goes on and on and *on*. Fifteen pages later Caroline says, 'I want to go home. Laurie put strawberry on my peepee.' And the interview ends. Finally. When she gave you what you wanted, you turned her loose, Dr. Roth. Is that how the evidence for this trial was gathered? Or manufactured?"

"Objection. Way out of bounds."

The judge asked, "How much more time do you think you'll need with this witness, Counselor? Do you have further questions that are relevant to the charges against the defendant?"

"The time I need will depend on how much time the witness is given before she has to answer my questions, sir. I can't control that." Mathes understood. Hull was implying that the bench was letting the witness pause to collect herself. How he was going to enjoy busting Harry. "Proceed."

"Forget the last question, Dr. Roth," Hull said.

"I won't forget it," the witness said. "You can't get away with that."

Chair Number One's nose was wrinkled in distaste.

"I know how defense lawyers try to tear down investigators who fight for injured children. Anything goes, doesn't it?"

"I can't answer that question. I'm not a witness."

The gavel sounded. As far as Hull was concerned, she could have gone on for fifteen minutes. He smiled at Laurie Coles and turned back to Dr. Roth.

For some reason not clear to anyone, Hull changed the subject. "Dr. Roth," he said, "you testified earlier that the children held back for a number of reasons in telling their parents about the molestation they suffered. How, then, did the parents get such information?"

The response was quick and firm. "We helped them obtain it. There is no other way in these cases."

"How did you help them?"

"Mr. Gunn sent a questionnaire to all parents who had children at Snug Arms during the time the defendant worked there."

Hull showed her a sheet. "This questionnaire says that the district attorney has evidence that Miss Coles committed crimes against three children at Snug Arms, does it not?"

"Certainly."

"And that many more children were probably abused?"

"Of course."

"And it asks the parents to pay special attention to their children's behavior. To look for tantrums, sulking, and fighting with playmates and brothers and sisters. Yes?"

"*Yes.*"

"So the parents were told that their their children might act up as a result of Miss Coles's crimes."

"Are you asking me to comment?"

"I'm asking you if it is true that it's an odd child who does not throw a fit or spat with a brother or sister. Isn't that what children are famous for?"

"That's a distortion. We meant unusual behavior."

"I apologize. But weren't you asking the parents to tell their children that Miss Coles had abused their schoolmates?"

"Of course. That's what the grand jury said, isn't it?"

"Ah. I can see that you're a psychological expert, not a student of the law. Do you believe the grand jury said Miss Coles abused children, Dr. Roth?"

She was clearly annoyed now. "The indictment said so."

Hull turned to Mathes. "Your Honor, the jury is being misled. May I have permission to point out that the grand jury said no such thing?"

"This is not a legal seminar, Counselor. I will make clear to the jury that an indictment is a finding that enough evidence exists to warrant a trial being held. Proceed."

"Thank you for pointing out that we are not in law school, Your Honor." He bowed and returned to the witness. "Where is your home base, Dr. Roth? That is, where is the bulk of your practice of psychology conducted?"

"From my home in Matawan, New Jersey."

"Yes. Well, people in New Jersey are as concerned about the sexual abuse of children as anyone in this courtroom, I'm sure you will agree. They are so concerned that your governor set up a task force on child abuse and neglect, and this group prepared a manual for interviewers. I now quote from those guidelines. 'Do not speak negatively about the accused.' Do you disagree?"

Silence.

" 'Avoid multiple interviews with different interviewers.' Do you agree with that?"

"Absolutely not. I appeared before that task force and argued against that position. One interviewer puts the child at ease and the other one gets the truth. The people who wrote that report are armchair psychologists."

Hull saw Anthony Sgueglia reenter the courtroom and froze,

realizing he had been about to make a major error. An unseen force must have directed the Squail to appear at this moment. "Your Honor, I request a delay of one minute. No more."

Mathes nodded and Hull approached the rail and motioned to Sgueglia, who came down the aisle. "Give me a piece of paper, Tony. Any piece of paper. And remember, you just gave it to me. The information on Roth. Just this minute."

Sgueglia handed him a blank sheet and Hull stood there as if reading it. His head was bobbing as his eyes moved across the sheet. Then he looked up and said, "Your Honor, I move that the entire testimony of this witness be stricken. Amanda Roth has misled this court. She is here under false pretenses!"

Whether it was his words or manner, demeanor in the courtroom disintegrated. Sgueglia smiled and the buffs shook their heads. The witness clasped her hands and Laurie Coles looked from face to face, trying to understand what was going on. Jurors turned to each other surprised, the judge reached for his gavel, and Pete Harmon swallowed.

The question among the spectators was uncomplicated: When would Harry Hull be carried off to the mental ward, lashed to a stretcher?

Justice Mathes decided to begin work that evening on a brief that would detail each of Hull's acts of misconduct. The attorney had turned outlaw.

He pushed his gavel away and waited until the buzz diminished, then said, "Explain the grounds on which you base this motion."

Hull was murmuring incantations. The Squail had better be right. If Tony is wrong, I can only ask a higher power for mercy. Be right, Squail! Feeling perspiration leaking from his armpits, he slipped his hand into the right pocket of his jacket and pulled out a piece of paper. It was the blank sheet, not the absolute gem Sgueglia had given him two days ago. He reached into his left pocket and the correct note emerged. Sweat was creeping down his arms now. God, what he would give for a cold beer! Jacko stopped everything when he wanted a coffee. Why couldn't Harry Hull bring a cooler to court with a few Buds in it? He looked at the witness and his mind cleared.

"Amanda Roth," he said, "you are not *Doctor* Roth. I'm going to address you as *Ms.* Roth from now on."

The gavel fell. "Address the bench, damn it! Excuse me, ladies and gentlemen. Mr. Hull, you have made a motion and it is on the record. You will bear full responsibility for any abuse of privileges during cross-examination. Do you understand the gravity of your remarks? Do you know what you're doing?"

"I hope so, Your Honor." If the Squail was wrong, the show was over. "Ms. Roth was qualified as an expert witness. A psychologist. She is nothing more than a self-appointed expert. She is *not* a psychologist and I will explain why. She has never earned a doctorate and is not a psychologist under New York statutes. I cite Section 7601 of the education law, which says and I quote, 'Only a person licensed under this title may use the title "psychologist" or describe his services by use of the word "psychologist." ' *Ms.* Roth has never earned or received a doctorate in psychology and she is not licensed in this state to appear here as a psychologist."

Harmon cursed the assistant D.A., Barney Rooney, whose responsibility it had been to check out witnesses' credentials.

"You are not a psychologist, are you, Ms. Roth?" Hull shouted. "You are what is known as a lay analyst or therapist. Isn't that a fact?"

Red spots dotted a chalky face as she shouted back. "I am a psychologist! We are permitted to use the term in many states. And you are injuring my professional reputation. I will come back here and sue you!"

Hull lowered his volume. "Sue on. This is New York, and under our laws you are masquerading as a psychologist. Now look, the judge just asked me if I knew what I was doing. Do you know what *you're* doing? Do you have the slightest idea of the preposterous nature of your testimony? You are a fraud before this jury, aren't you, Ms. Roth?"

"Don't answer that!" Mathes shouted. "Disregard this entire exchange, jurors. Recess and attorneys to chambers."

Harmon rose awkwardly, as if a leg had gone to sleep, and they trailed the judge through the door.

Chair One whispered to Two, "He stuck it in, didn't he?" Two replied, "I'm sick of technicalities. This has nothing to do with the charges. She's guilty or not guilty."

Mathes did not bother with coffee. Placing both hands on his desk, he rocked back and forth and glared at the district attorney, who stood stiffly and said, "I apologize. My assistant slipped. But the buck stops here."

Mathes turned to Hull. "When did you get your information on Dr. Roth?"

"On *Ms.* Roth, sir. Five minutes ago."

"Don't fuck with me, Hull. You're in enough trouble. Let me see it."

Which pocket was it in? Hull guessed correctly and the judge read the report. "Where did you get this?"

"From Mr. Anthony Sgueglia, a private investigator. He is licensed, properly, I might say, by New York State. You've probably heard about him. He was the one with Corky McGonigle when they rescued Mildred Cross from the school."

Mathes was still scanning the report. "You had this information before Roth took the stand, didn't you?"

Hull shook his head and delivered his line perfectly. "If I had it when she took the stand, I would have objected then and you would not have permitted her to testify as a psychologist."

"You're lying, you bastard!" Mathes glanced at Harmon, wishing he had not used that word with the district attorney in the room. "If you objected when she took the stand, you wouldn't have been able to put on your show. You're smarter than I thought, Harry. I'll give you that. You let Roth testify so you could tear down her credibility."

"I resent that, sir. With respect, of course." Hull felt the perspiration evaporating.

"Get lost, both of you."

Harmon was first out the door, winding himself up for a serious conversation with Barnard Rooney. Hull took more time. He thought he might ask Jacko for a coffee, then decided not to press his luck. He came into the courtroom, which quieted as he appeared, and halted behind the witness stand, where he stood motionless, knowing the jury's eyes were on him, until Amanda Roth turned her head. He smiled, then moved on and sat down beside Laurie Coles. "It's not over till it's over," he said as he passed her a stack of documents. "When we adjourn, go back over the interviews with the children. Memorize the exchanges."

It was a full five minutes before the black robes returned to the arena, seated himself, and told Amanda Roth, "You are excused at this time. If there is further need for your testimony, you will be notified."

She stepped down and banged the swinging gate open.

Mathes had regained tranquility as he spoke to the jurors. "At the end of the trial I will instruct you on how to deal with the testimony of the last witness. But I tell you now to disregard all side remarks made by the defense counsel during that testimony. You are not to discuss those remarks during your deliberations and I will remind you of that again later. Now, there is another matter before the court at this time and so you are excused."

The jurors filed out and Mathes said, "Is Anthony Sgueglia in the courtroom?"

Hull heard Sgueglia's deep voice. "Here, sir!"

"Come forward."

Sgueglia came through the gate.

"Are you employed by the defense in this case?" Mathes asked.

"I'm self-employed, sir. But I have been retained."

"Sit in the witness box. Bailiff, administer the oath."

Sgueglia was sworn in and turned to the judge. It was bristling red mustache versus black. "Are you licensed by the State of New York as a private investigator?"

"Yes, sir."

"Give the clerk your license."

He produced a laminated card and the clerk handed it to Mathes, who studied it and said, "Remember that you are under oath. What duties has the defense asked you to perform?"

"I decline to answer, sir. It's a confidential relationship. But I understand that I have to answer specific questions." Hull could see that the Squail was dying to add, "And you know that damn well, Judge."

"Where did you obtain the information about Amanda Roth?"

"At the education department in Albany, sir. From public files."

"I'm sure you know the penalties for perjury. When did—"

"I know the penalties for perjury, Your Honor."

"When did you turn the information over to Mr. Hull?"

"A while ago."

"I said *when*."

"I didn't look at my watch, but fifteen or twenty minutes ago. When Harry asked for a break and called me up to the rail."

"What did he say?"

"His exact words? He said, 'Squail, you worthless bastard, what have you got for me?' And I said, 'This is gonna cost you, Harry. Roth is a phony.' And I handed him the report."

Mathes said, "Step down. But leave word with the clerk of the court where you can be reached."

The judge told the spectators, "Technicians will install equipment this afternoon for the children's testimony. Court is adjourned until ten o'clock tomorrow morning."

As he left, the bailiff responded to a blinking red light on his desk, picked up his telephone, and listened. He hung up and went in to the judge's chambers. "There's a preliminary report on the psychiatric examination of Michael Strand." He consulted his notes. "They have made a finding that he was under heavy stress and had temporarily lost the ability to distinguish between right and wrong."

Mathes was not surprised. But another report was due soon, about the substance found in Mickey Strand's pocket.

Hull reminded Coles of her homework and called his office from the corridor. "Get hold of Stanley Schomburg," he told his secretary. "The shrink who talked to Coles in jail. Tell him to be here no later than one o'clock tomorrow, ready to testify. But it would be good if he got here for the morning session and listened to the kids. And tell Schomburg to remember what I said, about talking straight English when he's on the stand. I don't want to have to hire a translator."

He came out of the booth knowing he could no longer evade the judgment of the court buffs. "Harry," said one, "can I get an early ticket to your crucifixion? Jacko's going to nail you and I want an up-front seat."

Hull smiled. "The scalpers have got all the tickets."

There was more. "This is what you're still not getting straight, Harry. You kick their experts around. You poke holes. So an investigator tells the kid he'd go for her if he wasn't so much older. And she'll get an ice cream if she tells a good story about the bitch. Now, don't get mad, Harry. You were right to go after them. And you put a dent in the prosecution when you showed up the fake psychologist. But so what? No prosecution case is perfect. So in the end it's just holes. You haven't started thinking that you're winning this thing, have you? I'm sorry, Harry, but when the ruckus is over, the jury is still going to walk in and say she's guilty. You're doing a hell of a job. Just don't get your hopes up."

"Hey, friends, thanks a lot," Hull said, moving on to a waiting Corky McGonigle, who greeted him with a large grin. "What do I win for figuring out the Squail was your man, Harry? You owe me and you're gonna pay. Come on the six-o'clocker tonight and talk to the folks."

"I'd love to, Corky, but you know I can't. They'd saw my shingle off if I went public during the trial."

"Then let the Squail go on. He can tell how he tracked down the dirt on the expert."

"Cut it out, Corky. How do you think it went this morning?"

"You hit a home run. Right out of the ballpark. But that doesn't mean you can win the game, Harry. They've already put up the final score."

"Thanks a bunch," Hull said.

Chapter 26

STANDING BEFORE THE COURT BUILDING, THINKING ABOUT HIS NEXT MIS-sion for the defense, Anthony Sgueglia watched a video camera and five monitors being carted up the steps. The technicians were installing equipment that would carry the Snug Arms children's faces and voices into the courtroom in the morning. Then he strolled down River Road and scanned the Mexican blouses in the windows of Far-Flung Fashions. Ellen Strand was sitting at the back of the boutique, alone.

He went in and introduced himself, sniffed an ashtray full of crushed butts, and said, "I've been retained by the defense in the Coles case."

Eyes ablaze, she threw his card to the floor. "Get out! I have nothing to say to you."

He turned and walked slowly toward the door while saying, "I thought you might be interested in some information about your former husband."

She reacted quickly. "What are you talking about?"

He kept walking and spoke over his shoulder. "I don't want to harass you, Mrs. Strand. You can talk to me if you want to, but you don't have to." He was almost at the door. "One of the news people found out that I know why your husband was fired in Albany. He wants me to tell him about it, but I thought I should talk to you first."

She rushed up and grabbed his arm. "All right."

He turned to be sure his pocket recorder caught her voice. "You want to talk to me?"

"Yes! Sit down."

Sgueglia adjusted his belt, in the process switching off the re-corder, and sat down. The invitation was all he wanted.

She lit a cigarette. "Why are you telling me this?"

"Courtesy, I guess. I wanted to be sure it would be okay with you if I shared my information with the media guys."

"Stop the crap!" The cigarette glowed as she drew on it deeply. "I mean, what do you know? This is a very personal matter, and I have to live here."

She was gripping an arm of the chair. "There are people up in Albany who don't want to go public with this stuff," Sgueglia said, "but they tell me Mr. Strand was raising campaign funds for a legislative committee chairman."

"That was his job."

"Except, I'm told, he was hooked on drugs and needed the money for himself."

"I don't know anything about that."

"I didn't think you did, Mrs. Strand. But my sources say he walked off with close to two hundred thousand dollars."

"That's—!" She stopped, stubbed out the cigarette, and lit another. "I don't have any money, if that's what you mean."

"And when the legislator uncovered the theft, he threw Mr. Strand out."

She stood up and said ferociously, "What are you trying to get me to do?"

Sgueglia rose. "Don't get excited, Mrs. Strand. He's not your husband anymore. It's not as if you could be blamed. Or that anyone would call you a bad mother or say you let your child be exposed to drugs and try to take her away from you. Look, I'm going to think the whole thing over before I say anything."

He retrieved the business card she had thrown down and placed it on her desk. "By the way, Mr. Hull may want to bring you back into the trial and ask some questions about Mr. Strand. To test your credibility as a witness, I guess. And he can do it. Maybe you should get a lawyer. Listen, you can reach me at the number on the back of the card."

He left, uncomfortable. He did not like to manhandle people. But he had to do what he had to do. And Ellen Strand would not crack. There was no way she would change her story.

He drove down to Poughkeepsie, to see the people at Upstate Cable TV. Maybe they could explain why a family would plant a deep-dish antenna in the backyard when they were already receiving dozens of channels. He had Letty and Nick Andrews in mind. But the people at Upstate Cable couldn't figure it out, either. Or said they couldn't. He returned to Hudson Ferry and called a useful source in Albany, a young woman who worked for the state agency that monitored cable operations. Upstate made many mistakes in its billing, all in its favor, she said, and the agency might move in on it before long. Sgueglia filed that one away.

Harry Hull's energy had gone downhill. He went home from court and slept until eight thirty, then stared moodily at the parting rim of the sun and asked himself, "What is with me? Laurie sits in jail and I get in a night's sleep before bedtime." He showered and his mind wandered as he soaped up. How grand it would be if he awoke in the middle of the night tonight lying beside a woman. What might she look like? Speculating, he turned up the water pressure and suffered a delicious pounding.

He reached the Book Nook as pretty Polly Lennon was turning over the sign: CLOSED. She let him in and he paid a toll. "I don't carry law books, Harry, but they wouldn't help your client anyway." Still, there was a sympathetic quality to her tone.

Polly was an offbeat chick. She was about his age and had that laugh that sailed. Once she asked him why he had become a lawyer and he told her he wasn't sure. She said she had started out for a business degree, then woke up one morning and asked herself, "I'll spend this one life climbing the corporate ladder? In forty years I'll retire and ask what that was all about? One life and I spend it worrying about earnings per share? I'll blow myself away." So she went into books. She was the sweetest thing and he wanted to know her better. But she scared the bejesus out of him. Books? What would they talk about?

"Polly," he said, "who's the greatest writer of stories for children who ever lived? The champ?"

She gave him the laugh he loved. "Ask me a hard one. Hans Christian Andersen. You're into fairy tales?" She led him to the children's section and pulled down a tall volume. "Start with 'The Nightingale.' It's marvelous. But I'm having trouble putting you and fairy tales together, Harry."

"It's a hunch," he said. He felt anarchic forces carrying on in his head and could not stop his mouth. "What are you doing tonight, Polly? Close up and let's go over to the Ale House for a few minutes. And then we can get a bite."

She gave him small change from a twenty and her voice skipped up and down the scale. "So let's go."

As Hull walked into the Ferry Ale House with Polly on his arm, the regulars, who on this evening included a contingent of the court buffs, raised their steins, even though some felt more strongly than ever that Harry was making too much of a fuss over his dirty case.

"Bert," he said, "same deal as last time. "Serve 'em up until I go broke." He directed Polly's attention to the oil painting behind the bar, then raised his voice. "Some people around here thought Bert should take that thing down because the artist was a faggo."

"Don't start that stuff, Harry," said Joan, the wife of the Hudson Ferry policeman.

"Yeah. But it's true, isn't it? Somebody started that talk and everybody jumped on the wagon. All right, I'll drop it. So here we are again and you're waiting for another boring lecture from the lawyer for the guilty party. Right?"

"Right, Harry," he heard. "It's a frame-up, isn't it?"

"Hey," he responded, "don't you remember my last speech? The jury will figure out if she's guilty or innocent. All I'm saying is, she's got a right to a fair trial."

"Nobody has a right to put her hands on kids," Joan said.

"Have another drink, Dick." The policeman waved at Big Bert for a refill. Hull waited for relative quiet, then said, "Thank God you don't have my tomorrow. You know what I mean?"

"The kids are going on the witness stand," Joan said.

"Right. So I need some advice. How should I handle them?"

"Keep your mouth shut," Bert said. "You can only hurt yourself trying to make 'em look bad."

Hull raised his glass. "Good point."

Silence set in and Joan finally broke it. "You can't keep quiet. You have to say *something*, Harry." She shook her head. "But I don't know what."

Bert spoke up again. "Put a smile on your ugly face and ask the kids to tell you the greatest story they ever made up. And after the trial, give up lawyering and play softball for a living. You're a hell of a third baseman."

Silence again, ended by a voice that caused heads to turn. "It doesn't make any difference what you do, Mr. Hull. They're going to hang her." The voice belonged to a fellow who looked to be in his early twenties, probably a student at Wadleigh U.

The heads turned away and Polly whispered, "Let's go, Harry."

He told the bartender, "Another one all around, Bert, and anything the young fellow back there wants. See that he doesn't get arrested for opening his mouth. Good night, all."

At the Hendrik Grill they were greeted by the moonlighting court reporter, who seated them near the entrance to the facilities, where, in addition, the blower of the air conditioner changed the shape of hairdos. "Harry, you'll soon be the most popular man in town," Polly said.

Hull sighed. "I've quit caring. I think." She suggested a red wine and he startled himself by asking, "You've never been married, have you, Polly?"

There went the laugh. "Neither have you, I've heard. All right, I'll play. But you go first."

It came easily. "You have a date and a good time and then they get serious. Before you can even think."

"Who's they? Are they all the same? No, I take that back. I say it about men, too, the other way around. You have twenty dates and they never get serious."

He had a steak, she had a veal chop, and he went on. "I don't know how to talk to women."

"You're talking to me."

"Yeah."

"Maybe you worry too much." She hesitated. "Or maybe you don't think of me as a woman, Harry."

He laughed. "Cut it out. If I told you how you come across, you'd get scared and walk out."

"Take a chance."

He could not remember ever speaking to a woman this way. "You make me feel good, Polly. Things are going on in your head all the time. You make me feel great about myself. And I like your face and your voice." He saw himself approaching the edge of a cliff. "And I'd love to find you next to me in bed."

She studied his eyes and he did not blink. "I can make coffee at home," she said. "Let's go."

Pete and Serena were enjoying a cool evening. A full moon lit up the widow's walk and stimulated a question from Harmon. "How do you feel about kids, love? We've never talked about that."

"I like kids," she said.

"So do I. But just one."

"Two," she said.

"I meant two."

"Do you really want to get married, Pete?"

He sat up. "Are you saying yes?"

"I'm thinking about it."

"You want three kids? We'll have three."

"Two."

"Two."

In bed Serena threw off the sheet, tossed her pillow to the floor, and said, "I think I've figured out Harry Hull's strategy. The jury is supposed to decide between your witnesses and Laurie Coles, but he's changed the rules. He's turned the trial into a contest between him and the judge. Hull versus the Hangman. I'm not sure Harry knows that's his strategy, but the transcripts show it.

He's trying to provoke Mathes into doing something really rash that will show the jury how unfair he is."

"How can you sleep without a pillow?" Harmon asked.

In the morning, driving home from Polly's place, Hull was humming a tune, even if its composer wouldn't recognize it. Fingers tapped the wheel as he said, "Polly, pick out twenty tough books. I'll buy 'em and read 'em in six months." No! Everything doesn't have to sound like an arm wrestle at the bar. "Polly, could you suggest a few interesting books?" Better.

He took his new volume of fairy tales into the backyard and read the first story, the one Polly recommended, aloud, then read it again, and again.

On the way to court he reached two major tactical decisions. First, scrap the original defense witness list.

Letty Andrews: Laurie wouldn't let me in because she wanted to be alone with the kids. Mildred Cross in rebuttal: Mrs. Andrews was destructive and disturbed the classes. Not very exciting. Marla Burney: My son Tom said Laurie touched his penis on a specific date. Call her back and elicit the fact that by then little Tom had talked to dozens of kids who had been manipulated by Vince Garafolo, Liam Gunn, and Amanda Roth. No big deal.

None of it was strong enough to win an acquittal. He would call but one witness. Dr. Stanley Schomburg, the psychiatrist.

And under no conditions would Laurie take the witness stand. She would be chopped, diced, minced, and pulverized.

Then he reached a different tactical decision: Think hard about Polly Lennon.

Chapter *27*

Shortly before ten in the morning, a lighting man yawned a mighty "Yahh!" He had been in Justice Mathes's chambers with camera and sound men since six and the office was littered with cables. The bailiff arrived, observed the scene, and said, "Are you wiring the White House for a press conference? It's only kids and it's only going next door, into the courtroom."

The technicians exchanged smiles of pity and went on calculating angles of light refraction. "Hold it!" the cameraman yelled. "Right there. I can get them in tight shots and widen out when the lawyers do their lines." He asked the bailiff, "How close will the lawyers get to the kids?" The bailiff walked out without replying.

If permitted, it would be a standing-room-only crowd. Five monitors lit up with snow on their screens. Two huge panels faced the audience and another was mounted high on brackets at the front of the courtroom, before the jury and the press table. A monitor and a microphone sat on the judge's bench and Laurie Coles had a monitor of her own. She was also equipped with a small microphone, headphones, and a black box with a red indicator light.

Hull sat at the counsel table, angry that the children would be testifying from the judge's chambers, angrier still that the appellate division would not intervene.

The jurors quieted, the screens cleared, and a child was seen sitting at the judge's desk. Caroline Robertson's bright face was encircled by her winding curls. Perched on a pile of cushions, she was swiveling the chair. Suddenly she looked into the camera and said, "Boo!"

Light laughter rippled through the courtroom and lowered the tension, which was restored as Justice Mathes entered and said, "Turn it off!" He mounted the bench and addressed the attorneys. "I'm sure you gentlemen have considered the problems of dealing with child witnesses. Remember that you will be seen as authority figures. You must use restraint not only in your subject matter, but in your choice of words. And you must be as brief as possible." He turned to Hull. "The children may not be subjected to extended questioning. Is that clear?"

"Yes, sir," he said. "Are you going to ask the district attorney if it's clear to him, too?"

Mathes stared but said nothing. Then he explained the audio system. He and the attorneys would be able to communicate and their conversations would be heard in open court. In addition, Mr. Hull and the defendant could speak to each other over a private circuit. He told the attorneys to go to his chambers and Harmon left, with briefcase, followed by the clerk of the court. Hull scanned the audience. There in the second row was Stanley Schomburg, M.D., fingering a tuft of beard and staring back through the thickest glasses that might ever have been made.

Laurie Coles was left alone at the long counsel table.

The monitors lit up with a long shot of Harmon and Hull entering chambers. The clerk followed them in, sat beside Caroline, and looked at her tenderly. "You have to tell the truth," she said. "Do you understand what I mean?"

Caroline stopped swiveling and nodded. The clerk said, "I'm going to explain something about telling the truth. Do you solemnly swear to tell the truth, the whole truth, and nothing but the truth, so help you God? If you're going to tell us the truth, you can say yes."

Caroline picked up a large plastic paper clip and said, "Mommy says I should always tell the truth." In the front row of the courtroom, Lilly Robertson had tears in her eyes. As the clerk rose and Harmon replaced her in the picture, the child was attaching another plastic clip to the first one.

"Hi, Caroline," Harmon said. "I'm Pete. I'm going to ask you something about Laurie, your teacher. Is that all right?"

Hull leaned into his microphone. "It's not all right, Your Honor. "This is exactly what the investigators did. Planted a name in the children's heads."

Mathes replied quickly. "Let's not create an antagonistic atmosphere in front of the child."

Caroline looked up, startled, as she heard the judge's voice. "Oo-ooh," she said.

Harmon said, "Laurie was your teacher at Snug Arms, wasn't she, Caroline?"

She nodded, reaching for another paper clip.

Harmon said, "So she was your friend, and I'm sure you liked her. Did she ever do anything you didn't like?"

Too vague. But Hull kept his peace. The child looked away from the D.A. and said, "She yelled at me once. Yell-smell."

"Why did she yell at you?"

Caroline's eyes opened wide and she giggled. "I tripped Billy when we were playing out in back and he fell down."

"Oh. Can you remember anything else Laurie did, something you might have talked to your mother about?"

Hull leaned into his microphone. "He's leading the witness. He's leading the witness. I won't stop saying it, Your Honor."

That tore it for Mathes. "You'll stop if I have you physically removed from the room, Counselor."

"Mistrial," Hull said. "You can't say that in front of the jury. The defense moves for a mistrial."

"Denied. Proceed."

Harmon smiled at Caroline. "Do you remember anything about somebody taking her clothes off? And smearing something on herself?"

Hull said, "Leading again, Your Honor." But Caroline was already answering.

"She put strawberry on her peepee."

"Strawberry?"

She nodded. "She put strawberry on her peepee. Jam-ham."

"Ah. And then what happened?"

"She said for me to lick it off."

As the pictured widened, those in the courtroom saw Hull rubbing his eyes.

Harmon asked what Caroline did when Laurie asked her to remove the jam.

"I ran away." She was working on a string of four clips.

"I see. Were other children there when she did that?"

There was no answer.

"Were you and Laurie all alone when Laurie did that, with the jam?"

"No."

Harmon paused. Out in the courtroom one buff told another, "He didn't expect that one."

"Other children were there when Laurie did that?"

Caroline shook her head. "No."

Harmon did not pursue the contradiction. "Did she put the jam there just once? Or more than one time?"

Caroline said, "No. One time."

Harmon smiled. "Thank you very much for helping us. I have nothing else to ask you, Caroline."

"Can I have the beads?" she asked. "For Mommy?" She put the chain of paper clips in the pocket of her dress.

The clerk stepped forward and said, "I'll take you to your mommy soon, sweetheart."

Hull remained seated. "Caroline, I want to talk to you for just a minute. Do you remember if Laurie did that thing, with the jam, with any of your friends in school?"

Caroline nodded. "They told me."

"Okay. They told you she did. Did you see her do it with anyone else? Did you see that yourself?"

She shook her head.

"Do you remember that you talked to a tall man who had a little pin in his jacket?" Hull pointed to his own lapel. "A blue-and-gold pin?"

She looked reflective, then said, "Vince. He's high. He's like a mountain-fountain."

Hull laughed. "Yes. You told him the story about Laurie and the jam, didn't you?"

"Billy calls him Mr. Giraffe."

Hull laughed again. "That's good. But when you told him the story, you said that Laurie put the jam on you, not on herself. Do you remember that?"

Having finished defacing the judge's blotter with a felt pen, Caroline slid off the chair and skipped around the room as the camera followed her. Hull said nothing until she stopped and climbed back up, laughing. "Do you remember that, Caroline? You said Laurie licked the jam off *you*. Can you tell us which way it really happened?"

"Daddy said he wasn't home! Baddy-Daddy. He went in his office and wouldn't come out. I want my mommy!"

In the first row, Lilly Robertson leaned forward and nodded at Ellen Strand and Letty Andrews. Roy deserved it.

Hull looked into the camera. "I don't think further questions will be necessary, considering our inability to resolve this contradiction."

Caroline jumped off the chair and the cushions flew. She skipped to the door and the clerk took her hand and led her out.

Laurie Coles closed her eyes.

Bonnie Strand, who seemed destined for tallness, skipped into the picture and only three cushions were needed instead of the four Caroline used. She was sworn in, so to speak, and Harmon asked if she was comfortable.

She hunched up her shoulders and said nothing.

The D.A. wanted to make just one point with Bonnie. "Did you tell your mother that Laurie put something in your peepee?"

"I'm assuming the reporter is noting my objections to every single leading question, Your Honor," Hull said.

Mathes put a finger to his lips.

Bonnie seized her red hair and twisted it. "I told Ellie. Laurie put a pop stick in my peepee. I was scared 'cause Laurie might get me. Mommy said she would take care of me."

"Thank you for helping us," Harmon said.

Hull took over. "Bonnie, I'm Harry Hull and I hope you can help me, too. You like to explain things, don't you?"

The child picked up a red pencil from the judge's desk and scrawled on his blotter.

"Here's my question. You've told us what Laurie did. She put a stick in your peepee. Is that right?"

"Yes."

"How many times did she do that?"

"One time. No. A million times. Maybe it was Laurie."

"No further questions," Hull said cheerfully.

"Where's Ellie?" Bonnie asked. "Daddy Mickey's not here. He works far away. So he can't come see me. Ellie told me." The clerk led her out.

Billy Andrews's testimony was predictable. Defecation and cakes fashioned from Laurie Coles's waste material. The D.A. went briskly through the story and turned the witness over.

Hull decided that Billy's account of a monster room downstairs at Snug Arms had already been disposed of. He said, "Billy, you told Mr. Giraffe an interesting story. You know what 'number one' is, don't you?"

The boy wagged his head and pointed between his legs. He jumped down from the chair and pulled the cushions off, then climbed back up and stood on the seat, his little hands spread out on the desk.

Hull waited until he was calm. "You told Mr. Giraffe that Laurie did number one in a cup. Do you remember that?"

Billy looked like a lawyer in a movie as he nodded slowly, his weight on thin arms against the desk.

"And Laurie asked the children to drink her number one?"

"Laurie said so."

"Did you drink it, Billy?"

The boy pushed against the desk and stood straight in the chair. He laughed. "I was sick."

Hull was sorry he asked but had no choice but to continue. "You drank the number one and got sick?"

Billy laughed again. "I didn't drink the number one. I was home sick."

Hull gave the boy a grateful grin. "You weren't in school when Laurie did number one in the cup?"

"I was home sick."

"Oh. Well, I'm glad you're feeling better. Maybe you can help me some more, Billy. How do you know Laurie did number one in the cup?"

Billy leaned on the desk. "Somebody told me."

"Who told you?"

The boy seemed puzzled. "I don't know. I said that to Uncle Liam. I don't like Uncle Liam."

Hull shook his head, glancing at the camera. "I'm sorry to hear that. Well, thank you, Billy. You've helped a lot."

The clerk lifted the boy from the chair and he shouted, "I want to talk!"

Hull was equal to the occasion. "What do you want to say?"

Billy laughed wildly. "I want to watch TV!"

The clerk took the boy's hand and led him from chambers.

Laurie Coles was smiling, as if she had forgotten why she were here.

Another child appeared and said Laurie took her clothes off. Her mommy told her people shouldn't do that if they're not in their own rooms. Hull passed.

"Ten-minute recess," said Justice Mathes.

Out in the corridor Hull looked at the prosecution's witness list and was disturbed. The last child to appear would be Tom Burney, whose mother had probably given the most damaging testimony for the state. Searching for Sgueglia, he avoided the buffs. No Tony. But there was Corky McGonigle, angry. "Fucking Jacko. He's put the lock on the videotapes. Everybody in court can see the kids testify, but people at home can't. He pulled it at the last minute, so we wouldn't have time to get a court order."

Hull expressed sympathy but felt little. He was not happy with the children's testimony. He had made another dent in the façade, but the rest of it was there for the jury. Jam and stick and poop. "Corky, have you seen Tony?"

"He ran off to Albany. Maybe he's got a squeeze up there."

Hull went back into chambers and handed Harmon a copy of his own witness list. It contained only the name of Dr. Stanley Schomburg, psychiatrist. The D.A. looked disappointed.

The TV screens were turned on again and there was Tom Burney, a youngster with bright eyes that searched the judge's chambers and focused on Mathes's malacca walking stick. He seized it at its middle—it was an inch taller than he was—and strode to the judge's chair like a mountaineer. As he climbed into the seat, the cane was at his side. His mother wanted to cry, but she controlled herself. Grant Burney wanted to laugh and covered his mouth with his hands.

Harmon introduced himself as Pete and accelerated the formalities. "Hi, Tom Burney."

"Tom-Tom," was the immediate response.

Grant Burney winced and Marla said, "No big deal."

"Okay, Tom-Tom. I want to ask you about Laurie."

Tom raised the malacca cane and poked it to the floor. Few in the courtroom contained their laughter and Mathes withheld the gavel. Laurie was smiling again.

"Laurie is Tom-Tom's teacher," the boy said.

"Yes. Now, Tom—"

The walking stick rose and fell. "Captain Tom-Tom."

Serena Wiley was taking notes. Pete was going to get it in the ear tonight.

"Tom-Tom. Let's talk about Snug Arms. When you were there and you had to go to the bathroom, who took you there?"

"Laurie took Tom-Tom. Mommy says I wait too long."

"I see. When Laurie takes you to the bathroom, what does she do?"

Tom looked puzzled.

"I mean, where does she stand?"

"Mommy sits down when she pees."

Hull was beginning to enjoy himself as he considered the excursions this young fellow's testimony might take.

"Daddy stands up. Like Tom-Tom."

Harmon said, "Yes, you're some boy, Tom-Tom. Here's what I meant. When Laurie takes you to the bathroom—"

"Laurie doesn't go to the bathroom with Tom-Tom. I don't go to the school anymore."

Hull wondered what Jacko would do if he laughed out loud.

"All right," Harmon said. "But when you were going to Snug Arms, did Laurie go to the bathroom with you once and stand next to you?"

There went the walking stick. "Captain Tom-Tom goes to the bathtub by himself. With the dinosaurs. Tom-Tom swims with them." His eyes became slits as he told Harmon, "Dinosaurs swim in the tub and then they jump out."

In the courtroom, people were staring at each other and Grant Burney was squeezing Marla's arm. Laurie Coles was shaking her head and beaming.

"That a great story," Harmon said. "But do you remember Laurie taking you to the bathroom?"

"She doesn't swim good. She went to the bottom of the tub. Captain Tom-Tom told the dinosaurs to save her. But she flew. She was up on the ceiling hiding and Mommy came in and said too much noise. Then Mommy went away and Laurie flew down. Captain Tom-Tom shot her! *Zzzzz!*"

Harmon wanted to cut his losses but did not count on the boy, who pounded the walking stick and shouted, "Laurie went to the bathroom. I told Mommy I want her to babysit me. Mommy said no. Tom-Tom likes Laurie. Kids cry and she hugs the kids. Laurie is Tom-Tom's friend. Laurie showed Tom-Tom how to say God is good, God is great." He stopped and sat down.

Returning to the courtroom, Harmon received a severe glare from the bench. The D.A. said, "Your Honor, I ask that the testimony of the last witness be stricken from the record."

"Absolutely not," Hull said. "That child's testimony brings a lot to this case. It reveals the marvelous imaginations that have produced stories about Miss Coles, and it will give the jury something to think about. The defendant is entitled to have it on the record."

Justice Mathes's mustache was twitching. "The witness's testimony stands."

Harmon glanced toward the rear of the courtroom, at Serena, who was frowning at him, then turned to the bench. "Your Honor," he said, "the state rests its case."

Mathes spoke to Hull. "Is the defense ready to proceed?"

"We are, sir. I move that the jury be dismissed and that there be a directed verdict of not guilty. The state has not proved its case."

"Denied."

"Why, Your Honor?"

"Because your motion is not justified," Mathes replied.

Hull sat down. A motion to dismiss the charges is upheld on the night of every thousandth full moon. Then he stood again. "Your Honor, there is no corpus delicti."

"What are you talking about?" Mathes asked.

"Corpus delicti, sir. Where's the body? The state has presented all its witnesses and has not shown that a crime has been committed. Not a single piece of evidence establishes a crime. All we've heard is talk. The closest the prosecution came was when a general practitioner—not a pediatrician or a gynecologist—said that marks on a child's vagina might or might not have been caused by a stick. That's not substantial evidence that a crime was committed. And neither is anything else the state has said here. You have to prove there was a crime before you can ask a jury to convict a defendant, don't you? The motion is to dismiss the charges."

"Denied," Mathes said. "We are adjourned until one o'clock."

Wiley met Harmon in the cafeteria and complained that he hadn't warned her to dress for a kiddie carnival.

He asked, "Who was it who said kids say the darndest things? But remember, Serena. Everybody knows kids are kids."

"Including the judges on the court of appeals? Peter?"

Chapter 28

CHAIR NUMBER TWO: *HERE'S THE KIND OF THING THAT'S BOTHERING ME about this trial. The witnesses say Coles took off her clothes and did number one and number two in front of the children and told them to drink up and eat up. But that couldn't happen unless a person was completely crazy.*

Then why didn't she plead insanity? Because she didn't do it?

But how can I believe she didn't? The witnesses say she did those things to fifteen or twenty of the kids. Over and over for weeks and months. And finally, at last, one kid throws her jam away and says, "Mommy, Laurie plays weird games at Snug Arms. She does bathroom stuff on a table and licks things off us." And another one says she stuck things in them.

And Coles never thought a single kid might turn her in? That they were all so petrified they wouldn't dare talk? It doesn't make sense. Even a nut would know you can't get away with it forever.

So she might be innocent after all.

Still, crazy people do crazy things, even when they know they're bound to get caught sooner or later.

Look at Chair One, and that Number Nine. What did they do last night? Play dominoes? They're on a case where somebody could grow old in jail. They ought to be taking this thing more seriously.

The first ballot will be a pain. Number One will vote guilty. And Nine —Mister Einstein—he'll strut up and down and play devil's advocate. They're so predictable.

This is what's really bothering me. I heard a lawyer say on television that trials weren't held to find the truth. I thought that was the dumbest thing I'd heard in a long time, but then he explained it. In the outside world we get to hear and see everything, including some pretty good gossip. In court we can only hear and see what they call admissible evidence. There are rules about what can and can't be introduced because the law is trying to be fair to everybody. Some things may make a defendant look good or bad but have nothing to do with guilt or innocence of the crime we're talking about.

So what that lawyer said made sense, even if it sounded awfully cynical at first.

But it doesn't solve the problem this jury is up against. I just don't know who or what to believe. It's one word against another. I'd like to know a lot more about this Laurie Coles, for example. A whole lot more. What's she really like? I don't think I'm going to find out.

Chapter 29

"PLEASE TELL US YOUR NAME AND POSITION," HULL ASKED THE WITNESS.

"Stanley Schomburg, M.D., clinical professor of psychiatry and child psychiatry at New York University Medical School."

"How can we be sure you're what you say you are?" Hull asked. People walk into this court and claim to be psychologists and—" He heard the voice of Justice Mathes. "Counselor!"

"Excuse me. Dr. Schomburg, did you bring your credentials with you?" He felt he could get away with this one. "The defense wants to be certain of its experts' qualifications."

The witness handed several sheets to Hull, who said, "Your Honor, I present these credentials to the clerk of the court for verification." Mathes said nothing. "They show that Mr.—excuse me, *Dr.* Schomburg is what he says he is, and that he is also chairman of a committee of the American Psychiatric Association that was formed to study the sexual abuse of children. He hasn't come into court flying a false flag."

"Sidebar!"

Hull looked inquisitive as he moved to the bench with Harmon. Mathes spoke very softly. "Final warning, Harry. If your contemptuous conduct does not stop, I will cite you the instant the jury returns its verdict. But not before. You're not taking me down the path to a mistrial. So this is a formal notice and I'm putting it on the record."

Hull stepped back from the bench and announced, "I have been warned that if I persist in my conduct, I will go to jail when the trial ends." The judge raised his gavel, then lowered it as Hull went back to the witness, who seemed to be ignoring the sideshow. Having heard the morning news, he understood what was going on.

"Dr. Schomburg, please explain why you are a professor of psychiatry *and* child psychiatry? It sounds repetitive."

The witness looked up from his papers. "The position was created because of the high incidence of sexual-abuse charges. At one time those accusations were made mostly by a parent in a divorce suit. The children were caught in the middle and suffered greatly. If they agreed with one parent, the other became an ogre. It was extremely difficult to establish the truth. So a branch of psychiatry now specializes in the problems of children caught in those situations."

He was speaking English. But Hull did not want him wandering down unmarked trails. "Would you restrict your remarks to children in preschools?"

The psychiatrist nodded. "Yes. Recently there have been many cases in which sexual abuse has been suspected in nursery schools, and the truth there is just as difficult to determine. The children are caught in the middle again, so we're trying to find ways of preventing more emotional damage during the investigation of such cases."

"Do you mean investigators cause emotional damage?"

"Objection," Harmon said. "Generalization."

Mathes considered. "Go ahead."

"When a child is mishandled," Dr. Schomburg said. "For example, if a child is hungry and the interviewer says he can eat as soon as he tells the truth about the accused, the child is being badgered."

"And if you heard me tell a child, as the first thing I said, 'Hi. Tell me what Laurie did to you,' what would you say?"

"It's a loaded question. The interrogator should always wait to see if the child will identify the accused first."

"Ah. Well, Dr. Schomburg, let's say a small child sits down to testify and the first statement to the child names an accused person. Then comes a question. 'Did that person do anything to you that you didn't like?' What would you assume a child witness would think?"

Harmon was on his feet. "Too broad, sir."

"Much too broad. Strike it."

Hull stepped toward the bench. "Your Honor, are you saying I cannot ask an expert witness a hypothetical question?"

"Not if it's too general."

"Is that a new rule?" He hurried on. "Dr. Schomburg, let's say that an hour ago a child testified in this trial and the prosecutor said, 'Laurie is your teacher.' And then said, 'Did Laurie ever do anything you didn't like?' Are you in a position to assume what the child might think? By the way, the age is four and a half." He turned toward Mathes. "That's not too general, is it, sir?"

Mathes ignored him.

"Most children of that age would assume that the person named had done something bad," Dr. Schomburg said.

"And if an investigator said, 'Sure you'll tell me what Laurie did to you. All your friends have.' And if it was also said, 'You tell me what Laurie did and then we'll go out for ice cream.' What would you think the investigator was doing?"

"Coercing and bribing the child."

"And if an investigator said, 'You sure are beautiful, honey. Come sit on my lap and tell me what Laurie did to you?' "

The witness shook his head vigorously. "That person should not be near small children."

Hull favored the jury with a smile. "Have you testified in other cases in which a person was accused of sexually abusing small children? And if so, how many times, roughly?"

"In perhaps fifty cases. Thirty of them dealt with charges of abuse in preschools. The others involved accusations of molestation by one parent or another."

"And in the nursery-school cases, how many times have you been retained by the prosecution?"

The witness thought. "It's a guess, but I'd say a dozen times by the prosecution, in the rest by the defense."

"A dozen times for the prosecution. Okay. Now, Dr. Schomburg, were your comments about investigators' interviewing tactics based on your own observations, or on other research?"

"Both. In addition to my own work, the National Center for the Prosecution of Child Abuse has studied the problem."

"For the *prosecution* of child abuse?"

"Yes. The center was acting for the American Prosecutors Research Institute and the National District Attorneys Association. Those agencies have prepared guidelines to help prosecutors deal with cases of this kind."

"Well, let's get into that."

"Sidebar," the judge announced.

Hull and Harmon advanced to the bench and Mathes whispered gruffly, "Tell me what the questions are."

"First I'm going to introduce an exhibit that the state cannot object to. It contains guidelines for interviewing children involved in sex crimes, and it was developed by the organizations the witness mentioned. Prosecutors' groups. Then—"

"They'd better be certified copies," Mathes warned. "And I will not admit excerpts, only full texts."

Hull smiled. "Certified and complete, sir."

Mathes waved the attorneys away before Harmon could speak. The D.A. was relieved. He was not sure what to say.

Hull handed the exhibits to the clerk and a copy to Harmon, then turned to Dr. Schomburg. "Please read us the pertinent passages from those manuals."

Schomburg brought the papers close to his thick glasses and said, "I quote. 'As an interviewer, you must remain open, neutral and objective, and be aware of any reactions which could be interpreted as reinforcing certain responses and discouraging others.' In other words, you should not have made up your mind before you began the interview."

Hull remained low key. "That's what the prosecutors' organization says, is it? Please continue."

"Next. 'Avoid leading questions.' And then, 'Never try to force a reluctant child to talk or continue an interview.' Next, 'The investigator should refrain from telling one witness what others have said, so as not to influence the witness.'"

"But this case is full of exactly that kind of thing," Hull muttered. "Strike that. Forgive me, Your Honor. I forgot that such remarks belong in my summation." One of the buffs shook his head. Harry Hull should change his name to Hara Kiri.

Hull asked, "Do you know of other recommendations that would help investigators develop their cases fairly?"

"Yes. They are cautioned against exchanging children between investigators because they can be manipulated in that way, even if the investigators don't mean to do that."

"Thank you, sir. Now, have you spoken to the defendant?"

"Yes, on four occasions at the prison facility."

"Have you drawn any conclusions that you can share with us without violating professional confidentiality?"

"Yes. I concluded that Miss Coles does not fit any known profile of a pedophile."

Pete Harmon was trying to control his skeptical look.

"A pedophile?"

"A person with an abnormal fondness for children, an adult who desires sexual relations with children."

"These people have been profiled?"

"They've been studied for years. We have a good picture."

"And Laurie Coles doesn't fit it? How can you be so sure?"

He shook his head. "I would worry about anyone who was too certain in these situations. But nothing in Miss Coles's background or in the way she responded to questions indicated a sexual attraction to children. My impression is that she enjoys spending time with children, but that's true of many adults who grew up

without brothers or sisters, as Miss Coles did. They may not realize it, but it's an experience they've missed."

Hull began walking his circle, glancing up at Judge Mathes as
he said, "I have only one more question, Dr. Schomburg, and it's
another one of those hypotheticals. Here is Miss Coles, who
doesn't strike you as a child molester. And you've been around the
block and seen those types. Miss Coles appears normal enough to
you, and normal people aren't sexually attracted to little children.
You're following me?"

The psychiatrist understood that Hull was signaling the jury to
pay close attention.

"If that is so, in your expert opinion—not in the opinion of an
impostor who sat on that witness stand—" The judge cleared his
throat. "—How do you account for what Miss Coles is going
through? How could these charges have come about? I hope
you're good at mysteries, Dr. Schomburg. Can you solve that
one?"

The witness removed his seeing-eye glasses. "I'll describe an
experiment I conducted, a variation on an old study. A professor
tells a student a woman entering a taxi fainted. She was lying in
the street, with her dress torn, and the story ended unhappily.
Pass it along, he said. The students related the incident to each
other until the entire class had heard it. Then the professor asked
the last student for the story. He learned that a gorgeous woman
was entering a cab when a car stopped and the driver tried to
force her into his own vehicle. She fought him off and fell to the
pavement. The bad guy jumped into his own car and drove away
and the taxi driver raped the woman."

Hull decided to be thought dense. "That actually happened?"

"Of course not. Nothing happened. A story that invited fanciful
speculation grew and grew as it was passed along."

"Excuse me for interrupting."

"Those were college students, and I repeated the experiment
with small children. They were my patients, and I lengthened the
interval between their therapy sessions so they would have time to
pass the story along. I told the first child that an alien had landed
disguised as me. Well, the experiment ended in a strange way. I
wanted to let a couple of weeks go by and then ask the last child
what he had heard about an alien. Instead, my phone began ring-
ing three days later and parents asked me if I was crazy. Their
children told them that Dr. Schomburg was an alien who kid-
napped them and made them eat spinach twice a day."

Hull flogged the obvious once again. "Why do you say the experiment worked out in a strange way, sir?"

"Well, some experiments succeed when they fail. This one

showed that it doesn't take much for rumors to become facts, for a child to speak and a parent to draw conclusions and get in touch with other parents. Anxiety takes over, apprehension, and crimes are created."

Hull said, "Thank you, Dr. Schomburg. I believe you have reached the heart of this case, and I have no further questions."

The district attorney rose but remained at the counsel table. "Doctor, when you planted this story in your patients' minds, didn't it occur to you that you might harm them? That you might create anxiety about kidnapping, or that they would be terrified? In other words, that this was a destructive experiment that took advantage of those children?"

The witness replaced his glasses. "That did occur, and I would not have conducted the experiment without first consulting others in the field. I talked to a number of colleagues and the consensus was that the mere fact that an alien had landed and disguised himself as me was quite benign compared with what children see on television every night of the week and on Saturday mornings. When they describe their nightmares, you can just about name the shows they watch."

Harmon decided he had no further questions. He did, but he worried that he would lose more than he could gain from every moment this witness remained on the stand. The D.A. glanced toward the back of the courtroom and found Serena smiling—enigmatically, he thought.

The judge called a ten-minute recess.

Anthony Sgueglia and a woman who looked to be about Laurie Coles's age were waiting just outside the courtroom doors. And Sgueglia looked triumphant. "Teresa Vane," he said, "this is Mr. Hull, Laurie's attorney. Harry, Terry taught at Snug Arms."

Hull saw Wiley coming into the corridor and felt an impulse to run over and kiss the person who suggested he hire a private investigator. He shook the hand of a rangy woman who said, "I couldn't stand to read the lies about Laurie, Mr. Hull. I had to come back."

Sgueglia said, "Terry came in this morning and got in touch with Corky McGonigle. Instead of putting her on the air he brought her to me. But he's already taped her and I've seen it."

"I want to testify, Mr. Hull," she said.

Hull fought off ebullience and imagined the look on Judge Mathes's face when he announced a surprise witness at this juncture. Jacko would hold court all night if necessary to wind up the trial. He checked the time. "Problem. We have to talk before you testify and I can't get a delay."

Sgueglia broke in. "Harry, I've seen the tape. All you need to do is ask Terry a few questions about what went on at the school and she'll knock your socks off. Follow me? You won't be blindsided."

"Let's go," Hull said.

Sgueglia took his arm. "Something else. I don't know what it adds up to, but McGonigle laid another one on me. He says your judge, Mathes, was a close buddy of Mickey and Ellen Strand. But one day Mathes stopped coming around. Just like that. 'So what?' I asked Corky, and he said, 'I don't know. I'm just telling you.' The thing is, I don't think he does know anything else. He's thinking out loud. But Corky doesn't do that unless he smells something."

Hull was half listening.

"One more. Corky hears that the lab report on the stuff they found on Strand is coming back negative. Like, they don't have enough to make a determination."

Hull shook his head. "I can't handle that now. Tony, find out about Mathes and the Strands and think about Mickey Strand. Hard. And *move*." Sgueglia heard: Take the gloves off, Tony.

As Hull entered the courtroom with Teresa Vane, Laurie Coles was startled. He led the teacher to the counsel table and she jumped to her feet. They clasped each other and Vane whispered, "I'm sorry, Laurie. I was scared."

Pete Harmon seemed merely curious, but the judge walked in, stopped, and made it clear that he did not like what he saw. "Approach the bench!" he snapped.

The attorneys came forward and Mathes said, "What are you up to, Mr. Hull?"

"I have a witness we must hear, Your Honor. One of the missing Snug Arms teachers."

"How long have you had her?" Harmon asked.

"I just met her," Hull replied.

Mathes beckoned to Teresa Vane and she came forward. "How long have you been in Hudson Ferry?" he asked.

"I got here at ten o'clock this morning."

He stared at her. "When did you first make contact with the defense counsel?"

"A few minutes ago, in the hallway."

Mathes spoke to her sternly. "If you take the witness stand, you will be asked those same questions under oath and I will direct the district attorney to investigate your statements. If you are not telling the truth, the penalty will be severe. Do you still want to testify?"

"Your Honor," Hull said, "your tone is threatening."

"Do you still want to testify?"

"I do."

She was sworn in. Hull was silent, waiting for the judge to put his questions. Hearing nothing, and hoping he was not sliding into disaster, he said, "State your name, please."

"Teresa Vane."

"Are you a resident of Hudson Ferry?"

"I used to be."

"Have you been in town at any time over the past three months, for any period at all?"

"No. I came back for the first time this morning."

"On what date did you and I have our first contact, in any form?" He glanced up at the judge. "Please keep in mind that you are under oath."

"I never saw you or talked to you until a few minutes ago, just outside this room."

"Thank you. What is your occupation?"

"I'm unemployed. I was a teacher at Snug Arms."

Up came the audience buzz and down came the gavel.

"Did you work at the school while Miss Coles did?"

"Yes. She was teaching there when I came."

Hull was staring at the jury as he spoke to the witness. "I would like you to think hard before you answer my next question, Miss Vane. Did you at any time see, hear, or smell anything at Snug Arms that struck you as unusual? Please consider your answer carefully."

Teresa Vane was looking at the defendant. Then she turned slowly to face the jury. "Nothing. Ever."

"You never saw Miss Coles place a stick in a child's vagina, or defecate on a table and ask children to make poop cakes, or place jam on a vagina and lick it off or have it licked off? Excuse me, but that's what this trial is all about."

"I know what this trial is about. It never happened. I would have seen it if it did."

Hull thought of something. "Well, did you ever see Laurie Coles make physical contact with a child at Snug Arms?"

"Of course. We picked them up and hugged them all the time. When they did something well or were funny, or if they'd been having a tantrum. Little children love to be picked up and held. Ask their parents."

Hull turned the witness over to the prosecutor. Harmon would have to try to devalue the testimony in some way, probably by attacking Vane's character. Bad luck, Pete.

The D.A. was brisk. "Why did you run away when this scandal broke, Miss Vane? You knew the police wanted to speak to you."

"The police?" She bristled. "They did speak to me."

Harmon could not abandon that tack without losing points. "Why did you leave town so hurriedly and hide out?"

"Because I'm a coward. A policeman asked me what I saw Laurie do and I said nothing. He asked me ten more times in different ways and he was stomping around and shouting. I told him I never saw anything. Then he asked me if I'd been Laurie's lookout while she was molesting the kids. I jumped on the bus the next morning and got the hell out of here. I was *scared*."

Harmon left the witness and motioned that he was finished. He would have to sit down with the police chief and go head to head about overzealousness that could endanger cases.

Hull rose for redirect and spoke quickly. "Miss Vane, were you told by a police officer that if you did not implicate Laurie Coles you might be indicted yourself and therefore would not be able to testify in her defense?"

Harmon leaped to his feet but Mathes cut him off. "Don't answer that question, witness. If you have nothing for redirect, the witness is dismissed."

"I would like an answer to my question, Your Honor."

"You're not going to get one. That was not a question but an inflammatory speech."

"Sorry, Your Honor. No questions, but I'd like to cite a passage from a state exhibit." He rushed on. "A Snug Arms child is being questioned by Detective Garafolo on May twentieth"—his voice rose—"one day after the police decided that Teresa Vane was uncooperative. The child was asked, 'Did you ever see Laurie and Terry do anything to each other? Like things you might have seen your mommy and daddy do in their bedroom?' Can you believe such tactics, Your Honor?"

Teresa Vane left the stand and walked up the aisle and through the double doors.

Hull said, "The defense rests, Your Honor."

Chair Number Nine: *She's not going to take the stand. Is anyone surprised?*

But Hull felt a pull on his arm, saw a furious Laurie Coles, and realized he had goofed. Berating himself for assuming she had understood, he turned back to the bench and said, "We need five minutes in private, Your Honor. It's very important."

Mathes shook his head. "You have rested. Your summation, please."

Hull stepped forward. "The defense does *not* rest! I withdraw that statement and the record will show it!" He decided he might as well go down in flames. "Why the rush, Your Honor? Will the executioner go on overtime if we take another five minutes?"

The courtroom veterans had never seen the judge as irate, and they understood why. He could not force the defense to rest since the summations had not begun, and he would look bad if he denied a brief delay whose reason was apparent on the defendant's face: She and her lawyer were at odds.

"Five minutes!" Mathes snapped. "And it will be the last delay. But there will be no delay in dealing with your behavior, Mr. Hull. Make no mistake about that."

Mathes remained on the bench as Hull and Coles were led into the jury room. The attorney slammed the door hard—that might earn him an extra day behind bars—and stood before Coles. "I apologize, Laurie. I'm sorry we didn't sit down and talk about this, but I thought you knew. There's no way you can testify."

Her pale cheeks showed red blotches as she shook her head. "I'm not just going to sit there and keep quiet, Harry. I want to take the stand and tell them it's all a bunch of lies! And go to hell if you don't like it!"

"Sit down," he said. "We've only got a few minutes." She remained standing. "Do I have to spell it out for you? If you take the stand, you open up your whole life to the prosecutor. He can dig into every corner. The charge is molestation. That opens you up to questions about sex. Follow me?"

Her reply was a pair of blazing eyes.

"You're making me say it, Laurie. He'll ask about your personal life, including sexual experiences. And sooner or later he'll get around to Allison Wright."

She walked away from him, then turned and shouted, "What does Allison have to do with this?"

He dropped into a chair. "Nothing as far as I'm concerned. But if you testify, Mathes will probably let him put her on. Now please sit down and listen."

She reached for the back of a juror's chair.

"If he gets to put her on, he'll ask about relations with men, and eventually about where she lived and who she lived with. He'll hint at lesbianism and then put a shrink on the stand—one who'll cook up a connection between lesbians and child molesting. Who cares if it's true? Shrinks can get away with that, and the jury will hear it. It's tough enough now, but if you testify, it's all over."

"Allison wouldn't say anything that would hurt me."

There was a knock at the door. They ignored it, sitting silently until Hull said, "Those jurors will bring their prejudices into this room, and most people mix their prejudices up with facts." The knock sounded again and he rose. "I feel like a shit saying these things to you, Laurie, but I have to."

She leaned against the chair, eyes closed, and said, "I feel dirty.

All right, Harry. If that's the way it is." She turned away and said, "It won't make any difference anyway. I know what the verdict's going to be."

They returned to the courtroom and Hull said, "The defense rests, Your Honor."

"Summations in fifteen minutes," Mathes said. Hull wanted to grab the gavel and whack him.

Chapter 30

I<small>T WAS THREE THIRTY WHEN</small> H<small>ULL FACED THE JURORS, INCLUDING THE TWO</small> alternates who would soon be sent away, frustrated; they had heard everything and would be able to say nothing. Chair Number Thirteen had not wished illness on any of the first twelve, but he had been waiting for the moment during deliberations when Number One would pop off once too often. Thirteen, an oyster bar owner, had worked up some straighten-outeners for the yakky broad, and they were about to expire unused.

Hull, exhausted but exhilarated, stood with hands clasped, thumbs hooked behind belt buckle, surveying the jurors consecutively, giving each one a counted-out five seconds as he moistened a dry mouth. He would have given fifty dollars for the clean, crisp taste of a cold Bud. Pour, Big Bert.

"Ladies and gentlemen, I won't try to unravel the contradictions that make this case a farce. And I won't go back to each witness's testimony and demonstrate that the state's case is as strong as those castles kids build at the beach. The charges should have been thrown out, but the judge wouldn't do it."

He raised his eyes from the broad, stained planks of the flooring and stepped back, setting up a position midway between Justice Mathes and the jury box.

"I won't drag you back through it. Instead, I'm going to tell you a story, and I ask that you listen carefully." He knew Polly was in the audience, and he would have given twice the fifty to see her face. Staring up at Mathes, he said:

"Once upon a time in a faraway land, an emperor lived in a crystal palace. Lovely flowers grew outside, in a garden that ran all the way to a huge forest full of high trees. The woods stretched down to the ocean, where ships sailed in under the branches of the tall trees."

Chair Nine: *What is this?*

Hull: *What do you think of that, pretty Polly?*

Polly: *Do my ears deceive me?*

He turned to the jurors but spoke so softly they had to lean forward. "Up in the branches lived a nightingale whose songs were so charming that everyone stopped to listen. From all over the world people came to visit the emperor and admire his palace and garden. But when they heard the voice of the nightingale, they said, 'There is the emperor's greatest treasure of all.'

"When the emperor heard about the wonderful bird, he asked that it be brought to him. His chamberlain looked everywhere but could not find the nightingale. Then a little girl told him, 'I know the nightingale. When I lie down in the forest and listen to him sing, it feels as if my mother is kissing me.' And so the child led them into the forest and pointed up into the branches. There a tiny gray bird was singing a heartbreaking song."

Number Nine: *Will he do Hamlet next?*

"The chamberlain said, 'He's such an *ordinary* bird.' But the nightingale was taken to the emperor and placed on a golden perch. He sang at a great festival, so beautifully that tears came to the emperor's eyes. He told the little bird to stay in the palace, where he would live in his own cage and take walks twice a day and once at night. The nightingale wasn't happy with that plan, but he didn't want to offend the kind emperor."

Number Two: *I know this story. This is clever.*

Mathes: *I can't wait until the appellate judges read this stuff.*

"One day the emperor received a gift. It was a little mechanical toy, an artificial nightingale that had been made to look like the real one, except that it was decorated with many sparkling jewels. And when it was wound up, it sang one of the real nightingale's songs. The emperor said the two birds should sing together, and they did. But the real bird sang this way and that, while the artificial bird sang only notes that came from its mechanical insides. Always the same notes. But it sang well, and it was much prettier to look at. So the artificial bird sang alone."

Number One: *I'm making the connection. And so what?*

"Everybody praised the artificial bird. 'It not only sings beautifully,' they said, 'but its insides are perfectly arranged. You never can be sure what will come out of the real nightingale, but with the artificial bird, what's to come will come.'"

Number Two: *I see where he's going.*

"But when the artificial nightingale sang the same song over and over, always exactly in the same way, people became tired of hearing it. So the emperor decided that the real bird should sing again. But he had flown away, back to his forest home."

Hull stared out of the courtroom window, as if searching for the nightingale, then resumed, raising his voice. "But an awful thing happened one evening, when the artificial bird was singing at its best, each note perfect. Something inside the bird went *pop*, and there was a *whir-r*, and the music stopped. A watchmaker came in and fixed the bird, but he said it was wearing out and could now sing only once a year. Everyone was sad."

Polly: *So there's another Harry under there!*

"One day the emperor became ill and couldn't breathe, and that night he felt something pressing on his chest. He opened his eyes and saw Death sitting on his heart, and strange faces staring out at him from behind the bedroom curtains. The faces were talking and the emperor was frightened. He asked the artificial bird to sing, to drown out the voices, but it couldn't.

"Suddenly the sweet song of the real nightingale was heard at the window. Learning of the illness, he had come to sing for the emperor. And as he sang, the ghostly faces vanished, the emperor breathed easier, and Death floated away.

"The emperor's music director told him, 'With the real nightingale, you can never be sure what is coming. But all the sounds of the artificial bird have been concocted.' "

Polly: *I'm going to cry right now.*

"And so the emperor learned that it is better to listen to real voices, even if you can't always be sure what they will say, rather than to voices whose words have been arranged beforehand."

Hull canvased the jurors' faces, one by one.

"That story is by Hans Christian Andersen. Would you think about it as the prosecutor winds up those voices again during his summation. And please, during your deliberations, look at the videotape of the children's testimony. The experts said that when kids are making things up, they twist their hair and jump up and down. When they're telling a straight story, they're calm. Watch them and decide whether you've been told nonsense disguised as expert opinion."

Hull started toward the counsel table, but stopped suddenly. "And I ask you to remember, too, that in so many folk tales, villagers set out to find a devil who has harmed someone, or so they have been told. And they become angrier and angrier as they search. So in the end someone has to pay, and that's why so many witches have been burned and drowned so many times. But it never ends, does it? They keep coming back."

He faced the audience. "And now the latest villain." He pointed to Laurie Coles. "The Bitch of Hudson Ferry. That's her name all over town, isn't it? Everybody is angry, so *somebody* must pay. And it's Laurie Coles's turn. Right, folks?"

He turned to the jury again. "Thanks for listening."

There was no sound in the room until someone brought a pair of palms together. *Clap. Clap.* Justice Mathes tried to spot the offender, but Polly had kept her hands low.

Hull walked back to his chair and stood behind Laurie Coles. Her head was in her arms and she was sobbing in the silence.

Pete Harmon, never superstitious, was wearing the same jacket, tie, and slacks in which he had appeared on opening day. He remained seated at the counsel table, waiting for the judge's signal. Mathes appeared to be consulting a law book, but the pages did not turn. Only when Coles's sobs died out did he motion the district attorney to deliver the state's final words.

Harmon did the right thing. He told the jurors, "Rarely have I heard a summation as imaginative and moving as Mr. Hull's."

Unlike Hull, the D.A. was equipped with a sheet of notes, and he checked off the first one. "Let's be clear about something. The defense noted that this case has been surrounded by hysteria. That is true. I have heard shocking statements made all over Hudson Ferry. And my mail is filled with disgusting proposals about what should be done to the defendant. As far as the state is concerned, people who make such irresponsible statements do not understand the justice system that has served us so well for so long."

Serena Wiley: *Thank you, Pete.*

Harmon attended to business. "I was even tempted to call the defense counsel's remarks compelling. But I can't go that far. The fact that tongues wag does not mean that crimes have *not* been committed." He looked at Coles, then back at the jury. "We have presented convincing evidence that the defendant took advantage of small children under her care and abused them sexually. Fairy tales won't get around that fact."

Number Nine: *That is correct, sir.*

"I'll be brief. You heard that a child said she was molested and was told she would be hurt if she talked about it. An investigation started and parents and experts learned of the invasion of tiny bodies with foreign objects, and of games built around defecations and urinations and misshapen desires. And of the defendant parading in the nude. And yes, you also heard fanciful stories of underground rooms that do not exist. And of dragons and dinosaurs. But we're dealing with little kids here, and we know that once they feel free to tell what they know, their imaginations add to their stories."

Harmon attacked another point. "Let's get into the fanfare the defense made of whether Amanda Roth is a psychologist or a fake. While that was going on, I sat over there and thought a great impostor had been exposed. During your deliberations, ladies and gentlemen, think about the real value of Amanda Roth. Is it important whether she's a psychologist or a social worker? What's important is that she is a highly trained investigator, the one who brought this nation's attention to the alarming incidence of sexual molestation that nursery-school children are being subjected to."

Check. "You heard from Detective Garafolo, a veteran of our police department, a man who has never been accused of stretching the truth. And there was Liam Gunn, chief of the child protection unit at Princess County General Hospital, who is trying to bring an end to the kind of offensive acts we have heard about."

He paused to let it sink in and then went for broke. "And you have seen and heard the children themselves tell their stories. And I know you have all wondered, as I have, if they will ever forget their experiences."

The courtroom was as hushed as it had been for Hull. "And now I want to make a comment about Dr. Stanley Schomburg, the psychiatrist who appeared for the defense. A virtue was made of the fact that Dr. Schomburg has testified for prosecutors almost as often as he has for defense attorneys. Is that a virtue? Or should we ask if his testimony has the habit of agreeing with the viewpoint of the side that hires him? Are we talking about virtue, or a lack of credibility?"

Number One: *Wait a minute. When was the last time your investigators testified for the defense?*

Serena: *Cheap shot, Peter.*

"I leave you with a couple of thoughts, ladies and gentlemen. First, it is not important whether the defendant looks like a sweet person or a malevolent molester. What is important is the evidence. Did she or did she not commit the crimes? Of course she did, and we have proved that. Second, please forget about nightingales. The victims in this case are humans, little people. And anyway, we're here not to judge the value of fairy tales, but to seek the truth."

Polly: *Fairy tales are full of amazing insights, Mr. Harmon. Don't sound as dumb as Jacko Mathes.*

"Your mission is to deal with facts. And the facts prove that the defendant sitting here, Laurie Coles, did indeed commit the crimes stated in the indictment. And they prove her guilt beyond a reasonable doubt. She violated the privacy of children. We have laws against that. Thank you."

It was four thirty and, Sylvia be pleased, Justice Mathes was on schedule. The question in his mind was, is Sylvia on schedule? He was going to put the question to her at dinner this evening and then take her home and leave. Sylvia, too, would begin her deliberations.

"Members of the jury," Mathes said, "is there a reason why anyone who is sitting in chairs One through Twelve cannot now begin the process of deliberation?"

Silence, and anxiety.

"Jurors Thirteen and Fourteen are now excused, and the court wishes to thank them for their diligence. You may leave the courtroom."

Thirteen: *I'm going. Okay, the restaurant needs me.*

Fourteen: *They can't call me for another two years.*

Mathes delivered his charge. "My role is to interpret the law. Yours is to judge the truth or falsity and the weight of the testimony. So I will not comment on what any witness has said. But I will tell you as a matter of law that there was sufficient reason why the defense was not permitted to interview the children. You may draw no conclusions from that decision."

Hull looked at the jury with a curled lip.

"The children did not testify in the courtroom for good cause and the defendant's right to confront her accusers was not violated. That is not a proper subject for deliberation. You must remember that I am the keeper of the law and that you are to judge the facts."

Number Nine: *We might be out of here by noon tomorrow. Unless Number Two starts up.*

"Now," Mathes said, "one expert witness's credentials were challenged. That does not mean the witness is not qualified to deal with and observe abused children. The challenge had to do with the wording of a New York State law, and the court finds no reason to disqualify that witness as an expert."

Hull did a slow burn.

"Finally," Mathes said, "you may draw no conclusions from the defendant's failure to testify on her own behalf. The accused came into court with a presumption of innocence and did not have to prove it. The state had the responsibility of proving her guilty beyond a reasonable doubt. The law defines reasonable doubt as an honest and reasonable uncertainty as to guilt, after you have given full and impartial consideration to the evidence. Thank you."

The bailiff escorted the jurors to their sanctum. Serena was making notes, preparing for an evening of debate.

Polly was feeling low; Harry was going to lose.

Hull told Coles, "I can tell you this much. They won't reach a quick verdict." The matron led her away.

He busied himself with papers. With the jury out of the room, Judge Mathes would now punish the defense counsel for his transgressions. Many of the spectators felt that Hull deserved it. He had not just sassed the bench repeatedly but had called the townspeople a pack of witch-hunters. Lilly Robertson hoped he got a month in jail. Letty Andrews would settle for ten days and Ellen Strand for three. Marla Burney wanted an end to the whole matter. Harry Hull was supposed to defend Laurie Coles and that's what he had done.

Judge Mathes checked the time, then looked down at the counsel table. "I want to see the attorneys in chambers right now." He banged the gavel, rose, and walked out.

The court buffs arranged to reconvene over dinner, where they would begin their deliberations.

Mathes poured coffee and told Harmon, "I want an investigation of the circumstances surrounding Teresa Vane's testimony."

Harmon considered that. "The state did not object to her appearance, Your Honor, and it still doesn't."

"It was too convenient," the judge said, "and her testimony sounded as if it had been rehearsed for two weeks." He smiled at Harmon, humorlessly. "And you walked right into it, Prosecutor, with your question about whether the police had spoken to her."

Harmon nodded. "I blew it."

"I want an investigation."

The D.A. stiffened. "I have no grounds on which to act."

Mathes stared at him. "I *order* an investigation."

Harmon shook his head. "With all respect, sir, you cannot order me to do anything outside the courtroom. If you want an investigation conducted, you'll have to file a complaint, like anyone else."

Mathes nodded. "I see." He turned to Hull. "How did Miss Vane come to you?"

Hull was willing to spend all evening in Jacko's chambers. "She was brought to me by Mr. Sgueglia, my private investigator. But Sgueglia was just doing Cornelius McGonigle a favor. Miss Vane went to Corky and he sent her to me." He omitted *sir* and *Your Honor,* and Mathes did not miss it.

"Gentlemen, you will appear in my chambers at ten o'clock in the morning in connection with this matter. Will Mr. McGonigle be here, Mr. Hull, or must I issue a subpoena?"

Hull smiled. "He'll be here. Your Honor. Corky wouldn't miss it." Having expected to be sent straight off to jail, and to spend several days there for contempt of court, he walked out, free as a nightingale.

Laurie Coles was not told why she remained in the holding room for ten minutes before she was taken, handcuffed, downstairs and to the rear entrance of the criminal courts building. An officer she had not seen before, a middle-aged, nervous woman, led her through the door and into the parking area, where only one car remained. When they were well into the open, the officer stopped and said, "Hold it. Stay right here." Coles halted and the officer went back into the building.

She stood there, facing the door and waiting, when she heard a grunt behind her. As she turned, she felt a sting near her right temple and collapsed to the cement, striking her forehead again. A jagged piece of slate lay on the paving beside her.

The officer came out of the building, now accompanied by a man, another officer.

She pointed to a short, stout figure that was scurrying around the bend of the L-shaped parking area, but the other officer, bending over Coles, straightened and said, "She's out. Stay here. I'll get an ambulance."

She shouted furiously, "Are you crazy? We can't *do* this!"

He walked into the building without a sign of hurry.

The woman inspected a two-inch slash on the side of Coles's forehead and saw the skin laid back at its center and the temporal bone exposed. There was little bleeding, but she was extremely pale and breathing shallowly. The officer quickly removed the handcuffs to get a pulse reading and found it slow and erratic.

The ambulance did not arrive for fifteen minutes. Coles was taken to the General Hospital emergency room, where her forehead received twelve stitches and she was found to have suffered a concussion. She was placed on intravenous feeding and taken to the security ward. The woman officer, who was by then off duty, remained outside the door for a half hour. She was incensed that she had been made a party to an assault, and she remembered the explicit warning she heard as she climbed into the ambulance at the courthouse. "You want trouble? Just open your mouth!"

The report on the incident said the prisoner had stumbled, fallen forward, and struck her head on the pavement. There was no mention of a jagged chunk of slate, nor was it found.

As the ambulance was driving off, Coles's father was rushing through the bus terminal in Portsmouth, New Hampshire. Having stopped to pick up the afternoon paper, Fred Coles reached the ramp as the bus was pulling out, but the driver stopped and took him aboard. He found the story of yesterday's testimony, read it, and closed his eyes. A special investigator said Laurie put a stick in a child's—, and killed animals in front of the kids. God! And another investigator called this the worst case she had ever seen.

Coles did not want to think about it all, but sleep would not come and his mind repeated the stories he had been reading. They raced through his head, over and over until the dozing man beside him cleared his throat and he found that he had been rocking back and forth, with his lips moving.

Hours passed until he suddenly realized that a frightening idea had been trying to force its way into his mind. His hands were in his lap, clutching each other. His knees were clenched together, and his feet were pressed to the floor, as they had been in the courtroom days ago.

The idea was terrifying, as dreadful as the despair that had filled him when he found out that Laurie's mother was going to die.

The thought rushed in. Maybe the stories were true after all. Maybe Laurie did do those things, for some reason he would never be able to understand. Fred Coles arrived in Hudson Ferry hating himself.

Chapter 31

IT WAS PETE'S TURN TO COOK. HE WASN'T UP TO IT AND THEY WENT OUT, but not to the Hotel Champlain, home of the Laurie Coles jury. He had a different inspiration. Dutch's Oyster Bar.

Serena loved oysters, which he despised. "Great," she said, "but what will you eat?"

"Shrimp. Just a couple. I'm trying to lose weight."

"Cut it out, Slim. What's going on?"

"Lars Ost was Chair Thirteen. The alternate. I can talk to him now. Or I can listen, anyway. Did you ever know an alternate who didn't want to explain the whole case?"

Dutch's was a new old-fashioned place with sawdust on the floor and chopping blocks for tables, and Lars Ost, who greeted them, was one of those corpulent humans whose arms swung away from their bodies as they walk and whose hands face backward.

"You're the prosecutor," Ost said heartily. Harmon smiled and introduced Serena, and their host bowed. "Dinner's on the house, folks. My pleasure."

"Please," Harmon said, "we appreciate that, but we can't accept. My job, you know."

Ost laughed. "That's why I offered. Maybe I'll be in a jam some time, selling wine to a minor. And you'll go easy on me." He left, with his sense of humor.

"He'll be back when the entrées come," Pete predicted. "Now look, I'm an honest man." He laid a five-dollar bill before her. "You owe me forty dollars for four defense objections upheld and I owe you forty-five for nine denied. When I lose, I pay."

Serena pocketed the bill with a distant look. "Tell me you didn't know your witness had phony credentials, Pete."

"Of course I didn't know. Rooney screwed up. But I wish she had told me she wasn't a psychologist."

"You're off the hook, Pete. It was the Hangman's job to make sure she was qualified." She laughed. "Hull stiffed you. He knew Roth was open to attack before she testified and he didn't object. He walked you into it."

Harmon was chagrined. "But Jacko cleaned up the act. You heard the charge to the jury, that she's still an expert. That's not reversible, but I agree it wasn't evenhanded."

They ordered and Serena wanted to know what the hearing on Saturday morning would be about.

"Our favorite judge is freaking out about whether Teresa Vane was really a surprise witness. He wants to grill Hull's private eye, Tony Sgueglia."

"What the hell is the matter with Mathes? He should have doubled as the prosecutor and you could have taken a vacation."

"He ordered me to investigate Vane and I told him he wasn't my commander. So he's doing it himself."

"Something's got to be done about Mathes," Wiley said. "By the way, Peter." He heard the Peter. "I've reached a verdict in the case, and it has nothing to with whether Laurie Coles is innocent or guilty."

Harmon shook his head. "She didn't get a fair trial and you are now going to give me three reasons."

"More like six or eight. The Hangman mishandled the case. Nothing personal, sweetheart, but Coles should get a reversal."

He was smiling. "How do you know she'll be found guilty?"

Her smile was malicious. "You'll soon find out. Here comes our dinner and your alternate juror, on schedule."

They received their bibs as Ost sat down and wasted no time. "They'll have it wrapped by noon tomorrow."

Harmon's suspicion that it would not be necessary to ask questions was confirmed as the owner signaled for a beer.

"Hull did a good job for what's her name. I thought the judge would shoot him a couple of times. But it's a loser."

Wiley had a question. "How did you feel about that witness, Mr. Ost? The psychologist who isn't a psychologist."

He scowled. "She's a hustler. I was talking to my lawyer about the case, and I told him she drums up business by deciding everybody's been molested."

Harmon asked, "Would that have affected your thinking in the jury room?"

He nodded. "I hate fakes. It made me wonder. But I didn't hear much excitement about it. The jurors didn't like it, but they say so many experts and mothers and kids couldn't be wrong. And everybody wouldn't be making it all up."

Wiley asked, "What about the missing teacher? Didn't she give strong testimony?"

He drank his beer nonstop. "I haven't lifted a glass all week. The thing about the teacher is, you might believe her, except." He stopped and looked away from Wiley.

She almost laughed. You can say it, Mr. Ost. I'm a big girl."

"Yeah, well. The trouble is, that thing she said the cop told her, that maybe she was a lookout for what's her name." He looked around and lowered his voice. "See, the jury thinks Coles is a, you know, she hits from the other side of the plate."

Wiley felt her anger. "A lesbian?"

"You got it. There's a kind of look to her. So the jury is figuring, maybe, you know, the two of them."

Harmon did not confess he had wondered about that.

Wiley asked, as offhandedly as she could, "How do you know the way they feel, Mr. Ost? She only testified this afternoon."

He grinned. "It ran through the box like fire, the second she got off the stand. It started at one end and went around."

Harmon felt uncomfortable and wanted to leave, but Wiley had another question, and it would be the big one. "Have you figured out how you would have voted, Mr. Ost?"

He was genuinely surprised. "What else? Almost everybody knew she was guilty from the beginning. Look, the only reason I said the jury wouldn't be back until noon is because of a couple of windbags. They love to hear themselves. But there's another one in there, in the second chair, who may shut them up." He responded to a shout. "Hey, I'm holding things up at the cash register. Good talking to you. You sure I can't buy dinner?"

They declined, told Lars Ost how fascinating it had been chatting with him, and left.

"Let's walk down to the river," Harmon said.

"Makes you wonder, doesn't it, Pete? About juries."

"Tell me a better way," he said. "A jury of lawyers?"

At his office, Harry Hull was working on the idea that Polly Lennon might enjoy dinner with him. But first he had to find McGonigle, who had a date with Justice Mathes in the morning. Corky was not at channel 22 and no one knew where he was, so Hull went out and cased a few bars but suddenly found himself at a street phone, dialing the Book Nook. "Polly," he said.

"Harry!"

"I wanted to call you."

"I was hoping you would."

"I can't have something to eat."

"You can't. But you thought *I* could."

"Well. I thought."

"I want to have something to eat."

"I can't do it."

"Okay."

"Oh, Christ, there goes Corky. I'll call you back, Polly!"

There was McGonigle, stopped by a red light. Hull climbed in and told him about the command to appear in Mathes's chambers in the morning. "I think you'd better have a lawyer, Corky, and it can't be me."

"I don't need a lawyer. I don't molest children. That was a joke, Harry. So who's my lawyer?"

Hull had an idea. "Wiley. She's smart and right up your alley— she hates Mathes. And isn't it great? Pete Harmon's chick? I'm serious, Corky. Serena Wiley. Now let me out near my car. I don't want to be seen in public with you. So be there in the morning. I gave him my word that you'd show up. And don't start up that freedom-of-the-press jazz, at least until he asks you something."

"I'll be there, Harry, but I can't guarantee my conduct."

Hull parked before the Book Nook and watched Polly display- ing a volume to a customer, explaining it, and making a sale. When the man left, she was alone and he went in.

"Polly," he said, "you saw the performance and I have only one question for you. Can I tell a fairy tale?"

She kissed him. "You pulled it off." She backed away and said, "I don't know if it will help, but the jury was listening to every word. Most of them, anyway. There was a man in the second row with pens in his pocket, and his eyes were closed most of the time. But the women in the first two seats were paying close attention."

Hull laughed. "Choosing a jury is like picking a horse. You study the form until you get a headache and then somebody says, 'Look here. Drink Up! What a name for a horse!' You laugh be- cause that's silly. And then Drink Up wins."

That reminded Polly. "I don't really want to eat. I've started a diet."

"So have I," Hull said. "Just now. Let's go for a drive."

The sun was altering the color of the river ten miles above Hudson Ferry and he pulled off into a lookout. They watched the surface of the water change by tiny degrees from bright gold to pale yellow. Then, as a breeze whipped up, frills of white ruffled a dark blue that finally became black. The peacefulness of it all was disrupted as a high-sprung jeepster with an elevated front bumper chugged into the scenic area; its engine quit and tranquil- ity returned.

"Polly," Hull said, "I'm scared."

She said nothing.

"I should start work right now on Laurie's appeal. You're right. The verdict will be guilty. But I'm not up to it. I've never done an appeal."

She remained silent.

"I'm not even sure where to start. So Jacko didn't give her a fair trial. But you can't just say that. You have to lay it out, and cite earlier decisions to back you up. It's like going to school all over again, and it's not fair to Laurie."

Polly finally spoke. "How did you feel when you first took on this case?"

He thumped the steering wheel. "Like somebody had it in for me. Handing me a case where everybody was against me before I even went into court." He turned to her. "I thought Laurie was guilty. Look, I'm ashamed. I tried to get her to plead guilty. All right, now you know."

"You mean you thought she didn't have a chance of winning?"

"All right. That makes it sound a little better. But I was really thinking of everything but her. Like city contracts. So at first I wasn't even all that serious about it. But Jacko started giving me a hard time from the first minute. Giving her a hard time, I mean. I'm only the lawyer. And I started thinking. That wasn't right. Am I going to sit here and let him act that way? So I forgot about the contracts and the hard time I was getting all over town and I declared war. But now I'm not sure how to handle the rest. Do you know what I'm saying, Polly?"

She leaned forward and stared into the blackness of the river. The breeze had died and there was no moon. She said, "There's a great poem by Browning. 'Bishop Blougram's Apology,' about a man of the cloth who has lost the faith but goes on talking as if he still believes. Then he sees the light. There's a good line in it, Harry. 'When the fight begins within himself, a man's worth something.' "

"Jesus! How do you know things like that, Polly?"

"I read," she said. "Let's go to your place. I'll bet it's a wreck."

He pulled out and started down the road to town, amazed by the serenity he felt. Polly was something else. He drove unhurriedly, encountering little traffic behind or ahead, when his mirror suddenly filled with a blaze of blinding light. Swerving, he said, "Where did that crazy bastard come from?"

The beam flicked out and he accelerated. "Let's lose him!" He raced down the road, seeing nothing behind, but had to slow for a bend in the river. At that moment the rear of the car was hit. It jolted forward, then veered toward the river. He released the accelerator and straightened out on the shoulder. "Get out of your belt," he shouted to Polly. "Jump in back, on the floor!"

As she tumbled over the seatback he regained the roadway and pressed the accelerator, straightening the mirror and searching behind him. There was only intense blackness once more. But then the shape of the jeepster appeared. It was approaching fast and now he saw it was the one that had entered the scenic lookout. "Stay down!" he yelled. The high bumper hit, the rear window gave way, and glass flew through the car.

Hull found himself on the wrong side of the pavement and stayed there, fearful of the rocky riverbank, driving as fast as he dared on a road that wandered about. They were still five miles out of town when he heard a whine at the rear and saw the jeepster bearing down at an angle. He wheeled into the right lane, yelling, "Keep your head down, Polly!" It raced by.

They were four miles from town now and he felt secure enough to stay in the right lane. But the grinding whine sounded again and there was the jeepster, lights out, closing in from the left. He waited until their door handles were almost touching, then hit the brake pedal hard. It shot by and he heard the scream of its own brakes. He spun into a U-turn, but suddenly he heard nothing. Looking back, he saw an empty road.

Several hours later the body of Ike Brendelski, father of a Snug Arms child, was recovered from the Hudson River. The alcohol content of his blood was found to be twice the legal limit.

After finishing up with the police, Hull drove his smashed car slowly to his place, where he and Polly had a sandwich and coffee. They went to bed and held each other.

As Harmon and Wiley pulled into their driveway, two men left a car at curbside. "Relax," Harmon said. "It's McGonigle and Hull's private eye."

The newsman told Wiley, "Harry Hull says Jacko wants to see me and I shouldn't be in the same room with him without a lawyer. Are you for hire?"

Wiley asked if he could afford her and they all walked inside, where Harmon decided to lay low and act as bartender. This was not only Serena's party, but he knew what was coming.

And it did, in Corky McGonigle style. "In my open-minded opinion," he said, "Johnson Gillies Mathes is a low form of animal. Whoever sat him on the bench should suffer the torment of the damned."

"At least," Wiley said. "What's the problem?"

McGonigle explained what he expected Mathes to demand from him in the morning and added that if the judge could get it, a slug could dance. However, he conceded, it wouldn't hurt if an attorney were there to watch over him.

Wiley, watching Harmon studying titles in the bookcase, was amused. "I'd be glad to represent you, Mr. McGonigle," she said. "But I think you're being awfully easy on the Hangman."

They finished their scotches and left.

Most of the jurors were subdued during dinner at the Champlain. The exceptions were two who had arranged for the bailiff to comment on the freshness of the club soda as their sparkling white wine was served. Chair Number One, in a peppery mood, went to work on Number Two. "We can discuss the case now, dear." The loan officer ignored her.

"How are you voting?" Ten, the postal clerk, asked One.

"I haven't the faintest. We haven't begun to deliberate. Surely you don't know where you stand?"

The bailiff busied himself with the menu.

"All right," One said, "I'll tell you. The defense has the prosecution's number. You tell kids a story fifty times and they finally get most of it right."

Number Nine lifted his glass, which permitted him to loft his eyes.

Two was willing to let bygone go. "That makes sense. But do you think *nothing* happened?"

"Nothing. They were wound up and they sang, like in that nightingale story."

"It's possible. But could nothing have happened at all?"

"Zero. And the parents steamed each other up, too."

Number Nine had a question. "What about Marla Burney? She sounded as if her head was screwed on, didn't she?"

One signaled for another club soda. "Burney doesn't buy it, but no black family is going to fight this town. She knew she'd be cast out if she didn't go along. And her kid was somewhere between Mars and Jupiter. Laurie was in the bathtub with him at home, but she flew away, so he shot her down. He may be a nice boy to visit, but I wouldn't want to live with him."

Nine felt the time had come to correct One's thinking. "The defense lawyer has been praying for a juror like you. He only needs one, somebody who bounces one way, then the other. Why do you think Coles didn't dare take the stand? She'd have shot herself in the foot. So Hull's only chance was to snare a holdout, an opinionated person who doesn't let the facts get in the way. I guess he's found one."

Two noticed that One was now refusing to look at Nine.

The bailiff tapped his knife against his plate. "Order at the dinner table," he said. "I think we'd better leave this stuff for the morning."

Another jury, this one composed of four court buffs, was too professional to reach on-the-spot decisions. They reviewed their firm opinions for two hours before reaching a verdict of guilty.

Chapter 32

A DELUGE BOMBARDED THE HUDSON VALLEY IN THE WEE HOURS OF SATUR-
day and was still coming down as Serena tuned in channel 22's
early newscast and saw Corky McGonigle with a doomsday face.

"Two big stories," he said. "First, Laurie Coles, defendant in the
Snug Arms molestation case, was seriously injured last night in an
attack that took place behind the criminal courts building. While
she was in police custody."

"Pete!" He rushed in.

"The police did not report the incident until one hour ago,
which gave them about fourteen hours to put an explanation together." McGonigle looked angry. "They say Miss Coles fell
down." The camera closed in. "This correspondent does not mix
opinion and news. The following statement is opinion: I don't
believe the police version and I'm going after the facts."   .

Serena said, "Your fucking police, Mr. D.A."

Harmon said, "I'm going after the facts, too, Corky."

"Enough?" Corky asked. "No. Last night a man in a jeepster
tried to run Harry Hull's car into the river. That man ended up in
the water himself. His name is, or was, Ike Brendelski, and he was
a witness in the Coles case. Attorney Hull and a woman passenger
in his car were unhurt."

Pause. Wiley said, "My God! Polly!"

"Switching to opinion," McGonigle said, "a deadly virus has
crept into our town. Now back to the news. I have a date with
Justice Johnson Gillies Mathes in an hour. He's going to ask me
some questions about the Laurie Coles case and I'm not going to
answer him. And if any of you ever tell me something as a reporter, you can be sure that what you say will be held in confi-

dence. Don't miss 'News at Noon' on twenty-two." He winked. "If I'm not in jail, I'll be here."

As McGonigle gave way to a commercial, Harmon dialed the chief of police and said, "Harmon. This is to notify you that I am opening an investigation into the Coles incident behind the courthouse. I want a *complete* report by nine o'clock Monday morning." He hung up.

They ran through the rain from the kitchen door to the car. The drive was silent until Serena said, "Pete, will we become adversaries in the Coles case?"

"I'm not with Jacko on the Teresa Vane testimony," he said.

She felt a discomfort that occasionally visited. Would they face each other in an all-out legal tussle one day?

In the lobby of the court building they found Hull telling Tony Sgueglia about the ramming attack by Ike Brendelski. Wiley said, "Fear and anxiety make a climate for madmen. How's Polly doing, Harry?"

"All right. A bump or two, but she's good. She's feeling lucky today."

Hull told Harmon that Sgueglia would not be going up to Mathes's chambers. He had only been a conduit, having passed Teresa Vane from Corky to himself without talking to her. Sgueglia had a day of hard labor ahead of him, Hull said, and he had to get started. "I'll explain it to Jacko."

Sgueglia waved and they went upstairs, where they waited fifteen minutes for the judge. His secretary offered coffee, but Wiley declined and the rest followed suit. She did not want Mathes to feel clubby.

Hull was still in shock over the attack on his client. "I want this over with fast," he said. "I've got to get over to the hospital and see Laurie." Then he thought about Sgueglia, who was costing him big money each day, even at a discount. Whatever he discovered now would be too late. The jury was out. But there was the appeal. Okay. After the verdict came in, he would petition the court for funds disbursed and hope for the best.

The rain was still drenching the landscape when Mathes arrived, shaking out his raincoat and combing his wet red hair with his hand. Greeting no one, he buzzed for the inevitable java, then asked McGonigle to identify himself.

Corky turned to Wiley. "Should I answer?"

"If you wish."

"Cornelius McGonigle, newshound."

Mathes turned to Wiley. "Identify yourself."

"Serena Wiley, attorney-at-law, representing Mr. McGonigle."

Mathes gave no indication that he recognized the name. "Do you understand the rules that govern this hearing?"

"I understand out-of-court procedures, sir."

He stared, finally deciding he had not heard impertinence, and asked Hull, "Where is Mr. Sgueglia?"

Hull summoned calmness. "He would be a waste of your time, Your Honor. I will stipulate that Mr. McGonigle called Mr. Sgueglia and asked him to bring Teresa Vane to me, and I will tell you, under oath if you wish, that Mr. Sgueglia did not speak to Miss Vane. Mr. McGonigle talked to her at length."

Mathes worked on his mustache. "Mr. McGonigle, did Teresa Vane speak with you before she took the witness stand in the trial of Laurie Coles?"

"Yes. Listen, Judge, can I videotape this hearing?" Harmon and Hull were astonished, while Wiley was taken up with the effrontery of her client.

Mathes sipped his coffee. "I'll take that as a dumb joke. What did Miss Vane say to you?"

McGonigle replied in a rolling cadence. "I decline to answer on the ground that the First Amendment forbids Congress to make any law that would abridge freedom of speech. It says don't mess with the press, sir, and Congress hasn't. Yet. So I don't have to reveal a privileged communication and I won't."

"This is a special proceeding," Mathes snapped. "And don't you dare lecture me, young man."

"I'll tell you my rights six days a week and twice on Sunday," McGonigle said. "I only came in as a courtesy to Attorney Wiley, and I'll walk out if you get heavy. Sometimes you forget, Jacko. You're *only* a judge."

Wiley intervened. "The law is sort of on my client's side. His exchange with Miss Vane, if there was one, may indeed be privileged."

"Oh, there was an exchange," McGonigle said. "And a lot of it. I'll tell you that much, but no more."

"I have asked you what Miss Vane told you, Mr. McGonigle. I now ask what you told Miss Vane before she testified."

"Same answer, Judge."

"Same grounds, Your Honor," Wiley added.

Mathes stood. "That is not the issue here, Counselor. I am investigating the possibility that unlawful acts occurred in connection with a witness's testimony and I have wide latitude to proceed. You are giving your client poor advice."

"I ask you to apologize for that remark," Wiley said.

Hull entered the fray. "If Miss Vane was coached before she

testified, I would have been the one to do it. But she said under oath that we had just met."

"I did not address you, Mr. Hull."

"Now, Judge," McGonigle said, "don't get mad at Harry. I'm the one Miss Vane talked to. But I won't tell you what she said, or what I said to her."

The district attorney spoke up. "I'm surprised by the absence of a court reporter, Your Honor. I ask that this conversation be transcribed."

"That will not be necessary. Mr. McGonigle, do you understand the questions I have put to you?"

"I do."

Mathes was still standing, and his voice filled the room. "I serve notice that if you do not answer my questions, I will cite you for contempt and have you jailed while a warrant is prepared charging you with obstruction of justice."

McGonigle roared. "Do it! Mathes jails McGonigle! I love it!" He advanced on the desk, extending his hands. "I will not answer you. Cuff me! And let me tape it, Your Honor!"

Mathes buzzed and his secretary walked in. "Get the clerk of the court in here," he told her. The clerk entered and he told her, "You are now the court reporter. Take the following down. 'Mr. McGonigle, you are guilty of contempt and I order you confined to jail until you respond to my questions.' " He added, "That's it. Now get an officer up here."

Wiley rose. "We request a stay, Your Honor."

"Denied."

Harmon, shaking his head, circled the desk and spoke softly to Mathes but was quickly cut off. "Sit down!"

"Are you crazy?" Harmon shouted. "Stop this nonsense!"

Wiley looked perplexed. "I have an emergency, Judge. May I use your phone?"

He pointed to it and walked into the next room. She dialed a number and said, "Good morning, Judge Fisher. Serena Wiley here. . . . Fine, sir. And you? . . . I have an urgent request. Justice Mathes of Princess County Supreme Court has cited my client for contempt and remanded him to jail. His name is Cornelius McGonigle and he is a member of the press. Mr. McGonigle has invoked his First Amendment right against revealing privileged information. I know a full hearing will be required, but since he is highly unlikely to leave the area, I would like to request a stay of execution pending the hearing."

A policeman walked in as Wiley was saying, "Yes, sir, he's here." She told the officer, "Please ask the judge to come in."

Mathes appeared and she handed him the phone. "Judge Arnold Fisher is on emergency call and is sitting in Poughkeepsie, sir. He would like to speak with you."

He seized the phone and Wiley studied the torrent outside as he said, "Mathes here." They watched his face tighten. "The issue is obstruction of justice, sir. It supersedes the press issue." He listened again. "Of course. Yes, sir."

He thrust the phone at Wiley, who listened and then said, "We should make it by eleven thirty. Thank you, Judge Fisher." She hung up and handed Mathes a note. "His address, Your Honor."

"Get out," he said.

They left, but McGonigle lagged behind and they heard him. "Jacko, you're not bright. You've reduced a constitutional issue to an ego-freaking feud and you can't win. Eat it!" He closed the door and joined them at the elevator.

"That was not wise," Wiley said.

He laughed. "I was defending your honor. He wouldn't apologize for saying you were giving me bad advice."

They got into Harmon's car with McGonigle shaking his head. "I'm not sure I like this. I'd get a charge out of sitting in Jacko's jail. What a story!"

Wiley was stern. "There's more involved here than your kicks, Corky. Mathes can't mess with the First Amendment. You owe it to your colleagues to see this thing through in a dignified way. Oh, and leave that fucking camera in the car."

"Yes, Your Honor," McGonigle said.

The rain slowed them and it was almost twenty minutes of noon when they rang Arnold Fisher's bell. He was an elderly, frail man with a weak voice and rimless glasses that dangled from a ribbon. He had been chief judge of the court of appeals for many years and was highly regarded. He was retired, true, but it was no secret that Fisher's views were often sought by his successor.

He accepted apologies for their tardiness and led them haltingly into a study crammed with law books. The room contained a wheeled step ladder, a small-screen television, and an elegant Regency desk before which sat a group of high-backed chairs. Mathes had beaten them there and sat in one.

"Justice Mathes has been here a few minutes," Fisher said, "and we have not discussed the case. We can begin now, but I must say something first. This is an extraordinarily irregular session. You have bypassed the appellate division and come to me, and I am not empowered to hear such disputes. So I must set some ground rules." His reedy voice was difficult to make out. "I am only trying to help and cannot get into the merits of the contempt citation. So we need only cover the broad outlines of the matter. And when we conclude, I may offer advice. I am in no position to hand down rulings. If that is clear to all, please proceed, Justice Mathes."

Corky removed his watch and placed it on the desk, noting that it was a quarter of twelve.

"Thank you, Judge Fisher. Briefly, we concluded a criminal trial in Hudson Ferry yesterday afternoon and the jury is out. However, the defense brought in a last-minute witness who gave exculpatory testimony in a manner that appeared to be carefully rehearsed despite its supposed spontaneity. I asked District Attorney Harmon to investigate the circumstances surrounding the preparation of that testimony and he declined to do so. I am therefore proceeding myself."

"Any disagreement so far?" Judge Fisher asked. Hearing none, he gestured to Mathes.

"After the testimony was given, I learned that the witness, Teresa Vane, had spent time with Mr. McGonigle before she appeared in court. I summoned Mr. McGonigle and asked if he and Miss Vane had spoken to each other and he conceded that they had."

Wiley broke in. "He said without hesitation that they had."

Mathes waved her off. "I asked him what they had discussed and he refused to answer. I intend to apply for a warrant that will charge him with obstruction of justice and meanwhile have cited him for contempt."

Judge Fisher nodded to Wiley.

"My client declined to answer on First Amendment grounds and still does," she said. "The witness went to him as a member of the press and their conversation is protected—"

Mathes interrupted. "She did not approach McGonigle as a newsman. I have reason to believe she sought his advice, and I want to know what he told her to say on the stand. His refusal to answer my questions constitutes a clear obstruction of the judicial process."

"That's blather," McGonigle said. "What I mean, Judge, is that he has no evidence that the witness came to me for advice, which she didn't." His watch showed ten minutes of twelve.

Fisher said, "Thank you all. I now understand the basis for the contempt citation and for Mr. McGonigle's refusal to respond, and I suggest we move on. Would you explain, Justice Mathes, why it is urgent that this man be detained immediately, prior to a full hearing?"

"Yes, sir. I am going to place the witness under bond to dissuade her from leaving the state before this matter is resolved. And I don't want her to have contact with Mr. McGonigle in the meantime. Furthermore, I will issue an order forbidding Defense Counsel Hull to be in contact with the witness."

"I'll fight that!" Hull said. "She's my witness."

Judge Fisher held up a hand. "Don't be premature, please. You're shaking your head, Mr. McGonigle. Do you wish to say something? Something constructive, sir?"

"Yes, sir. This controversy will be a dead mackerel in another four minutes."

No one understood the remark and Fisher let it go, turning his attention to Wiley. "Counselor, what is your response to Justice Mathes's argument that there is a need for the immediate detention of Mr. McGonigle?"

She was staring at McGonigle's watch, wondering what her client was up to. "We've heard two issues, sir. One is that Justice Mathes fears the witness may leave the jurisdiction. I spoke to her this morning and have her assurance she will remain in Hudson Ferry until the question of her testimony is resolved." I will guarantee her availability. As for Justice Mathes's second point, that he doesn't want the witness to speak to either Mr. McGonigle or Mr. Hull, I fail to see how she can be silenced. She can speak to anyone she wishes to unless Mr. Mathes can find a way of putting her into solitary confinement without visiting privileges. And I doubt that he can. The trial is over and Mr. Hull can talk to Miss Vane as often as he wishes. If his client is convicted, he will want her assistance in an appeal. Her testimony raised the possibility that Miss Coles did not receive a fair trial. The witness said under oath that she was threatened with arrest if she did not provide evidence to support the charges against Coles. So I am not challenging the judge's contempt citation at this time, merely saying that there should be a stay of execution pending a formal hearing."

McGonigle rose and told Fisher. "Please listen to me, sir. I am not a nut. I'm a careful newsman and no one has ever called me a liar. If I may turn on your television, you'll have the whole story" —he picked up his watch—"beginning in ninety seconds. If you don't agree five minutes from now that we've all been spinning our wheels, I'll go directly to jail with no argument, sir."

Judge Fisher, tilting precariously in his swivel chair, turned to Wiley. "Shall I take your client seriously, Counselor? Would you like to confer with him?"

She led McGonigle to the other side of the room, where they whispered animatedly. Then Wiley returned and said, "I urge you to grant Mr. McGonigle's request, sir."

He nodded and McGonigle switched on the miniature TV and tuned in channel 22 just as he appeared on the screen, seated at the anchor desk. "Corky McGonigle with a 'News at Noon' special," he said. "It's all on tape." The camera pulled back and revealed two women and two men seated across from him. Logos came and went and they heard him say, "The woman across from me, on my left, is Teresa Vane, who was a teacher at the Snug Arms nursery school. Next to her is Ginny Bracci, our receptionist here at channel twenty-two." He pointed to a clock on the studio wall. "It is now five minutes past three. Ginny, what time did Miss Vane walk up to your desk this afternoon?"

The receptionist looked puzzled. "Five minutes ago. Just before three."

"Who did she ask for?"

"For you, Corky."

"Thank you." He pointed to the security guard. "Paul, were you in the reception area when Miss Vane walked in?"

"Yes, sir."

"Is Ginny right? Miss Vane arrived just five minutes ago?"

He nodded.

"Say yes or no," McGonigle said. "Did Miss Vane arrive just five minutes ago?"

"Yes. What's going on?"

"What did you do when Miss Vane asked to see me, Ginny?"

"I came in and told you. Oh, my God! Corky, are the cameras on?"

"They are. And what did I say?"

She giggled. "You screamed for David."

"Thank you." He looked into the camera. "David is channel twenty-two's news director. What did you do, David?"

David took a quick swipe at his hair. "I came in a minute ago and you said one of the missing Snug Arms teachers was in the studio and you wanted to be sure somebody wasn't setting you up."

"And?"

"And you told Ginny to bring Miss Vane in and asked all of us to stay here."

"When was that?"

"Oh, two minutes ago."

"What did Miss Vane say when she came in?"

"She said Laurie Coles was innocent and she wanted to tell her story."

"Did she say anything else, or did I say anything to her?"

David laughed. "You said what you always say. 'Action! Camera!'"

"Thank you, Ginny, David, and Paul. Go have a drink on me. Now, Miss Vane, what story do you have for Hudson Ferry?"

McGonigle lowered the volume. "Miss Vane then told me what she testified to later in court. Enough?"

Judge Fisher nodded and McGonigle snapped off the TV. "I refused to show the tape to Justice Mathes because I was sure he'd seize it before we could put it on the air." He turned to Mathes. "That's what I mean by freedom of the press."

Judge Fisher rocked back and forth and in the silence they heard the rain letting up. Then he said, "Mr. Harmon, you're the district attorney and you've hardly spoken. Why is that?"

Harmon shook his head. "I'm not a party to the contempt citation, sir. I'm here out of courtesy to Justice Mathes. And I agree, for whatever it's worth, that Mr. McGonigle is not obliged to answer his questions. To tell the truth, Your Honor, I'm not really sure why I'm here. I have no argument with Miss Vane's right to testify."

Judge Fisher rocked again. "Justice Mathes?"

Mathes had his eyes fixed on the exquisite desk. "I will think this matter over. Meanwhile, I will stay the contempt order."

"I think the rain has stopped," Fisher said. "I hope everyone has a pleasant afternoon."

As the four of them left, Mathes remained in his seat.

McGonigle bounded out to the car. "Fisher's going to carve him up now. He should feed him to the raccoons."

Hull, thinking of Laurie Coles lying in a hospital bed, was silent all the way back to Hudson Ferry.

Serena and Pete were subdued as well. She felt as if a magnet was drawing her ever deeper into the case of Laurie Coles; Pete felt its force pulling at her.

Chapter 33

BREAKFAST DID LITTLE TO LIGHTEN UP CHAIR ONE. NINE HADN'T knocked. Not that she wanted him to. She wouldn't have let him in. But he hadn't knocked. She had wanted to say, "Get lost." She hadn't slept well.

They were strangers in a crowd as the jurors were driven a rainy three blocks from the Champlain to Deliberation Summit. One and Nine sat apart, which did not escape Two. If either of them ever asked Third Federal Savings for a loan, the meaning of scrutiny would take on a new dimension. In the circumstances, she took the liberty, as they arrived in the jury room, of urging Number One along. "Why don't we get started?" She received a glare from the foreperson.

The bailiff, cheerful because he would get a vacation day and a half for working on a Saturday, checked around, making certain everyone had a pad and pencil, then approached the door and said, "I don't suppose you'll be needing lunch today, folks? I'm sure you'll have it wrapped up this morning." He smiled and closed the door behind him.

One said, "He's speaking for the hurry-up judge. Look, why don't we take a quick vote? It'll give us a clue."

"No," Two said. "We haven't reviewed the evidence yet."

"Does anyone else object?" One asked.

Except for a yawn, there was silence in the paneled room.

One smiled. "You're outvoted, dear."

"Voting has nothing to do with it. The rules say we have to review the evidence."

"You are a *pain*," One said. But they reviewed the evidence for a half hour. Then Two agreed to a vote.

The foreperson went around the long table and heard unanimous guiltys except for Two and Nine, who gave no response. "Okay," she said, stretching out the *O* and clipping off the *kay*, "so a lot of you like wound-up nightingales. Well, since we're two votes short, it doesn't make any difference which way I go. So I won't say anything right now."

A storm broke. "What the hell?" shouted Five, the advertising copywriter. "You get us to put ourselves on the line and then you clam up?"

"And what did that remark about the nightingales mean?" asked Eight, the retired secretary. "You don't have to be insulting, you know."

"Free speech," said One.

Eight, aged and slight, rose. "If you don't act properly, I'm going to tell the judge I want to be sent home."

"Sorry," One said. "Anyone else?"

Silence ended the squall.

"Listen," said Four, the construction man. "We can't let those kids down. This stuff is going on everywhere. You hear about it all the time. Teachers have to stop monkeying with kids and we have to send a message."

"Good point," One said. "But what do other cases have to do with whether Laurie Coles monkeyed around at Snug Arms?"

Four got up and circled the table slowly as Five spoke up. "You people like it, being locked up in a two-bit hotel room? Is this a vacation? Let's get back to the evidence. But can I say something first?"

"Who's stopping you?"

"Okay. Picking the kids' testimony apart will waste time. It's garbage. Secret rooms and cutting off squirrels' heads. We'll still have to get to the big question. Did something happen at Snug Arms or didn't it? Well, of course it did. So many people wouldn't get together and make it up. That's too crazy to think about."

"She's guilty," said Four, still circling.

"We have to look at the children's testimony," said Ten, the postal clerk. "We can't get around that. The kids are what this case is all about."

Five slapped the table. "Here we go again!"

"Let's listen to the kids," said Eleven, the grocer. "Who wants to see the video?"

Seven hands were raised and One went to the door and knocked.

"I don't believe it," said Five.

The bailiff sighed but rolled in a small monitor and a VCR. He placed a finger on START and said, "Here's the rule. If you see some of it, you see all of it." He pointed and winked. "But if it gets too loud, here's the volume switch."

There was Caroline Robertson in the judge's chair saying, "Boo!" into the camera. This time when she was confronted with the confusion about who put jam on whom and ran around the room, she did not get a laugh. She was followed by Bonnie Strand and the ice-pop stick.

"She's twisting her hair," said Five. "Does that mean she's telling the truth?" When Bonnie said Laurie did it and then asked if Laurie did it, Five asked, "Does that mean she told a lie the first time? We're wasting our time, I tell you!"

Time went by and on went the tape, with comments interspersed. Billy and poop cakes and Laurie urinating in a cup. Billy drank the urine and it made him sick. No, what he meant was that he was sick at home that day.

"Where is this getting us?" Five asked.

"Hit the volume," One told Five. He did.

"That didn't do a damn thing for us, did it?" Five asked. "We can argue this stuff for a week. But how would little kids know anything about sticking things in vaginas unless it happened? So however they tell the stories, we know damned well she did it. Let's vote and get out of here."

One held up her hand. "It's not that easy. We can't just walk in and say guilty. Of what? We have to say yes or no to every count of the indictment. So we'd better look at it."

"It's high time." Everyone looked at Nine, who had finally broken his silence. "Those kids would have been more sensible than we've been." He looked at his watch. "It's almost noon and we haven't read the counts yet."

Without acknowledging Nine, One went through the indictment. The moment she finished, Five said, "Let's vote."

"Why not?" She pointed to Two, who said, "I don't think she got as fair a trial as she could have. The defense should have been allowed to interview the children, just like the prosecution. But I suppose it would have come out the same way. So I guess I say guilty on all the counts."

"Got your courage up, did you?" said One. She pointed to Three. "Guilty."

Four. "Guilty."

When she reached Nine, she said, "And how do you vote? Did they prove it, prove it?"

Nine said, "Two and two equals four. Guilty."

Ten, Eleven, and Twelve agreed.

"So," One said, "eleven votes for guilty. If I say guilty it's over, and if I vote not guilty, we sit here. Well, well. Do you remember the last thing the judge told us, friends? In order to find Laurie Coles guilty, we have to be convinced beyond a reasonable doubt. I'm not, and I'll tell you why."

"Shit," Five said, not too softly.

The foreperson brought him to heel. "Watch your language." She smiled. "I started out thinking Coles was guilty as hell. You knew how I felt when we first sat down. You thought I was horsing around. Well, I wasn't. The truth is, I still think she's probably guilty. But a doubt has crept in."

"A reasonable doubt?" Five asked. "Or do you just like going the other way? What's with you? Do you always have to be the center of attention?"

One would not let it pass. "Do you want to talk about me or the case?"

"Sorry," Five said. "But I think . . ."

"I haven't noticed you think yet," One replied.

"What's the matter with you?" Two asked. "Why don't you let him finish what he's saying?"

"Because he bores me. All right, if you care what my doubt is, listen. Remember that last witness? The missing teacher? Up to that point I was only thinking how convenient it all was. Moms and pops get up there and shock us and the experts show up and say, goodness, this is the worst case I've ever seen. I'd like to hear their testimony on other witness stands. Is it always the worst case they've ever seen? Forget nightingales. Are they parrots? And then the little ones come running in and tell us the awful things Laurie did. It was all so pat. So I had my doubts. But as the judge said, any old doubt isn't enough. *Reasonable* doubt. So I was going to send Coles up anyway. But then this teacher, Teresa Vane, testified that when she told a cop she had never seen Coles do anything to the kids, he asked her if she'd been Coles's lookout. Now, that got me mad."

"May I interrupt you?" It was quiet Six, the woman who fashioned costume jewelry. "I was disturbed by that, too. I want to be fair, and I know we've got somebody's future in our hands. But how do we know Miss Vane was telling the truth?"

One was gentle. "We don't *know*. And we'll never really *know* whether Coles is innocent or guilty. All we'll know for sure is what we thought and how we voted. But all right. Vane sounded convincing, and I noticed that the prosecutor didn't go after her. He looked like he swallowed his gum. And then the defense read us something from an exhibit. Remember? The very next day after the cop threatened to make a defendant out of Vane, the detective, Garafolo, asks a kid if he ever saw Laurie and Terry do things like Mommy and Daddy do in the bedroom. Well, son-of-a-bitch!

Excuse me. I don't think the police ran their investigation in a professional way. It's not up to them to decide who's guilty. But they tried to stick Coles from the start, and this town can stand on its head before I'll change my mind. I can live somewhere else, too. But do you see what I mean? That whole business changed my doubt to the reasonable kind. What do you think of that?"

One looked around, passing Nine quickly, until Four spoke. "They're butches. One was doing the other one, if you know what I mean. And you know those people. They stick together."

"I don't know the faintest thing about those people. Are you a psychologist, sir, like that Amanda Roth? The phony?"

Eleven, a grocery clerk, asked the foreperson if there was a chance she might change her mind. One replied, "As soon as hell freezes over. Meanwhile, I want to hear Teresa Vane's testimony again."

They went to lunch, dispirited, and while walking by the newsstand in the hotel lobby, Number One lagged behind and detoured. Minutes later the jurors knew about the courthouse attack on Laurie Coles, and about how Ike Brendelski had died while trying to run attorney Harry Hull into the river.

Chapter 34

PETE HARMON LEARNED EARLY ON SATURDAY AFTERNOON THAT THE GENeral Hospital laboratory had failed to detect any illegal compounds in the substance found on the person of Michael Strand. The amount submitted for testing, the laboratory said, was insufficient to yield a conclusive determination.

Harmon hung up on Assistant D.A. Barnard Rooney and found Serena on her lofty outdoor perch, closing out her reading of the summations in the Laurie Coles trial. "Love," he said, "something's going on backstage. Behind the scenery of the trial."

"You've noticed, sweetheart?"

"I'm noticing. Look. Mickey Strand walks into the courtroom with a gun full of bullets. He wants to shoot Laurie Coles. Barney Rooney asks the grand jury to indict him and they don't. Strange? Rooney says hang on, I'll be back with proof of coke in his possession. But the jurors say their term is expiring and they don't want to hang around. Meanwhile the shrinks decide Strand was crazy when he walked into court, but he's as sane as they are now. Strange? And none of it makes the slightest difference because the lab says it can't find any evidence of drugs. Am I paranoid?"

"Paranoia isn't all bad, Pete. And while you're at it, what do you make of the fact that you still haven't received your reappointment?"

"Thank you. That's another one. They tell me I'm a great guy but not that I'm D.A. for four more years. Strange? And I'm sure it hasn't escaped you that Jacko would like to do me in. Do I see a pattern?"

She was amused by a thought. "Did you notice Mathes looking back and forth from you to me in his office this morning? And again when we were down at Judge Fisher's? I was reading his mind. This chick is the D.A.'s girlfriend and she's giving me a hard time over the Coles case. What's going on here? The Hangman wanted to jump all over you."

"Jacko has lost whatever objectivity he ever had. The man is hopeless."

She was shading her sensitive eyes from the afternoon sun. "Would you lower the awning, please? I want to talk to you about something important, Peter."

Peter. He cranked the awning out over the widow's walk and sat down. "You want to get married."

She laughed. "I take the Fifth. It's not a great time to bring this up, sweetheart. You've got a lot on your mind. But it wouldn't be fair not to tell you. You know you'll get a conviction against Coles. Well, I'd like to pass Harry Hull a tip or two for his appeal. Now, don't get mad."

He wasn't exactly neutral. "Me, mad? Jesus! You want to do the appeal for the other side? Why should I be mad?"

"I didn't say that. It's that Harry has very little background in criminal law and no help. He could use some."

He conceded, if not wholeheartedly. "Okay, what are you going to zap me on, love?"

She shook her head. "You wouldn't want an unfair advantage, would you?"

"Do what you have to do. But I'll be rooting against you."

She rose. "It wasn't an easy decision. But Mathes didn't let Coles defend herself. He's a disgrace to the bench. Now tell me you mean it—no hard feelings."

"Almost none. Where are you going?"

"Downtown. I want to look in on Polly." Serena drove off feeling lousy. She had not lied, but it was the first time she had told Pete anything less than the whole truth.

Polly had a bruised cheek and a splint on her left wrist, but it was only sprained, she said. "Serena, it was the oddest thing. When the first bump came and I saw what was happening, I decided we were going to die. I'm scared when I think about how calm I was. When Harry told me to get in the back, I just jumped over the seat without thinking about it and lay there, hoping he was going to be all right."

She went to the door and locked it. "Come here," she said, leading the way back to a tiny office whose floor was stacked with books and required careful navigation. She poured tea and said, "How do you size up Harry, Serena?"

Wiley laughed. "Girl talk?" But she knew Polly was not in a flippant mood. "I'll tell you if you'll tell me where I can find him."

"I know where he is. Now be honest."

"Okay. He strikes me as someone who walked into the biggest crisis of his life without knowing it was there." She stopped. "You said be honest now."

Polly nodded.

"I don't know if he really wanted to fight or if he saw that he couldn't get out of it without fighting. Anyway, he got stuck with the worst possible case and put up a terrific scrap."

Polly was excited. "He did a good job, didn't he?"

Wiley smiled. "I might not have done everything the way he did, but that's lawyer talk. Lawyers are quibblers. Listen, he not only had heavy charges to fight, but he was up against the Hangman. Yes, Harry put it on the line. But he's going to lose. You know that."

"I've known it from the beginning." She smiled. "You're still being honest, Serena. Do you think you could have won?"

"Never. The jury's out but the verdict is in. But hold on, Polly. What are these questions for? Is something going on?"

The owner of the Book Nook stood up and shouted, "I'm in love! I'm in love, Serena!"

Wiley felt the flow of a current. It was the way she felt about Pete Harmon. "Tell me about it."

They neglected the tea as Polly scrambled for words. "Something must have happened to Harry way back when. He thinks he's got the best second-rate mind in the world. He's been coming into the shop for a long time. He pretends he's looking at books, but he's peeking at me. What he doesn't know is that I peek back. It's like playing tag in the book racks. For a long time he was afraid to talk to me, as if he'd say the wrong thing and I'd think he was a horse's ass. But a couple of nights ago he walked in and asked me about fairy tales, of all things."

Wiley was tickled. " 'The Nightingale.' I wondered how he got on to that. It was perfect, Polly!"

She winked and feigned modesty. "I know. Then we went out and had a good time and he opened up and talked about himself and, Serena, I've never been in love and I'm in love!"

They hugged and laughed, and Wiley became serious. "Where can I find him?"

"He left five minutes before you got here." She dialed a number and said, "Sally, is Harry still there?" She listened and said, "Tell him to sit there for five minutes, will you?"

She told Wiley, "Sally says he's been making a speech about the Founding Fathers and driving customers away. You're going to help him, aren't you, Serena? Wow!"

"I think he's a good guy with the deck stacked against him," Wiley said.

Sitting alone in a booth at Speedy Sally's, Hull was surprised when Wiley walked in. "The news has spread," he said. "Polly gave me this terrific book on how hard the framers worked to protect people from the power of the state." He showed her the book. "I've been giving readings from it, but I'm not deaf from the applause."

She sat down and ordered tea. "I'm going to get a court order to keep Harry out of this place," Sally said. "Will you get it for me, Harry?" She laughed uproariously and retreated to the far end of the diner.

Wiley saw that Hull was strung out. She remembered her first appearance before the Supreme Court, where she argued an appeal from a death-penalty conviction. She was in a room at the Hay-Adams and was getting her things together when she dropped her hairbrush. Then she banged an ankle against the bed frame. Tears rushed to her eyes as she slipped into her skirt and the zipper stuck. She finally checked out and, ignoring the taxis in front of the hotel, walked rapidly, trying to calm herself. When she reached the Supreme Court she discovered that her appeal brief and notes were in her suitcase instead of her briefcase. She argued nervously and the decision went against her and the prisoner was executed two months later.

"You've got the jury jitters," she told Hull.

He drank his coffee in a series of gulps. "And I'm lost. I saw Laurie this afternoon, in the hospital, and she's bad. Listen, if they can do this to her—and you know damn well the cops set it up— think of what they'll do to her in the big place." He yawned. "I'll tell you the truth. After I saw Laurie I went to my office and reviewed the case. Don't give me any stories now. That jury is going to get her and everybody knows it. So I started outlining the appeal and I couldn't do it. I don't know the case law, the childhood exceptions to the hearsay rules, and all that."

He wiped his forehead and yelled, "Turn up the air conditioner, Sally! I'll pay for it." They heard a sparse laugh.

"Maybe I can suggest a line of attack," Wiley said.

He looked up from an empty cup. "Hey! You're the one who put me on to the private eye. Talk!"

"One," she said. "Access. There was no reason you couldn't have had your own experts, excuse the expression, interview the children. They could have been watched every step of the way. So she was deprived of due process. You got your objection on the record, so you can use it. You might work on that. I think I've got the case law."

"Access," he said. "All right."

"Now, confrontation. Remember *Maryland versus Craig?* The High Court said that trial judges must determine that each child, individually, might be harmed by emotional stress if required to face the defendant by testifying in open court. Mathes just said they'd all appear on closed-circuit TV. And you reserved your right of appeal on that one, too."

"Confrontation. Okay." He was scribbling on a napkin.

"Experts who aren't experts. Amanda Roth. Mathes qualified her."

"Right."

"I wouldn't spend a lot of time on the hearsay stuff, like the parents testifying to what their children told them. The hearsay rules have been banged around in these cases. I'd put it low on the list."

He looked up. "You're right, Serena. Check. Sally! What the hell do I have to do to get more coffee?"

"And the manipulation of the children. Leading questions and coaxing. Coercion and planting of ideas and the defendant's name in their minds."

Hull put down his pen. "All right, I've got it. But I want to ask you something." He waited while Sally banged his coffee down. "Why are you doing this? I mean." He gulped the coffee. "What about you and Harmon?"

Wiley was expecting it. "You're forgetting. You asked me that a few days ago and I told you Pete's Pete and I'm Serena. But you're not carrying a grudge, are you?"

Hull pushed the coffee away. "No." He smiled. "Pete was as fair as a D.A. can be."

"I agree with you." She reached into her purse and handed him a sheet. It was a typed summary, with case citations, of the points she had made.

She stood up. "I have a fair vocabulary," she said, "but it doesn't quite meet the need here. The best way to say it is that you've done a ballsy job, Harry, but it would take a miracle to win on the trial level. Still, on appeal, win or lose, you can show that Mathes pisses on the justice system."

Hull stood up. "Thanks, Serena."

"And there's someone else you might want to give a different sort of attention to. I'm talking about Polly. There's a person really worth thinking about."

After Wiley left, Harmon cranked back the awning and sunned himself for five minutes, until four thirty. Then he went inside and phoned Bob Kirk, chairman of the Princess County Board of Supervisors.

"I'm fresh out of gin," he said. "How about asking me over for a quick one, Bob?" He did not laugh. "An ounce and a half."

Kirk did not respond immediately and Harmon tapped a fingernail against the mouthpiece. Then he heard, "I'd love to have you over, Pete, but there are people here right now."

Harmon said, "I'll tell you what, Bob. I have to run an errand near your place. I'll stop by in a half hour and ring the bell. If company's still there, don't answer and I'll go away. How does that sound?"

Hesitation, followed by what might have been a laugh. "Yes, Pete. Sure."

He drove along the riverbank and at five climbed the slope and pulled into Kirk's empty driveway. The door opened and the supervisor, bald and round, greeted him with an explanation that the guests had just left.

Harmon received his gin and asked, "Who's going to be the new district attorney, Bob?"

Kirk remained standing. "What are you talking about?"

"Will it be Barnard Rooney? The one who couldn't get an indictment on the man who barged into court with a loaded thirty-eight? I'll make you an offer, Bob. I'll drop the whole thing if you'll answer some questions that are bugging me. Who intervened for Mickey Strand with the grand jury? And who got the lab to say it couldn't find any drugs on Strand? The only one I can think of is Mathes. But if so, why? My imagination is working and I'm thinking that Mickey might have something on Jacko. Do you think I should ask Mr. Strand?"

Kirk was too calm and spoke too softly. "Pete, you sound as if you're asking for trouble."

"I guess I am. And was the Strand matter worked out last Wednesday afternoon, after Jacko canceled the afternoon session of the trial and played a round of golf with Barney Rooney at the Rhinebeck Club?"

"I don't know anything about that. Cut it out, Pete. You know better than this."

"Where's my reappointment, Bob?"

Snappy time had arrived. "I don't think this is the time or place to discuss that matter."

"Okay, here's the deal. You should be able to round up your supervisors by nine o'clock Monday morning and get a yes or no in five minutes. My record is not exactly a mystery around here. So if I haven't been confirmed by nine thirty on Monday, consider that I have resigned as of one minute later. You'll need a new D.A.

And I may not keep my mouth shut." He grinned. "Maybe I'll run for chairman of the board of supervisors."

He walked out, not having disturbed the gin.

Serena had returned, and her reaction to the news did not surprise him. "I hope you resign."

He felt giddy. "If I do, will you marry me?"

"I've been taking your proposals seriously, Pete. Let's keep talking." She was cooling him out. "What will you do all day if you're not district attorney?"

She was roasting duck and thumbing through the index of a cookbook. Dill, dip, doughnuts, dressing, duck(ling). He could taste it. "Ask me what ticked off Bob Kirk the most, love?"

"What ticked off Bob Kirk the most, sweetheart?"

"I told him I was wondering if Jacko had butted into grand jury proceedings, when they didn't return a gun indictment against Mickey Strand."

Her eyes widened. "What made you say that, Pete?"

"I told you I thought something was going on backstage in this town. Didn't you wonder why Strand wasn't charged?" He gave her a big grin. "You could have defended him."

"Cut it out. Tell me what you're talking about."

"Get your transcript."

"Watch the bird," she said. "And don't baste it."

"Baste? Don't worry."

When she returned with the document, he flipped through it and said, "Mickey Strand told Mathes, 'You know my name.' And he called Mathes a son-of-a-bitch. Forget the gun. Can you see Jacko letting anyone get away with that in open court?"

She shook her head. "So you think there might be something between them?"

"I don't know. I'm guessing. More and more I'm guessing."

"Do you think you're going to be D.A. after Monday morning, Pete?"

"What does unemployment insurance pay these days?"

The duck equaled the creations of the great chefs and the wine was brilliant. They talked on and called it an early Saturday night.

In bed, Pete said, "Good-night, snapdragon."

"Why that?"

"Because when I pinch your ass, your mouth opens, like a snapdragon. Don't you know anything about flowers?"

Her mouth opened and their legs twisted around each other. A kiss began that would not quit and he threw his arms around her and lifted her over him, but she suddenly gasped. "My God, Pete!

Do you realize what you said?" Disengaging herself, she ran to the telephone and dialed Hull.

"Harry. Put that fellow Sgueglia on Mathes. See if anything was ever going on between him and Mickey Strand. I'll talk to you tomorrow."

She returned to bed. "Where were we, Pete? Where's that funny place between your teeth?"

Chapter 35

SUNDAY BREAKFAST WAS CHILLED BY CHAIR NUMBER EIGHT'S ANNOUNCE-ment to the bailiff. "I want to go to church."

Number Five's spoon reached the skin of his grapefruit. "And I want to go home. But we can't until we reach a verdict."

"She has a right to go to church," One said.

"That's correct," the bailiff said.

"Why?" Five asked. "What about church and state? What if I want to play racquetball? My joints get stiff when I don't play. Do you hear me complaining?"

"Relax," the bailiff said. "She can go to church."

"I want to talk to the judge," Five said. "Do you really have to go?" he asked Eight. "Don't you want to get out of this place?"

"I attend church," Eight said.

She was driven to Our Lady of Good Counsel and they waited in the rooms they had come to hate. Then it was off to the jury chamber, where the foreperson notified the bailiff that the jury wanted to hear the testimony of Teresa Vane. Then she asked if any juror had something to say that hadn't already been said.

"Damn right," Four said. "Why didn't Coles have the guts to get up on the witness stand? What was she afraid of?"

"The judge said we couldn't consider that. We can't hold it against her and you know it."

"She was afraid to testify," Four said.

"I hate to tell you," said Eight, "but I've forgotten most of the testimony. It was so filthy." There were tears in her eyes. "But I feel so sorry for that young woman. I prayed for her this morning."

"Saints be praised!" Five said.

At eleven thirty the bailiff rapped on the door and One let him in. "Judge Mathes is in court," he said. "You can hear the testimony of that runaway teacher."

"Watch your mouth," One told him. "It's the testimony of Teresa Vane."

He laughed and led the group to the jury box. Harmon was at the counsel table with his fresh and cool look. Down the line was Hull, who seemed to be aging day by day. The clerk and the steno were in place and the media people were at their table; a couple of them were yawning, as if Saturday night had been devoted to activities other than sleeping. The rest of the huge room was empty.

Judge Mathes appeared and did away with formalities by waving the bailiff back to his seat and addressing the foreperson. "I understand the jury wishes to hear the Vane testimony."

One thought that was strange. Had the bailiff been eavesdropping on them? How did the judge know they wanted to hear that witness? All she had said was *some* testimony. And had the bailiff also told the judge she was the holdout? "Yes, your honor. Teresa Vane."

There were murmurs among the correspondents and One noticed that the court reporter was already holding the transcript open at a particular page. She read the preliminary exchanges swiftly, not even letting up when Vane was asked if she had worked at the Snug Arms school with Laurie Coles.

One interrupted. "Excuse me, but could you go just a little slower, please?"

Number Five massaged his face as the reporter looked up, offended. But she slowed down. "Mr. Hull: 'Did you at any time see or hear or smell anything at the Snug Arms school that struck you as unusual?' Witness: 'Nothing. Ever.'"

Number One was thinking more about Judge Mathes than the testimony as they heard Vane reply to Hull's question about sticks, defecations, and jam: "It never happened. I would have seen it if it did."

Then Vane was heard telling the district attorney about a police officer's threat to implicate her in the crimes when she did not incriminate the defendant. Finally: "I jumped on the bus the next morning and got the hell out of here. I was *scared*."

The reporters were composing lead paragraphs about an apparent deadlock in the Laurie Coles jury, with, just possibly, a swing toward a verdict of not guilty.

The jurors went off to lunch, where One and Nine continued to ignore each other. On their return, the bailiff took One's arm and held her back. "I want to tell you something," he said. "This judge hates deadlocks. If you people end up telling him you can't reach a verdict, he'll poll the jury one by one and find out who the holdout is. And Jacko never forgets."

She pulled free and said, "If your buddies had just killed Coles last Friday, we wouldn't have to go through all this."

The bailiff backed away and closed the door.

One decided to say little about the Vane testimony. If the rest of the jurors didn't get it, it was hopeless. The wrangling continued and at four o'clock another ballot was taken. There were still eleven votes for guilty. She opened her mouth and closed it, then sighed. "Okay. You're going to go right on being deaf, dumb, blind, and stupid. It's no use." She looked deflated as she regarded Number Two. "Guilty. Are you satisfied?"

Cheers broke out and the bailiff grinned and reached for his phone.

"All *right!*" Five was shouting. He asked Eight, "When you were at church, madam, did you pray for this, too?"

"Let's go," Four said. "I want out of here."

"Not so fast," said Two, whose eyes had never left One. "We have to take another vote." She pointed to the instructions that lay before them. "The rules."

"Whatever," Four said. "Do it!"

One saw immediately what was coming and almost laughed as she asked Two, "How do you vote?"

"Not guilty."

The bailiff, who had come to recognize the voice of Number Five because of its carrying power, dropped the phone as he heard a shout. "Sweet mother of Jesus! What in the goddamn hell are you talking about?"

One was silent as Four strode around the mahogany table and stood behind Two. "You switch *now?* Are you crazy?" He seized her shoulder and she jerked away and stood.

"If you touch me again, I'll have you arrested! I say there's a reasonable doubt."

Five was holding his head in his hands as Nine came around the table to the new problem child. "Madam, we can work this out with common sense." He motioned to Four, who stalked back to his seat. "We've been through the evidence. The investigating detective." A finger came up. "The parents." Another finger. "The experts who interviewed the children. The children themselves." He held four fingers before her, then placed a hand under his chin. "You have to understand. These are only humans. They're not calculators." He smiled. "Let's say you're multiplying six digits by eight digits. You have forty-two calculations to make plus twenty-one carryovers. That's sixty-three separate mathematical processes." Number Five thought that if he screamed, Nine might stop. "If you make a single error, the result will be incorrect."

"What are you talking about?" Two asked.

"A calculator doesn't know how to make an error. But humans do. You give them a chance to flub one and they will. Still, the evidence is overwhelming and leads to only one rational conclusion. The defendant is guilty on all counts. Now do you understand, dear?"

Two had not resumed her seat. She lifted a finger and said, "First, do not call me dear. Second, you're rattling on about numbers. We're talking about people. Third, the inconsistencies in the testimony are *ir*rational. Fourth, I believe the kids were led on by experts who were beating the bushes for business. Fifth—I think you only had four points, sir—it was unfair not to let the defense talk to the children. The point is, we have the rest of someone's life in our hands and we can't give in to emotions and prejudices. Do you realize that woman could sit in jail for years and years if we convict her? Coles has her rights, whether we like her or not. Put that in your calculator." She sat down.

Nine gazed around the room and saw that everyone but Two agreed with him. Sometimes people just didn't make sense.

Number One moved in. "Addressing the point you made about the defense and the kids, friend—"

"Don't call me friend."

One was feeling restored. "Have it your way, but you're out of order on that one. The judge instructed us that his decision to keep the defense away from the children was a matter of law, and he's the law person. We can only deal with the testimony that we heard. Surely you can follow that?"

"Don't talk down to me! Are you steamed up because you and the numbers man aren't making it anymore? Are you as bored with each other as you are with this case?"

Number One rose so quickly that a coffee cup went over and a black stream flowed half the length of the long table. "What did you say?"

Hullabaloo. The bailiff called Justice Mathes and broke the bad news.

Nine was trying to figure out how to look as if he hadn't heard Two's remark and the others were studying the false beams across the ceiling. One leaned over and asked, "Did you drill a hole in the hotel wall, dear? Listen, tell the truth. You only switched because I did, right?"

Number Four pounded the table as Six returned from the bathroom with paper towels to dam the stream. He said, "Let's not get sidetracked again. We have to make sure the defendant doesn't fool around with kids again. Let's stick to the point."

Two could barely be heard. "It wasn't fair. Those interviewers put words in the kids' mouths. If they won't say something happened, the experts can't get a job straightening them out."

The noise did not abate until the bailiff banged on the door and said, "Break it up. Dinnertime!"

Five was whispering to himself. "No, *no!* This can't be happening!"

Chapter 36

IT WAS ALMOST NOON ON SUNDAY WHEN LAURIE COLES LEARNED THAT HER father had tried to see her the day before. A nurse told her that no visiting was permitted in the security ward of General Hospital and he was sent away. He had come back this morning and been refused entry again. He was out in front, the nurse said, sitting on a bench.

The headache returned and Coles closed her eyes. The intravenous setup had been removed and she had eaten an early lunch. And while she no longer felt pain around the stitches on her forehead, a throbbing had kept her awake much of the night; now it came and went.

The pulsing eased. She rang for the nurse and found out that her father was still out front. She asked if she could send him a note and the nurse hesitated, then looked at her watch. "Do it fast," she said. "I'm off in five minutes. And if you tell anybody, I'm in big trouble."

She left, and Coles, despite a dizziness, made her way to the window and looked out. There he was. Dad sitting up straight on a green park bench, hands folded in his lap, ankles crossed, head cast down. It gave her great comfort to see him there. And, she realized, her room was on the ground floor of the hospital.

A plan formed and she wrote, "Dear Dad. I'm all right. Go to your motel and stay there as long as you can. I'll try to get permission to call you. Thanks for being here. Love, Laurie."

Minutes later she watched the nurse pass by and speak to him. He rose and followed her, and they passed out of sight.

The headache came back and she sat at the edge of the bed and waited. It passed and a fuzzy sensation remained, but she went to the closet and found that her court clothing was there, hung up.

The blouse and suit, underwear, stockings, and shoes, and her purse. She decided she would dress and wait until the corridor was clear, then walk out quickly, call Dad, and arrange a meeting place.

She had to get out. She could not remember what happened at the parking lot of the courthouse yesterday. Something had fallen on her, she thought. A heavy object, sharp at the edges.

She lay down and a realization filled her mind. She was not going to be acquitted. She knew it from the looks on the faces of the jurors. And Harry Hull knew it, too. She remembered his walking in. It had to be yesterday because it was in this room. He was sympathetic, but all he said was that the jury was still out.

The taunts about the penitentiary came back. A new cellmate every night. And the rest of it.

She fell into a heavy sleep from which she did not emerge until five o'clock, when she was awakened and told to dress herself. She was being returned to the prison. As she walked out of the hospital, handcuffed again, she realized that her plan had been nonsense. The only way out was through a locked and guarded door.

Fred Coles had learned of the attack on his daughter when he stepped from the bus on Saturday morning and saw a newspaper. He hurried to the hospital and asked to see her. That was permitted only if a patient was in critical condition, he was told, and Miss Coles was out of danger. He pleaded, then raised his voice, and finally was led from the building. He sat on the green bench most of the day.

On Sunday the nurse slipped him Laurie's note. He rushed back to his motel and checked out, but left word that he was expecting a phone call. He waited in the lobby within sight of the desk until five o'clock.

On his way to the bus station, Coles began to think about killing himself. But then he wouldn't be able to help Laurie.

Chapter *37*

A MAD PLAY WAS BEING CONSTRUCTED IN HUDSON FERRY. IT WAS AS IF actors were working from utterly different scripts. Disconnected scenes were being built, as if they, too, were meant for different works. And yet the outcome of each scene would affect everyone on stage.

Harry Hull walked in for breakfast, and Speedy Sally waved him toward a booth. She meant, say nothing, be quiet. He started to sit down, but she motioned to the far, unoccupied end. He wondered but obeyed.

Sally was talking to a woman hunched over the counter. Hull recognized her as a police officer, and that was no surprise. Cops loved Sally's. No matter what they ate, the price never varied. If they gave her a five, they got four dollars back in change. A ten brought back nine.

But Hull noticed that the officer seemed to start and stop speaking, resuming as if under Sally's urging. Sally glanced at Hull and whispered. The woman did not reply. Sally spoke again and she straightened and nodded. She was led over and Sally said, "This is Margaret Little, Harry. She knows who you are and wants to tell you something. Maggie's a cop, except that she just quit." Sally went off to pour coffees and urge the cook to keep the bacon and eggs moving.

Hull tried to put Little at ease. "Didn't I talk you out of a speeding ticket? About six months ago?"

Her faint smile was brief. "I was in charge of returning Coles to prison on Friday afternoon. She didn't trip and fall, Mr. Hull. She was set up. And so was I. I won't go along with that. We were trained never to mishandle prisoners, no matter what they'd done."

He thought it wise to remain silent.

She spoke more quickly. "I was told to leave her in the parking area for a minute. When I came back out with my partner, she was on the ground, bleeding. I saw a man running away, but my partner wouldn't go after him. He told me to help her and he would call the ambulance. That's not our training. One calls the ambulance, the other one goes after the attacker."

Hull's anger was rising.

"I think the man who attacked her was the one who went after you. Short and stout. That crazy Brendelski."

Hull no longer cared about Ike Brendelski.

"She was hit by a piece of slate, jagged around the edges, maybe nine by six inches. Slate carries fingerprints, but somebody got rid of it. I don't know who."

Hull said, "You're a courageous lady, Miss Little. But why are you telling me this?"

"I thought about it the whole weekend, and this morning I walked in and told the chief what happened. He said I must have been high on drink or dope, and he was going to put me on limited duty while he looked into my case. So I quit. I decided that if I went along with this one, I'd buy the next one. And I wouldn't be able to stop because once you're in, you're in all the way."

"Will you give me a sworn statement, Miss Little?"

She sighed. "Sure I will. Assaulting prisoners just isn't right. I think everybody should know what happened."

Minutes later, in Hull's office, she gave a statement, with his secretary as a witness. He listened carefully and agreed with her. Everybody should know what happened.

A half hour passed and ex-officer Maggie Little was speaking into a channel 22 camera and undergoing questioning by Corky McGonigle.

Harmon reached his office at eight thirty and did not find the report, as requested, of the circumstances under which defendant Coles was injured Friday afternoon. He gazed at a photograph of Serena on his desk. Oh, that fine, elegant nose, that creamy cheek. He slipped it into his briefcase. At nine o'clock, on the dot, he called the chief of police and said, "I haven't seen a memo on the Coles affair."

"The department has investigated and found no reason to alter its original report, Mr. Harmon." The chief didn't talk that way. He was reading. And he had not said "Mr. Harmon" in three years.

"I hope you're taping this," the D.A. said. "A formal request for a full report will be in your hands shortly. The records will show that it was issued by the district attorney at five minutes past nine this morning." He hung up.

He sent off the memo and learned that his secretary had received neither a call nor any correspondence from Bob Kirk, chairman of the county board of supervisors.

It was ten past the hour and he called Corky McGonigle, who sounded out of breath. "If you want a good story, be in my office in no more than twenty minutes, Corky."

"You can't beat the one I just got!" McGonigle replied. "I mean, I don't think you can."

At twenty-eight minutes past the hour McGonigle walked in with a camera crew and sat down. Neither man said anything.

As nine thirty passed, Harmon nodded, the camera rolled, and the newsman spoke. "Corky McGonigle, 'Channel Twenty-two News,' in the office of our district attorney. Mr. Peter Harmon has something to tell us this morning."

The red light swung to Harmon. "I am announcing my resignation as district attorney of Princess County. You will be told shortly that I have resigned for personal reasons. That would be like announcing that a tornado has struck and umbrellas are getting wet. I'm resigning for two reasons. First, the time by when I should have been notified of my reappointment passed long ago. No one has complained of my work, but evidently somebody around here doesn't want me in this job."

McGonigle was nodding and grinning.

"Second, I asked the chief of police for a detailed report of how serious injuries were sustained last Friday by Laurie Coles, whose prosecution I have just completed. Miss Coles was in police custody at the time. The chief told me this morning that he has no intention of reopening the investigation. Evidently somebody around here doesn't understand that the district attorney is obliged to look into *all* crimes. I will ask my successor to press for an investigation, and if the board of supervisors doesn't do the same thing, the residents of this county should ask why. Thank you."

The familiar coda came. "Corky McGonigle, 'Channel Twenty-two News,' at the D.A.'s office. That is, the office of the former D.A. of Princess County. You heard it here first."

McGonigle told Harmon about his tape of officer Margaret Little's statement and left.

Chapter 38

NUMBER TWO IGNORED HER BREAKFAST AND A QUESTION FROM SIX ABOUT whether she was feeling all right. Pushing away scrambled eggs with hash browns, she drank coffee and waited for barbed remarks that did not come. While the jurors were unhappy, they could not muster the animosity they had shown the foreperson during her holdout period. At least Two, unlike One, stated her views without trying to make a fool of everyone. And the other jurors were in fact uncomfortable about the way the investigators had acted. A case could be made that the Snug Arms children had been somewhat manipulated. Still, the weight of the evidence was crushing. It couldn't all have been made up.

As the bailiff was signing the check at the cashier's desk, Two finally found the energy to speak. "I've gone over and over this reasonable-doubt thing," she said, "and I've finally decided I can't honestly say that's what I've got. So I'm switching. She's guilty."

Not a word was said, but the speed with which everyone rose indicated a belief that the sooner they left the restaurant and took a formal vote, the less time there would be for another change of mind.

In the jury room, it required exactly a minute for twelve guiltys to be tallied. Number One opened the door and the bailiff was aware of the silence. "We have a verdict," she told him.

"Hold it right there. I'll call the judge." He closed the door and they waited. A sudden desire for tidiness seized them and they arranged clutters of paper into neat piles along the mahogany table.

The word spread quickly and the courtroom was packed; several spectators carried thermos jugs, in case this was another false alarm and the jury continued to delay the inevitable. At front row left were the Snug Arms parents, but the buffs noticed that Marla Burney had again chosen a seat in the second row. They also saw that D.A. Pete Harmon, who had not yet arrived, was evidently in a generous mood. He had invited his assistant, Barnard Rooney, to hear the verdict from the counsel table.

But no sooner had they made that observation than Harmon walked in through the double doors at the rear. Rooney hustled through the gate to greet him and they remained at the back of the room, talking. Then Rooney returned to the counsel table, where Hull was seated. Harmon came down the aisle to the second row and spoke to Mrs. Burney. She seemed puzzled, then squeezed over and he sat down beside her, behind Lilly Robertson. As a buzz ran through the room, Corky McGonigle, at the press table, ran through the gate and spoke briefly to Serena Wiley, who looked at Hull, then nodded.

McGonigle reached the press table just as the black robes entered. The bailiff raced through his incantation and Justice Mathes said, "Present the jury."

Hull was on his feet. "Your Honor, I don't understand why the district attorney is not at the counsel table."

Mathes said, "Present the jury." Hull sat down, baffled.

In came the dozen in a solemn procession. When they were seated the judge said, "Bring in the defendant."

As Laurie Coles entered from the holding area, all eyes were fixed on the bandage over the right side of her head. She seemed steady enough on her feet, and as she sat down, Hull smiled and squeezed her hand. Lilly Robertson told Ellen Strand, "Hull is a bastard!"

"Madam Foreperson," Justice Mathes said, "has the jury reached a verdict in the matter of *The State of New York versus Laurie Coles, defendant?*"

Number One rose. "We have, Your Honor."

"Please give your verdict to the bailiff."

She handed him the ballot and he delivered it to the judge. Mathes adjusted his glasses and studied it. He handed the sheet to the clerk of the court, who showed no emotion as she read. "The jury finds the defendant guilty on each of the thirty-nine counts in the indictment."

Hull had taken Laurie Coles's hand again as the clerk began to speak. He held it firmly as the eruption came.

There was disorder in the court and no way to stop it. Lilly Robertson stood up and screamed at Coles. "Now you'll pay! You thought that bump on the head was something? You'll pay now!"

Ellen Strand and Letty Andrews were applauding along with

the other parents in the front row. Behind them Marla Burney moved past Harmon and left the room.

Mathes waited it out and rapped his gavel only after everyone had sat down. "Members of the jury," he said, "I will now ask each of you individually if that is your verdict." He did and heard unanimity. "The court thanks you for your diligent work at a difficult task, and you are now discharged."

They rose and returned to their room to gather belongings and, in the words of Number Five, get the hell out.

Hull sprang to his feet and advanced to the bench without asking the usual permission. He laid a document before Mathes and said, "We serve notice that the verdict will be appealed, sir, and we now ask that reasonable bail be granted during that process." He placed a copy before Barney Rooney.

Mathes studied the written motion and looked up as Harmon came through the gate. "Your Honor," he said, "as the prosecutor in this case, I would like to make a statement."

The buffs still could not understand what was happening. Inexplicably, Barney Rooney, second banana, was sitting in the prosecutor's chair and Pete Harmon was acting as if he were a visitor in court. The commanding look was gone.

Rooney shrugged and Mathes signaled Harmon to proceed.

"I see no reason why the defendant should not be granted bail in an amount she can meet. After the injuries she has suffered while in police custody, I fear for her safety. We have had a gunman in the courtroom and an attempt has been made on the life of the defense counsel."

As Harmon passed back through the gate and returned to his seat, Mathes asked Barney Rooney for his recommendation, and finally the audience understood. Peter Harmon was no longer the district attorney.

Rooney rose and said, "Your Honor, the state opposes any reduction of bail. The evidence in this case has been overwhelming and the possibility of a reversal is remote. We therefore ask that the motion be denied."

Hull was on his feet. "A refusal to grant reasonable bail may become a death sentence for the defendant. I would like to call a witness who will give evidence to support that statement. And you will see that under the circumstances you must reduce Miss Coles's bail."

Mathes's voice rose, "This is not a formal bail hearing. And you have already stated your motion, Mr. Hull. Sit down!"

Hull came around the counsel table. "I will not sit down while this woman's life is in danger! You cannot leave her in the custody of the police, whose role in her so-called accident is questionable.

My witness will testify to that. If you will not listen, you will be personally responsible for any further injuries she may suffer, Justice Mathes!"

Mathes stood up. "That's it. Mr. Hull, I find you guilty of contempt of court and sentence you to serve five days in jail, effective immediately." He boomed, "Take this man into custody and remove him from the courtroom."

Laurie Coles was sobbing, her head in her arms, but suddenly she jumped to her feet and shouted, "Why didn't you let that man shoot me? It would have been better!" She fell back into her chair.

Mathes was still standing. "The defendant is out of control," he said. "Remove her to the holding area."

Hull, sneering at the judge, held out his hands to an approaching officer.

The officer reached out with handcuffs, then hesitated and looked at the judge, but Mathes's eyes were on a figure coming down the aisle. It was Serena Wiley, who said, "Your Honor, may I approach the bench?"

"No!" Mathes shouted. "You are not a party to these proceedings."

Harmon leaped up, banged his knee against the gate, and limped to the bench, lips moving as he leaned forward. Mathes held up a hand and said, "You have no standing here. Return to your seat."

Harmon stepped back. "So you already know I've quit. You didn't even ask Barney why he was sitting there, did you?"

"Your Honor," Wiley said, "these proceedings have become a travesty. Please reconsider your actions."

As Mathes's gavel struck the bench, its head split away and flew across the room toward the press table. Reporters ducked and could not restrain their laughter. "One more outburst," Mathes said, "and I will clear the court, press and all."

Corky McGonigle was laughing as more policemen came through the double doors. The judge said, "There will be a fifteen-minute recess, and any unauthorized person who is on this side of the gate when I return will also be guilty of contempt and will be jailed immediately. Take Mr. Hull away but hold the defendant here." He walked out.

Hull leaned over Coles and whispered. She raised her head, nodded, and tried to smile. He pulled two sheets from an inside pocket, gave them to Wiley, and once more extended his hands. The officer who had been standing beside him applied the handcuffs, but in front rather than pinning the attorney's arms behind him, and led him down the aisle and out of the courtroom. Exiting, Hull turned and swung both arms over his head, shouting to Coles, "It ain't over till it's over, Laurie!"

When Mathes returned, Wiley had left and Harmon was seated among the spectators once more; there was a look on his face the judge did not like.

"After careful review," Mathes said, "the application for a reduction in bail is denied, but not on the grounds the state has suggested. Miss Coles is entitled to appeal the verdict, and we cannot predict the outcome of that action." He was being ever so careful. "However, the defendant has no firm roots in the community and she is unemployed. Those factors encourage a convicted person to remain in the court's jurisdiction. Further, the penalty for the charges in this case is substantial, and therefore the incentive to flee is increased. For those reasons, bail will remain as originally set."

His pace quickened. "Sentencing will take place in ten days. Counsel will be notified. The defendant is now remanded to the custody of the bailiff and will be removed to the state penitentiary."

The gavel came up, but Harmon was striding through the gate once more. "Your Honor," he said, "you can't move the defendant out of the Hudson Ferry area after taking her attorney out of the courtroom. She is entitled to counsel to object to that ruling and she is not represented."

Mathes held the gavel high. "You're certainly not representing her, Mr. Harmon. Are you forgetting something? You prosecuted her."

Harmon turned to Coles. "Will you permit me to raise an objection and make a motion on your behalf, Miss Coles?"

She seemed confused, and before she could reply, Mathes said, "This trial has concluded and the court is now adjourned." He banged the gavel and walked out.

Bewildered, then looking terrified, Coles was handcuffed and led away.

Harmon turned to Rooney. "Where the fuck were you, Barney? Why did I have to stand up and object?"

Rooney was putting papers into a briefcase and did not look up or reply.

Chapter 39

WILEY WAS IN HARRY HULL'S OFFICE BY THE TIME MATHES CONCLUDED the court proceedings. She had considered driving down to see Arnold Fisher, then decided that the phone was the way to go.

The retired judge greeted her graciously and heard her out. The jury in Hudson Ferry had found Laurie Coles guilty. Hull asked that bail be reduced and Justice Mathes refused. While a bail reduction after conviction would be rare, after conviction, Miss Coles had been severely attacked while in police custody, as Mr. Fisher knew. Hull asked that a witness be heard in support of the bail motion and the judge said no. The witness was a police officer, Margaret Little, who quit the force this morning. When Hull persisted—as he should have, Wiley editorialized—he was cited for contempt and taken off to jail.

She read Fisher the statement Officer Little had given Hull and told him that the policewoman had repeated her accusations on television. Wiley, a bit embarrassed, said, "I know some of this case is being tried on TV, sir, but the circumstances have become more outlandish every day. Anyway, I have a transcript of what the officer said."

"Please read it to me," Judge Fisher said.

Over the sounds of puffing as he lit his pipe, she read both Corky McGonigle's questions and the officer's responses. He asked to hear several sections again and she read them.

There was no reaction at first, and as the pause lengthened she hoped Fisher had not nodded off. Then he spoke. "I must explain something again. I cannot hear cases. I'm hearing emergencies on weekends just to help out. So I should not even be talking to you now, and if I have a comment to make on what you've said, I will make it off the record to Justice Mathes. But I imagine he will be attentive."

"I understand, sir," Wiley said. "In case you can't reach him at the court, I'd like to give you a number. It's for the Rhinebeck Club."

Fisher laughed. "You are thorough, Counselor."

She was about to hang up when he asked if she could spare a minute. "Let's have a truly private conversation. Serena, I respect your work and appreciate your point of view, but I'm curious. What the hell is steaming you up about this case? What's going on in that town?"

He had called her Serena and she was embarrassed. "That's not an easy question, sir. Where do I start?" She settled down. "Every day there are new charges of sexual abuse in a nursery school somewhere around the country. It would be foolish to think that the stories are never true, even if so many cases end with juries not believing the prosecution after lengthy trials. But the very idea of such crimes is so devastating to parents, and they often become prey to professionals who have made molester-hunting a trade."

She heard him puffing and thought he really should give up tobacco. He said, "I'm sure you're going to get more specific now. Aren't you?"

She found a laugh. "End of speech. Cases of this kind need excruciating care on the judge's part because the defendant is guilty in the public mind before the trial even opens. It's a good thing we don't use public opinion polls instead of courts. Oops, there I go again. Okay. I wasn't surprised that the town convicted Laurie Coles the day she was arrested, but the law has to be above the mob. And Justice Mathes is not, in my firm opinion." She stopped. "Am I out of bounds, sir?"

"No, we're just chatting. And my name is Arnold."

She laughed. "I can't say it. I'm a prisoner of habit. But thank you. I think the judge has conducted the Coles trial unfairly and I plan to help Mr. Hull with the appeal."

Fisher said, "Yes, the law must remain above the mob, despite all temptations. Now, keep this in mind, Serena. I cannot hear further motions in this case, and yet, I'm concerned." She heard a small laugh. "So, you gave me a phone number, I'll give you one." He did. "You know Ab Rusk, don't you?"

Did she know Abner Rusk, chief judge of the court of appeals? "I wear a suit of armor when I appear before him."

"I'll let Ab know you might call. Good luck, Serena."

She was elated. Judge Abner Rusk followed the law wherever it led and took even slight instances of unfairness as a breakdown of the justice system. Quick access to Rusk was a big plus.

She turned on Hull's radio and heard a news bulletin. Peter Harmon had resigned as district attorney of Princess County—for personal reasons. Barnard Rooney had been appointed to succeed him.

At home she found the ex-D.A. snapping his fingers to a rap group. He reminded her that he, at least, had the afternoon off. She chased his shots around the tennis court and then he chased her around the shower. As they stretched out on the widow's walk in the late afternoon she asked, ever so cautiously, what he planned to do with the rest of his life.

He seemed to be counting clouds in a cloudless sky. "The truth is, love, I haven't decided on that. But I might be interested in taking a look at the other side of criminal law—I think it's called the defense side."

She was pleased. "I'd be happy to be your guide, Pete."

They heard a two-sentence radio report. Attorney Hull had been released from the lockup after serving three hours. Justice Mathes said he felt his point had been made.

The judge also announced that Laurie Coles would remain at the nearby prison until her sentencing, to be available to her attorney.

"I'm glad Arnold Fisher is retired," Serena said. "Now he has time to hear important matters. And he scares the Hangman."

That evening Hull and Polly Lennon dropped in at the Ferry Ale House, where he received a new nickname: Harry Jailbird. Later they wound up at his place, where she picked up *The Baseball Almanac* and asked, without opening it, "What was the longest nine-inning ball game ever played at night?"

He was astonished. "That's the last question I ever thought you'd ask."

"Don't stall."

"Exactly? Hours and minutes? I give up."

She grinned. "The record is six hours and fourteen minutes, and it was between the New York Mets and the Atlanta Braves."

He snatched a mitt from the closet, put it on, and pounded it. "Polly, I'm suspicious. You looked it up this afternoon."

"Yes, but I had a reason. Something's been on my mind for a while. I was at your opening game in April and I saw that freak double play you made. The manager kept telling you to play in against the bunt and you kept moving back. And I was yelling at you to stop playing it safe." She cupped her hands. "Move up, Harry! Move up!"

He laughed. "I *thought* that was you. All right, Polly. What's this all about?"

"About you, Harry. You win the contest for caution. But you didn't play it safe in the Coles trial. You knew you were only supposed to go through the motions and not get aggressive, but then you saw that the umpire wasn't going to play fair and you moved in on him. Coles didn't win, but you did. You took a chance."

Hull thought that over and made a large statement. "I want to know you better, Polly. You make me feel good!"

She said, "Harry, I already told you. If there's one thing you definitely have, it's possibilities. Do you know what Alfred North Whitehead said?"

"Who?"

"He said our minds have limits, and yet our possibilities are unlimited. Keep stretching, Harry."

Leave it to Corky McGonigle. At ten o'clock channel 22 interrupted another rerun of "MASH" and showed the newsman striding back and forth in front of two men and two women who were seated in what looked like a hastily constructed jury box. "Here they are," he said. "Four of the twelve men and women who heard the Laurie Coles case and found her guilty this morning. We're going to find out what went on in that jury room over the long weekend." He stopped and pointed. "Let's start with the foreperson. What took you folks so long? This town thought you'd be in and out of there in a couple of hours."

Number One wore a sober look, "It wasn't an easy case. There were many complications."

McGonigle turned to the woman beside One. "You were the second juror in the box. What was so complicated?"

Two pursed her lips as McGonigle continued to pace. "We spent a long time discussing the fact that there were no eyewitnesses to the crimes. No one saw them committed. And the witnesses kept telling us what the children told them, instead of what they knew themselves. We didn't like that."

Number Five cut in. "I think you feel a special responsibility when you're sitting on a jury. There were disagreements, of course, but everyone was reasonable."

McGonigle stopped and gave Five a look of astonishment. "Were you at a tea party? Are you telling us that these were the first deliberations in history in which no one called anyone else a bleep-bleep?"

Number Two looked away as the other jurors shook their heads. "That would have been a waste of time," Number Five said. "It never got personal. For example, there was a difference of opinion over how much weight to give the testimony of that psychologist whose credentials were challenged. But we resolved it by talking it through."

McGonigle turned up the heat. "What was your reaction to the Snug Arms teacher who testified? Teresa Vane. The one who never saw or heard anything going on for nine months. And, I might add in view of the testimony, never smelled any evidence of a crime. What about that, Juror Number Five?"

He smiled. "That was difficult to deal with. But in the end we decided that the fact that someone *didn't* see anything happen didn't mean it didn't happen. It just meant she didn't see it. If you follow me."

McGonigle gave the camera a raised eye. "All right, let's add it up. You were bothered by the absence of eyewitnesses and all that hearsay testimony. And they gave you a social worker who was wearing a psychologist's hat. Didn't you have an awful lot to worry about, even without the teacher who said nothing happened? With all those problems, it sounds as if you could have acquitted Laurie Coles as easily as you convicted her."

Number Nine saw that the situation might be getting out of hand. "Sitting on a jury is an awesome responsibility," he said. "In the end we handled the problems as a matter of logic. We weighted each offer of evidence made by the prosecution and defense. That took a lot of time. Then we added up the weights, and the prosecution was ahead by a convincing amount. In other words, beyond a reasonable doubt. It was a matter of probabilities. And I want to tip my hat to my fellow jurors. They're a mature, rational group of people."

Corky McGonigle, who thought he was hearing balderdash, was ready to write the show off as a dud and get off the air, but Juror Number Two spoke before he could.

"We found Miss Coles guilty, but there was a terrible part to this case. The way the investigators acted. They made suggestions to the children, and children believe what they hear. They shuttled stories between those kids until they were all repeating them. I wouldn't want those investigators near my children, I'll tell you that. And if I had the chance to do it again, I think I'd vote not guilty." She was crying. "The jury did the best it could, but I'm just sorry about the whole thing."

McGonigle got off the air with a sober look and channel 22 returned to "MASH."

Chapter 40

IT WAS A TEDIOUS TUESDAY FOR HARRY HULL. A TRUCE HAD BEEN REACHED in the war with Judge Mathes, although it would not remain in force for long. He would appeal the contempt citation quickly, as much to keep the needle in Jacko as out of a concern for his reputation; at the moment Hull was wearing his three hours in the lockup as a Purple Heart. Still, the end of the trial had left him with a flatness that accompanies failure.

His mood was not enhanced by two sheets on his desk, one of which carried Serena Wiley's suggested grounds on which to appeal Laurie Coles's conviction. Each point would require a thorough study of how the Constitution had been applied in other cases. He would have to find strong support for each claim to prove that Mathes had flouted the doctrine of *stare decicis,* under which a judge must follow precedents set in similar cases unless he can show good reason to write new law.

The other sheet contained just one word. Bail.

He went to work on the appeal but soon found himself wandering. Bail had priority; Laurie was sitting in jail and that was a dangerous place for her. But his concentration was clouded again, this time by doubts that he could win her freedom before the appeal was heard. If Jacko feared he might be reversed on his refusal to lower bail, he would go ahead and grant it—a bond of one million dollars in negotiable assets or a hundred thousand in cash. Forget it. Winning a reversal of that sham would take a long time.

His thoughts were interrupted by the arrival of Anthony Sgueglia, whose report did little to raise Hull's spirits.

"I've been back down to the cable company people, Harry, and this time I had real dirt on them. Deceptive practices and more. I sat down with the boss and told him I would put the evidence in front of the cable commission and he'd lose his franchise—if he didn't cooperate. So he did. I told him about the dish antenna I spotted in the backyard of the Andrews house and asked him why they'd install one of those when they were already getting dozens of channels. What do they want? Snowball fights from Iceland? So he checked it out. I know it's too little and too late, Harry, but listen anyway. Letty and Nick Andrews belong to a porn club. The antenna brings in dirty movies. Freaky shows that not even cable would put on. Girls and guys, guys and sheep, guys hand-jobbing each other. So here's Mommy telling what happened to her little boy at the school and the parents are as kinky as anything she testified to."

Hull's sigh was heavy. "It's not little, Squail, but it's definitely too late."

"I know. Take me off the payroll, Harry. But I owe you, and there's an unfinished piece of business. I'm going down to the city and look up the man with the habit."

"Strand?"

"Mickey Strand. A guy who can mess with Jacko Mathes and walk away."

Hull got to work dictating an appeal brief, thankful that he had substituted so many hours of research for so many beers. And a tip of the hat to Serena, he added.

Wiley spent most of Tuesday morning at the kitchen table, but only because her desk would not accommodate the range of paper mountains she had constructed. She was performing major surgery on the transcripts of the investigators' interviews with the Snug Arms children. First she laid them out by the date on which the conversations took place. Then she scissored them up until each child's interviews had been separated from those of the others.

At eleven o'clock she was studying the interviews, child by child.

At noon she was angry.

At one o'clock she was furious.

At two o'clock she asked Pete to rub the sleep from his eyes and come down to the kitchen. "Here is what happened to one child, selected at random," she said. "Billy Andrews. Garafolo saw him first. The detective told Billy that Laurie did bad things to the kids. Then he asked the boy what Laurie did to him and didn't get an incriminating answer. So he told Billy about more nasty things Coles had done. Finally, after some bribery talk about ice cream and candy, Billy began to agree with Garafolo. When he got what he wanted, he passed Billy to Liam Gunn, who reinforced the stories and said the older children had already told what Laurie did. And he said, 'You don't want to be a little baby, do you?' Billy said he wasn't a little baby and picked up on the stories. So Gunn handed him off to Amanda Roth, who kept at the child until the story was being told the way she wanted it testified to in court. Then the parents took Billy and the other kids to the prison and showed them that Laurie was locked up tight and couldn't hurt them. And the pattern is repeated with child after child."

Harmon's discomfort grew as he listened. He picked up pile after pile and went through each. "Serena," he said, "please believe me. I did not see the pattern. Or I wasn't looking for it. A little of both, I suppose."

"You're not on trial here, Pete. Anyway, I think the children *were* harmed."

Now he was baffled. "You show me this and then you say Coles is guilty?"

"I wasn't talking about Coles. I think crimes were committed by the investigators. They injected harmful stories into gullible minds through repetition, manipulation, and coercion. I believe a formal investigation should be conducted to find out whether criminal acts were committed."

He marched around the kitchen. "Investigate the investigators?" He sat down and stared at her. "I see what you're up to. If Barney Rooney refuses to investigate, Hull will tie him up in litigation. And if he agrees, even for the sake of appearances, Hull will get the right to have his own experts talk to the children, to get their version of what happened during the interviews."

She nodded. "And something else. Can you see the parents agreeing to turn their children over to Hull's experts?"

He said, as jovially as he could, "I didn't miss that, love. I didn't mention it because it struck me as the kind of legal cunning you usually associate with prosecutors."

"Maybe that's where I learned it, sweetheart. Sometimes you talk in your sleep."

He changed the subject. "I can see our shingle now. Pete and Serena, Attorneys-at-Law."

"How about Serena and Pete? It has a certain ring."

An hour later, after calling Hull and making his day, Wiley and Harmon were sitting across from Barnard Rooney, district attorney of Princess County, as he read a citizen's complaint that had been signed by two residents of Hudson Ferry, Serena Wiley and Peter Harmon. The complaint named Detective Vincent Garafolo, Special Investigator Liam Gunn, and a social worker who called herself a psychologist, Amanda Roth.

Rooney looked up as he finished and they saw surprise and disbelief. He picked up the Billy Andrews chronology, went halfway through it, and pushed it back across the desk with the complaint sheet. "I'm feeling polite today," he said. "Are you crazy, Miss Wiley? And have you lost your mind, Pete?"

"I'll be polite, too," Wiley said. "I don't believe your response will advance our discussion."

He shook his head. "It's the best I can do. I was told you had quite a reputation, but I can't remember ever seeing a set of allegations this preposterous."

She pushed the complaint back across the desk. "Bullshit, Rooney. Let's not waste time with politeness. What about the statement by the police officer, Margaret Little? The *former* police officer. Her account of the attack on Laurie Coles. That the cops set her up. Was that preposterous, too?"

Harmon said, "Let's get something straight about those investigators, Barney. They fucked up, but it's not their fault. It's mine. I should have studied the transcripts more closely. Especially since I wasn't tied up playing golf with Mathes."

The D.A. stood up, signifying that the conversation was at an end. "This is a warning to both of you. If you persist in trying to bring this frivolous action, you will probably face charges yourself. Your allegations are likely to cause monetary harm to well-regarded reputations. I hope you can afford the damage award."

"I'm in danger of yawning," Wiley said.

"In addition, your charges are libelous and slanderous." He smiled and sounded friendly. "Ask Pete to explain that to you when you get home." The smile vanished. "Your conduct in this matter is unprofessional. As attorneys, you're opening yourselves up to proceedings that could take away your licenses to practice law."

Harmon nodded. "Except that the transcripts back us up, allegation for allegation. And that's not all. We suggest you study the trial record and the exhibits very carefully. You'll find that for some reason certain conversations with the children were not recorded. So what we have here is a selective recall of events. Were the censored interviews the ones in which the investigators put heat on the children? Injured them emotionally, beyond a doubt?"

Wiley went for the last word. "I'll tell you what. We'll leave the complaint with you, and after you've ordered your drinks at the nineteenth hole, why not show it to Jacko? Maybe he can figure out a way to put us in jail for contempt, or gag us." She headed for the door. "I don't envy the spot you're in, Mr. District Attorney."

Wiley only thought she would have the last word. Harmon said, "It's a hell of a way to start your first term, isn't it, Barney?"

Chapter *41*

Anthony Sgueglia loved the Big Apple in August. It wasn't the heat but the humidity that he liked. Mugginess put his targets into scratchy moods, and people were more vulnerable to pressure when they were suffocating.

He came down lower Broadway with his jacket over his shoulder and passed a street vendor selling auto decals: RADIO ALREADY STOLEN. Cute. At ten minutes of five he stopped at a phone booth, called Strand Consultants, and asked if Michael Strand was in. When a voice said, "One moment, please," he hung up and continued down to Trinity Church, whose towers he admired briefly before turning into Wall Street. He passed the Stock Exchange, where young clerks in gray gowns, released from their stocks and bonds, were exiting to have postponed cigarettes. At Hanover Square he turned down to Beaver, where at five o'clock he took a final look at a photograph of Mickey Strand, pocketed it, and set up watch as very important executives rushed from air-conditioned office buildings into air-conditioned limousines.

Five minutes later Strand emerged and bustled down Hanover Street with Sgueglia in step behind him. The young man was lean and had a long, quick stride; Sgueglia was glad they didn't have far to go. As they neared Pearl Street he came abreast and said, "Let's have a drink, Mickey."

Strand jumped as if he were about to be mugged in broad daylight and Sgueglia offered his version of an engaging smile. "Relax, guy. I don't want your wallet. Just a talk, Mickey."

Strand continued backing off and came up against a granite building wall. "Get the hell away from me!" he snapped. "What do you want?"

A young woman walked between them and stared at Sgueglia,

who gave her a jaunty tilt of the head. She continued on rapidly and he placed an arm against the rough wall, leaning in on Strand and searching his eyes for dilation, the telltale sign of drugs bounding through the blood. "Joseph sent me, Mickey."

Strand shook his head and black curls bounced. "Joseph who?" His good-looking but pale and pinched face was wet with perspiration.

"Joe from Albany, Mickey. Your boss from the banking committee. Joe would feel lousy if I told him you didn't remember him. He thinks it would be a good idea if we sat down and talked about something."

"About what? Baloney. He can't touch me. He'd be blown out of the water."

Sgueglia was genial. "You're right. If he went public. I mean, about the money and the shoot-up stuff. He'd look as bad as you for letting it all happen on his turf in the first place. So call yourself lucky. Joe's mouth is closed. But mine isn't, Mickey. How long do you think you'd hold on to your biggest account if I dropped the word to your clients?"

Sweat gathered along Strand's dark hairline. "Who are you and how much do you want?"

Sgueglia handed him a business card. "Stop the bribery talk, you goombah. I don't want money. Look, unless you want to yell for a cop, let's go across the street and have a drink. I need some information." He turned and crossed narrow Hanover Street without looking back and walked into Stub's Pub. As Strand followed him in, he went to a booth at the rear, past the dart-board gang and away from the buzz of the stock jobbers at the bar.

Sgueglia had a beer while Strand chose a nonalcoholic brand; evidently he had learned that the distillates of grain and the product of coca leaves are poor mixers. A leg was jiggling and Sgueglia set out to relax him. "Mickey, stop worrying. I'm not here to hurt you. I just need some information."

Tension turned to sullenness. "Forget it. You won't get anything out of me."

"Oh, you'll talk," Sgueglia said. "But first you want me to tell you what I know. Nobody tells me anything until I show them I know plenty. Okay. You took in over six hundred thousand bucks in illegal cash contributions for Joe the Senator and you forgot to turn in almost two hundred thou of it. And I know you're a financial public-relations consultant to a bunch of companies. One of the networks is your biggest client. If I have to take it out in the open, I'll do it." Sgueglia crossed his legs; he didn't know he always did that when he was bluffing. "I don't want to do it,

Mickey, but if I have to, I will. And you'll be out of business in thirty days."

"Fucking blackmail," Strand said.

Sgueglia frowned. "First you talk bribery and now it's blackmail. I don't like to even hear that word. Why don't we call my proposition a fair exchange? You open your mouth and I'll shut mine. Something like the deal you made with your ex?"

Strand pulled out a handkerchief and ran it across his face. The collar of his white shirt, with thin blue stripes, was limp with sweat. "What do you want?"

Sgueglia was watching him closely. "I'm interested in Justice Johnson Gillies Mathes of Hudson Ferry."

Strand set his glass down. "Jacko? Why?"

"I've got a theory, Mickey. Everybody thinks you walked into the courtroom up there to shoot Laurie Coles because she messed your daughter. I'm not sure that's the story."

Strand pushed his ersatz beer away and grinned without humor. "You're not, are you?"

"No. And you stood there in the courtroom and called Mathes a son-of-a-bitch. And he let you get away with it."

"Go on."

"And that psychiatric report that said you were under a lot of stress was an out-and-out cover-up. All the Snug Arms parents were stressed out. But there's more strangeness. I gave big odds that the lab report wouldn't hang coke possession on you. And it's a fact that you were higher than an astronaut that day, weren't you, Mickey?"

"I thought you said you weren't trying to do me in." Then he blurted, "All right. Maybe I was."

That was the first communicative reply. Sgueglia spoke above the raucousness of the room; it must have been a good day for the stock-and-bonders. "So somebody put the fix in, to get the whole matter dropped. And I have an idea that won't go away no matter how hard I step on it. It was Mathes. But if I think that way, I have to wonder why he'd do that. It's dangerous. What have you got on him, Mickey? I'm told that Jacko is hot to sit on the court of appeals. Are you holding a piece of information that would kill that chance?"

The leg was jiggling violently again. "Give me a smoke."

"I'll get some. What's your brand?"

"I don't care."

Sgueglia went to the bar. He looked back and saw Strand slipping something into his mouth. He returned empty-handed and said, "You don't smoke, Mickey." Then his voice dropped and hardened. "I don't give a damn what you swallow or shoot, guy.

Shoot your brains out if that turns you on. But if you don't talk, I walk." He looked at his watch. "And I'm ready to move out."

Strand leaned back in the booth and relaxed for the first time. His lips played with a smile and he said, "You're on the right track, mister. I was in orbit when I went up to that jerkwater town last week. I didn't know what I was doing and I didn't care. I don't give a damn about that woman they're trying. I went in there to give Jacko a bullet in the head. But I couldn't handle the gun." Now he laughed outright. "So you want to put him up the creek."

"Isn't that where you want him?"

"Tell me again I'm safe. You're not going to my clients. How can I be sure?"

"What would that get me? Talk, Mickey!"

Strand retrieved his drink and banged the glass down. "Mathes is Bonnie's father."

The air conditioning had nothing to do with a shiver that swept through Sgueglia. He went back to work. "I don't believe it. You're doing a number on me." He rose.

"Sit down!" Strand said. "God damn it, Bonnie's not mine. Jacko's her father. I knew it from the day Ellen said she was pregnant, and then she finally admitted it. That's why I finally walked out."

"Drugs had nothing to do with it?"

"Maybe." He laughed again. "In fact, it proves it, wiseass. I was so gone on the stuff that I couldn't get it up. There was no sex during any possible time that Bonnie was conceived. So Ellen played games with Jacko. He was always hanging around. For Christ's sake, look at the kid's hair. Direct from the balls of the redhead." He finished off his so-called beer.

Sgueglia tried to control his excitement as images of Harry Hull appeared before him and caution restrained him. There was a difference between gossip and admissible evidence. He said, "Forget it, Mickey. You're telling me Mathes sat on a case in which his own daughter was involved?" He shook his head. "You'll say anything. You're whacko. And saying it doesn't prove it."

"What the hell is your name? Tony? Don't be stupid. What could Mathes do? Jump off the bench and explain it to the folks? 'I can't preside over this case, ladies and gentlemen, because, you see, I fucked Ellen Strand. And then I walked out on her when she got the preggers.' He had to shut up and sit there whether he wanted to or not."

Sgueglia considered that, but his problem was not solved. "That's still us talking. It's not proof."

Strand's demeanor was fraying. "You know damn well there are only two ways to prove it, and they go together. Ellen admits it out loud and genetic tests back her up. You're going to have to get it out of Ellen, aren't you?"

"Thank you," Sgueglia said. "And I want to tell you something. If you hadn't talked, I wouldn't have gone to your clients anyway, Mickey. I talk blackmail, but I don't do it. Life's too short."

Strand shrugged and Sgueglia had a parting word. "Speaking of which, you sound like a smart guy, and it's your life and none of my business. Be my guest and blow it. But did you ever think about not ripping yourself to pieces, the way you're doing?"

He was out of the booth when Strand jumped up and grabbed his arm. "Listen, I'm trying. I'm on some pills to keep me clean. I was flying with the kites when I went in there to shoot Mathes. I was crazy. It got to me later because I couldn't even remember buying the gun on the street. So, believe it or not, I'm trying like hell to break it off."

Leaving New York from lower Broadway at six o'clock consumed a full hour. But it was a jubilant hour, Sgueglia's excitement dampened only by a return of doubts. He had uncovered an extraordinary story, and genetic testing, now over nine-five percent accurate and specific, would confirm Justice Mathes as Bonnie's father. But what if Jacko refused to give a blood sample? Then Ellen Strand would have to stand up and point a finger at him. Would she do it? Sgueglia went back to his unrewarding chat with Ellen at Far-Flung Fashions and found little reason to think she would. So once more he might be riding into town with too little, too late. Sorry, Harry.

He stopped for a bite along the Saw Mill Parkway and made meticulous notes of the conversation with Strand, then called Hull and gave him the gist of the story. Hull interrupted several times with brief comments. "You're making it up." "Sure, Tony." And, "This is your idea of funny?" But suddenly he exploded. "Do you know what you've brought in, Squail? This blows Jacko into the river. Get up here fast. The speeding tickets are on me, you beautiful son-of-a-bitch!"

Chapter *42*

SERENA AND PETE WERE BRUSHING THEIR TEETH AT MIDNIGHT WHEN THE phone rang. They hustled back into clothes, put on coffee, and greeted Harry Hull, who with a winged hat and sandals would have resembled Mercury riding breathlessly into Rome. Sgueglia followed him in as a plain citizen.

Flushed with excitement, Hull motioned to the private eye, who recounted his conversation with Mickey Strand. Consulting his notes, he omitted nothing, which meant it took a fair amount of time to arrive at the revelation. Wiley and Harmon were puzzled until the magic words were spoken:

"Then Strand said, 'Mathes is Bonnie's father.' "

There was silence in the living room and Hull looked triumphantly at his listeners and asked, "Did you hear that? Jacko Mathes is the father of a complainant in the Laurie Coles case."

Harmon's head was tilted to one side, Wiley's to the other. Harmon went for the coffee and returned chortling as he poured. "Priceless. Jacko, you turkey! How dumb can you get?"

Wiley shook her head. "What else could he have done? What explanation could he have given? He was trapped." There was excitement in her voice. "But we're not, Harry."

Hull was less buoyant. "We've got a big problem. "Corky McGonigle told Sgueglia that Mathes was once a close friend of the Strands but stopped coming around all of a sudden. So Tony talked to Ellen, but she clammed up. And she's the only one who can prove it, or at least raise it."

Harmon dissented. "No and yes. No one can produce absolute proof for such a claim. But it's true that if she'd name Jacko as the father, the verdict would probably be dead." He asked Hull, "Have you ever seen a prosecutor enjoy the collapse of his own case? Mathes is some son-of-a-bitch! But Tony, how can we be sure Strand wasn't just trying to get rid of you? He's loony but smart. Right?"

"I've been lied to by half the swindlers in this state," Sgueglia said. "I'd bet my license on it."

They drank coffee and talked. Midnight became one o'clock and ideas flew and were shot down. Finally Wiley said, "The logical route would be a paternity suit at which Mathes would have to testify under oath, but that would take forever."

Harmon noted that even if Ellen Strand were to bring such a suit, husband Mickey would not be regarded as a credible witness. "He walked out on her and the child. He'd be considered biased. And you can't bulldoze her, Harry. Her lawyer would charge you with harassment."

Wiley gave Hull a breather and asked how the appeal brief was coming along. He produced two copies and handed one to Harmon.

"For the prosecutor?"

Hull grinned. "Yes. The enemy of the enemy is a friend, Pete." He'd have to ask Polly who said that.

Harmon and Wiley read the document and made notes in the margins.

"It's terrific," Wiley said. "One suggestion. Put the defense's inability to talk to the children first. And I'd include the investigators' tactics with the children. That should curdle the judges' blood."

Harmon nodded. "I agree. And not to get too clever, but you might want to observe that you gave Mathes a chance to take himself off the case on the first day. And he didn't take it."

"That's right," Wiley said. "But be careful not to leave yourself open to an accusation that you were manipulating the court. In other words, that you knew Mathes was Bonnie's father from the start. So I'd be careful to get all the dates straight. As I remember the record, you asked Mathes to disqualify himself when he said you were frivolous and unprofessional during your cross-examination of Detective Garafolo."

"Good point," Harmon said. "So Sgueglia would be prepared to swear that he received the information from Strand and passed it on to you subsequent to your disqualification motion."

"I know how to testify," Sgueglia said.

Hull recovered the briefs and Wiley said, "Can you get it into shape fast, Harry? By tomorrow afternoon?" She yawned. "I mean this afternoon."

Sgueglia, who had been searching in his memory, broke in. "Wait a minute. I don't know if it'll help, but here's another one from McGonigle. The IBM guy's wife. Your witness, Pete. Marla Burney? Corky said she's a pal of Ellen Strand's."

"Burney's sensible," Harmon said.

A new silence set in until Wiley stood up. "Holy smoke! Marla Burney." They waited. She grinned, remembering her conversation with Polly Lennon. "Listen, I'm embarrassed to talk this way, but this is girl stuff. Will you hold everything till noon, Harry? Do nothing till then?"

"You're on."

She reflected. "Another thing, and it's hard to say. I think I see where we're going, and you may have to take a backseat. You're Coles's attorney, and you wouldn't be seen as exactly neutral. Does that bother you?"

"Just do it, Serena. Get her out of jail!"

Hull went home to labor on the appeal brief after telling Sgueglia, "You're back on the payroll. Squail, I'm beginning to think you might be worth a damn."

Wiley introduced herself and said, "Mrs. Burney, I'm going to be upfront, as they say. I'm trying to get the verdict against Laurie Coles reversed, and I want to tell you something I'm sure you already know. If I didn't believe that, it would be unethical for me to be here. I heard you testify. I know you're a thoughtful person, and I'm not just saying that to warm you up."

Marla Burney glanced through the kitchen window and saw Tom showing Bonnie Strand how easy it was to hang by one arm from the branch of a tree. They heard him yell, "Captain Tom-Tom on guard duty! Mom and Dad put me in bed at night, but I sneak out and guard the house. All night!"

Wiley opened a file folder and related Mickey Strand's information. She did not need her notes but kept her head down; watching for a reaction would be like eavesdropping. Then she looked up and saw a hesitation.

"You're wrong about something important, Miss Wiley. I didn't know."

Wiley was shaken as she realized what they had all missed the night before. "I apologize, Mrs. Burney. I just got the information and haven't had a chance to think it through."

Burney was studying her closely. "So you didn't assume I knew this and said nothing while that man presided over the trial."

Wiley was intensely embarrassed. "I'm mortified, Mrs. Burney. We were all so stunned by the news that we didn't realize the implications. If you want me to leave, I will. But I hope you don't feel that way."

Mrs. Burney sighed and looked out the window again. "No.

Some things are more important than others. The truth is, I knew that Bonnie wasn't Mickey's child. Ellen told me that much. But she never said who the father was and I didn't ask, of course." She paused. "My God, she's in a terrible position!"

"That's why I'm here, Mrs. Burney. I understand why Mrs. Strand kept it to herself. But I'm sure you agree that something has to be done. Laurie Coles is also in a terrible position. Whether she's guilty or innocent is—well, I'll say it—is irrelevant right now. The first thing is, no one should ever be convicted without a fair trial."

"I agree."

The children were dropped off at the home of Bonnie's nanny and minutes later Wiley and Marla Burney walked into Far-Flung Fashions. Wiley halted inside the door, thankful there were no customers in the shop, as Burney went to the desk at the rear and hugged Ellen Strand. Burney spoke and Wiley saw Strand turn pale. Burney kept speaking and finally Strand darted a glance at Wiley, who was inspecting a sweater from Scotland.

Burney motioned and Wiley came forward and said, "I'm sorry. I know you're caught in the middle."

Strand burst into tears. Burney embraced her and held her until she dried her eyes and told Wiley, "It's been torturing me for months. You must know what I went through on the witness stand, with him sitting right there. He hasn't even spoken to me since the day I told him I was pregnant." She spoke through sobs to Burney. "It's been driving me crazy, Marla. I wanted to tell you. I almost did. You would have made me do the right thing."

Then she said to Wiley, "All right. What do I have to do?"

Wiley told her, gently and hopefully, but avoiding promises she could not guarantee, what she had to do. Strand, through more tears, said she would do it.

Chapter 43

It was almost eleven o'clock when Wiley left Far-Flung Fashions and hurried over to Harry Hull's office. She received the Laurie Coles appeal brief and dialed an Albany number as Hull watched, amazed when he heard her ask for Abner Rusk. She gave her name, the chief judge came on, and she said, "I have an unusual request, sir. I have a copy of the appeal from a criminal conviction and would like to fax it to you. It's the Laurie Coles case in Hudson Ferry."

She waited and Hull went on marveling.

"Thank you, sir. It's only twenty-two pages. If you would have time to read it quickly, I would also appreciate having a few moments with you this afternoon. That is, the prosecutor in the case and I would like to talk to you. I assure you it's a true emergency, sir."

She grinned at Hull as she said, "Sweeney's? Yes, I know it. I had dinner there a few months ago, just after I argued before the court." She waited, then said, "No, I lost that one." She waited again, then held the phone over its base before dropping it. "Quick, Harry. Copies."

As the machine cranked, she said, "The most important thing that can be done for Laurie Coles today is for Ellen Strand to be home this evening. If you tell Marla Burney we may have found a way out for Ellen, she'll understand and make sure she's home."

Hull, collating pages as his secretary brought them in, found his hands trembling. "If you pull this off, Serena . . ."

She succumbed to impetuosity. "One more copy, Harry. The district attorney should have his immediately. I'd love to drop it off myself."

He handed her the briefs and hugged her. "You're crazy, Serena. God bless."

Five minutes later Wiley introduced herself to Barnard Rooney as a messenger for Harry Hull and placed a copy of the brief before the D.A., who could not hide his puzzlement. "I suggest you look this over as soon as you can," she said. "You might be asked about it rather quickly."

She walked out and told herself to settle down.

In Albany, at a few minutes before seven o'clock, Harmon and Wiley approached the impressive edifice that housed New York State's highest court. They passed the white marble structure and continued on for a block since Judge Rusk was not going to hold this illicit meeting in official quarters.

At Sweeney's, elegant and hushed, they were shown into an alcove at the rear, where two men rose to greet them. The chief judge of the court of appeals, a gangly fellow with a gray cowlick, was holding the fax sheets of the Coles appeal and, to their surprise, stood next to the man whose fine hand lay behind this dinner.

"Counselors," Rusk said, "I thought it might help if Judge Fisher sat in with us." Arnold Fisher lit up his pipe, pointing to a framed no-smoking sign on the wall. "I am above the law," he said.

Both Wiley and Harmon recalled Judge Rusk's performances during their appearances before the high court. He ambushed attorneys by concealing a bounty of legal knowledge while assuming the manner of a country lawyer awed by extraordinary minds. He would scratch his head and appear to be puzzled during oral arguments and never interrupted. But as presentations ended, he struck with one or two questions, rarely more, and attorneys had to admit, privately, that he had found the strengths and weaknesses in their arguments and discarded the oratory.

Apologizing for having taken the liberty of ordering his favorite wine, he pushed the brief aside and asked Wiley, "What's your strongest point, Counselor?"

She would not be had. "The Coles verdict should be set aside for reasons of equal importance. Access is one. The defense had as much right to have its experts see the children as the prosecution. They could have been supervised as they interviewed the children. Denial of access violated due process." She wanted to use the exact words but didn't dare: ". . . nor shall any state . . . deny to any person within its jurisdiction the equal protection of the law."

She went on. "The lower court also made a blanket ruling that the children would not confront the defendant and used closed-circuit television. Before that can be done, the judge must determine for each child that harm would be done if he or she were to testify in open court. Failure to do that violated the confrontation clause." She offered a peace token. "I'm sorry, sir, but I can't rank them one over another. Due process and confrontation are both compelling grounds for reversal."

The wine was indeed good and they ordered dinner as Judge Rusk made a losing argument for the barbecued catfish. "And I suppose you'd like to tell us what support you have for your confrontation argument, Counselor?"

Harmon saw the route Rusk was taking and knew Wiley was ready for it. "*Maryland versus Craig,* sir. It's in the citations."

Rusk seemed disappointed. "That's a loser. The *Craig* conviction was thrown out by the Maryland high court, but the Supreme Court reinstated it and said confrontation didn't necessarily mean face-to-face. So why cite *Craig?*"

"Because the Supreme Court noted in its decision that each child, individually, was found to be in danger of being injured by direct confrontation. They pointed that out."

Rusk turned to Judge Fisher. "Stir the pot, Arnold."

Fisher stoked his pipe. "I have a feeling that we're sort of paddling up a quiet stream. Perhaps as dinner goes on, we'll find out what brings these thoughtful people to Albany. How does that strike you, Serena?"

She was cool. "I rest on the law, sir."

Rusk turned to Harmon. "You prosecuted the Coles case, sir, and you're still the attorney of record. Where do you stand? Now please don't make a speech about the district attorney's dual obligations. We know about that and we're off the record anyway. I hate to see speeches wasted on small crowds."

Harmon smiled. He had been waiting for the question. "I felt a conviction was justified on the merits of the case, sir. But Justice Mathes was in a hurry. A case that should have taken two months to try ran one week. And he made one error after another. But, and please excuse me for being direct, no one tells Justice Mathes how to run his court, and that includes the prosecutor. I believe he was unfair to the defendant all along the line. And to make it worse, Justice Mathes insulted the defense counsel repeatedly in front of the jury. That's where I stand, gentlemen."

Rusk nodded. "Excuse us for a moment. The captain is waiting for me to compliment the wine." He and Judge Fisher left the alcove.

Wiley said, "Bravo, Pete."

Harmon was tapping the table. "Thank you. But Fisher's trying to hurry things along, isn't he? They don't really want to talk about the law."

"Can you blame him? We shouldn't be here and Rusk shouldn't be listening to us. He knows we've got something up our sleeves. He just wants the law points in case we're for real."

The judges returned as the entrées were served and Abner Rusk confirmed Wiley's supposition in his plainspoken way. "Why don't we get to your real argument, Counselors?"

Wiley watched him closely as she said the words: "Justice Johnson Gillies Mathes is the father of one of the children in the Laurie Coles case. He should not have sat."

The chief judge's eyes narrowed and there was silence until they excused themselves again.

"He's asking Fisher if it's certain beyond a doubt that we're not crazy," Wiley said. "He's got to cover every base. I can hear him asking Fisher what the chances are that if we lose here, we'll take the dirt to the federal district court."

"Where they'd throw us out, love. They'd find a reason to keep the case in the state appellate division. But meanwhile the scandal would make it to Siberia in an hour."

The judges returned more quickly this time and Rusk did not sit down as he asked, "What's your evidence, Counselor?"

"Will you accept the word of the mother, sir?"

He did not reply.

"She has every reason not to lie. Her daughter is one of the children the defendant is accused of sexually molesting. She wants to see justice done."

"Go on," Rusk said.

"Her name is Ellen Strand. She understands the gravity of what she did in remaining silent when Mr. Mathes did not disqualify himself. And to save you from having to ask me, the only promise I gave her was that we would do all we could to keep this matter private. She agreed that if I failed, she would bring a paternity suit against the judge or face the consequences of public disclosure by the Coles defense."

Wiley handed him a sheet containing Ellen Strand's phone number and the office and home numbers of Barnard Rooney and Justice Mathes. "In addition, sir," she said, "I told Mrs. Strand she might receive a call, but I did not use your name or position. I said the caller would ask if she knew Miss Wiley. If she said yes, the caller would ask her a couple of questions about this paternity matter."

Rusk sat down, his anger showing. "Judge Fisher tells me you would not lie, Counselor. He vouches for you. I ask you and Mr.

Harmon if there is anything you've said that you wish to withdraw. Think about that, please."

"We're aware that our professional futures are on the line, Your
Honor. What we have told you is true and there is nothing we
wish to withdraw."

He looked at Harmon, who said, "We stand by every word."

"Thank you," Rusk said. "And also for your discretion in this
matter."

Most of the drive back to Hudson Ferry was silent until Harmon
said, "Serena, if you don't marry me, I'll swear out a statement
that you made this whole thing up."

The tension was relieved and they stopped at Harry Hull's office to catch him up on the news.

Hull said, "I'm going to jump in the river. I'm going to swim to
Bermuda and get drunk every day for a week."

Chapter 44

Hudson Ferry was tranquil on Wednesday evening.

At 8:15 P.M., Ellen Strand was sitting by the telephone and Marla Burney was reading to Bonnie before bedtime; it was a special treat. The phone rang and a man with a weak and reedy voice asked Ellen if she knew Serena Wiley. Yes, she said. He asked if Johnson Gillies Mathes was the father of Mrs. Strand's child. Yes, she replied. He asked if there could be the slightest possibility of an error. None, she said. None whatever. The man thanked her and suggested that, for her own sake, the conversation remain confidential.

At eight thirty, the phone rang at the home of the district attorney. Chief Judge Abner Rusk of the court of appeals asked Barnard Rooney if he had had an opportunity to review the defense counsel's appeal brief in the Laurie Coles case. Rooney dropped his golf book, sat up straight, and said yes, sir. Rusk asked that the district attorney's response be rushed to Albany. Rooney excused himself for asking, then asked if he did not have the customary sixty days in which to reply. The answer was no. His brief should be in Albany by nine o'clock the following morning. And Rooney should understand that he was volunteering to respond by that time. Rusk added that the D.A. need reply only to the argument on the question of access, whether the defense was deprived of due process by being denied the right to have its experts interview the Snug Arms children. Rooney was thanked for his cooperation and heard a click.

At eight forty, Justice Johnson Gillies Mathes received a phone call and found Judge Rusk on the line. Mathes's heart fibrillated at the thought that he was about to be asked if he was interested in sitting on the court of appeals. Instead, he was asked if he was the biological father of Bonnie Strand, a complainant in the Laurie Coles case. Mathes's atrial valve did a click and a drum roll, but only briefly. He asked if he was the target of some sort of practical joke and Judge Rusk said he did not want to be fucked with. Mathes asked if he could call back in fifteen minutes and Rusk said no. Mathes wondered if Bonnie Strand's mother had made some outlandish claim. Rusk said she had not but would file a paternity suit if asked to. He added that he wanted to see Mathes's resignation from the bench instantly. By morning. After an extended pause, Mathes said he had been thinking of resigning anyway and asked if that would close the matter. Rusk said it appeared that it would and suggested that their conversation remain confidential for Mathes's own sake.

Otherwise, Hudson Ferry was tranquil on Wednesday evening.

Corky McGonigle walked into Speedy Sally's a few minutes before nine the next morning and caught Harry Hull and Tony Sgueglia laughing it up in a rear booth. "What's funny?" he asked.

Sgueglia stopped chuckling. "Sit down or you'll fall down laughing, Corky. A guy walks in and says, 'B-b-bartender, g-g-give me a s-scotch and s-s-oda.' The bartender says, 'S-scotch and s-s-soda c-comin' up.' Another guy walks in and says, 'Bartender, give me a scotch and soda.' The bartender says, 'Scotch and soda comin' up.' The first guy looks up and says, 'S-s-say, b-b-bartender, w-were you m-m-mimicking m-m-me?' The bartender says, 'N-n-no. I w-was m-m-mimicking *him.*'"

"What's funny?" McGonigle asked. "You lose the biggest case of your life, Harry. The judge is going to put a match to your lawyer's license and they're going to ride you out of town on a rail with nails in it. And you're swapping jokes. That can't be. Something's going on." He set his camera on the floor and yelled. "Sally! Where's the coffee?"

Hull reached a decision. "Can you keep that big mouth of yours shut if I tell you something, Corky?"

"If Mathes couldn't get my mouth open, nobody can. Talk, Harry."

"It's a coincidence. You just mentioned Mathes's name. Do you know his secretary?"

"I take the Fifth. I never talk about girls. Maybe once in a while."

"Go over to Jacko's chambers and camp out, Corky. Get his secretary alone and pump her. That's all I can tell you, but you could walk into a good one. I can't guarantee it, but there might be a strange story popping."

"That swaggering mutt got a seat on the court of appeals? No, if that was it, you wouldn't be clowning. Has Harry been in the bottle all night, Squail?"

"He hasn't touched a drop in years."

"Corky," Hull said, "don't sit here. Get over to Mathes's chambers!"

McGonigle looked suspicious. "Whatever happens, I'll get the official version. But you'll give me the real story later. Right, Harry?"

Hull shook his head. "Corky, all I know is what I read on television."

McGonigle grabbed his camera and dashed out as Sally arrived with his coffee.

At ten o'clock McGonigle appeared on channel 22 with a scoop and a comment. "Rumor: Justice Johnson Gillies Mathes, who presided over the Snug Arms child molestation case, has quit. His resignation from the bench will be announced later today. Rumor: The judge has asthma and can't stand our climate. He's going off to Arizona to practice law. Fact: This is the first time anyone has ever heard that Justice Mathes suffers from asthma. You heard it first on twenty-two."

The newsman set out to find Hull again and couldn't. His secretary hadn't heard from him.

The motel desk said Mr. Anthony Sgueglia had checked out at eight o'clock that morning.

Nor could McGonigle raise Mathes, once upon a time a judge. He was at Sylvia's castle on the river explaining his abrupt decision to start a new life in Arizona.

She sipped an espresso from a colorfully glazed ceramic demitasse and startled him with a question. "What happened, Jack? Did you take a bribe?"

He laughed. "Sylvia! What kind of a joke is that?"

She looked more appealing than ever, her luxurious form half reclining on the cushions of a honey-leather sofa. "What's the real story? You had your heart set on Albany and suddenly it's the Painted Desert. I don't get it."

He stroked the red mustache. "Well, I had a blowup with the softheads in the appellate division. They're all wrapped up in the rights thing. Rights for criminals. That's all they talk about these days and I couldn't take it anymore."

She sipped. "To put it another way, Jack, you blew up your chance for a seat on the court of appeals."

He smiled. "It was a matter of principle."

Five minutes later she had made it unmistakably clear that she had no interest in starting a new life in Arizona with an ex-judge who would be scrounging with the pack for cases and fees. And she detested smoky, greasy barbecues on the terrace.

Jacko walked out and counted up his losses: Everything.

Sylvia had not told Mathes everything. That afternoon she had learned that she was pregnant. He didn't have to know about it. He'd be far off, and anyway she could have the baby in London, or Paris. Paris in the springtime.

McGonigle reached Serena Wiley and asked for her reaction to Mathes's resignation. She sounded surprised, but added, "He won't be missed." Replacing the phone, she told Harmon, Hull, and Sgueglia, "The joint is jumping."

They were finishing a shrimp salad at one o'clock when the phone rang again. It was a law clerk in Albany who asked for Mr. Hull. "In special session this morning," he said, "in very special session, the appellate division reversed the conviction of Laurie Coles. The decision will not be announced until two o'clock, but would you like to hear a summary?"

He jumped up and gave his audience a wildly waving V. "Please," he said.

"The court finds that the defendant was denied due process under the Fourteenth Amendment when the lower bench denied the defense access to the child complainants without first hearing expert testimony that they might be harmed by such a procedure. The conviction is set aside and the defendant is to be released pending a decision by the district attorney as to whether he will retry the case."

"Thank you. But there may be a problem. The judge in the case has resigned."

"I understand that, sir. I have been instructed to call the prison superintendent, Mr. Hull, but I thought you might want to suggest a time."

Hull heard the message. The decision would be announced at two o'clock. "If Miss Coles is released at two thirty, sir, I will meet her and see that she is removed from the Hudson Ferry area. I think we'd better have her out of here. And I will personally vouch for her return if she's needed again."

"Thank you. Is Miss Wiley available?"

Serena took the phone and was surprised to hear Arnold Fisher. "Serena," he said, "I know you're aware of the extraordinary nature of the action the appellate division has taken. A majority of the judges on the court of appeals were not absolutely convinced of Judge Rusk's position on the access issue, but he was insistent. In the end they realized that more was going on here than they were being told about, but their respect for the chief judge is so great that they did not press him and went along. And Judge Rusk laid down the law to the appellate division. He spelled out the decision for them. Now I'll get to the point. This is all highly irregular, and to put it mildly, Judge Rusk would be most upset if the confidential aspects of this matter were to become public."

"I understand, sir. That won't happen. And I want to thank you for your help."

"There's nothing to thank me for." He shorthanded the Rusk Amendment. "If we tolerate misconduct on the bench, all is lost."

Hull was in Barnard Rooney's waiting room when the D.A. walked in from lunch and snapped, "What do you want?"

Hull said he was amazed by the speed of the appellate division's decision and did not realize that Rooney had been able to respond to the defense brief so quickly. He was here to get a copy of Rooney's reply.

"Give me no shit," Rooney said. "You people pulled some kind of a stunt, and if you think I won't retry this case, you're dumber than I thought, Harry."

Hull couldn't resist. "Maybe you should have let Harmon write the brief, Barney. He has more experience."

Rooney walked into his office and slammed the door. Hull was given a copy of the brief by the secretary and rejoined Sgueglia, who trailed him as he drove out to the jail in the loaner the insurance company had provided.

Shortly after two they saw the superintendent and Hull said, "We're here to pick up Miss Coles when she's released. She will get into this man's car and I will watch them drive off. If another vehicle leaves the prison within fifteen minutes, I'll follow it, and if anything happens to Miss Coles on the way to her destination, you will be held responsible. My witness to this conversation is Mr. Anthony Sgueglia, a private detective licensed by the State of New York."

Sgueglia dropped his card on the superintendent's desk and they went back out to the guardhouse.

At two thirty Laurie Coles was escorted through an archway into an open area that lay between the prison building and the surrounding walls. She was carrying clothing and walking unsteadily. A bandage still covered the left side of her forehead and tears were coursing down her face.

Hull moved toward her and heard a command. "Stop! Keep away from the prisoner until she signs out."

"Sure," he said. "Excuse me."

They stood outside the guardhouse as Coles signed a release

form. Then she fell into Hull's arms and he helped her into
Sgueglia's car.

"Laurie, I can't spend time with you," he said. "We want you
away from here right away. Mr. Sgueglia is going to drive you to
Albany. But you have to keep in touch with me. Will you be with
your father?"

She nodded. "I thought I was dead. How did you do it?"

"I had a lot of help." He reached in and held her hand. "Look,
this is not the time for speeches, but I want to tell you what I really
believe. Our laws are okay. But sometimes they get bent by people
who aren't okay." He kissed her cheek. "Your dad will know
you're coming, Laurie. Say hello."

Sgueglia pulled onto the road in the wrong direction. That was
the Squail, dropping a false scent on the trail. Hull watched for
twenty minutes. No vehicle left the prison gate.

Chapter 45

HULL APPEARED AT THE DISTRICT ATTORNEY'S OFFICE ON FRIDAY MORNING at Barnard Rooney's request and was surprised by a handshake. "Let's call off the war," the D.A. said. "It's just a case. Another docket number."

"Peace," Hull replied. "Hey, Barney, I'm not trying to be funny, but have you seen Jacko?"

Rooney shook his head. "I called him last night to find out what this was all about. There was an intercept and the operator said the number was disconnected. So I told the wife to put dinner on hold and drove over. The house was lit up but he wasn't there. And an hour later I got a call from a friend who's a real estater. He said Mathes put the house on the market and told him he'd be in touch. He's gonesville." Rooney banged a drawer shut. "Harry, you know why I asked you to drop in."

Hull wore the mask of curiosity.

"If you went over the record of every criminal trial in this country, in this whole century, you wouldn't find a case like this one. The verdict comes in on a Monday and two days later I get a call from the chief honcho in Albany. He tells me in a nice way, as if he's helping me, to rebut only one point in the defense brief. Then he plays tough guy and says in effect for me to butt the hell out. Don't even appear. The next day they throw out the conviction and turn the defendant loose without even a bail hearing. You know the story behind this thing, Harry, and I want it."

Hull moved from curiosity to puzzlement. "I thought you were going to tell me about the status of the case, Barney. *The State of New York versus Laurie Coles.* Are you going to get it put back on the docket?"

Rooney sighed. "Shit! Some day, Harry. Some day, if I'm really nice to you, if you mug a ninety-year-old woman and kill her and I let you off, will you tell me what was really behind this reversal? I mean, Jacko is acting like a fugitive. We were golf buddies and he resigns and cuts out without even saying so long." Hearing no response, he said, "Okay. On Coles. You know I have to try her again, so let's talk about access. It's no mystery that I can put a hundred experts on the stand who'll testify that the kids would be emotionally harmed if your experts were allowed in the same room with them. All they said in Albany was that Mathes didn't hear testimony on that danger in each case. I'll make sure it's done. So you won't get anywhere pushing that one, Harry. You'd drive into a dead end."

Hull shook his head. "No good. You put on a hundred experts and I'll put on a hundred and one who'll say the interviews can be videotaped and it'll all be out in the open. So the kids will be safe. Barney, I'll have to take that route. I have an obligation to my client and I'm in this thing to the finish."

Rooney rubbed his eyes; he was weary in the morning. "I know. Listen, when you see Pete Harmon, tell him thanks for me. I'm really enjoying his leftovers."

In the lobby, Hull walked out of the elevator and there was Lilly Robertson in the midst of a cluster of people waiting to go up. "Pig!" she yelled. She swung her purse and shouted and he ducked. "You feel great, don't you? Do you know what you've done to the children?" Everyone moved out of range and she was in the elevator alone. The doors closed.

Rooney faced Robertson, Letty Andrews, Ellen Strand, and Marla Burney and summed up the problem in a dispirited way. "If we go back to trial, the defense will drag out the proceedings with appeals on the access issue. And in the end they'll probably win the right to see the children. The odds are heavily against us on that one."

"You sound like Harmon," said Lilly Robertson. "Backing off before you start."

"I'll give it to you straight," Rooney said. "Something's going on in this case. You know it as well as I do. But I can't find out what. I think it's connected with Mathes." He searched each of their faces as he spoke. "If any of you know what I'm talking about, tell me and we won't spin our wheels."

Robertson was furious. "What the hell are you talking about?" The others said nothing; Ellen Strand lit a cigarette.

"You don't have to be a lawyer to know there was an under-ground motive behind the reversal of that verdict. And you must realize they were in a godawful rush to do it. Those judges would have gone to the moon to find a reason."

"They don't give a damn about the children," Robertson said.

Rooney waved that off. "Let's get down to business. If the case is retried, defense experts will spend time with your children. That had better be all right with you. If you won't allow it, say so now, because if you back off later, that will be the end of the case."

"Of course we'll permit it," Robertson said. "We're not going to let her get away with what she's done."

Marla Burney spoke hesitantly. "I don't know about subjecting the kids to that. Tom's going to a new school next month and I wonder—"

Robertson cut her off. "You were trying to escape your responsibility from the beginning, Marla. You didn't want to testify, and when you finally got up there, you went this way and that way. You were terrible."

Strand balanced embarrassment against anger, and embarrassment lost. "You have no right to say that, Lilly! Marla did a terrific job. There were more interviews with the jurors and they said she was the strongest witness they heard."

"Let's stick to the point," Rooney said. "I have to know if the children would be made available for defense questioning."

Letty Andrews shook her head. "No. Billy's just starting to settle down."

"I won't let Bonnie go through it again," Strand said.

Robertson flared. "Well, you can run away, but I won't. Caroline will be available when she's needed, Mr. Rooney, so you have no excuse not to keep after the bitch! Don't be a coward like my husband." She walked out and the others left minutes later.

At three o'clock Rooney announced that the charges against Laurie Coles were being dropped. He appeared with Corky McGonigle on channel 22, explained that legal obstacles stood in the way of a new trial, and gave roundabout answers to the newsman's questions. McGonigle got him off the air and glared into the camera.

"The following is opinion," he said. "The real story is missing from the official version of what happened in the Laurie Coles case. Something's buried in the woodwork, and that's not all. I still can't understand why Justice Mathes blew town as if a posse was after him. When I dig it out, you'll hear it on channel twenty-two. This reporter doesn't like secrets."

Most of Hudson Ferry, from River Road up to Utopia Lane, felt a loss in the demise of the Coles case. Some townspeople, pleased to see it over with, drank iced tea and beer and played softball and shopped as August blazed down. But others asked questions that would not depart with the case. "How will we ever find out what happened? She did it, didn't she? It's not right that we can't find out. I mean, for sure. Did she do it?"

The *Tribune* observed their distress with a one-line editorial on its front page: "The law is an ass."

Still, forgiveness for Hull was quicker than he expected. The first sign appeared at Speedy Sally's as Dick, the policeman who had given him a hard time at the Ferry Ale House, paid Sal the usual one dollar for bacon and eggs, started to leave, then turned and threw the attorney a wave.

Later that morning Hull was passing the criminal courts building when he encountered a group of the law buffs and found them unusually subdued. "Harry," one said, "the law's the law, but did she mess with the kids?"

They followed as he walked along, bursting to tell them the story. Finally he said, "Who am I? God? Who are jurors? God times twelve? You know the system. Juries get as close to the truth as they can. But nobody ever *knows.*"

Belligerence returned as the buff said, "You didn't hear the question, Harry. "Is she a pervert? Did she tinker with those little kids?"

He turned and smiled. "You didn't hear the answer because you didn't like the reversal. You're going to believe what you want to believe and so will everybody else. But there's a worse part. You say the law's the law, but that's just easy talk. When the law gets us mad, we wish a gang of Brendelskis would move in and hang somebody and sneak away in the night." Recalling one of Polly's pearls, he said, "Remember a skinny guy in the White House? Abe Lincoln. You know what Honest Abe said? He said, 'There is no grievance that is a fit object of redress by mob law.' So here's the point: This time our laws protected Laurie Coles. The next time they might protect you. People keep forgetting that."

His yearning to reveal the true story was laid to rest when his antagonist took a deep breath and said, "Forget it, Harry. The hell with it. Let's be a town again."

At his office he received a phone call that sent him rushing down to the Book Nook. "Polly," he said, "did I ever tell you about a lawyer down in the big city who chopped me up every time we came up against each other? He drove me crazy, like the rest of them."

She had no time to reply.

"He runs a big law firm now and he just offered me a partnership."

Polly tried to smile.

"A full partnership. Criminal law. He said he followed the trial every day and knew Laurie was a goner. And then the verdict gets thrown out. He said, 'Whatever you did was brilliant, Harry. You've got what I need.'"

She was frowning and he noticed.

"Hey, that's not the point. All I did was the best I could. Serena pulled off the reversal. But something happened to me while this macho man was talking. When he was finished, I said, 'Thank you very much, but I like it up here. I don't think I need the big town.'"

Polly reached out for him.

"I don't feel as if I was run out anymore. I did a good job. When I first walked into that courtroom and read the indictment, I almost dropped. But then I stood up to Mathes. I'm an okay guy and I can do more than mortgages. Now listen to me. Why don't we take a break? How about a trip to Paris, France? Or Madrid. In Spain. Let's see the world."

Polly laughed and hugged him.

That evening Grant Burney told Marla, "I'm still not sure what to believe. We're never going to know, are we?"

"No," she said, "but here's what I think. *Something* probably happened. To one child, I'd guess. I don't know what it was or who did it. Maybe Laurie Coles, but it could have been a babysitter, or a nanny or a gardener." She shook her head and closed her eyes. "Or some crazy mother or father. No, that's too awful to think about. But when the news came out and the kids heard about it, they did what they're famous for. They topped each other's tales. And the parents panicked. Which is understandable. I felt it myself. But then those investigators took over and the children's tales began to sound more and more manufactured. As if they were coming out of machines."

"The nightingale," Burney said. "Let's read that story to Tom."